A SMALL CASE OF MURDER

A SMALL CASE OF MURDER

Lauren Carr

iUniverse, Inc.
New York Lincoln Shanghai

A Small Case of Murder

All Rights Reserved © 2004 by Lauren Carr

iUniverse, Inc.

For information address:
iUniverse, Inc.
2021 Pine Lake Road, Suite 100
Lincoln, NE 68512
www.iuniverse.com

ISBN: 0-595-30253-X

Printed in the United States of America

Be on your guard against false prophets; they come to you looking like sheep on the outside, but on the inside they are really like wild wolves. You will know them by what they do. Thorn bushes do not bear grapes, and briers do not bear figs.

—Matthew 7:15-16

PROLOGUE

▼

Spring, 1970

Lulu didn't even try to hide her amusement about the young man's fascination with her breasts. It was clearly the first time the kid had ever seen a bra-less woman in a see-through top.

The postal clerk was so rattled by Lulu Jefferson's fashion statement that he almost forgot to stick the stamp she bought onto her envelope before posting and tossing it into the local mail bin.

The bra-less look was all the sensation in California. It just hadn't reached Chester, West Virginia, yet. With its cobblestone streets and churches on every corner, some people would think the small town was still stuck in the fifties.

Singer-songwriter Lulu Jefferson kept up with the latest fads. It was essential in her line of work. On her way to being the next Nancy Sinatra, Lulu wore her sun-bleached hair down past her waist and her skirts up above the middle thigh. Her bare feet were more of a statement of her generation than her country roots. Lulu preferred the Rolling Stones to Hank Williams.

The singer hummed her next would-be hit (if it ever reached the ears of the right people) as she strolled up Second Street Hill to her rented room over the Langley's garage nestled under an old maple tree.

Sometimes Lulu thought Chester was surrounded by a force shield, like something out of *Star Trek*, which kept the rest of the world out. Her friends were selective about the outside influences they let inside: like marijuana that tunes you in, miniskirts and hot pants that threaten to show more than thigh, and see-through tops that make postal clerks swallow their chewing gum.

Not that that was all bad.

Somebody had to stay sane in the midst of the chaos created by the changing times.

The small town way of life suited Lulu's best friends, Claire and Johnny Thornton. Marriage and a kid worked for them. They were so into it that they ran off to the Grand Canyon to make another kid.

"Good for them!" Lulu thought. "But that Ozzie and Harriet Nelson stuff is not for me. Hollywood, here I come!"

She sighed in admiration of the green on the trees. The blossoms were gone. Spring was over. "When did that happen?" she wondered as she crossed Indiana Avenue.

Time sure does fly.

Man, does it fly! The bus for her gig in Philadelphia was leaving at five o'clock in the morning, and she still had to pack.

As she hurried up the shady street to her apartment, Lulu made a list for the first time in her life, even if only in her mind, of what she had left to do before leaving town. Mentally, she checked off her meeting with Reverend Orville Rawlings to go over the music for the wedding.

"What a trip!" Lulu giggled to herself. "Wait until Claire reads about that."

Lulu reminded herself that she had to take all of her miniskirts and halter-tops. Her long legs and breasts were her biggest assets, as the kid in the post office would testify. The singer/songwriter wanted to believe that she would make it to the top in show business on her talent, but she couldn't deny that sex sells. Good thing she enjoyed it as much as the next guy did.

Chester was still getting used to the "open sexuality" thing, Lulu observed, when she caught her landlady's disapproving gape at her bare legs accentuated by her bright purple hot pants.

The mature woman shook her head at Lulu's skimpy attire and made a "tsk, tsk" noise with her tongue before resuming the chore of weeding her flowerbed.

"Kicking and screaming all the way into the twentieth century," Lulu giggled as she ran up the steps to her apartment.

Lulu told herself that she could check another item off her list. She wrote and mailed that letter to Claire. She wished she could be around to see all the excitement when the Thorntons read it.

Lulu opened the door and stepped into her apartment. She didn't bother digging out her key because people didn't lock their doors in Chester. There was no reason for security in this burg. Lulu tossed her bag to the floor like she always did and slammed the door to make sure it latched.

That was the last thing Lulu did before the hand clamped the handkerchief over her face.

Lulu's guitar hit a sour note as her bare feet struck the strings in her struggle to break free from the muscular arms that had seized her. The instrument made an odd musical sound as it tumbled to the floor from where she had set it up against the wall.

The chloroform rushed up her nostrils, down into her lungs, through her bloodstream, and hit her brain.

In her unconscious state, Lulu Jefferson was unable to enjoy the trip on which the hottest recreational drug—all the rage in California—took her.

CHAPTER 1

▼

Summer, 2004

"Smile and say good morning," Beth Davis ordered the reflection in her compact's mirror when the bell over the front door signaled her first pharmacy customer of the morning. The grind of working for a living put a crimp in her nightlife. The druggist flexed the muscles in her cheeks to curl the corners of her lips into a smile.

On the corner of Carolina Avenue and Fifth Street in the heart of town, Chester Drug Store had been owned and operated by the Martin family since 1960. Since the closing of the steel mills in the early eighties created an exodus of each new generation to the surrounding cities of Pittsburgh, Cleveland, and even Washington, D.C., in the fight for financial survival, business ownership in the valley was in a state of constant turnover.

The 1990 census indicated that senior citizens were a majority in the small town, but the 2000 census showed that the tide was shifting. Young families were moving into town to seek sanctuary from the very forces Chester's eager younger generation was pursuing in the metropolis.

Another sign of life returning to Chester was evident in the landscape. Housing developments dotted the countryside where farms used to lie. An imaginative real estate contractor even managed to squeeze a townhouse development in place of some long-abandoned railroad tracks behind Martin's drug store.

Beth Davis had just finished her sixth mug of coffee and put on her white pharmacist's smock when Joshua Thornton and his sixteen-year-old son Murphy came in and made their way down the center aisle to the pharmacy counter at the back of the store. Beth kept her back to them while she transformed her mood from sulky to perky.

Joshua tapped his knuckles on the counter. "Excuse me?"

Beth snapped the compact shut and turned around. When her sleep-filled eyes met Joshua's clear blue ones, she shrieked.

The former naval officer, trained always to look perfect, had on the same rumpled clothes he had worn the previous day and had slept in on a filthy hardwood floor. The day's growth of beard was evidence that he couldn't find his shaving kit. Despite his unkempt appearance, Joshua Thornton was still as handsome as he was the day he graduated as valedictorian from Oak Glen High School. There were a couple of crow's feet in the corners of his blue eyes and strands of gray hair at his temples; but he still had the same finely-chiseled features that made Beth's heart skip a beat when he had first invited her to go with him for an ice cream cone.

It took a moment for Joshua to see the cause for the pharmacist's startled reaction. Her long, thick, strawberry-blond hair was lighter and shorter, but freckles were still splashed across her upturned nose.

"Josh?" the druggist whispered for assurance that the image before her was not a fantasy.

"Hello, Beth." Joshua couldn't help but smile back.

Beth lunged across the counter, grasped his neck, and kissed him on the mouth.

The sight of the woman's open display of affection for his father prompted the teenage boy to raise an eyebrow.

Joshua flushed at the sight of his son's surprise. "Murphy, this is Beth Davis. She's an old friend of mine from school."

Beth laughed out loud at Joshua's introduction. "Old friend? Is that all I am?" She confided to Murphy, "We almost got married the night of the senior prom."

"You don't have to tell my son about that." Joshua studied the few changes he could see in Beth since the last time he had seen her. Tiny lines had formed around Beth's mouth and there were dark circles under her eyes. The youthful pinkness in her cheeks had disappeared.

"Well," he reminded himself, "aren't we all getting older?"

Joshua told Murphy, "That was a long time ago. Beth and I dated before I met your mother."

The teenager wasn't going to let his father off so easy. "Dad, she said you just about married her."

With pleasure, Beth noted the striking resemblance the boy bore to his father. Murphy had inherited his father's wavy brown hair, blue eyes, and fair complexion. Joshua Thornton's genes also showed in the boy's lean, athletic build. Just inches shorter than his father, the boy was still tall for his age.

Beth giggled girlishly. "You mean he never told you? Oh, we were the couple in high school. Your father was the quarterback, first string in his junior year—"

"Yeah, Mom told us about that."

"—and I was a varsity cheerleader." Beth struck a pose with her hand on her hip and an imaginary pompom in the air. "Go, Bears! Oh, those were the days!"

The bell over the door at the front of the store jingled. In the security mirror, Beth saw Jan Martin studying the headlines in *The Pittsburgh Gazette* while making her way down the aisle. She yelled louder than necessary and waved to her boss. "Hey, Jan, guess who this is. You'll never guess."

In an attempt to place a name with her face, Joshua studied the rail-thin woman with brown wire-framed glasses perched on her nose and long copper-colored hair tied back with an elastic band into a ponytail. She was dressed in a pair of khaki pants a size too big and a plain, white, button-down shirt.

Instantly recognizing her former childhood friend, Jan ripped off her glasses and smoothed her ponytail in one swift action. "Josh? Josh Thornton? So that moving truck did belong to you."

"It wasn't mine personally," Joshua joked. "It actually belonged to a government contractor."

"What moving truck?" Beth asked.

"Didn't you see it?" Jan fingered her dowdy clothes. "Last night, the biggest moving truck anyone in this town ever saw was unloading all this stuff at Grandma Frieda's old stone house up on Rock Springs. I saw it on my way home after we closed."

Beth smirked. "Some of us have better things to do than watch movers unloading junk."

Ignoring Beth's biting comment, Jan told Joshua, "That black antique Corvette must be yours, too."

"Corvette? Nice, Josh." Beth leaned on her elbows against the counter and swayed sideways on her heels. "Tad told me that you quit the Navy."

Joshua nodded his head. "Tad has been a big help since Val died. He met the movers yesterday to unload my stuff. We didn't get in until one o'clock this morning and spent the night on the floor in sleeping bags." He indicated his and Murphy's bedraggled appearances. "That's why we look like we just went on a forced march across the country."

"I imagine that big old house is going to need a lot of work," Jan observed. "It's sat empty ever since Grandma Frieda died."

"Over ten years." Joshua suppressed a gasp of recognition when he finally recognized her. "Jan Martin literally grew up down the street from me," he told Murphy as proof that he did remember her.

Jan told Joshua solemnly, "I was sorry to hear about your wife dying. I'm surprised that you left the Navy, though."

"Valerie's death forced me to examine my priorities. It is impossible to raise five kids alone while putting in eighty hours a week and traveling for JAG."

"JAG?" Beth asked.

Joshua explained, "I was a lawyer assigned to the Judge Advocate General."

Murphy told them with pride, "Dad convicted an admiral for murder and sent him to Leavenworth for life."

Despite Murphy's announcement, Beth appeared disappointed. "So you never saw any action?"

"Only in a courtroom," Joshua demurred.

Beth abruptly changed the subject by stating in a perky tone, "Jan manages the store now."

"Mom is semi-retired," the store manager explained. "I write for the paper."

Giggling, Beth interjected, "She writes these charming little articles for *The Evening Review*."

"Where are the rest of your children?" Jan asked suddenly.

"They are sorting out the furniture and crates back at the house. I left J.J. in charge. He's Murphy's twin. I also have two daughters, Tracy and Sarah, and another son, Donny."

Amused, Jan said, "Figures that an orphan and only child would have five kids."

Joshua chuckled at the irony of his life before telling his old friends, "We're on our way to my new office. I bought Doc Wilson's old place." He didn't miss Beth's and Jan's exchange of raised eyebrows.

"No one has been in that place since Doc died four years ago." Beth giggled.

Joshua rationalized, "George warned me that it was a fixer-upper, but the building is solid, and it is a good location right here in town."

Jan reassured him. "I'm sure it will be a gem once you fix it up. Is there anything we can do to help?"

Reminded of what had brought him into the store, Joshua turned his attention to Beth. "My son Donny has asthma. Tad told me he called in a prescription for his medication, and I want to make sure you have it." He was aware of Jan's watchful eye on the druggist while Beth stood up from where she had been leaning against the counter to check her computer to find that she did have the prescription ready to fill.

After the father and son left the store, Beth mused, "He still looks great, doesn't he?" She noted that since they were last lovers, Joshua Thornton still had his slender waist and fit well into his worn jeans.

Jan groaned and slunk back to her office with her newspaper clutched against her flat chest.

$*$ $*$ $*$ $*$

Swoosh!

At the west end of Rock Springs Boulevard, the box Joshua Junior (J.J.) held, propelled by the force of ten-year-old Donny Thornton's blow aimed for his sister's head, flew across the stone house's attic. The collection of letters and pictures inside scattered like falling leaves in an autumn breeze. A stack of letters tied together with a pink ribbon hit the floor to create a mushroom cloud of dust.

Thirteen-year-old Sarah retaliated with a fist to the side of Donny's head that knocked him into a stack of boxes. The whole stack tumbled over, and their contents spilled out across the floor.

It was an easy task for Sarah Thornton to win in a physical challenge from her plump, bookish, little brother. Sarah was an athletically muscular girl. She always wore her straight blond hair in a ponytail, and no makeup ever touched her face. Cosmetics were for prissy girls, like Tracy, her sister who was older by two years.

"Knock it off!" As J.J. inserted himself between his battling siblings, he mentally recalled the moments before the fight broke out to determine what had prompted it. Was it really because Donny was standing in Sarah's way when she was getting ready to go downstairs?

While her brother scolded Donny and Sarah after breaking up the fight, Tracy Thornton knelt in the blanket of dust that covered the floor to repack the overturned boxes.

Tracy Thornton was a girl on her way to womanhood. Like her late mother, Tracy was petite and delicate-looking. Even with only a touch of makeup, she was pretty. Exposed by the tank top and shorts she wore for relief from the misery of the summer's humidity, Tracy's flesh was the color of milk in spite of the California sun of their last home in San Francisco. She had pulled her long auburn hair back into a ponytail in anticipation of a day of hard work.

In the attic dimly lit by a single bare light bulb and the sunlight able to fight its way through the bug and dirt-encrusted windows, it was difficult for her to tell if she was finding everything that was spilt onto the floor.

"Sarah, why can't you just let him go?" J.J. asked his sister.

Tracy retrieved an envelope from under the dresser. Observing that the seal was unbroken, she studied the address and postmark.

"He took a swing at me!" Sarah stated her case for justifiable assault.

The postmark on the envelope was Chester, West Virginia. It was mailed from in town.

J.J. reminded her, "You knocked him down first."

"I barely touched him," Sarah scoffed.

"Hey, guys, look at this!" Tracy stood up and showed them the letters bound with the pink ribbon and the unopened envelope.

"These letters are all addressed to Claire MacMillan. That was Dad's mom. They're from overseas." Tracy shifted through the pictures from the box. "And these pictures are of a young couple. I think they're Dad's parents."

"These are Grandpa's letters to Grandma," J.J. confirmed as he read the front and back of the envelopes in the stack. "Dad will get a kick out of seeing these."

"Let's read them." Sarah grabbed for the letters.

J.J. held them out of her reach. "No, they're personal. We'll give them to Dad, and, if he wants us to read them, he'll let us."

Tracy pointed to the front of the envelopes. "Look at the date on those letters. They're from the sixties." She showed them the envelope she had found separated from those tied with the ribbon. "But this envelope is postmarked 1970. It is addressed to Claire Thornton from someone named Jefferson. The return address is Chester, West Virginia. It was never opened."

"Maybe the humidity resealed it?" Intrigued, J.J. studied the envelope. He noticed the post date. "May 8, 1970. Why does that date ring a bell?"

"That was before you were even born," Sarah stated.

"Yeah, but I heard that date about something before," J.J. countered. "Why would someone write a letter to someone right here in town in 1970 when they could call them on the phone? It doesn't look like a card. I wonder what this is about?"

*   *   *   *

"So this is a fixer-upper?" Murphy tried unsuccessfully to lighten his father's mood by asking the question in a Brooklyn accent.

Joshua failed to see any humor in the quip.

During the whole one-and-a-half-block walk to his new office, Joshua reassured himself that he was wise to invest in Dr. Wilson's two-story office building in the heart of Chester. He had a waiting area and two examination rooms on the ground floor. The doctor's private office and a lab, which Joshua could convert into a break room for himself and the associates he planned to hire eventually, was upstairs.

Dr. Russell Wilson had been an institution in Chester for over seventy years. When Joshua Thornton was in high school, the doctor showed his young patient a yellowed diploma to prove that he had graduated from medical school in 1928. In his later years, the town's only doctor suffered from arthritis so badly that he was forced to give Joshua his physical for his Naval Academy application from a desk chair. Despite the breaking down of his body, the doctor's mind had remained sharp. He never had to check his files. He could recall every detail about his patients, right down to their parents' and ancestors' medical history.

One of Chester's most respected citizens, Dr. Wilson was as much a role model to Joshua Thornton as his grandfather, uncle, and cousin. It wasn't until Joshua went to Annapolis that he discovered that not all doctors were stout men who smelled of a mixture of schnapps and cigars and made house calls in the middle of the night.

All of Joshua's efforts at self-encouragement about his investment failed at the sight of the abandoned building. The wooden siding was discolored and weather-beaten beyond repair. The windows were so caked with filth that they had become opaque.

A moose head greeted Joshua and his son in the front foyer. A huge bookcase with a broken glass front sat right smack in the middle of the bare, splintered, hardwood floors in the reception area. Murphy counted three roll-top desks overflowing with stacks of files and papers.

The young man watched his father from over the junk piled up between them.

Joshua firmly ground his teeth in an effort to control his rising frustration over what was clearly an unwise investment made from across the country during what had to be the most traumatic year in his and his family's life.

Joshua responded to his son's quip by turning around in a complete circle as he took in the monumental task that lay before him to make the building suitable for his place of business.

Murphy picked up an old ceiling lamp that sat on top of a scarred examination table. The teenager's action caused an avalanche of junk from the table and two stools on either side of it.

"Leave it!" Joshua ordered when Murphy attempted to restack the junk. "Damn it! George must have seen me coming from a mile away!"

"Betcha didn't know Mrs. Wilson was a pack rat?"

Not recognizing the jovial voice that interrupted his father's curse, Murphy sought to see who had joined them.

A man dressed in jeans and an oversized white tee shirt had come through the open door behind them. He strolled around the office while picking up files and studying their contents like a patron perusing a shop open for business.

Except for additional smile lines and a few extra strands of gray hair that added character to a handsome face, the visitor resembled Joshua in his coloring and features. The most notable difference was that while Joshua was muscular from a lifetime of athletics, their visitor was a full head shorter and slightly built. Whoever the stranger was, Murphy sensed by the smile that came to his father's lips that he was friend rather than foe.

"I've been dying to see what was in here." The visitor petted the moose head.

"Why didn't you warn me?" There was a note of affection in Joshua's curt question.

The visitor reached out and patted Joshua on the cheek. "Because if you bought it; lock, stock, and barrel, then I could get my hands on these files." He indicated the folders and papers overflowing from the roll-top desks, boxes, and crates scattered around the room.

"What do a bunch of old files mean to you?" Murphy asked.

"Most of these patients, the living ones that is, are now mine."

Joshua turned to his son. "You don't know who this is, do you?" He smiled in response to the shake of Murphy's head. "This is the guy I've been exchanging e-mails with for the last six months. Dr. Tad MacMillan, my cousin, your second cousin. He's the town doctor now since Doc Wilson died."

From where he was studying the moose head between himself and Murphy, Tad winked at the teenager. "I'm the only doctor who has an office here in town and will lower himself to make house calls," he added jokingly, "when I'm not sitting around empty houses all afternoon waiting for movers. You know those guys didn't show up until six o'clock last night? It was dark by the time they got all that stuff out of that truck."

Joshua told him with sincerity, "And I thank you for being there to let them in."

Murphy gasped at Tad. "Now I remember you. You were at our great-grand-mother's funeral. You had long hair then, and gave me and J.J. rides on your motorcycle."

"If your dad will let you, I can give you another ride. The bike I have now is even bigger and badder than the one I had back then." While Murphy grinned in anticipation of another exhilarating ride on his cousin's Harley, Tad held up a file he had picked up from one of the desks and returned his attention to the boy's father. "So can I relieve you of these old files?" he asked the building's new owner.

Joshua didn't answer right away. "Why didn't you just have your patients request them after Doc died? Then, his office would have had to send them over."

"I did that, but Mrs. Wilson refused to send them. She was very eccentric."

"I don't remember that."

Tad swore. "Oh, Josh! Come on! She washed her hands every five minutes, if not more—"

"She was a nurse."

"She was a compulsive personality and she never forgot about the sins of my youth."

"One of the curses of being a legend."

"Are you a legend?" Murphy interjected.

"You're too young to know," Joshua answered. "I'll tell you about the infamous Tad MacMillan when you're thirty-six."

Tad rolled his eyes. "I'm a good guy now! Anyway, Mrs. Wilson never let me forget about my wild days. She wouldn't let anyone else forget it, either. She always called me 'that junkie down the street'. After Doc died and I told my patients to request their files be sent over, Mrs. Wilson claimed in every case that she couldn't find them. Then, after she died, her daughter—You remember Paula?"

Joshua answered the sudden question with a nod of his head.

Tad resumed his explanation. "Paula moved to Baltimore. She came back home for the funeral, took one look inside that house, which Mrs. Wilson never let anyone in after Doc died, and about fainted. That was when Paula discovered that her mother was a major pack rat." Tad gestured with a wave of his hand at the contents of the room as proof of his statement.

"So I see," Joshua responded.

"Paula hired a professional cleaning crew to clean out all the junk at their house. She had them bring all the stuff they didn't take to the landfill down here and sold it to George."

"Who unloaded it on me—on your recommendation." Joshua pointed a finger of blame at Tad. "I trusted you."

Murphy and his siblings would be intimidated into compliance by the glare Joshua aimed at his cousin. They called it "the look."

Instead of backing down into a gesture of passivity, Tad MacMillan responded to Joshua's glare with a smile that lit up the dingy room. "Josh," he purred, "have I ever let you down?"

A grin fought its way to Joshua's lips.

Murphy could now see why his second cousin was a legend. Tad MacMillan was clearly one of the most charismatic men the teenager had ever met. He could even charm Joshua Thornton.

Tad went on to offer, "I'll help you clean this place out and buy the stuff that you can't use if you will let me have these files."

Joshua smirked mockingly at his son. "Should we?"

CHAPTER 2

▼

"The good news is that all of our furniture made it here in one piece," J.J. reported to his father upon his and Murphy's return home.

Joshua wiped a drop of dirty sweat from his brow and inspected his children's progress in unpacking their belongings. Five days of driving across the country in a van filled with five kids and a dog were catching up with him. Joshua was physically and emotionally drained.

Slumped in his recliner with a beer bottle braced between his thighs in lieu of a cleared-off end table on which to place it, Joshua observed Admiral, their big mutt, eying a spot on the sofa as if to determine if he would fit on it.

Seeming to sense his master's eyes on him, the dog turned his head to see that his instinct was right.

"Don't even think about it," Joshua warned the canine.

Admiral retreated to his doggy bed that had haphazardly landed in front of the fireplace after being yanked out of a moving crate.

The Thornton children rescued the funny-looking puppy with huge paws from the pound. It was only after the children had bonded with him that a dog breeder informed Joshua that his family's new pet was a Great Dane/Irish Wolf-hound mix. Within a year, Admiral resembled, in looks and size, a wire-haired Scooby Doo.

"What's the bad news?" Joshua took the clipboard that held a list he had made of all their belongings before turning them over to the movers to be transported across the country. He tasked J.J. and Tracy with checking off the items on the list as they unpacked those boxes that had arrived the night before.

"Seven boxes are missing," J.J. reported.

Joshua studied the inventory list. J.J. had checked off every item except for seven boxes. He read the contents of each box: legal documents (will, birth certificates, etc), photo albums/family videos, diplomas, puzzles, and the CD collection.

"How important is the stuff that's missing?" Donny asked from where he sat upside down in a wing-backed chair that belonged in the study. The boy rested with his back in the seat part while his legs were raised up above him across the back of the chair.

"They only include the birth certificates for you guys." Joshua didn't tell them about the lump he felt forming in his throat as he noted that one of the missing items was the framed picture of their mother that he always kept on the corner of his desk. "I'm going to have to call them."

"I already did," J.J. announced. "They promised to call back first thing in the morning."

Pleased with his first-born son's initiative, Joshua sat back in his chair and took another swallow of his beer.

As if it would be news to her family, Sarah told her father, "You are aware that this house only has one bathroom." The girl was practicing her juggling skills with some ping-pong balls she had found.

Joshua moaned. "Yes, Sarah, I am aware of that." Additional bathrooms were top priority in renovating the house built before multiple bathrooms became a necessity for large families.

"Who ever heard of a mansion with only one bathroom?" Sarah scoffed.

"This isn't a mansion," Joshua countered. "It's a house. It's a big old stone house built over one hundred years ago when indoor plumbing alone was a luxury."

With a note of admiration in her tone, Tracy added, "And it was built by our great-great-great grandfather, Jeremiah Thornton, as a wedding gift for his bride, Rachel. He even laid the cobblestone driveway. And she planted the lilac bushes out front and the rose garden around the wrap-around porch."

Sarah rolled her eyes. "I don't care about that. I just know that if we don't get another bathroom, one of these mornings I'm going to kill you for using up all the hot water like you did this morning."

Tracy countered, "Well, if you didn't sleep so late you wouldn't be the last one to get the bathroom."

Exasperated, Joshua announced, "We will get more bathrooms."

J.J. tapped Murphy on the arm. "I guess we better start cleaning out that attic if we want to put our room up there."

Before his sons could ascend the stairs to go up to the top floor, Joshua asked with a wicked chortle, "By the way, did you find any skeletons up in that attic that I should know about?" When he consented to the twins rooming in the attic, Joshua already knew the monumental task before them.

From where she sat in the living room's window seat looking out onto the rolling front lawn, Tracy answered her father's question by handing him the stack of letters tied with the pink ribbon. "They seem to be letters your parents sent to each other while your dad was in the Navy."

Joshua smiled as he studied the writing on the envelopes. When it came to his parents, he had vague memories of a young couple very much in love.

Tracy handed him the unopened envelope. "There's one letter that wasn't opened. The return address is Virginia Avenue right here in Chester."

Joshua observed the difference in the handwriting across the front of the envelope from those in the stack bound by the ribbon. "This was written by a leftie."

"A leftie?" Murphy asked as he and his twin came back into the room to learn more about the unread letter.

"I can tell by the slant in her writing." Joshua showed them the handwriting across the front of the envelope. "This was addressed by a left-handed woman."

Then, Joshua noticed the post date: May 8, 1970. Struck by the date, he dropped back into the recliner. He studied the handwriting on the envelope more closely.

J.J. noticed the color drain from his father's face. "What's wrong, Dad?"

"This was mailed the same day my parents died."

Tracy caught her breath. "The same day they died? I'm sorry, Dad. I didn't realize."

"I knew that date sounded familiar. That must be why the letter was never opened," j.J. concluded. "The addressee was deceased by the time it arrived."

"Didn't Grandma and Grandpa die at the Grand Canyon?" Sarah asked.

"They were on a second honeymoon after my father got out of the Navy and were killed in a car accident on their way back." Joshua opened the envelope and took out the letter written on two sheets of purple stationery. "Grandmomma must not have had the heart to open this so soon after they died and then forgot about it."

Silently, Joshua digested the contents of the letter while his children studied the changes in his expression as he read and reread every word. In an attempt to read over his shoulder, they moved in closer. Donny rolled out of the wing-backed chair to turn himself right side up.

Joshua muttered, "I didn't know about any of this."

Demanding to know the contents, his kids crowded closer around him.

"It's from a Lulu…" Joshua checked the last name written on the return address on the envelope. "…Jefferson. I never heard of her."

Unable to summarize the letter in only a few words, he read the letter out loud:

"Dear Claire,

Tomorrow I'm leaving for Philadelphia. Would you believe I got a singing gig at a real club? Things are really looking up.

Anyway, I tried to call you but Frieda…"

Joshua stopped reading to remind his children that Frieda was his grand-mother, their great-grandmother.

"Anyway, I tried to call you but Frieda told me that you and Johnny are on a second honeymoon in the Grand Canyon. You two must be serious about giving Josh a little sister.

Remember that dead body we found in the Bosley barn? How could you ever forget? His face is seared into my mind. Well, I saw him today in Rev-erend Rawlings's office. I went there to talk to the reverend and Marge and Al about the music for their wedding, and there was his picture on the wall. It was a picture of Reverend Rawlings and Sheriff Delaney and some other guys in army uniforms. Reverend Rawlings said it was a picture of him and some of his buddies from the Korean War. That's why Sheriff Delaney said we lied. Our body and them were all war buddies. Figures!

It was him! I'm positive! Tell Johnny and see what he thinks. I tried to call Ricky Pendleton about it, but since he moved to Youngstown I don't have his phone number. Maybe Johnny has it. I'm sure Johnny will be able to make sense out of all this.

Call you when I get back.

Peace & Love,

Lulu

P.S. Good luck on that baby sister for Josh."

Joshua folded up the letter and put it back into the envelope. Once again, he studied the handwriting on the front of the envelope.

J.J. spoke first. "So your dad died before he could check into it. I wonder what she did about it."

Sarah asked, "Was this body in the barn murdered or—?"

After Tracy pointed out that Lulu referred to it as just a body in the barn, her sister proposed that they go find Bosley's barn to see where the body was discovered.

"That was over thirty years ago. That barn is probably long gone by now." J.J. asked his father. "Who is this Reverend Rawlings, Dad?"

That was one question to which Joshua knew the answer. "Now, there is a piece of work," he replied to the question with a grin. "Reverend Rawlings has a church in New Cumberland. He's very influential in the valley. I went to school with his son, Wally."

"Were you friends?" Tracy asked.

Her father laughed. "Not exactly. Wally always tried to make me feel like there was something wrong with me since my parents were dead. He is now the county's prosecuting attorney."

Joshua dismissed the contents of the letter in his hand with a single shake of his head. "We're talking about a thirty-year-old letter from some lady I never heard of that is about a body that may not have been murdered. It was probably a vagrant who crawled into the barn to keep warm and died of natural causes."

"If that was the case," Murphy argued, "why would it be so important to this Lulu to tell your folks that this Reverend Rawlings knew the guy? She couldn't even wait to get back from this singing gig to tell them. She had to write them a letter to make sure they knew about it as soon as they got back from making you a sister."

Joshua confessed to his own curiosity. "I will find out what happened when Mom didn't get this letter."

That prospect was promising to the children.

"How are you going to do that?" Murphy wondered.

Joshua smiled slyly. "One of the advantages of small towns over the big city is that in every small town there is one person who knows everything." He winked at his children. "Fortunately, I know him."

*   *   *   *

Late that night, after his children had fallen into an exhausted sleep after their move, Joshua used the excuse of taking Admiral for a walk to go visit the best source in town to inquire about the contents of Lulu Jefferson's letter.

Dr. Tad MacMillan's office was on the ground floor of a two-story cape cod tucked between two red brick houses on Indiana Avenue, near the corner of Sixth Street. When he wasn't tending to his patients, Tad lived in an apartment on the second floor with a separate entrance behind the house on Church Alley. A bachelor, Tad had no reason to demand more space for himself and Dog, an unruly stray he had nursed back to health after it was hit by a car.

"I'll get it!" a feminine voice called out from the back of the apartment when Joshua knocked on the screen door at the rear of the house.

When Admiral saw Tad's shaggy mongrel peek out from under the kitchen table, the large dog hid behind his master's legs and stuck his head between Joshua's knees to peer back at the dog half his size. Admiral was a coward at heart.

Tad sat back in a kitchen chair with his bare feet perched up on the corner of the table and one eye aimed at the news on the portable television set hooked up under the cupboard. Even though he was just a few feet away, he didn't make any movement to welcome his cousin into his home. Instead, he laughed at the size of Joshua's pet. "What is that? A pony?"

"He was much smaller when Valerie and the kids picked him up from the pound," Joshua told him through the screen door between them.

Her long legs gracefully swishing under an oversized nightshirt, Maggie Mac-Millan hurried in from the living room and through the kitchen to answer Joshua's knock. The hairbrush the beauty wielded in her hand told Joshua that she had been brushing her long, wavy, strawberry-blond hair. Her golden tan revealed that she had not spent much of the early summer indoors.

Joshua looked quizzically at the girl who could not have been out of her teen years. Despite Tad MacMillan's reputation for going through women like disposable syringes, Joshua considered the beauty too young for the attractive doctor who was in his mid-forties.

After their guest stepped inside the apartment, Maggie threw her arms around his neck. "Uncle Josh! Come in! How was the move?" She kissed him on the cheek.

"Maggie?" Joshua looked the young woman up and down and suddenly felt very old.

"Yes, it's me," Maggie giggled softly. "Who did you think I was?"

"I haven't seen you since—" Joshua held his hand out to his hip.

Aware of his cousin's assumption, Tad laughed loudly. "This is what they grow into."

Seeing that they were blocking her father's view of the television, Maggie led Joshua by his hand across the kitchen to the living room doorway. "I'm just passing through on my way to Penn State."

"Pennsylvania State?" Joshua gasped. "That's where I went to law school." He shook his head in disbelief. "I can't believe you've graduated from high school. Seems like only yesterday your dad called me to say he was a father and I fell out of my chair."

"So did my mother," Tad cracked.

Maggie excitedly asked Joshua, "Did you see the car Dad bought me for graduation?" After Joshua answered her question with a shake of his head, she led him back across the kitchen to show off the blue coupe parked next to her father's motorcycle in the alley. "I wanted a convertible, but Dad said it isn't safe."

"This from a man who only drives Harleys?" Joshua snickered when he heard Tad growl in response to the joke made at his expense.

Maggie laughed huskily.

Excusing herself with the explanation that it had been a long drive up from Florida and she was tired, Maggie disappeared into the back of the apartment after once more kissing Joshua on the cheek and giving Tad a quick kiss on the lips.

"She's a lovely girl," Joshua complimented her father as he sat at the table across from Tad. He added with a sly grin, "She must get her looks from her mother."

"She gets them from me."

"You ever hear from her mother?" Joshua asked casually.

Tad responded with a single shake of his head and a sideways glance in his cousin's direction before quickly returning his attention to the television set. "You never stop, do you?"

"No, I don't." Joshua chuckled. "Look, it's been eighteen years, and you have never once referred to Maggie's mother by name. It's only been 'the mother'. You never even told your own mother—Maggie's grandmother—"

"It was a one-night stand, ancient history, and none of your business." Tad snickered, "You just can't stand it when you don't know something."

"No, I can't. That's why I'm so good at what I do."

"What do you want besides to pick a fight?" Tad pushed against the table with his feet to expertly balance his chair on its hind legs. As a further sign of his coordination, Tad shoved a box of Pepperidge Farm cookies across the table to Joshua in the form of an offering while performing his balancing act.

While he accepted the offer, Joshua noticed that Tad was not eating the cookies himself, but instead feeding them to Dog, who was under the table. "I saw your light was on while I was walking Admiral." He gestured to the dog that had lain down dangerously close to the only two legs of Tad's chair touching the floor.

Keeping an eye on the television, Tad plopped the chair down onto its four legs and got up to pour two cups of tea for himself and his cousin from a kettle warming on the stove.

Joshua nodded towards the portable set. "What are you watching?"

Tad set a mug with the tea bag seeping in the boiling hot water in front of Joshua. "The news. I don't mean to be rude, but I've been watching this series they've been running. Tess Bauer, she's a local girl, went off to Pittsburgh and is with the station out there. She's been doing an in-depth investigation into the drug traffic here in the valley. She even interviewed me, but not on camera."

"Why not? Aren't you pretty enough for on-camera interviews?" Joshua took a cautious sip of the hot tea.

"I'd love to clean up the drug traffic in the valley, but that's for the law, not the news media. All I can talk about are my own addictions and the usual crap about how dangerous they are." Much to Dog's dismay, Tad tossed a cookie to Admiral. "She did find a source willing to go on camera. They've been showing interviews with her all week." With the remote resting at his elbow, he turned up the volume on the television. "There she is."

Joshua turned his attention to the portable set.

The woman appeared to be barely out of her teens. Her hair, a reddish hue that matched that of freshly spilt blood, was cut just a fraction of an inch longer than a crew cut. She wore a skimpy black top with spaghetti straps, which revealed a black widow spider tattoo on her bare left shoulder. Her stark, black makeup, including black lipstick, on her pale skin made her appear eerie. She wore a thick collar of dozens upon dozens of black strings, leather straps, and silver beaded necklaces; matching bracelets on her naked arms; and rings on every finger and thumb. Her hands were further adorned with black fingernails that looked more like the claws of a carnivorous beast.

Observing her high cheekbones and facial bone structure, Joshua thought the subject of the interview would be pretty if it weren't for the morbid makeup and attire.

Journalist Tess Bauer contrasted her source's appearance in a conservative pale blue women's suit. She wore her honey-blond hair straight down to her shoulders, with bangs chopped straight across her forehead. Tess was what Joshua called "handsome".

"The girl she's been interviewing is Amber. She doesn't give her last name," Tad told Joshua.

The interview took place in what appeared to be someone's living room. The conservative furniture was not at all what would be found a drug addict's home, at least not Amber's.

"So you have been heavily involved in the trafficking of drugs in the Ohio Valley?" Tess was asking from off camera.

Amber's expression was between that of a sneer and a smirk. "I don't do the trafficking myself. Let's just say that I'm real close to one of the top people."

"Who is that?" Tess asked from off-camera again.

"Why," Amber jeered, "Vicki Rawlings."

"We have talked about Victoria Rawlings before," Tess told the audience on camera. She was sitting in a chair with a forest of house plants behind her. "You said in previous interviews that Victoria Rawlings, the granddaughter of the Reverend Orville Rawlings, is heavily involved in the drug trade in the Ohio Valley."

Amber was on camera again. "You might say she is the manager and Reverend Rawlings is the CEO of the company."

"Do you believe—?" Joshua started to ask Tad, who held up his hand to hush him.

"Now, as I told you before off-camera, Amber, you can't make statements on-camera that you can't prove."

"Oh, I can prove everything," the girl said mockingly as she slapped a micro-cassette tape onto the glass top coffee table. "Here's your proof."

The setting changed. Tess Bauer was now speaking to the viewers from behind the news desk. "I brought the tape that Amber gave me during that interview here to the studio. It is of a telephone conversation between Amber and a woman she identified as Victoria Rawlings. We will play that tape for you now."

"But—" Joshua tried to object only to have Tad hush him again.

The transcript of the telephone conversation on the tape was displayed on the screen as the audio played. Amber was talking to Victoria about a drug shipment they had just delivered.

"I never saw so much money in my life," Amber was saying. "So what do you do with all that cash? Why don't we go to Hawaii?"

"Someday, girlfriend, some day," Vicki responded.

Joshua noted that her voice sounded younger than Amber's.

"But there was so much. How much was there there?"

"Two hundred thousand."

"Two hundred thousand? Damn! Let's move to Hawaii."

"I wish I could, but I don't get to keep it. I only get to keep my cut. Ten (bleep) percent."

"How many ways is the cash split?" Amber asked.

"Two. Three, if you count that man they call my father." Vicki giggled, "But he doesn't really count because I can usually get him to give me some, if only to shut me up."

"That's Wally Rawlings, the county prosecutor," Tad whispered to Joshua.

"And who are the other two?" Amber was asking.

"Aunt Bridgette and Grandfather," Vicki laughed girlishly. "If his congregation only knew that their leader was the biggest (bleep) drug lord in the whole (bleep) valley!"

Tad shook his head while Joshua looked at him with surprise. "Did you know that?"

"It's common knowledge in drug circles."

"They're going to get their butts sued." Joshua indicated the television station playing the news broadcast.

Tad turned off the set. "I know. Even though it's true, it is also common knowledge that Vicki Rawlings hates her family. Rawlings's lawyer can make a case that she made it all up and sue the pants off Bauer."

"How about this Amber? What family is she from?"

"I have no idea. I never heard of her before, and I thought I knew everyone in this valley. Probably just some barfly wanting to get her face on television. When Rawlings sees this, she may find the price for her fifteen minutes of fame is too high." Tad took his now empty mug to the sink. "Want some more tea?"

"No thanks."

Tad washed his mug and the couple of other dishes in the sink. "How are you doing?"

Joshua avoided the real topic about which Tad was asking. "My back is killing me."

"That's old age."

"It is not." Joshua revealed his somber mood. "When is the pain going to go away?"

"It won't." Drying his hands on the dishtowel, Tad turned back to Joshua. "It will become livable, but it won't ever go away."

Joshua sat back in his chair. "I seem to recall you being more help when you drank. At least I liked your advice better then."

"Hey, blame yourself if you don't like me this way. If it weren't for you, I wouldn't even be here, let alone drinking tea while watching the nightly news."

"Are you sorry that I dragged you out of that shack and took you to Glenbeigh?"

"No." Tad grinned fondly at his cousin as he sat across from him. "I never did thank you for that, did I?"

Feeling uneasy with the topic, Joshua shrugged off Tad's gratitude.

In spite of his younger cousin's discomfort, Tad continued, "How many men would get on a plane and fly across the country to break into a house, drag a guy out kicking and screaming, and take him to rehab?"

"I couldn't let you die." Joshua felt brave enough to ask about what he had been wondering for over a decade. "Were you trying to kill yourself?"

"Maybe. I don't know." Tad sighed and looked at his savior. "Life isn't fair, Josh. You read the Bible, didn't you?" Before Joshua could answer, Tad told him, "The word 'fair' isn't in there. God never promised that life would be fair. I mean, why is it that a bum like me has someone like you go out of his way to save him, while a good person like Valerie—?" His voice trailed off.

Joshua looked down at his hands. "I wish I knew."

Tad watched Joshua study his hands as if he had suddenly noticed a malformation in his palms. "Why did you come back here?"

Joshua paused a moment. He blinked before rubbing his palms together as he answered, "I always said that I would come back."

"You had a very successful career in the Navy."

"Valerie and I agreed that we would come back here to live after I retired."

"You had five years left to retirement, and Valerie is dead." Tad asked again, "Why did you pull up all the roots you had in San Francisco to come back here and start over again?"

Joshua shook his head. He wanted Tad to move on to another subject. "I wanted to come home."

"Why? You haven't been back here since Grandmomma died."

With effort, Joshua tore his eyes from where he was looking at the wall next to where Tad sat to meet his cousin's suspicious gaze. "When Valerie did something that made no sense to me, she used to say that God tugged at her heart until she felt like she had to do what He wanted."

Tad slowly nodded his head. "Did God tug at your heart to make you come back?"

"You just said it. What sensible man leaves the Navy five years from retirement and uproots his kids to move into a drafty, old house with only one bathroom and no central air?"

"God doesn't always make sense. Only He knows how everything is going to come together in the long term. We only see it in the short term."

Joshua sighed as he quoted his late grandmother. "God does everything for a reason."

"Yes, I believe He does."

"Why did He take Valerie from me?"

"I don't know."

Dog came out from under to table and put his front paws in his master's lap to beg for another cookie. His plea was met with one for him and another for Admiral.

Joshua quietly watched Tad pet the grateful dogs.

"It seems to me," Tad said when he resumed their conversation, "that you never would have come home until after you retired unless something happened to make you come back sooner. Valerie's death was that something. But why now? Why would God want you to come back now instead of in five years?"

"Why don't you ask Him?"

"You ask Him," Tad countered playfully. "You're the one He's been talking to."

Joshua sat back and sighed with relief. He saw by the soft grin on Tad's face the answer to his next question. "Do you think I'm nuts?"

"Why would I think you were crazy?"

"I just told you that God has been speaking to me through my heart."

Tad scoffed. "God speaks to me all the time."

"The last man who told me that God spoke to him, I put away for life for a double homicide." Joshua explained, "He said that God told him to beat his stepdaughter's and her boyfriend's brains in with a rock because they committed the sin of adultery."

"Is God telling you to kill anyone?"

Joshua quickly shook his head.

Tad chose his words carefully. "I can't tell you if your grief over Valerie has put you over the edge. Hell, maybe what you think is God tugging at your heart is really homesickness for the family you left behind twenty years ago when you went off to the academy." He smiled as he added, "I can tell you that if you are basing your questions about your sanity on God speaking to you, then you and I should look into a double-occupancy in the psyche ward at East Liverpool Hospital because God has spoken to me every single day of my life."

"Every day?" Joshua swallowed.

Tad whispered, "It was only after He humbled me into sobriety that I was able to comprehend what He was telling me."

"What was He telling you?"

Tad sucked in his breath and sighed as he responded, "That He loved—and loves—me very much—too much to let me keep screwing up." He laughed softly. "But that doesn't always stop me."

"Does it stop any of us from screwing up?"

"Nope. That is the human condition, my son."

Both men became lost in their own thoughts.

Afraid that he would break down if Tad continued to talk about Valerie, Joshua abruptly changed the topic by asking, "Did you know Lulu Jefferson?"

Tad repeated the question with a naughty tone, "Did I know Lulu Jefferson?" He smiled broadly until the younger man caught the meaning behind his expression.

"Wait a minute. Lulu was Mom's friend."

"She was also a good teacher," Tad snickered.

"What kind of teacher?"

"Guitar." Seeing Joshua's doubtful expression, Tad went on, "I mean it. She did teach me how to play the guitar…and other things. Let me set it up for you. She was twenty-five with a tiny waist, big soft breasts, and legs that didn't stop. I was fifteen and eager to learn." Tad sighed dreamily.

"Do you mean that she—?"

"I was her toy," Tad declared proudly. "Yeah, I knew Lulu. Aunt Claire didn't know anything about us. She would have killed her." He paused thoughtfully. "Now if they didn't make an odd pair."

"Why did they make an odd pair?"

"Lulu sang folk songs and played the guitar and knew all the guys. Now, Aunt Claire only dated your dad from the time they were old enough be boyfriend and girlfriend. She dressed more like Laura Petrie than Joey Heatherton, which was how Lulu dressed, but they were the best of friends."

Tad took two cookies out of the bag and gave one to Joshua. He stopped and mused, "Too bad." He shook his head before biting into the cookie. "I remember that was so bizarre."

"What?" Joshua prodded him.

"Lulu and Aunt Claire were best friends, and they died separately on the same day." Tad put his feet back up on the table and pushed his chair so it teetered back on its hind legs.

"How did Lulu die?"

"A drug overdose. She died the exact same day your parents were killed in that car accident out West." He sighed. "That was one awful week."

Intrigued, Joshua sat forward.

Struck by a realization, Tad asked him, "Why do you want to know about Lulu?"

"I heard the name."

"You heard the name from whom?"

"Around." Joshua stood up and stretched. "Thanks for the tea." He patted Tad on the shoulder and headed for the door. "I'll see you tomorrow."

Admiral waited for his master to open the door to make his escape from the other dog.

"Want a piece of advice?"

To answer Tad's question, Joshua stopped at the door and turned around.

"Watch with whom you spread certain names around. The more things change, the more they stay the same. Reverend Rawlings may be old, but he's not dead."

"I said nothing about Reverend Rawlings."

"You didn't have to. A mysterious death in Chester? You don't have to look long before Reverend Rawlings's name creeps up like a cancer. He didn't become a drug lord by quoting Jesus."

Admiral looked longingly up at the unopened door.

Joshua put his hand on the doorknob to leave, but stopped. "Did Lulu ever mention a dead body to you?"

Tad responded with a wicked grin, "We didn't talk that much."

When Joshua turned back to the door, Tad interrupted his departure by asking, "Are you talking about the body your folks found on their prom night?"

Joshua whirled back around. "Prom night? They found a dead body on their prom night?"

Tad looked questioningly at him. "I thought you knew about it. You brought it up."

"All I know is that Mom and Dad found a dead body, and Lulu and a Ricky Pendleton were with them."

"I didn't know that. I assumed they were alone."

"But you know about the body." Joshua gave up on leaving and leaned against the kitchen counter across from his cousin.

With a groan, Admiral plopped down onto the floor between the two men.

"I remember your folks talking about it like once. They didn't like to talk about it because it really scared them," Tad said. "Lulu never mentioned it to me at all."

Joshua chuckled naughtily, "Because you two didn't talk that much." He turned serious. "How did they come to find a dead body?"

Tad shrugged and shook his head. "All I know is that it was the night of their senior prom and your folks went to Bosley's barn to make out—"

"Make out?" Joshua repeated.

"That wasn't the way they put it when I was in the room," Tad chuckled, "but I assume they wanted to have sex."

"I know what making out is. So what happened at Bosley's barn?"

Tad shrugged again. "They found a dead body. It was a man."

"Murdered?"

"I don't know the particulars, but I assume so."

"Did they know who he was?"

"Never saw him before," Tad answered. "They went to get the sheriff. Chuck Delaney was the sheriff then. When they came back the body was gone and the sheriff threatened to arrest them for filing a false police report." Tad threw up his hands as a gesture of completing the story, as he knew it. "That's all I know."

Joshua squinted questioningly. "The body was gone?"

"Yep."

Joshua sighed and stared at Tad thoughtfully. After a moment, he asked, "Who is Ricky Pendleton?"

"Maybe Jill Stewart's brother. Her maiden name is Pendleton."

"This guy moved to Youngstown after he graduated from high school."

Nodding his head, Tad said that he was thinking of the same person about whom Joshua was asking. "This guy moved to Ohio to work for General Motors."

"He was there," Joshua muttered.

"If you want to know more about it, I'll ask Jill for Rick's phone number. You can call him but be discreet. Your kids already lost a mother. You're all they've got left."

CHAPTER 3

▼

"Think."

"I'm tired of thinking," Donny told his father. "I don't know where it is." Then, in the same breath, he asked, "Are we going to McDonald's for breakfast?"

Before checking the time on his watch, Joshua observed the two pharmacy customers in line ahead of them. It was already mid-morning. The whole family had wasted most of the morning searching for Donny's asthma inhaler, purchased right before they departed San Francisco, which the boy confessed had been missing for twenty-four hours. After their search turned up nothing, Joshua took Donny to the drug store to get the prescription Tad had called in filled.

While they waited at Chester Drug Store to pick up Donny's medicine, Joshua acknowledged Beth's smile with a slight wave of his hand. He frowned when he noticed that her grin did not reach her eyes. Despite the air conditioning that was on so high that goose bumps formed on his forearms, Joshua saw beads of sweat form on Beth's forehead and upper lip.

Suddenly, Bridgette Rawlings Poole blew in and back to the pharmacy. With the attitude of a woman to be reckoned with, she willed the other customers out of her way.

Even though she was only in her late thirties, Bridgette Rawlings Pool did not hold her age well. Her crimson hair did not match her olive skin tone. She did not stop with her hair when it came to drastically enhancing her appearance. Her silicone breasts were out of proportion with her malnourished body.

Her entrance caused Donny to stop thinking about his anticipated breakfast to adjust his glasses to watch the entertainment that commenced when Bridgette

Poole slapped her hand onto the countertop and demanded, "I want my prescription."

"I'll be with you in just a minute," was Beth's response.

"I don't have a minute," Bridgette snapped. "All you have to do is hand it to me."

Lured by the threat of a scene, Jan Martin came out of her office located behind the pharmacy.

Beth gritted her teeth. Her smile more closely resembled a sneer. "I'll be right with you, Mrs. Poole, as soon as I'm finished with this customer." Ignoring Bridgette's eyes that had widened with outrage, the druggist returned her attention to her previous customer. "Now, that is erythromycin—"

"Ms. Davis! I never—"

Bridgette Poole's lid blew just as Jan slapped a bag onto the counter and stated in a low, yet pleasant, tone, "Your prescription is right here, Mrs. Poole."

With no sign of gratitude, Bridgette snatched up the bag and checked the pharmacy slip stapled on the front.

While giving her pharmacist a warning glance, Jan punched the buttons on the register before further enraging their customer by stating, "That will be forty-six, ninety-eight."

Bridgette shouted, "What?"

Jan repeated the amount of the prescription in a calm tone.

"I have insurance," the customer argued.

"I'm afraid your insurance doesn't cover this prescription, m'am."

"You should be afraid."

"I called to confirm it myself, Mrs. Poole." Jan offered her the phone. "If you would like to call the insurance company, you are welcome to use our phone."

Bridgette grumbled as she dug her checkbook out of her purse and wrote a check. "Never mind. I'll pay you. It's obvious that you need the money more than I do."

Calmly, Jan retaliated, "It isn't because we need the money, Mrs. Poole. It's because your insurance doesn't cover elective drugs. But I must say that this ointment has done a wonderful job in erasing your frown lines."

Bridgette thrust the check at Jan, grabbed the bag containing her prescription, turned to leave, and physically collided with Joshua, who was stepping forward to take his turn at the counter. Like the changing of a dead light bulb, Bridgette's arrogance was replaced with congeniality. "Josh?"

Embarrassed to acknowledge he knew the unpleasant woman, Joshua murmured a greeting.

A smile came to her lips. "Visiting the old homestead, huh?"

"Moving back into the old homestead."

While Bridgette stood her ground to keep Joshua's attention, his son asked Beth if they had time to fill the order for his inhaler. Joshua saw the druggist's hand tremble when she took the insurance card he reached around Bridgette to hold out to her.

"I heard Jan call you Poole." Joshua divided his attention between Bridgette and Beth, who was inputting his insurance information into her computer database. "I guess you married Hal."

"Yeah, I married Hal," Bridgette responded without any pride. "He handles all of Father's publicity. I manage the church's finances."

"I'm not surprised you two kids got married. I remember how Hal followed you around like a lost puppy all through school."

Bridgette showed no fondness at the memory. "He's still devoted." Her grin was like that of a predator as she admired Joshua's firm body. "I heard you got married. Are you divorced?"

"She passed away. It's just me and the kids now." Joshua gestured towards his youngest child.

Their business completed, Donny returned to his father's side.

Bridgette's smile contorted at the sight of the boy. "How sweet," she squeaked before she appeared to recall why she was in such a hurry. "I have to go. I have a breakfast meeting at the club. Give me a call and we'll get together, Josh." With a wave of her hand, Bridgette flew up the aisle and out the door.

"Some people never change," Joshua muttered before turning his attention to his son. "Ready to go?"

"To McDonald's," Donny answered. "I'm hungry."

Joshua squeezed Donny's shoulder as he ushered him up the aisle towards the door. "I could go for an Egg McMuffin myself."

Donny asked along the way. "Who was that witch, Dad?"

Beth and Jan heard Joshua inform his son that Bridgette Poole was Reverend Rawlings's daughter. He waved farewell to his friends back in the pharmacy before exiting the store.

"He has a nice-looking family," Beth mused after the father and son disappeared from sight.

"Yeah," Jan responded with equal wistfulness.

"Could have been my family," the druggist muttered.

"Mine, too," the manager said in an attempt at empathy.

Beth laughed at her. "Like you ever stood a snowball's chance in hell with Joshua Thornton. He asked me to marry him."

Wounded by the shot, Jan reminded Beth of her role as employee. "Next time Bridgette comes in here, just wait on her. Don't get into a debate."

"I was in the middle of waiting on Mrs. Frost."

"You know that Bridgette throws a tantrum when she doesn't get what she wants when she wants it. The sooner you can get her out of here, the better it is for everyone."

Beth sighed with disgust and returned to the supply of pharmaceuticals to fill waiting orders.

Jan observed Beth's trembling hands. "What's wrong with you?"

"Just leave me alone!" Beth snarled. "I have a lot of work to do."

Jan returned back to her office and slammed her office door to mark the end of the discussion.

Alone at last, Beth sat down at her desk and opened the bottom drawer. She took out an unmarked prescription bottle, popped the lid, shook out two pills, and put them into her mouth.

*   *   *   *

Ideally, Joshua hoped to return home with Donny to find a stack of empty moving boxes collapsed and piled up on the front porch waiting to be hauled away with the trash. Instead, the boxes were only slightly less filled and repositioned from one room to another.

Joshua was shocked to discover the twins and their sisters huddled together in the study on the first floor. Murphy manned the laptop concealed behind stacks of Joshua's law books that had yet to be shelved in the built-in bookcases. "What are you doing?" their father demanded to know. "I leave you alone for a few hours and what do I find? You're in here playing computer games."

"We're taking a break," Sarah explained. "We've been working ever since Donny woke us up with his crisis this morning."

"We found Rick Pendleton," J.J. announced proudly.

Joshua's heart dropped into his stomach.

After Tad's reminder of his responsibility as a single parent, Joshua dropped the issue of the letter. Lulu Jefferson was a hippie who died of a drug overdose; the body in the letter was not a matter of any official record because it disappeared before the sheriff could see it; and Reverend Rawlings was not someone anyone wanted as an enemy.

"Why are you looking for Rick Pendleton?" Joshua demanded to know.

Murphy stated the obvious, "Because he was there when Lulu and your folks found that dead body. He's the only one still alive to tell us what happened."

All at the same time, Joshua's four older kids told him about how after talking more and more about Lulu's letter, J.J. decided to check out the Internet for news articles about Lulu's death. Discovering that the local paper's web site had no articles dating back that far, he went to the library in East Liverpool to check their newspaper archives.

J.J. plunged on with his report. "They didn't have anything on file about Grandma and Grandpa finding a dead body, but there was a lot of stuff on Lulu." He handed his father a folder full of copies of newspaper articles.

Joshua was tempted to read the contents of the thick folder, but knew that as soon as he did he would be drawn into the case. "Feels like she got a lot of press," he observed while balancing the folder in his open palm like a human scale.

"Unfortunately, she got all of her publicity after she died," J.J. observed. "In a nutshell, her death was ruled an accidental overdose of heroin or a suicide, but her sister, Karen Jefferson, campaigned to have it changed to murder."

"Heroin?" Joshua raised an eyebrow.

"Lulu was a party girl," Sarah said. "Alcohol, pot, party all night."

Murphy added, "The newspaper editor agreed with the sister that it was murder." He yanked an article out of the stack Joshua held in his hand. "You were right, Dad. Look at her publicity picture."

Joshua studied the sizable clipping that included a picture of Lulu, an attractive young woman with long blond hair sitting cross-legged with a guitar perched across her lap. It was a left-handed guitar. He was pleased with himself for his deduction when he first saw Lulu's handwriting on the front of the envelope. She was left-handed.

"The heroin tracks were in her left arm," Murphy pointed to the section in the article that reported details from the autopsy report, "which means she would have had to inject it with her right hand."

Joshua read on. "The sheriff theorized that she just had a friend do the injection and when she OD'd the guy split."

Tracy presented their hypothesis. "Yeah, but if she was serious about her career, she would not have put tracks in her arms. She would have had the injections where the tracks would not have shown, like between her toes or under her arms."

Even though he agreed, Joshua shrugged. The point about the tracks being in the left arm was not grounds enough for an investigation. "There were a lot of singers and performers back then, and even today, who let their addictions override common sense: Janis Joplin, for one; Jimi Hendrix, for another." He fingered through the collection of articles. "So this sister, Karen, got nowhere?"

J.J. reminded his father that the sheriff was the same Sheriff Chuck Delaney mentioned in Lulu's letter. "He claimed no one had a motive to kill her, of course. He's a suspect."

Joshua was nodding his head. It became clear in the clippings that Lulu was killed before she had a chance to tell anyone about seeing the picture in Reverend Rawlings's office.

Apparently, no one knew about the letter.

"The whole case was dropped after Karen Jefferson was killed in a car accident," J.J. said. "Her car went off the road about eleven months after Lulu died. Then, when the newspaper editor tried making a case for that being murder, he died in a fire when his house burnt down just six weeks after Karen was killed."

Joshua didn't think it was possible for his heart to sink any lower into the pit of his stomach. "So doesn't that tell you something?"

"Yeah." Murphy's face was flushed with excitement. "Lulu was murdered because she saw that guy's picture in Reverend Rawlings's office."

Sarah added, "And we need to bring him to justice."

"We?" Joshua scoffed. "There's no 'we' here. You're missing something. If what you have found suggests what you think it means, and I'm not saying I disagree with you, then this evidence means that we are dealing with a very dangerous man here. I don't want you kids asking questions or stirring up trouble." He made his point by dropping the folder onto the top of his desk and slapping the laptop shut. "Now get to work," he ordered with a gesture towards the study door.

"Ah, come on, Dad," J.J. scoffed. "You've investigated conspiracies and brought down serial killers. This is nothing compared to that." He held up his forefinger and thumb to symbolize a miniscule quantity. "For you, this is just a small case of murder."

CHAPTER 4

▼

Valerie Thornton used to joke, half-seriously, that her husband was obsessive. Once he got on a case, he could not think of anything else until he was satisfied that he had uncovered every minute piece of the puzzle that made up the truth.

Now, sleeping alone in the bed he used to share with his wife in what used to be his grandmother's bedroom, Joshua Thornton wished that he had never opened that envelope and let his children read the contents of Lulu's letter. He realized with dread that he had passed the gene of obsession onto his offspring. He recognized the spark in their eyes as they argued that it was just too much of a coincidence that Lulu Jefferson died the very same day she saw that picture in Reverend Orville Rawlings's office.

One could argue that coincidences, unbelievable ones, do happen. Lulu died on the same day her best friend and her husband were killed while driving across an Oklahoma interstate by a truck driver who had fallen asleep at the wheel of his rig after twenty-two hours without sleep.

Claire and Johnny Thornton weren't murdered. Joshua knew that for a fact. As a curious teenager, he requested a copy of the accident report from the Oklahoma state police and called the witnesses to question them—much to his grandmother's dismay. Their deaths were just a tragic accident.

Why couldn't Lulu's death by a heroin overdose also be a horrible accident like that of so many other talented young artists of her generation back in a period of drug experimentation?

In that case, her death would just be a coincidence, along with the deaths of both her sister and the newspaper editor who claimed it wasn't an accident.

Their deaths crossed the line of coincidence into the territory of suspicious.

Joshua sighed and climbed out of his lonely bed to pace. When he swung his feet to the floor, Admiral awoke with a yelp.

"Sorry," Joshua muttered to the dog while wondering why Admiral, with all the children sleeping in their rooms down the hall, chose to sleep next to his bed. He was the one who objected to the animal's addition to the family.

Admiral gazed longingly up at his master and laid his head on his leg.

With a sigh meant to come across as grudgingly, Joshua stroked the top of Admiral's head and scratched his ears while he debated with his obsession.

It was a short debate.

"Come on," Joshua ended up telling the dog. "We're going for a walk."

It was not long before Joshua found himself knocking on Tad MacMillan's door.

Through the kitchen door, Joshua saw his cousin peer in from the living room to see who was knocking. Then, instead of letting him in, Tad rushed back into the rear of the apartment.

Joshua checked out the driveway at the bottom of the steps. Maggie's new car was gone. Just the day before she had stopped by his house to visit with the kids before continuing on her way to Penn State. So, he concluded, it was not Maggie whom he heard arguing with Tad from inside the apartment before the doctor returned to crack open the storm door.

"What's wrong?" Tad inquired if Donny was having an asthma attack.

After assuring the doctor that his son was fine, Joshua announced, "I have a couple more questions about Lulu." When he stepped forward to invite himself inside, Tad blocked his entry with the door.

"Now?" Tad looked back over his shoulder into the apartment.

Joshua saw a woman's white macramé purse on the kitchen table. "I'm sorry. I didn't realize—"

Tad smiled awkwardly. "It is Saturday night." When Joshua apologized and took a step down the stairs, Tad stopped him. "If it's only a couple of questions, go ahead and ask."

Even as Joshua declined, Tad waved to invite him inside. Yet, while he had let Joshua enter his home, Tad guarded the living room doorway to prevent the visitor trespassing any further.

"I thought you dropped this stuff about Lulu." The dismay in Tad's voice was unmistakable.

"I can't. You know how I am."

"Even if—" Tad shook his head with a sigh. "Forget it. What do you want to know?"

"Did Lulu Jefferson shoot heroin?"

Tad's answer was quick and to the point. "No. She drank a lot of booze and smoked pot, but she didn't do anything that involved needles. She fainted at the sight of needles."

"She had a track in her—"

As Joshua started to explain about the tracks in Lulu's left arm, Tad glanced into the living room. Whatever he saw over his shoulder prompted him to halt the interview. Abruptly, Tab grabbed Joshua by the arm and escorted him to the door. "Listen, can we finish this later? Are you going to church tomorrow?" After Joshua answered that he was taking his family to the First Christian Church, the church both of them had attended while growing up, Tad told him he would see him there and ushered him out.

The latching of the door in Joshua's face signaled the end of their conversation.

It was close to midnight and Joshua still couldn't sleep. So he took Admiral the long way home. They strolled up Sixth Street past Oak Glen Middle School. Donny and Sarah were going to go to the same school Joshua had attended over twenty years earlier.

Joshua heard his name called out when they turned onto Rock Springs Boulevard. He stopped on the corner and peered through the darkness.

Across the street, a street lamp lit up the boulevard's dead end at the opposite end of the street from his house. Rock Springs Boulevard was three blocks in length.

Joshua recalled when the dead end was the entrance to Rock Springs Park. A wooden roller coaster once took up most of the hillside behind the school. The park's carousel that he used to ride with his grandfather every weekend was now in the Smithsonian Museum in Washington, D.C. All evidence of the park was destroyed during the construction of Route 30's three mile path through West Virginia between Ohio and Pennsylvania.

"Josh?" Jan was waving to Joshua from her front porch. "Is that you?" Her home on Rock Springs Boulevard was built onto the hillside. She was cooling off with a tall glass of iced tea. "Couldn't sleep either, huh? I guess the time has come for that old house to get some air conditioning."

Joshua led Admiral up the walk and steep steps to Jan Martin's porch. Judging by her glasses, wet hair clinging to her head, and the short cotton bathrobe that appeared to be the only thing she was wearing, he guessed that Jan had just taken a shower or bath. He explained the reason for his walk at such a late hour. "I'm still getting used to sleeping alone."

Jan held up her glass. The ice tinkled as it collided with the sides of the glass "Have you tried herbal iced tea? I have a blend made especially for relaxation. I'll pour you a glass." She slipped off the railing and went inside to get the tea.

After leaving Admiral on the porch, Joshua followed her into the quaint little cottage. The mementos in the house reminded him that Jan had lived with her mother in the two-bedroom home her whole life. Jan's father died of cancer just three months before she was born.

"How is your mother doing?" Joshua called into the kitchen where his hostess was pouring the tea from a pitcher into a glass. In the living room, he fingered a couple of porcelain thimbles in a glass case on the wall next to a corner curio cabinet filled with Fenton ware.

"She's on a bus tour in Branson, Missouri. She's been traveling a lot lately."

"So you're running the drug store?" Joshua studied the collection of Fenton ware. Judging by how filled the curio cabinet was, he concluded the Martins had almost every piece of the rose-colored blown glass works collection.

"I guess." Jan came out of the kitchen and handed Joshua a frosty mug she had taken from her freezer.

Joshua studied the cold, red colored liquid. The flowery scent reminded him of something Valerie used to drink hot on occasion before going to bed. "What's in it?"

"Chamomile and hibiscus flowers, peppermint, spearmint, and a bunch of other spices. Try it. You'll like it." Jan pushed the mug towards him.

Joshua took a cautious sip and waited to feel his body relax. It didn't happen, but he couldn't complain about the taste. "Not bad," he relented.

"How do your kids like Chester?" Jan asked on their way back out onto the porch to sit in the swing and enjoy the summer night air.

Joshua shrugged. "Donny and Sarah are having the roughest time. They have lived in San Francisco most of their lives and they aren't accustomed to moving every few years like the other kids. Lately, it seems like they're always at each other's throats."

"They just lost their mother," Jan explained simply.

"Yeah," Joshua agreed. "That was rough on all of us."

Jan queried gently, "I heard she had a heart condition."

"No one knew about it. The weird thing is she worked out four times a week. There was no—" Joshua stopped speaking to battle the emotions that always welled up when he had to recount the worst time of his life. "Well," he breathed, "there's a reason they call it the silent killer."

"Yeah." Jan wondered if she should change the subject.

Joshua relieved her of the dilemma when he continued: "We had a date that night. We went out to dinner and a show." He stopped to swallow his tears. "The kids were in bed when we got home, and Val and I went in to take a shower together."

Even though it was dark, Joshua turned his face away so Jan couldn't see his pain.

"One minute everything was perfect. I felt Val's breath on my neck and, the next thing, she was limp in my arms. The water was coming down on us, and she was slipping away from me. I got her out of the shower, and carried her into the bedroom, and laid her on the bed."

Lost in his memory of that night, Joshua took a deep gulp of the cold tea. The sweat from the mug dripped across his fingers and down his wrist.

"The doctors told me it happened so fast that she didn't even know what happened. I went ahead and told the kids that. She didn't suffer. She was just suddenly gone." He shook his head. "But that isn't true. She was talking to me."

Jan whispered her question. "What did she say?"

"That she'd always love me. Those were her last words." Joshua stopped speaking. He sat back and took another gulp of the tea.

Jan tried to think of something, anything, to say.

"Ain't life ironic?" Joshua chuckled in spite of his pain. "Val was the one who wanted a house full of kids. I didn't care one way or the other when we got married. I mean-I love them with all my heart. I'm just saying, Val was the one who wanted to have them, and all I wanted was to make her happy. So, we had a house full of kids." Joshua laughed hollowly. "I never, in all my life, ever felt so clueless."

"Joshua Thornton clueless?" Jan breathed. "I never would have thought it possible."

"Do you have the confidence to raise five kids?"

"Don't you think I should get a husband first before I consider having the five kids?" Jan smiled in an effort to lighten the conversation.

"Well, when you do get that guy, if you convince him to have five kids, if you have a heart, you won't die until after they are raised."

The two old friends laughed as if no time had passed since their youth when they used to kill time on lazy summer nights on the same porch swing on which they now swung.

"I went to see Tad but he seemed to have a date tonight," Joshua told her.

Jan welcomed the change to a lighter topic. "I'm not surprised. Tad Mac-Millan does have a certain reputation. Of course, in this town, once you get a reputation it sticks to you like glue."

Joshua grinned. "Yeah, well, I'm not completely innocent there. I still think of him as the cigarette-smoking, beer-guzzling, motorcycle-riding hound."

"Well, he still has the motorcycle and, as for the ladies—" Jan said, "You still hear things about him."

"What? What do you hear?" Joshua asked naughtily.

"I'm not a gossip."

"You're a journalist. That makes you the same thing in my book."

"I never made it as a journalist." She drained her glass. "Who was Tad with tonight?"

"I never saw her."

"Maybe she was Maggie's mother?" Jan grinned questioningly at Joshua.

"Maybe. What have you heard?"

"I hear things all the time about Tad and his women."

"I mean about Maggie's mother."

"Oh, that. You mean you don't know? I was hoping you'd tell me. I would have thought Tad would have told you of all people."

"He doesn't tell me everything."

Jan smirked. "He told you it was none of your business."

"Yep," Joshua laughed. "I half suspect he's keeping it a secret just to make me crazy. It happened so suddenly. Here I am in Annapolis, planning to marry Val the day after graduation, and Tad calls and announces that he's a father. Boom! No nine months to prepare for that, especially from a wild man like Tad."

"Maybe she was married," Jan suggested.

Joshua shook his head. "Even Tad, at his wildest, had principles. But there is one thing I do know. After he sobered up, Tad became a good father. Maggie has turned out great."

"Yes, she did. She's gorgeous. She was in buying sunscreen the other day. A boy knocked over a display while watching her."

"I think this helped." Joshua drained the mug and set it on the porch rail and stood up. "Thanks for the tea and conversation, Jan."

"Anytime."

Joshua took up the dog's leash. "Come on, Admiral. Let's go to bed."

Unaware of Jan's longing gaze, Joshua led Admiral off the porch, down the walk, and on home.

CHAPTER 5

▼

The sprawling red brick church on top of the hill along Indiana Avenue between Third and Fourth Street was a center of social activity on Sunday mornings. Church members would greet each other in front of the First Christian Church and catch up on the news from the week. It is the same way at all the churches, representing almost every orthodox religion all along the street.

Conversation momentarily stopped when the single father marched his five children up the sidewalk of the tree-lined, cobblestone street and through the First Christian Church's double doors.

Jan Martin watched the Thorntons approach from the church foyer where she greeted fellow members of the congregation as they came inside to the sanctuary.

"Did you get any sleep last night?" Jan handed her childhood friend a bulletin. After Joshua answered that he did, Jan offered him a plastic sandwich bag filled with herbs that she had removed from her pocket. "I made up some tea for you. Have a cup before you go to bed at night and it might help."

The Thornton children admired the oak interior of the old church building. The floors were hardwood, the walls paneled, and the pews constructed of matching oak. Even the high cathedral ceilings were oak paneled. Four glass lamps hung from the ceiling over the center aisle.

Joshua led his children down the aisle to a pew at the front of the church. The father then stood aside to let them file in before sitting next to Tracy at the end.

"So this is where you went to church when you were growing up, huh, Dad?" Tracy's voice, as well as those around her, bounced and echoed off the paneling around them. The echoes caused a dull roaring effect inside the sanctuary.

Joshua pointed out the baptistery behind the altar. "That is where I was baptized."

"Hey, Jan, how are you doing?"

Recognizing Tad's voice, Joshua turned around in his seat to watch his cousin come down the aisle. Tad was rolling up the bulletin Jan had just handed him. Chester's most notorious doctor greeted and was warmly greeted by various members of the congregation. Tad MacMillan knew everyone.

When he saw his cousin, Tad smiled fondly and surprised him with a hug. "Sorry about last night," he whispered into Joshua's ear.

"Hey, I'm sorry I didn't call first. I should have known better than to drop in on you on a Saturday night."

"Don't worry about it. How about if I take you and the kids to brunch after the service?"

"That will put you in hock," Joshua objected.

"Can you think of a better way to go?" Tad chuckled before going through a door next to the pulpit. A moment later, he came out from behind a curtain on the altar to sit at the keyboard.

Dressed in a plain black robe, the youthful-looking pastor, Stephen Andrews, came out from behind the curtain, stepped up to the oak podium, and put on his reading glasses.

The appearance of the pastor prompted the congregation to hurriedly quit talking with their neighbors. Those who weren't already seated rushed to their pews. The sanctuary ended up filled with a mixture of elderly church members (some of whom Joshua recognized from his youth) and young families with children.

Reverend Andrews signaled Tad with a nod of his head to start playing the opening hymn on the keyboard. The choir stood and sang at Tad's direction. On a cue from the minister, the congregation stood and joined the choir in singing the opening hymn.

*   *   *   *

Downstream, along the Ohio River, another congregation sat in rap attention as the Reverend Orville Rawlings shouted his sermon from his pulpit high above them.

"And then Jesus told his flock to beware—Hear me! He warned them to beware of false prophets!"

Valley of the Living God was an institution in the Ohio valley. The marble and brass church building was the largest in the area. The ceilings seemed to reach the heavens themselves, and the worship center (the church leaders preferred the term "worship center" to "sanctuary") was so large that the reverend's booming voice, unnecessarily assisted by a state-of-the-art sound system, echoed endlessly during his sermons.

Worship services at Valley of the Living God were a production unrivaled by any of the smaller, less affluent churches in the valley. Besides having the largest building and congregation in the area, they also had a full-time staff, whose sole purpose was to produce and direct the worship services performed three times every weekend.

Reverend Rawlings's sermon was only a small part of their productions.

Valley of the Living God did not have worship services. The church put on full theatrical productions aimed to make their audience fully experience the Reverend Orville Rawlings.

Their services consisted of a music team, which, dressed in black jeans and blazers over white tee shirts, resembled a rock group more than a church choir. The professional musicians were hired during a countrywide talent search. No one asked, and the musicians didn't tell, if they followed their employer in his preachings.

At the back of the stage, a projection screen continuously showed graphics, videos, and close-ups from on the stage shot by any one of the cameras set up throughout the auditorium and manned by members of the paid production staff.

Center stage, at his pulpit, Reverend Orville Rawlings was the star of the show. The spotlights reflected off the gold jewelry he wore on his fingers and wrists. The gold trim on his black robe sparkled on the stage. Even his hair was black, with only a touch of gray standing out at the temples.

A giant of a man, Reverend Orville Rawlings used as much money as needed to conceal his age. His wrinkles were instantly removed with creams and lasers, and a personal trainer assisted him in banishing fat from his body while building up muscle. Even his own family could not guess his age. The Reverend Orville Rawlings was ageless, just like a star should be.

Every Sunday, Reverend Rawlings had his perfect family lined up in the front pew. After his wife's unfortunate drowning, the reverend's daughter, Bridgette Poole, became the hostess. She sat next to her husband, Hal.

Amongst the church's first members, Hal Poole's parents were very proud when their son dedicated his life to Reverend Rawlings's mission. Actually, Hal dedicated himself to the reverend's daughter. It was a commitment the wisp of a man, who started going bald at twenty-one, had made when he was still in junior high school.

Wallace Rawlings sat on the other side of Bridgette.

Unlike his father, Wallace Rawlings let age have its way with him. He loved the fine rich food and spirits served at the cocktail receptions and luncheons that were a way of life in the world of politics and high society. His love for the good life and lack of ambition in athletics showed on his waistline. In the two decades since Wallace Rawlings and Joshua Thornton were high school rivals, Reverend Rawlings's son had ballooned up to become one of the valley's biggest politicians.

Like his father, Wallace suffered the loss of his wife. The choir's late lead vocalist, Cindy Rawlings had a voice like an angel and the hearts of everyone in the congregation. Her death was a blow to everyone who had ever met her.

Hal Poole, Valley of the Living God's public relations director, ignored reporting anything to the media about why Victoria Rawlings, now seventeen years old, had not attended her family's church since she became a teenager, nor did they acknowledge Amber's bomb dropped on the news. Other than asking for prayers for their family, they pretended Wallace's daughter didn't exist.

*   *   *   *

Reverend Steven Andrews gave his customary sigh of relief upon hearing the opening notes of the closing hymn. He closed his eyes and silently thanked God for letting him live through another sermon without throwing up on the pulpit. After six years as a church pastor, the young reverend still had stage fright when it came to giving his sermons.

While he played the keyboard, Tad tried in vain to get the pastor's attention.

Reverend Andrews was unaware of the choir's questioning gaze at the back of his head while they led the congregation in song. At the close of the hymn, he lifted his arms up towards the ceiling. "And now, may the Lord go forth with you and be with you. Amen." He smiled a farewell to the congregation and waited for them to file out.

Instead of going forth, the members of the First Christian Church looked expectantly up at their pastor. A murmur rose from within the sanctuary.

Perplexed, Reverend Andrews turned to Tad, who hissed, "You forgot the offering."

The pastor gasped.

Laughter rippled throughout the church.

The ushers rushed down the aisle, grabbed the offering plates, and haphazardly passed them to the pews.

The Thornton children giggled while Joshua fought to not chuckle himself while he dropped a check into the plate.

When Joshua turned around in his seat to hand the plate to the family in the pew behind him, he noticed a girl dressed in a black skimpy shirt with baggy pants slung so low on her bony hips that it was a mystery as to how they kept from falling down to her ankles. The only color on her body was her poker-straight hair, which was the color of a new copper penny. It was bluntly cut short at her jaw.

The girl dressed in black came in at the back of the church and walked down the aisle at the far side of the sanctuary.

Other young people in the sanctuary were dressed in the dark, revealing style of their generation. Some had tattoos and body piercings. While greeting those who sat around him, Joshua noticed that the woman behind him had her tongue pierced. Unfazed by the sight of the gold stud stuck on her tongue, Joshua introduced himself and his children to the mother of two.

The father of teenagers, Joshua thought that he was incapable of being shocked by anything done in the name of fashion. He realized that his assumption was wrong when he laid his eyes on the girl in black.

Joshua saw the scales of a black snake draped across her stomach from under her midriff top. The snake wrapped itself around her body, up her back, over her right shoulder, and across the front of her throat. The serpent's head, his mouth open in mid-strike, was illustrated on her left shoulder.

Her glassy gaze was fixed on Tad, whose concentration was directed at the song he was playing on the keyboard.

The image of the girl in black with the snake wrapped around her body caused a stir amongst the congregation. All eyes were fixed on the visitor to their service.

Could she be going up to the pulpit to plead for the reverend to save her from the serpent that had taken control of her body?

Joshua saw beyond the body art to notice her hand in her shoulder bag as she moved in the direction of his cousin.

A family made up of three generations was in the pew between Joshua and the girl with the snake. He didn't have time to go around them.

"Excuse me," Joshua said repeatedly as he squeezed his way in front of the seven people blocking his path.

The grandmother with a purple hat perched on top of her gray head sputtered when she lost her balance and landed on her rump in the pew. "Joshua Thornton, didn't they teach you manners at that academy? I never!" Joshua instantly recalled when the elderly woman had once complained to his grandmother about him being "mouthy".

Tad saw the girl just as she pulled her hand out of her bag to reveal a handgun. She aimed it at him.

"She has a gun!" The keyboardist threw himself at the pastor and shoved him down onto the floor.

Joshua heard the roar of the congregation in his ears as he dove like a player racing for home plate. In midair, he reached for the arm in which the girl held the gun and thrust it upwards towards the oak ceiling above them.

As the man and girl hit the floor, the bullet discharged from the barrel, struck one of the hanging lamps, and sent a shower of glass down onto the shocked congregation. The bullet continued its flight upward until it planted itself into one of the oak panels high above the church members.

As a unit, the congregation scattered. Their screams bounced off the wooden interior around them until it built to a crescendo. The men sheltered the women who sheltered the children. The Thornton twins shielded their younger siblings.

On the floor at the foot of the altar, the man and the girl wrestled for the weapon.

Her high-pitched screams sounded like that of a wild animal fighting a fellow predator.

While Joshua fought to keep her finger from again squeezing the trigger of the gun, he felt a sudden pain shoot up from his groin to his chest. She had kneed him between the legs. That pain was instantly replaced by another in his upper arm where she planted her teeth. Determined to win the fight, she bit down harder.

"She's biting me!" Joshua kept his grip on the gun that she refused to release while he called out for help.

Her teeth tore into his flesh.

Murphy and J.J. ran to their father's aid. J.J. attempted to pry her jaws open while Murphy pounded her wrist with his fist to force her to let go of the weapon.

"Bastards!" she cursed in a shrill voice.

She lunged at J.J. when Joshua took possession of the battle's prize. The wild look in her eyes and the sight of Joshua's blood on her lips caused the teenager to retreat for safety behind his father.

"Stop it!" Joshua landed a punch across her jaw.

The girl with the snake tattoo collapsed to the floor in a heap.

The intended victim was the first to his feet. A doctor first, Tad leapt over the railing between him and the congregation to get to the fallen girl.

The pastor picked himself up from the floor and looked down at the girl lying motionless below the pulpit like some sort of dead animal sacrifice.

The skimpy top had become disheveled in her collapse to reveal another tattoo. At first glance, the serpent seemed to be protecting the prey he had captured for himself. A closer look revealed a pentagram tattooed on the girl's left breast beneath the head of the snake. The serpent was guarding the symbol of Satan, the lord of the underworld.

The stunned silence evaporated into a hum of murmured questions that built to an echoing roar.

"Wow!" Donny exclaimed. "Dad hit a girl!"

"I'm sorry, Reverend. She left me no choice." Joshua apologized to the pastor, who stepped down from the pulpit on trembling legs.

Tad pointed to Jan, who Joshua suddenly noticed was by his side trying to examine his bite wound. "Call 911. We have a potential drug overdose here."

Jan rushed back to the office to make the call.

"What's that?" Donny pointed out the tattoo that adorned the young woman's left breast.

"It's a pentagram," Joshua answered.

"She worships Satan," the pastor whispered, while looking around as if searching for other members of her "church".

Tad motioned for the crowd to step back. "Give her some air, please. Stand back."

"Who is she?" Joshua asked anyone who would answer.

Tad responded to the query. "She's Vicki Rawlings, Reverend Orville Rawlings's granddaughter."

✶   ✶   ✶   ✶

Joshua watched Tad speak to the emergency room doctor in the seemingly quiet reception area. He still had to get accustomed to seeing his cousin behave in a professional manner.

At the church, Joshua watched with awe while Tad tended to the unconscious Vicki Rawlings. The girl's attempt to kill him was irrelevant to saving her life.

While the paramedics loaded the assailant into the back of the ambulance, Joshua observed the stark contrast of Vicki's roots from the girl with the serpent tattoo wrapped around her body. A shiny black MG convertible was parked in front of the ambulance. Next to the personalized tag that read "RWLNGS4", was a bumper sticker that proclaimed "Jesus Lives!" Joshua assumed the car belonged to Vicki.

"She's out of danger," Tad announced when he joined his cousin in the waiting room at the hospital after Joshua was treated for his bite wound. The doctor examined the damage Vicki had managed to do to Joshua while he was disarming her.

An emergency room nurse had sterilized and bandaged the injury with liquid stitches. Vicki Rawlings bit Joshua so deeply that she left a perfect impression of her dental mark on his upper arm.

Murphy and J.J. excused themselves from the two nursing students entertaining them by the vending machines to learn what Tad had to report about the girl with the gun.

"Medical danger," Joshua clarified. "Where's her family?"

"It's Sunday," Tad reminded him. "They're all at Rawlings's church putting on a show of a functional family."

"So they're just going to leave her here?"

"At least until after their Sunday night service. Then, one of them will slip in under the cover of darkness and whisk her away to a psycho ward someplace for the customary three days of confinement until they have to take her home."

"And what about the police?" Murphy wondered. "I mean…she shot up a church, man."

"She bit Dad," J.J. added.

Tad sneered, "Vicki is the county prosecuting attorney's daughter."

Joshua was not satisfied with the explanation. "She took a shot at you!"

Despite his attempt to appear unaffected, Tad uttered a sigh that betrayed a note of emotional exhaustion. "That girl has been stalking me for over three years, and no one has been able to stop her yet."

As Tad expected, his cousin picked up the distress he had learned to expertly conceal from the outside world. "You have a whole church full of witnesses who saw that girl pull a gun and try to shoot you." Joshua's next statement was delivered with the force of a declaration of war. "My children were in that sanctuary."

"And by the time Rawlings's lawyer is through, they'll all have new cars and amnesia."

"Maybe Wally won't do anything about his daughter, but I will." Joshua demanded to know, "Have you filed any complaints with the sheriff about her? Do you have copies of them?"

Tad's voice faded as his attention was drawn to an ambulance that had pulled up outside the emergency room doors. The attendants were unloading a gurney with a middle-aged woman on it. "I documented everything. I even saved the e-mails she's been sending."

"Good. The state attorney general will be very interested in why the prosecuting attorney has not done anything about controlling his daughter."

The doctor was studying the patient on the gurney racing by him. "I have to go." He caught up with the emergency room doctor who met the gurney. "Excuse me, but this is one of my patients. What seems to be the trouble?"

"Looks like an allergic reaction to medication," Joshua heard the doctor tell Tad.

CHAPTER 6

▼

Joshua Thornton was not having a good Sunday.

After leaving Tad at the hospital, Joshua took the twins to his office to continue wading through the junk left by the building's previous owner. He had yet to feel as if he had made any progress when it was time for them to return home to wash up for dinner.

Joshua was looking forward to a cold beer and Sunday dinner. Since her mother's death, Tracy did her best to continue with the tradition of cooking a special dinner every Sunday for the family to sit down and eat together.

However, as soon as her father came through the door, Sarah told Joshua that Tad needed his help right away. Without even changing out of his dirty, sweaty work clothes, Joshua left behind a home-cooked dinner of baked chicken and potato salad and went to his cousin's apartment.

For the first time, Joshua wished Tad hadn't quit drinking. He really wanted a cold beer.

Tad answered his door on the first knock and yanked Joshua inside the apartment.

The woman at Tad's kitchen table held little resemblance to the girl Joshua had almost married the night of their senior prom. Beth's unkempt hair hung in her eyes. The makeup that had not dripped off in her nervous sweat was smeared. Her fingernails, which Joshua remembered as being always neatly manicured and painted to match whatever she was wearing at that time, had been bitten to the quick. Chips of polish hinted at the pink color they had once been painted.

After peering into the alley like he was harboring a fugitive, Tad closed the door behind Joshua.

Meanwhile, the doctor was explaining their dilemma at a hundred miles an hour. "I asked you over here because we need some good advice. This afternoon one of my patients was brought into the ER—"

"Was that the woman I saw them bringing in when we were talking?"

Tad nodded in response to Joshua's question. "Gloria Frost. Nice lady. She has a chronic sinus infection. I prescribed erythromycin for it because she is allergic to penicillin. She even wears a medic alert bracelet. What happened was that she was given amoxicillin, which is penicillin-based, and she had an allergic reaction. She's in serious condition, but I think she'll make it."

"Did she know that amoxicillin is penicillin-based?"

"Didn't matter," Tad shook his head firmly. "The bottle was marked erythromycin by the pharmacist who gave her the wrong pills."

Joshua followed Tad's gaze to Beth, who wrung her hands while staring with wide eyes at her former lover across the table.

"How could you make a mistake like that?" Joshua asked her.

The pharmacist whined helplessly, "I don't know." As she continued with her explanation, Beth spoke with more conviction. "Mrs. Frost came in with her prescription. Then, Bridgette Poole came in and—You were there. She was yelling at me, and I got all confused, and I just grabbed the wrong pills." Beth concluded, "It wasn't my fault."

Tad spoke softly, "Of course, the emergency room doctor had to call the authorities. The police are going to want to talk to Beth. Mr. Frost has already said he intends to sue."

"Why did you call me?" Joshua wanted to know. "If you wrote the right prescription—"

"I have no doubt but that Wally Rawlings will want to press charges of criminal negligence against Beth."

"Wally has been out to get me for years." Beth picked up her purse from the floor and dug through it.

Joshua recognized it as the same macramé handbag he saw on Tad's kitchen table the previous night.

"Why?" the lawyer asked.

Beth removed a bottle from her purse and popped two pills into her mouth. "How should I know?" She spoke around the pills while gesturing to Tad, who shot her a look of displeasure before filling a glass with water from the tap.

"A woman almost died because of your mistake," Joshua argued.

Beth's wide-eyed stare changed into a glare. "Aren't you supposed to defend me?"

"At this point, only if I choose to. It would be easier for me to decide to help you if you showed at least an ounce of remorse for what happened."

"She should have looked at the pills before she took them."

"The bottle label read erythromycin and the information sheet in the bag was for erythromycin," Tad said. "It was your responsibility to make sure erythromycin got into the bottle."

Beth jumped to her feet. "I thought you were on my side!"

"I said I would help you. You're my friend—"

"You certainly don't sound like it!" Beth put her purse on her shoulder.

Tad yelled back at her. "Don't give me that shit! I didn't have to warn you about what was coming down the pike! I could have just sat back and let you shit your pants when the deputies showed up at your door to question you."

Beth stepped around the table and headed for the door.

Tad blocked her escape. His voice took on a pleading tone. "Beth, you have to take responsibility for your actions, especially when it comes to messing up other people's lives."

"I made a mistake!" Beth rolled her eyes.

"You screwed up!"

"Like you never screwed up!" Beth pushed past Tad to the door.

"You go through that door, then don't come back! I won't be here to clean up your messes anymore, and neither will Josh! You'll be on your own, babe!"

Beth slammed the door on her way out.

"Screw it!" Tad picked up Beth's glass and threw it against the door behind her. The glass shattered.

Joshua wondered what he had just witnessed.

After he got hold of himself, Tad sighed and picked up a dishtowel. "I'm sorry I got you over here for nothing."

Still hot and thirsty, Joshua poured himself a glass of milk from the refrigerator. "Tell me about your relationship with Beth."

Tad was on his hands and knees cleaning up the spilt water and broken glass. "We're friends."

"Yeah. Right."

Tad sat back on his haunches and watched Joshua gulp down the milk. "Is that green I see in those baby blue eyes?"

"Beth's purse was on this kitchen table at midnight last night. If it was completely innocent, you wouldn't have been so shy about letting me know Beth was here."

"It wasn't what you think." With a sigh of defeat, Tad pulled himself up to his feet. "I've been trying to get Beth into rehab for years." He deposited the broken glass into the trash.

Joshua didn't want to believe him. "She's an alcoholic? Come on! We dated all through high school. I drank more than she did."

"Beth took it hard when you dumped her to marry Valerie. That's no excuse, but she used it as one. And then, she said her nerves were bad. So, she went to a quack therapist who got her hooked on Valium. Then, since she was a pharmacist, she went on to become hooked on her own pills. Diet pills. Sleeping pills. She uses a pill for everything."

Tad poured himself a glass of milk and refilled Joshua's empty glass. He sat on top of the kitchen table to drink it. "I got a call from a bartender buddy of mine last night. Beth was getting herself into trouble. So, I went and got her, and brought her back here."

"What was she on when she gave Mrs. Frost the wrong medication?"

Tad shrugged. "She could have been trying to get off them. She yo-yos. One day, she's going to get herself clean. The next day, she slides back to where she was before."

"Why don't you send her to rehab?"

"I'm not her keeper. I can advise her. As her doctor, I can commit her the way you did me. But then, according to the law, they can only keep her there three days. Then, they have to let her go. You got lucky with me. After three days in detox, my survival instinct kicked in. I had bottomed out and was ready to sober up. I can tell you right now that Beth won't stay in rehab. I'd bet money on it. She hasn't bottomed out yet. So, all I can do is be here for her when she does."

Joshua's legal mind signaled danger. "Does Jan Martin know about Beth's problem? You know the Frosts can sue her, too, since her and her mother own the drug store."

"Jan just thinks Beth has a drinking problem. If she knew Beth was stealing pills, she would have had her out of there years ago."

"Well, she's going to know now. Beth and I have a past, but Jan doesn't deserve this." Joshua headed for the door. Remembering Vicki Rawlings, he stopped. "Did you print up those e-mails?"

"E-mails?"

"The e-mails from Vicki. Any letters you may have saved will be helpful, too."

Joshua followed Tad into the living room.

The living room was cluttered. Tad had several patients and was active in the church and drug abuse counseling centers. That left him little time to notice, let alone clean up, the clutter in his cozy living space.

Dog was stretched out on the sofa that, from the looks of it, was more of a dog bed than a sofa. It looked like something Tad must have picked up, along with the recliner, from off a street corner on garbage day. Magazines, books, medical journals and patient folders were stacked on every flat surface.

Tad was rummaging through a box that had originally been a container for a new pair of boots. It contained a stack of paper that had been printed from his computer, which he kept in his office downstairs.

"Here they are. They're all here." Tad handed the box to his cousin.

"Thanks. I'll have to read them."

Joshua's cousin shrugged off any explanation. "Go ahead. I have nothing to hide. Do whatever you want with them. I just want that girl out of my life."

"I'll get right to work on it." Joshua went back into the kitchen with Tad behind him.

"Wait."

Expecting Tad to have changed his mind about reading the e-mails, Joshua turned to him. He was prepared to argue his case.

Tad tore a sheet of paper off a memo pad on the kitchen counter next to the answering machine. "Jill left a message for me today. She says Rick would be glad to talk to you about that dead body. He lives in Cleveland now." Tad gave him the slip of paper. "Be careful."

"I didn't get where I am today by not being careful."

"If you were so careful you wouldn't have five kids."

CHAPTER 7

▼

Joshua finally got his beer.

Joshua placed his oak computer desk in the same spot in the study where his grandfather used to have his. Fondly, he recalled when he was small enough to play underneath his grandfather's desk while waiting for him to finish his paperwork before they went fishing at the river.

The house was quiet while everyone was digesting his or her Sunday dinner. J.J. and Murphy went up to their room to continue cleaning. The attic windows were still encrusted with decades of dirt. Donny and Sarah went to the school down the street to play basketball. Tracy was relaxing on the front porch with needlepoint. Admiral's snoring from the middle of the bare floor was the only sound in the study.

Joshua was unaware of how much he resembled his grandfather as he alternated between chewing on a pipe and nursing a mug of beer while he sorted the stack of papers Tad had given him. Based on the sent date, he sorted the e-mails from Reverend Rawlings's granddaughter into the order in which his cousin had received them.

"What interest would Vicki have in Tad?" Joshua asked himself as he studied the messages.

Tad wasn't the Rawlings family doctor. Vicki couldn't possibly run with his crowd. They were of different generations, and Tad didn't hang out in bars or with drug users anymore. How did she even know him?

Joshua read an early e-mail Vicki had sent to Tad in mid-June, more than three years earlier. "Hello, Daddy, Happy Father's Day from Your Baby."

Joshua scanned the rest of the messages. Each one made some reference to father or daddy.

"Okay, Tad," Joshua asked his absent client as he tossed the stack of papers back into the box, "What have you done now?"

*   *   *   *

"The doctor said that Victoria should wake up this afternoon," Orville Rawlings reported to his son.

After leaving the hospital, Orville Rawlings made a detour to his son's office on his way to his mansion overlooking the Ohio River. He made no pretense of looking through the papers, which included arrest reports, on the prosecuting attorney's desk.

The reverend observed the cramped space of the prosecutor's office and frowned. While the title of county prosecuting attorney sounded influential, Hancock County was not big enough or rich enough to supply its lawyer with any more than a corner office in the basement of a school building next to the courthouse in New Cumberland.

Orville Rawlings was insulted every time he visited his only son's dingy workplace. The valley's richest and most influential citizen's son had a staff consisting of one secretary and two part-time assistants, who made more money with their own private legal practices.

Any other father would insist his son quit, but Orville Rawlings needed Wallace to be the county's top legal officer.

"Good," Wallace Rawlings muttered at the news of his daughter's release from the hospital.

"I expect you to go with me to pick the child up."

"I have an appointment."

"Who with?" Orville took a thick Cuban cigar out of his pocket. "Better not be with that new music director I hired."

"What if it is?" Wally grinned at the thought of how well the singer filled out her black jeans.

"Because I forbid it." The church pastor bit off the end of the cigar and spat it to the floor as if to comment on the county government's rule against smoking in public buildings. "We will not have another Steubenville."

"Cindy died over ten years ago, Father. No one can fault me now for seeking companionship."

Reverend Rawlings put the cigar between his teeth and formed his words around it. "You'll seek companionship when and with whom I say, and not until I tell you." Orville leaned into the flame from the lighter Wallace held out to light his father's cigar.

"Why can't I choose my own women, except for those I have to pay for by the hour?"

The reverend laughed cruelly. "Need I remind about the last woman you picked to keep for yourself?" He muttered, "She almost ruined all of us."

Wallace responded in a low voice. "That was a long time ago, Father."

"I did not work fifty years cultivating this valley like a dedicated farmer to build this church only to have you and your perverted weakness for the flesh bring me down."

"No, better to have a satanic junkie do it."

"Say things like that in public and kiss all this goodbye." Orville indicated Wallace's office with a sarcastic chuckle. He sat down in the chair across from Wallace's government issued desk. "Despite all the trouble Victoria has caused, I preach about family loyalty. She can't do us any harm as long as we put on the show of sticking by her. We show that by being there at the hospital, looking grief-stricken for the cameras, and giving the statement I had Hal write for you." The reverend pointed to the words on the sheet of paper he had handed his son.

Wallace read over the statement about the difficulty of parenthood, the vulnerability of youth to Satan's temptation, and how his daughter needed him to stand by her now more than ever. "Did Hal compose what I am to say to Joshua Thornton?"

"Who?"

"Joshua Thornton. Oak Glen's Golden Boy." Wallace's tone betrayed remnants of childhood envy.

"The orphan who beat you out for student council president?" Orville frowned.

Wallace's frown matched his father's. That was one thing Orville Rawlings ordered and did not receive. "He's back."

"So?" The reverend's eyes betrayed only a hint of concern. "He isn't planning to run for prosecutor, is he?"

It was Wallace's turn to chuckle sarcastically. "Of course, Father. Thornton left the Navy and came home because he wanted this job." He gestured to indicate the shabby office.

Reverend Rawlings responded with no hint of humor. "Sarcasm does not become you."

"Joshua Thornton is Tad MacMillan's cousin. He's the one who stopped Vicki from shooting him." Wallace leaned towards his father. "He knows Vicki wasn't going to church to kill herself to end the inner battle between the devil and God for her soul." He pointed to the section of Hal's statement that explained why his daughter went to the church with a loaded gun.

"People will believe me before they believe him."

"He's a lawyer, Father. He's coming here," Wallace indicated his office by pressing his index finger against his desktop, "to talk about Vicki. If he wants to cause trouble, he can do it."

"No one can prove anything."

"That interview with Amber the other night caused a lot of problems."

"When I'm through that news station will be history."

"Amber got Vicki to admit to being a drug dealer. She said you were her boss."

Reverend Rawlings laughed. "And you saw how many people believed her. We had more people in our church this weekend, at all three services, than we have since Easter. They were all there to show their support for me against my spiritual enemies. Satan knows that I am winning my battle against him and he's been sending his demons into battle against me."

"Please, Father," Wallace groaned, "I'm not Bridgette's doofus husband." He gritted his teeth. "It is common knowledge that Vicki has been stalking Tad MacMillan for years."

Reverend Orville Rawlings's eyes narrowed as he muttered, "Would have been easier for us all if she had just killed him."

Wallace Rawlings snarled, "She'd never kill him. He's her daddy." Seeing that mincing words didn't work, he shot it straight to his father. "If Joshua Thornton insists on taking this to the mat, we're all going down, and he's the man to take us there."

Orville stood up. The large muscular man dwarfed his soft, robust son behind the shabby little desk. The father ordered his son. "You make sure that doesn't happen." It took only one step across the small office for him to reach the door.

At the door, Reverend Orville Rawlings turned and smiled paternally. His expression almost looked sincere. "I'll be picking Victoria up at the hospital at five o'clock. Be there and wear your best look of fatherly concern."

*   *   *   *

Joshua Thornton grinned at Wallace Rawlings. After shaking hands like a pair of boxers at the beginning of a match, Joshua sat down in the same chair Reverend Orville Rawlings vacated just before giving his order to get rid of the very problem the lawyer was now handing Wallace.

Even though he had been a government employee, Joshua still had difficulty containing his surprise to find Hancock County Prosecutor Wallace Rawlings tucked away in a basement. Joshua knew that the county was not rich, but he thought they could at least have found room for their prosecutor in the courthouse.

After recomposing himself from the shock, the former Navy commander fired his first shot across Wallace's bow by dropping a thick folder in the center of the prosecutor's desk.

"I have compiled a stack of copies of police reports that Tad has filed with the sheriff's department since your daughter started terrorizing him three years ago. Yet, she has never spent one minute in jail. Vicki has been very busy, as you will see in those reports, if you choose to read them."

Wallace refused to touch the reports. It was a mental tactic. By refusing to acknowledge the folder, the county prosecutor was non-verbally telling Joshua Thornton that his charges were so unimportant to him that they weren't even worthy of reading.

Instead, Wallace rationalized the reason for his inaction. "Vicki is ill. Sick people belong in the hospital, not jail. She has been hospitalized repeatedly."

Joshua was not intimidated by Wallace's lack of response to the file on his desk. He was too seasoned to let a bush-league stall like that make him edgy. "Vicki has never been hospitalized for longer than three days, at which time you take her home and she's loose again. She has followed Dr. MacMillan. She has broken into his home and office. She has tried to run him off the road and sent him threatening e-mails." Joshua tossed another folder filled with copies of the e-mails Tad had received from Victoria. "That's stalking. There are laws against stalking."

"She's a kid. She's infatuated."

"So was Amy Fisher." Joshua pulled out his big gun. "Listen, Wally, I'm not going to sit here and get into a pissing contest with you. The stakes are too high, and I don't have the time or the patience for it. I called the attorney general in Charleston this morning. Guess what? He's an academy grad, too. We kind of stick together. I told him about the shoot-out at the First Christian Church in Chester yesterday. I faxed him copies of every one of these police reports in which nothing was ever done. In each case, the ball drops once it hits your court. The attorney general found that interesting. Then, I told him that the perp was your daughter."

"Did you tell the attorney general about your assault on a teenaged girl? You almost broke her jaw."

Joshua snickered. "That was self-defense. I have the bite wound to prove it. I also have dozens of witnesses ready to testify about that if you choose to make an issue of it."

"And once we get her cleaned up and dressed in a white dress with a strand of pearls around her neck, a jury will think that you are some sort of pervert attacking an innocent virgin."

Joshua reminded Wallace of the less-than-pure tone set by his daughter's body art. "Pearls don't go with snake skin."

"Give it up, Thornton."

"This is going to stop, here, and now," Joshua ordered Wallace.

The prosecutor was so shaken by the force of Joshua's glare that he retreated back in his chair.

Wallace's reaction pleased Joshua. "The attorney general is sending a special prosecutor up to handle this case." He checked his watch. "She'll be here by the time Vicki is released from the hospital. There will be two state troopers there to take her into custody for stalking, assault with a deadly weapon, and attempted murder. She's seventeen years old. That means she'll be tried as an adult." Joshua stood up. "Good day, Wally. Nice seeing you again."

With that, Joshua Thornton left.

For the first time in twenty years, since the two rivals went up against each other at their last high school debate in their senior year, Wallace Rawlings was speechless.

When he found his voice, the pastor's son dialed the phone. He listened to it ring three times before Reverend Orville Rawlings answered his private line. "Father, we have a big problem."

✴   ✴   ✴   ✴

"He's going to have the cleanest car in town."

J.J. and Murphy were trimming the hedges and trees in the front yard. The freshly mowed lawn looked like a lush green carpet.

Sweat rolled down the boys' bare chests and backs in the summer heat.

J.J. stopped to pour himself a glass of lemonade from a pitcher Tracy had set for them on the front porch. While draining the glass, he chuckled at the young man washing his blue Chevy in the driveway to the cedar-sided house across the street.

Murphy mopped his dripping face with a towel before taking J.J.'s glass from him to drink the inch of cold liquid his twin had left at the bottom of the glass before sucking an ice cube into his mouth.

The neighbor checked his reflection in the side mirror of his car.

"Tracy must be coming," J.J. concluded.

As if on cue, Tracy came around from the back of the house with a tray of grapes and a pitcher of ice. "You guys ready for a break?" The twins launched themselves at the fruit. Tracy freshened their glasses with ice while reporting on her and Sarah's progress in sanding the kitchen cabinets. Donny had been tasked with washing the second floor windows.

Murphy raised his glass in a toast and called across the street to their neighbor. "Hi."

The young man accepted Murphy's invitation by dropping his sponge into the bucket and crossing the street. "Hi. I guess you're moving in." He offered Tracy his hand. "I'm Ken Howard."

Tracy shyly looked down into her glass.

"Yeah, we just got here last week." Even as he shook Murphy's hand, Ken continued to gaze at Tracy while her brother introduced his siblings.

Ken asked Tracy, "You going to Oak Glen this fall?"

J.J. answered, "We'll be juniors. Tracy is going to be a sophomore."

"Really?" Ken's smile widened. "I'm a senior this year." He took a deep breath. "I'd be glad to show you around and introduce you to everyone."

Even while J.J. and Murphy nodded for her to accept, Tracy murmured, "Thank you. Maybe." She hurried inside while Ken held onto the hope of "maybe" as he watched her leave.

"She's really shy," Murphy offered Ken another glimmer of hope.

Disappointed by Tracy's lack of enthusiasm, Ken stepped down off the porch and crossed the street back to his own driveway.

Before the twins could comment on their sister's shyness, Joshua whipped his Corvette into the driveway and swung it around to the bottom of the steps of the front porch. In the summer heat, the lawyer had taken off his suit jacket and tossed it behind his seat. As he stepped out of the car and up the steps to the porch, Joshua observed with pleasure the pile of trimmings his sons had stacked up in the yard during the course of the day.

"It's looking good." The place resembled more the cheery home of his childhood.

Joshua poured himself a glass of lemonade from the pitcher and sat on the swing to drink it while his elder sons gave him a progress report from their seats on the porch railing.

Murphy dug a slip of paper, soggy with sweat, out of his pocket. "Rick Pendleton returned your call. I got the directions to his place and said we'd be there tomorrow afternoon for him to tell us all about the body."

Joshua took the slip of paper. "Is this the royal we?"

"No, it's the literal we," J.J. said.

Joshua sidestepped the issue of taking his children to speak to Rick Pendleton about the body he had found forty years earlier by stating that he would change his clothes and come back outside to help them with the yard work.

Before Joshua could step inside the house, Murphy stopped him to inquire about his meeting with his old high school rival.

Pleased with himself, Joshua announced, "It went very well. Victoria Rawlings is spending the night in the county jail."

"But since her dad is a lawyer, can't he defend her?" Murphy suggested.

"No, he's the county's attorney. His contract with the county does not allow him to take any other legal cases, including his daughter's. If he does anything to hamper the special prosecutor's investigation, then he'll look bad for the next election. Yet, if he doesn't help his daughter, then it will look like the Rawlings are not the close knit family that his father preaches about."

Joshua added with a snicker, "I'd hate to be in his shoes right now."

*   *   *   *

The vase barely missed Wallace Rawlings's head and shattered against the wall behind him. Even though Vicki was his daughter, he stood back and let the two West Virginia troopers wrestle the girl to the floor to handcuff her.

Reverend Orville Rawlings had chosen to stay as far away as possible from the scene he predicted would be ugly. He ordered Hal Poole to spin the situation into the best possible direction. Meanwhile, the pastor hid in his home, out of sight of the media cameras.

Since Wallace was afraid to say anything about the arrest warrant, Vicki Rawlings did not know about being taken into custody until the state troopers entered her hospital room to take her away.

The county prosecutor wished he had the courage to disobey his father and meet with the music director instead of coming to the hospital to play the role of the concerned parent.

"You son of a bitch!" Vicki shrieked at him. "You're going to pay for this!"

"It wasn't my fault," Wallace argued weakly, "You went too far this time."

"Too far?"

Vicki kicked one of the troopers in the stomach. The police officer refrained from doubling over and wrestled her face down while she continued to curse at all of them. After cuffing her hands behind her back, the troopers yanked her to her feet.

Vicki cackled. "If you think I've gone too far this time, you just wait! You ain't seen nothing yet!"

CHAPTER 8

▼

"I don't think Vicki Rawlings will be a problem anymore."

The morning following Vicki's arrest, Joshua proudly told Tad about his meeting with the county prosecutor.

The lead story on the local evening news covered Victoria Rawlings being taken into custody. The two troopers had to carry Vicki, kicking and screaming, to the patrol car. Tess Bauer and her news crew were only able to garnish a series of "bleeps" from Vicki as her statement about her arrest. Tess's coverage of the story was aired both on the evening and morning news.

Marjorie Greene, the no-nonsense prosecuting attorney sent by the attorney general, told the media that she intended to go for the maximum sentence. A known drug dealer who goes around shooting up churches during Sunday morning service, Victoria Rawlings was a public menace.

Through a statement, the Rawlings family apologized to those their lost lamb had hurt. However, they insisted, jail was not the answer for poor Victoria. She did not intend to hurt anyone. She was trying to kill herself to end the inner battle between God and Satan for her soul. They requested prayers and understanding.

Tad didn't appear impressed by Joshua's accomplishments.

Dressed in his soiled work clothes to continue cleaning out his office, Joshua reported his progress on his cousin's behalf while taking a coffee break in his somewhat cleaned up reception area.

Besides updated plumbing, Dr. Wilson's office also lacked air conditioning. The humidity was stifling even though it was not yet eight o'clock in the morning.

Feeling like his toes were being smothered, Joshua stopped to remove his shoes and socks. He used his socks as a fan for his feet while he gave his cousin his report.

Tad wasn't even listening to him.

Joshua had collected the late doctor's papers, put them into boxes, and stacked the boxes in a corner in the reception area. Piled three boxes high, the folders took over a quarter of the downstairs office. Over fifty years of medical records for the population of a whole town makes for a lot of paper.

Realizing he was not receiving any gratitude for getting rid of Vicki Rawlings, Joshua sat up in his yet-to-be-hired secretary's chair and observed Tad digging through the papers. After searching through one folder, the doctor, crouched on his knees, would put the file back into the box before taking out another folder to check the contents.

"What are you looking for?"

Tad answered, "My patients' records."

"No," Joshua shook his head. "You're looking for something in particular. Tell me what it is, and I might be able to help."

"No, you can't."

"Then maybe you can help me. Want some turn-of-the-century medical journals?"

Tad yanked the next folder from the box and opened it. "Which century? Twenty-first or twentieth?" He shoved the folder back before looking up at his cousin for the answer to his question.

Joshua crooked a finger at Tad and led him up the back staircase to the room that was to be his legal office, Dr. Wilson's former private office. Joshua opened the door and stepped back for Tad to step in and gasp.

All four walls of the office were lined with floor-to-ceiling built in bookcases filled with books, plus more in crates on the floor.

"Looks like Mrs. Wilson was not the only pack rat." Joshua observed. "He never threw away any medical journals. We also have old books, and some of them are first editions of novels that are now classics."

Tad took two books down from a shelf and examined them. They were in mint condition. "Don't you collect books?"

"Yes, but I'd have to add on another room to the house for all of these. Some of them are valuable. Others are junk. Why didn't Paula get rid of them?"

"She didn't want to deal with it. She hated this town and wanted to get out."

"Since when?"

"Since I slept with her."

The bell over the front door jingled to signal the arrival of a potential client.

"Are you open for business?" Tad dropped the books he was examining back into a crate.

"I might as well be. Someone has to pay for two bathrooms, new plumbing, and central air conditioning for this place." Joshua held open the door for Tad to lead the way down the stairs.

Beth Davis was waiting for them in the reception area. She wore the same clothes she was wearing at Tad's apartment two days before. Her makeup was completely worn off to reveal a pale, splotchy complexion and dark bags under her eyes.

"Josh?"

Afraid that Beth might collapse in her disoriented condition, Joshua guided her to the sturdiest chair available for her to sit down.

Tad gazed at her with concern. "Are you okay?"

Beth ignored Tad's question. Instead she clutched Joshua's hands with clammy, trembling, fingers. "Are you open for business yet?" She seemed unaware of his less-than-professional attire.

Tad picked up one of the boxes. "Thanks a lot for saving these papers for me, Josh. I'll be by with a truck later on to get the rest." He shot a smile at Beth on his way out the door.

"I'll pick you up at ten o'clock to go to New Cumberland," Joshua reminded him of Vicki Rawlings's arraignment. Tad acknowledged the reminder with a single nod of his head before closing the door behind him.

"I've been worried about you." Joshua poured a cup of coffee for Beth.

"Have you really?" she scoffed.

"Why wouldn't I be?" He handed her the coffee, which she gulped down. Deciding the desk was safer than the old chair with wobbly legs, Joshua leaned against the corner of Dr. Wilson's nurse's desk. "You didn't show up for work yesterday."

"What was the use? Why get dressed and go to work just to get fired? Jan did fire me, didn't she?"

"You could have called. Jan was worried. She went by your house and you weren't there."

"If Jan was really my friend, which she isn't, she would have stuck by me. So would Tad."

"Beth," Joshua asked as gently as possible, "how bad is your problem?"

"You're the lawyer."

"I'm talking about you stealing pills."

"Is that what Tad told you? Did he also tell you that alcoholics are the world's best liars?"

"So I guess that means I can't believe anything either of you say."

"I am not an addict."

Joshua crossed his arms and looked down at the woman who tried to appear in total control. Her wringing hands gave her away. It was a nervous habit he recognized from their days together in high school.

"Well," Beth's lawyer and former lover sighed, "the only one who could have put amoxicillin in that bottle was you. So if you didn't screw up because you were under the influence of something, I guess that means you screwed up just because you are a screw up, period."

"Oh? And I guess you never screwed up."

"What happened to you, Beth? You used to have it together."

"You happened to me," she answered in a low voice. "I loved you. You promised to come back and marry me, or did you forget all about that promise when you met Valerie?" She spat his late wife's name with disdain.

Joshua refused to react to Beth's accusation. "I'm not taking the blame for your sickness. The next thing you'll be telling me is that it's my fault Mrs. Frost is lying in that hospital bed thanking God that she's still alive."

"I was a virgin when I met you!"

"That was twenty years ago! Get over it or get therapy!" Joshua gritted his teeth. "Okay, I'm the lawyer. Here's where you stand. You're in deep shit, lady! You'll never work as a pharmacist again. Mr. and Mrs. Frost are suing you for all they can get!"

"Well, that's not much."

"The sheriff is looking for you for questioning, and they have a very good case for criminal negligence. Plus, Jan went through the pharmacy inventory yesterday and a hell of a lot of pills are missing. She is legally obligated to report it. She called me last night to ask me what to do. If she doesn't report it, then she'll look like she's involved. So, are we looking at drug dealing here, as well as negligence? Think carefully before you answer that question."

Beth drained her cup of coffee. Her question out of left field knocked Joshua off balance. "Did you hear about Vicki Rawlings?"

"Yes. What does that have to do with this?"

"Can you defend her?"

Joshua laughed. "Who do you think called the attorney general?"

Beth looked up at him. Joshua could see that her green eyes were filled with fear. "Why did you call the attorney general?"

"Because she took a shot at Tad in a church filled with people, including my children."

"Do you know what you've done?"

"Yes, I got a menace off the streets."

"Oh, my God! Oh, my God! You have no idea what you've done!" Beth got up out of the chair and dug through her purse. When Joshua stepped towards her, she pulled away and rushed to the door while blubbering hysterically. "How could you do this? How could you have done this to me? You've ruined everything!"

Beth Davis was gone.

*   *   *   *

It was during a weak, sympathetic moment that Joshua agreed to let his children tag along to Vicki Rawlings's arraignment. He rationalized that the trip afforded him a chance to show them their new home town.

While the father drove the Thornton van through the rolling countryside along the Ohio River to the courthouse in New Cumberland, Joshua and Tad pointed out the various sights.

In Newell, the first town downstream from Chester, they passed Homer Laughlin China, where many of the local residents worked. The china plant's wares were used in some of the finest restaurants in the country.

Then, there was the former Waterford Race Track. Now, it was called Mountaineer Park. Since Joshua left the area after high school for Annapolis, the popular track used for horse racing had more than doubled in size with the addition of a health spa, gambling casino, and entertainment facility. Even though it was not yet ten o'clock in the morning, the parking lot was packed with cars.

The courthouse's parking lot was also packed. There wasn't much parking to begin with. The lot consisted of a few spaces squeezed in along the edge and behind the school building where Wallace's office was housed. Every space was taken up with spectators to see Reverend Orville Rawlings's granddaughter arraigned for attempted murder, assault with a deadly weapon, and stalking. Joshua ended up parking the van down the street.

Tad and Joshua herded the children into the courtroom and took up the back row in the gallery. The children craned their necks to take in the action while Tad announced the players in the show they were about to see.

Orville and Wallace Rawlings were in a conference at the defense table with an older, short, robust man with thin gray hair, and a bushy salt-and pepper-colored mustache that looked like it belonged on a walrus.

As always, the reverend stood out. His black hair was slicked back without a strand out of place. His black suit with a stark white shirt and red tie was as expensively tailored as their lawyer's suit. Joshua could tell by the way the reverend slapped his leather driving gloves into his palm that he was annoyed about the whole situation.

"That's Clarence Mannings," Tad indicated the man with the walrus mustache in conference with the reverend.

"I know Mannings." Joshua squinted at the high priced attorney. "He's from Philadelphia. Very expensive. He defended an admiral I prosecuted about three years ago."

"Did you win?"

Joshua chuckled, "How do you think I got my promotion to commander?" He turned serious. "Mannings's technique is to confuse the issues and muddy the waters. The court martial panel was too bright to fall for it, but a civilian jury can be more easily confused. Greene will have her work cut out for her."

The special prosecutor was already at the prosecution table conferring with her co-counsel.

"Do you remember Hal Poole?" Tad indicated Bridgette's husband.

In the gallery's first row of seats behind the defense table, Hal Poole sat at Bridgette's side. He sat up so straight in his chair that he looked as if he had a steel rod down his back. With his hands neatly folded in his lap, he stared at the empty judge's bench at the front of the courtroom. Motionless in prayer, he looked like a robot on stand-by.

Hal was perfectly groomed. The few hairs left on his head were combed neatly into place. Even the purple handkerchief in his breast pocket was pressed and folded. Joshua noted that the enlisted men who served under him in the Navy weren't groomed as well as Hal Poole.

Joshua observed, "I'm surprised that Hal handles the church's public relations. You'd think a spinmiester would have to have his own mind to be able to cover up for the Rawlings."

Tad disagreed. "He's perfect for the job. He never questions anything the Rawlings do. He just parrots what the reverend and Bridgette tell him to say." The doctor continued with the update. "Bridgette is the church's business manager."

Tad studied the crowd in the courtroom with a touch of awe at the large attendance. "It's usually not this crowded."

"Do you make it a habit of sitting in on courtroom trials?" With a wicked grin, Joshua hinted at his cousin's colorful past.

"No, I'm usually here for professional reasons," Tad responded, "not for raising hell—" Conscious of the children, he corrected himself, "heck. I have been the county medical examiner ever since Wilson died."

Tad indicated a man wearing a white cap over a bald head sitting in a wheelchair in the aisle in front of them. "That's Leo Walker. He's suing Wallace Rawlings for ten million dollars."

Leo turned and looked around the gallery. Joshua saw that he had a round face and coal-black beady eyes. When Tad acknowledged Leo's presence with a slight wave of his hand and a cocky grin, the man in the wheelchair scowled and turned back towards the front.

Tad whispered to Joshua, "Last year, Vicki ran into his Toyota and totaled it. She was drunk at the time, but didn't spend even a night in jail. The sheriff just drove her home. She was never charged with DUI."

"What's wrong with him?" Donny asked.

"From what I hear, not a thing," Tad remarked. "I know his doctor; first doctor, that is. Doug Longstreet. Walker kept saying he was in pain and couldn't walk. Doctor Longstreet said there was nothing wrong with him. So, Walker fired him and is suing him for malpractice. Then, Walker found a doctor who would say he had some nerve damage in his back."

"But if Vicki Rawlings hit him, then why is he suing her father?" Donny wanted to know.

"Because," Joshua answered, "her father has all the money and the van was registered to him." He wondered how long Wallace Rawlings had been the prosecuting attorney.

Tad told him Wallace had only been in office three years. "Before that, he was struggling. He's not that good in a courtroom. He comes across as slimy, and juries just naturally hate him."

"Daddy's money doesn't guarantee you free admission on all the rides."

"Not when you're a defense attorney and your acquittal record is only thirty percent. However, Daddy's money and influence was a big help in his election campaign."

Tess Bauer sat on the other side of the courtroom. In a turquoise suit, her appearance was so polished that she looked out of place amongst the local media in the small country courthouse.

"Tess graduated from Oak Glen about…" Tad paused thoughtfully, "I think about eight years ago. She comes from a family of six kids out by Birch Hollow. Her younger sister was friends with Vicki." He added sadly, "She was a real looker. After Diana died, Tess tried to get Vicki arrested. Everyone knew she was Diana's supplier, but Tess couldn't prove it. She declared war on the Rawlings. They haven't been able to make a move without her covering it ever since. She probably feels like throwing a party."

Jan slipped into the courtroom and took the seat across the aisle from Joshua. She had taken special effort that morning to apply new cosmetics. She had also spent some time with the hair dryer and curlers, something she had not used since her cousin's wedding months earlier.

When Joshua turned to greet Jan, he paused to take in the change in her appearance.

"What's wrong?" Jan smoothed her hair. She wondered if there was a detail that she had failed to address in applying her makeup.

"You look different." Joshua gasped as he realized what was different. "You're wearing makeup."

Jan was as flustered as she was when they were twelve years old and she wore her first bra to Sunday school. Upon noticing the strap peeking out from under her sleeveless baby blue sundress, Joshua announced her new undergarment to the whole class. Maturity prevented her from reacting the same way she did back then. Instead of giving Joshua a bloody nose, she stuttered, "Do you like it?"

Joshua shrugged. "It just takes some getting used to."

Before Jan could retort, Beth Davis staggered down the aisle between them. She was visibly more frazzled than when Joshua saw her hours earlier. She squinted against the lights in the courtroom and tried unsuccessfully to cover up her lack of balance as she made her way to the front of the gallery in her search for a seat.

Jan reached across the aisle to grab Joshua's wrist. "You need to get her out of here."

Tad was already taking action. He caught up to Beth and took her by the arm. "Come on, Beth," Joshua heard him say. "Let's go get some air."

While Beth tried to pull away from the doctor who attempted to keep the scene quiet, the bailiff brought Vicki Rawlings, her hands cuffed behind her back, into the courtroom.

"All rise!"

Everyone in the courtroom rose for the judge's entrance.

Vicki regarded the judge and her audience with disdain.

Tad forcibly shoved Beth down into a vacant chair just a few feet from Vicki and sat beside her with his arm draped across her shoulders to keep her still.

For Joshua, it looked like the average bureaucratic procedure he had witnessed and participated in regularly for the last decade.

Marjorie Greene read through the list of offenses with which Victoria Rawlings was charged. Mannings declared that she pleaded not guilty and requested bail. The prosecution objected, saying the defendant was a menace to society. Mannings then pleaded that the defendant was a misunderstood child in need of psychological help. He claimed she suffered from some chemical imbalance and was in need of medical examination and treatment.

Tess Bauer glared scornfully at Vicki.

Leo Walker shook his head and laughed.

For his part, Reverend Orville Rawlings sat in the seat directly behind his granddaughter, who slumped in her chair. Slapping his palm with his driving gloves, Orville Rawlings watched the proceedings like the captain of a ship supervising his underlings in a clean-up operation after an accident that was the result of negligence on the part of his crew.

Looking the part of the concerned matriarch, Bridgette patted her father's arm while at the same time looking annoyed.

The judge set bail at fifty thousand dollars and then scheduled the trial date for September 9.

This was the point when things changed from business as usual.

Vicki turned to her lawyer and exploded. "What do you mean the trial date is set for September 9?"

Mannings tried to hush her, but Vicki would not be hushed. She jumped up and turned to the gallery behind her.

"So you think you can just lock me up and all your troubles will disappear! Nah! That's not the way it works!" she appeared to say to her father.

Vicki shook off the bailiff attempting to lead her out by the arm as she directed her curses to each family member in turn. "If I go down, you're all going down with me!"

The guard joined the bailiff in wrestling Vicki towards the door to go downstairs to the jail on the second floor, but she broke away and lunged at Reverend Rawlings. "You can lock me up, but you can't shut me up!"

Vicki's struggle with the guards got her to the other side of the gallery. "You know what they say, the word is mightier than the sword! My words are downright deadly!"

Joshua followed her eyes and saw that it seemed her last remark was directed at Tad. Or was it Beth?

As her blood drained from her face, Beth clasped Tad tightly with her arms around his neck and screamed into his chest.

The guards picked Vicki Rawlings up and carried her through the side door. It clanged shut.

With a weary shake of his head, the judge adjourned the court and left.

With Vicki gone Orville Rawlings covered up his face and his shoulders shook. Joshua leaned forward to take a look at Wallace Rawlings for his reaction. His face was as white as a sheet, which was the case for the whole Rawlings family.

"Judging from that performance," Jan told Joshua when everyone stood to leave, "it isn't going to be much of a stretch for Mannings to convince a jury Vicki Rawlings is crazy."

Joshua saw that Marjorie Greene was already conferring with Clarence Manning at the front of the courtroom. He imagined she was warning the defense lawyer not to make Vicki's emotional state the issue during the trial.

A cry rose from across the courtroom. The Thorntons craned their necks to see through the crowd gathered in the aisle.

Beth Davis had collapsed at Tad's feet.

While Tad ordered the spectators to stand back to give Beth air, Joshua fought through the crowd to get to their side. "What happened?" he asked the doctor.

"She passed out." Tad pointed to Jan and ordered her to call an ambulance. Quickly, she disappeared into the crowd.

"If you don't mind," Joshua heard an impatient voice from behind them. "Can't you put her someplace else?"

Joshua looked up at Wallace and Orville Rawlings. "Can't you see that she is unconscious?"

"She can't be moved until the ambulance gets here," Tad stated firmly while he tended to Beth. "There's another door right behind the jury box."

"We have to go out the main exit." Reverend Rawlings clasped Hal Poole's wrist to stop him when he started to follow the doctor's suggestion. "The media will think we are ducking out the back way if we go out the other door."

Tess Bauer and Leo Walker lingered nearby while the Rawlings family tried to force their way over Beth's unconscious body.

Joshua blocked the reverend's path. "I'm afraid you have no choice, Mr. Rawlings, except to take the other exit or wait until after the ambulance takes her to the hospital."

"It's *the* Reverend Rawlings!" Orville Rawlings barked. "I am *the* Reverend Rawlings and don't you ever forget it, boy." He waved his arms and shook the spectators away with his large bulk. "Get away from me!"

Joshua noticed the gloves he had previously seen the reverend slapping in his hands were now gone.

"I'm sorry if I said anything to offend you." Joshua's children were disappointed to hear their father apologize. "But I will not let you endanger this woman in the name of taking advantage of a good photo op. If you try," Joshua put his face into Wallace's double-chinned face, "I am warning you right now, you will find out exactly how little boy there is in me."

Wallace regarded Joshua and his equally tall sons flanking him. "Father, let's go out the side door. We can go around and meet the press out front." Wallace gestured for the family to turn around.

Before following his son's suggestion, Reverend Rawlings hesitated long enough to give Joshua a hard glare that warned his son's childhood rival that he had just crossed swords with the wrong man.

CHAPTER 9

▼

Joshua was not as gullible as his children thought. He knew when they talked him into taking them to Vicki's arraignment that they would want to continue along to see Rick Pendleton. He didn't intend to take them with him. However, by the time Tad escorted Beth to the hospital in the ambulance, it was late, and Joshua lost his resolve.

Rick Pendleton was a retired autoworker who, after leaving Chester in his youth, made his home in an upper-middle-class housing development in one of Cleveland's suburbs.

From an enclosed patio furnished in blue-striped furniture, Rick, his wife Ruth, and their guests watched the Pendleton's two grandsons play on a wooden playground set in a lush green back yard. Joshua's children sipped iced tea while the two men drank beer from frosted mugs.

"I have two other friends who are raising their grandchildren," Ruth, a robust woman with short salt-and-pepper hair, was telling Joshua, who sat between Sarah and Donny on the swing bench.

"We were looking forward to my retirement to go off and see the world. Instead, we're going off to play dates." Rick's laugh was good-natured, but Joshua detected a note of disappointment. Remembering his guest, Rick changed his tone and sat forward. He rested his elbows on his knees. "I'm sorry, I forgot. I'm sure, knowing Johnny's momma—"

Joshua shrugged off his apology. "Don't be sorry. Grandmomma always made sure I felt wanted."

"Yeah, well, she had a good excuse for having to bring you up. Our Chelsea is alive."

"Rick, don't air our dirty laundry." Ruth Pendleton squeezed her husband's forearm as if it had a shut off switch.

Rick sat back in his chaise with a grunt. He looked Joshua up and down and shook his head. "Damn! I can't get over how much you look like your daddy. I remember your grandmother wanting Johnny to go to the academy, but he was head over heels in love with Claire and just had to marry her." Rick sipped his beer. "They were destined to be together. Nowadays, they use the term 'soul mates'. That was Johnny and Claire all right." He sighed. "He'd sure be proud of you."

Impatient, Murphy asked, "Can you tell us about when they found the dead body?"

"Can he?" Ruth smiled.

Rick shook his head with a small laugh. "I can't believe you came all this way to ask me about that. I gave up on that years ago."

"Gave up?" Tracy repeated with a questioning tone.

"Trying to convince people there was a body. You see, no one ever did believe that we found a body that night."

Joshua sat forward. "You found it in Bosley's barn? I assume that was on Jim Bosley's farm out on Locust Hill?"

Rick confirmed Joshua's assumption. "It was an old barn by the stream. He didn't use it anymore because he had built a new barn across the lane. He just let the other one go and it was all overgrown. It was next to the woods and had lofts. It was a good make out spot, a lot more comfortable and private than trying to do it in the back seat of a car on a double date."

Joshua concealed his understanding of Rick's prelude with a soft smile. He didn't want his children to know how much he empathized with what Rick was saying.

Rick sighed and began his story, "It was the night of Oak Glen's senior prom, back in 1963. Johnny and Claire had been going together all through school, so they were naturally going to go together. Me, I felt like I was king of the world when I got a date with Lulu Jefferson." He added with a laugh, "Johnny set it up for me through Claire. Lulu was a hot number back in those days. We used to call her Lulu Sinatra because she was every bit as sexy as Nancy Sinatra."

Joshua and his children waited patiently for him to continue.

Rick was deep in thought as he took another swig of his beer. "It was my idea that we go to Bosley's barn. They were in Fox's nursing home because one of them had a stroke and the other had Alzheimers, so that whole farm was abandoned. I remember that Johnny and Claire went up into the loft, and Lulu and I ran back to this stall in the far corner."

"Were there any lights in this barn?" Joshua interjected a question. "Did the barn have electricity?"

Rick answered with a shake of his head. "The place was ancient. Johnny and I had flashlights. I remember I had taken off my tuxedo jacket and put it down on the hay for Lulu. When she laid down on it, she felt something. When she felt the hay under the jacket, she shrieked." He chuckled at the memory. "She thought it was a dead animal. At the time, I thought it was funny. It was such a high-pitched shriek. Johnny was getting a little annoyed with all the noise we were making."

"I can imagine," Joshua commented in a soft voice.

Rick stared into space as he recalled what happened next. "The way Lulu screamed when we saw those eyes on that man's face when I shone that flashlight on him, I'll never forget it."

Murphy reminded them of Lulu's words in her letter. "Lulu said that the memory was seared into her brain."

"I believe that." Rick cleared his throat, sat up straight, and went on. "He had been shot or stabbed. There was all this dried blood on his chest." He let out a single chuckle. "I thought it was a joke, and he was a store dummy because he was so stiff, but then—We went and got Sheriff Delaney."

"All of you together?" Joshua asked.

"None of us had the guts to stay alone with that dead body."

"Then what happened?"

Rick let out a quick breath. "There was no body."

"It was gone?"

Rick nodded his head. "I led Delaney right back to the stall where we all saw it. Johnny and I even dug through that old musty hay with our bare hands looking for it, but it was gone. The sheriff made some sort of joke about him going back to the cemetery on the hill where he belonged, but that was all the joking he did. He threatened to take us all in and call our folks for filing a false police report."

"Why didn't he?" Joshua wanted to know.

"I think it was because he did half-believe us. I mean, your daddy never lied. He told me once that when he was just a young kid that his mom caught him in a lie and he couldn't sit down for a week. He never told another lie ever again and everyone knew it. So, when Johnny told Delaney that there was a dead body there, he had to have believed him, and us."

Ruth went into the kitchen to retrieve another beer for her husband. When she wordlessly asked if he wanted another, Joshua declined with a shake of his head while he mouthed, "No, thank you."

"So what happened to it?" Joshua knew that it was a question that Rick was still struggling to answer decades later.

Rick's tone held just a hint of fear despite the safety of years and distance. "The killer had to have moved him. That's what Johnny said…" His voice trailed off.

Joshua sat forward to prompt Rick to verbalize his thoughts. "What did my father say happened?"

"That the killer moved him," he whispered.

"But he was as stiff as a board. That means rigor mortis had already set in. It takes a while for rigor mortis to set in."

J.J. was puzzled. "But if he had been dead for a while, why would the killer have moved him after they found him?"

"Because he didn't want him found." Rick accepted the beer his wife handed him.

"My son's point," Joshua explained, "is well taken. If the killer left the victim in an abandoned barn long enough for rigor mortis to set in, how did he even know you found him? Plus, why go to the trouble of moving the body again after you left to get the sheriff?"

"Like Johnny said, the killer was there when we found him." Rick looked questioningly at Ruth. She appeared equally puzzled.

"He stuck around in an abandoned barn hours after offing the guy?" Joshua shook his head in disbelief. "That makes no sense. If I was the killer, I would have been long gone."

The Pendletons didn't offer any other suggestion.

Joshua's mind was already working on the answer to his own question. He stood up and looked out across the yard at the two young boys going down the slide.

Murphy voiced a thought. "Someone had to have told him that the body had been found. The killer returned to the scene of the crime and moved it before they got back with the sheriff."

"Who told him?" Joshua asked his son.

Rick interjected, "The only ones who knew we found the body was us four and we stayed together all the way to the sheriff's office and back to the barn. None of us told anyone."

"No, you did tell someone," Joshua argued. "You told the sheriff. Did Sheriff Delaney call anyone before going back to the barn with you?"

Rick gazed up at him. "Yes. He called his deputy at home and told him that he was going out to the barn with us because we found a dead body. He told us it was because he needed the deputy to come in and hold the fort while he was gone."

"But you don't know for a fact that that was who he called." Joshua frowned.

"Who else could he have called?" Donny asked.

"The killer or an accomplice to give him a heads up to get rid of that body."

"Damn!" Rick gasped. "Johnny was right!"

"My father was right?"

"After we left the barn, on the way home, Johnny was driving. I remember he had a death grip on the steering wheel. We could all see it. Claire asked him what was wrong and he said, 'Don't you get it?' like we were stupid. Lulu went nuts. She said, 'You mean the killer was there?' and Johnny said yeah. Dummy that I am, I still didn't get it. I asked him if he saw the killer and Johnny said, 'Yeah, he was standing right there. He was the one wearing the badge.'"

*   *   *   *

"I want to go home!" Jan could hear Beth screaming from the examination room. "Now!"

Jan silently made her way down the hall towards the room to see what the medical staff was doing to her friend.

"Calm down!" Jan heard Tad yell over his patient's shrieks, "You can't go any-where until we bring you down to earth!"

Jan peered around the corner into the examination room.

A nurse and an orderly pinned Beth down onto the examination table. She was seemingly naked under a thin, blue cotton robe. Her bare legs flailed from under the white sheet draped across her lower body.

Jan saw hate in Beth's glazed eyes as she watched Tad struggle to inject an IV into her arm. She managed to break an arm loose and slapped the doctor square across the face. The unexpected attack caused him to drop the needle and recoil from the patient. The orderly pulled her back.

"I hate you!" Beth spat at the doctor. "And I'll make Maggie hate you, too! I'll tell her the truth! I'll tell her everything, and then she'll hate you, too, just like me!"

"Shut up!" Abruptly, Tad grabbed Beth by both shoulders, his hands almost at her throat. Fear shot through her drugged haze, and Beth dropped back down onto the table.

The nurse and orderly gazed at the doctor in stunned silence as he peered down at the patient. His angry eyes bore into hers.

"Shut up and keep still," Tad's voice dropped to a low threatening tone, "unless you're ready to die here and now."

Beth became still.

"May I help you?" Jan shot through the ceiling when the curt voice barked into her ear.

"I was just looking," Jan stammered out an excuse to the nurse, who reminded her of a particularly nasty English teacher she had in junior high school.

The nurse's stern expression was enough to send Jan hurrying back to the waiting room where she obediently sat down and picked up an eighteen-month-old magazine to read an article about the new and exciting life of an actor who killed herself a few weeks ago.

CHAPTER 10

▼

"I have a job for you kids," Joshua told his children as he scooped French vanilla ice cream into a row of bowls lined up along the kitchen counter.

It wasn't the diet kind of ice cream.

A connoisseur of ice cream, Joshua considered low fat, frozen yogurt, or fat free, sacrilege. His ice cream sundaes were a family event. The children would, as they were now, gather around the kitchen to watch him make their frozen delicacies per their instructions.

"Go through all the books Doc Wilson left in my office, pull out the medical books and journals, and pack them up. Tad is taking them."

"And what about the rest?" Tracy took the hot fudge sauce off the decades-old stove and set the pan on the table next to the ice cream carton. She missed the luxury of a microwave oven.

Frieda Thornton did not believe in microwaves, bread makers, or other modern conveniences when it came to cooking.

"Well, it's going to take me a lot of time, but I'll have to go through them and determine what ones are worth anything. The rest I'll donate to the library."

Donny whined, "Dad, all those books are going to take a week."

"So, for a week, I'll know you kids aren't getting into trouble," Joshua replied. "It has to be done. I can't put my law books in that office until those are out." He waved a cream-covered scoop at them as he made his point. "This is what happens when you don't buckle down and do what has to be done. Wilson's daughter didn't want to deal with it, so now I have to."

"Is that a fact of life?" J.J. smirked as he eyed the butterscotch sauce.

"Yes, it is."

Murphy illustrated to his siblings, "And now Dad doesn't want to deal with it, so we have to."

Joshua put the lid on the carton of ice cream and handed it to Tracy to put into the freezer. "That's the way it works."

He grabbed the first bowl in the line and proceeded to ladle thick gobs of hot fudge sauce onto the ice cream. It oozed to the sides. He then topped it off with whipped cream, nuts, and a spoonful of chopped cherries with one whole one carefully placed on top. He presented the sundae to Tracy.

Joshua selected the next child in line for his sundae. "Okay, Donny, what do you want on your sundae?"

"The usual." Leaning across the counter, Donny licked his lips as he watched Joshua dole out the whipped cream.

Sarah perched herself on the kitchen stool. "Dad, I don't understand how the sheriff could have killed that man. Lulu's letter said that Reverend Rawlings was the murderer."

"No, Lulu's letter didn't say Reverend Rawlings killed him. She only said that she saw a picture of the dead man in the reverend's office," Tracy reminded Sarah while Joshua presented Donny with his sundae and proceeded to the next one.

J.J. added, "That picture proved that the reverend knew the victim."

Murphy patted their dog on the head. "I'll bet that picture is long gone."

Admiral stomped his large feet to signal his growing impatience. He couldn't believe all this food was just inches from his mouth and he got none.

Donny was already devouring his sundae. "Why would the sheriff warn the reverend to get rid of the body?"

Joshua handed a banana to J.J., who proceeded to slice it for his twin, himself, and their father's sundaes. "Because Reverend Orville Rawlings is a powerful man in this valley. You saw him today. He's used to everyone following his orders. And don't forget, Lulu said in her letter that she saw Sheriff Delaney in that picture, too. Those two went way back."

Their father went to work on his own delicacy while the offspring worked out the scenario amongst themselves.

"So the sheriff could have been the killer," Sarah concluded.

"Yeah, but, as far as we know, the sheriff didn't know that Lulu saw the picture," J.J. disagreed. "Rawlings did. She says in the letter that she asked him about it when she saw it."

Murphy pointed to his twin with his spoon as he told him, "Reverend Rawlings could have ordered Sheriff Delaney to kill Lulu to keep her quiet. Can you think of a better hit man? The sheriff. If he says it was an accidental overdose who's going to argue?"

"The victim's sister," Tracy answered with a note of sadness.

"Then she conveniently bites the dust," Donny reminded them.

"And then the newspaper editor's house gets torched," J.J. completed the scenario.

Murphy snickered, "And since the sheriff is the one who does it, every murder is ruled an accident. It's perfect!"

"Except for a little piece of mail that they don't know about." His masterpiece completed, Joshua leaned against the kitchen counter while ordering with only a hint of a grin. "And they won't know about it until I say so."

"But if these murders are perfect, then how are you going to nail them?" Sarah wanted to know.

"Whatever happened to this sheriff?" Murphy asked.

"He died years ago," Joshua told them. "But Reverend Rawlings is still around and he is still very powerful. Clarence Mannings doesn't come cheap."

"But you can get him, can't you, Dad?" Donny grinned with pride at his father. "You brought down an admiral."

"Before I brought down that admiral, before I even thought to bring him down, I made sure I had all my facts straight. When you go up against the big players, you don't want to miss with your first shot, because they'll crush you before you get another one."

"So what do we have to do to bring down the reverend?" Sarah asked.

"Why do we even want to?"

"Because he's crooked," Donny stated, matter-of-factly.

Tracy agreed. "Think of all those poor people who have given him their support because he's supposed to be a man of God and he's probably ripping them off."

Joshua shook his head. "Many people have tried to put the reverend out of business. He has been checked out financially in and out, up and down, and no one has ever found any indiscretion in his business dealings."

"But he lives in that big mansion. Pastor Andrews lives in that little house behind the church. Doesn't that say anything?" Donny wondered.

"Wise investing is not a sin," Joshua countered.

"Does this mean that you're not going to do anything, Dad?" Murphy was surprised.

"I have a business of my own to set up and I need clients who can pay me. Right now, I maybe have one client who is probably not able to pay me for a long time to come, if ever. We need at least two more bathrooms in this house before one of you kids commits your own murder. These appliances in this kitchen are on their last legs."

"You're saying that you don't have time to work on this," J.J. translated.

"Not without a paying client, I don't, and neither do you kids."

"Well," J.J. asked, "if, say, you were going to prosecute this case, what would you do?"

Joshua caught the meaning behind the question. "Nothing."

"But, if you were going to prosecute, what would you do?"

"First, I would need to know who was killed. It's bad enough that there is no body. Not only is there no body, but, to my knowledge, there is no missing person's report to go with the disappearing body."

"But we have an eyewitness who says there was a dead body," Sarah told him.

Joshua chuckled as he shook his head. He swallowed a mouthful of ice cream before he explained the reason for his quiet laughter. "Kids, contrary to what the general population believes, eyewitness testimony is considered to be one of the least reliable forms of evidence. Rick Pendleton is a very nice man, and I believe he is sincere. However, it was dark when he saw this body almost forty years ago. So identification will be questionable, if it ever came to that." Joshua added with a wave of his spoon, "Not only that, but, for all we know, he could be lying for any number of reasons."

The five children looked at each other while Joshua gave them a final warning. "Don't go any further with this. That is an order. If Rawlings or Delaney killed this man for whatever reason; and Lulu Jefferson for seeing a picture; and her sister and the newspaper editor for seeking justice, then that means Rawlings is more than capable of murder. It has been my experience that if a man is capable of killing once, twice, four times in this case, then life is very cheap to him. He can kill, or order a person killed, as easily as squashing a bug under the heel of his shoe. Get my drift?"

Before the kids had a chance to respond, Tad knocked on the back screen door and stepped inside without waiting for an invitation.

When he saw that the doctor had his own dog on a leash, Admiral scurried to hide behind the protection of the children's legs under the table.

"Hey, gang! I was just out walking Dog." Tad stopped when he saw the size of Joshua's sundae. "Oh, man, I can hear your arteries clogging over here."

"The man stops drinking and gives up drugs, and suddenly he's a purist," Joshua told the kids.

Tracy was already taking the tub of ice cream out of the freezer. "What do you want on your sundae?"

"Just one plain scoop is fine for me." Tad leaned against the kitchen counter next to Joshua. "Have you heard from Beth?"

Joshua continued eating his sundae. "The last time I saw her she was with you."

"What did she tell you this morning?"

"You know better than that. That's confidential."

"Did she hire you?"

"That's hard to say," Joshua squinted. "She got mad and walked out. What happened at the hospital?"

"She left. Jan and I have been looking for her all afternoon."

"Did you make Beth mad?" Joshua asked with a teasing tone.

Tad wasn't joking. "Yes, I did. I told her I was checking her into detox to get dried out. She's been living on booze and pills since Saturday. That's why she fainted. I left her with a nurse to go call Glenbeigh and tell Jan what was happening. When I came back, Beth was gone."

"Why did the nurse leave her alone?"

"She got called away to help with another patient. It is an emergency room." Tad shook his head in disbelief. "It wasn't the nurse's fault. I didn't think Beth had the strength to sit up on her own, let alone get dressed and walk out."

"Where would she have gone?" Tracy handed the bowl of ice cream to their guest.

"I don't know, but I have a good idea." Tad looked down into the bowl of ice cream. Worry had robbed him of his appetite.

"A bar?" Joshua suggested.

"No. To go find Vicki Rawlings."

"Vicki Rawlings is in jail," J.J. reminded him.

"Not anymore," Tad told them. "Grandpa paid her bail. She was out an hour after the hearing."

Joshua looked at Tad with furrowed brows. "I'm afraid to ask, but I have to know—what is Beth's connection to Vicki?"

"I think you know."

"What?" Donny asked.

Joshua looked to Tad for confirmation as he answered his son. "Beth Davis is a pharmacist. Drugs, more pills than one person can possibly imbibe, were missing from the pharmacy when Jan did an inventory yesterday. Vicki Rawlings is a known drug dealer. Beth was very upset upon learning that Vicki had been arrested and asked me to defend her. Why would she do that? Because she is terrified that Vicki Rawlings would name her as one of her suppliers. If that happened, we would be talking about something much bigger than criminal negligence. We're talking about hard time in prison."

Tad nodded sadly. He handed his ice cream over to Donny. "Will you go over to Vicki's with me to find her?"

Joshua looked down at his sundae. There was a little less than half left, but he now didn't have the appetite. Much to Admiral's disappointment, he set the dish on the floor for Dog to finish.

*   *   *   *

For a seventeen-year-old girl, Vicki Rawlings had a nice place, if she took care of it. The drug dealer lived on the other side of Newell in a doublewide trailer set back in a hollow off Route 208, nicknamed the Race Track Road because the road led straight to the Mountaineer Park. Traffic was fast and heavy on the country road on race nights.

Woods surrounded the bare lot that was void of grass and vegetation. A wooden tool shed was erected behind the trailer. Even though the home was relatively new, it appeared run-down due to neglect. Maintenance was not on the teenage homeowner's list of priorities.

Dusk had turned to dark by the time Joshua and Tad arrived in search of the doctor's patient.

Joshua stopped his Corvette in the driveway at the edge of the woods. Beth's five-year-old white sedan was parked next to a dirty four-wheel drive truck in front of the trailer. The truck bore temporary tags.

"She's here all right." Joshua coasted up to the trailer. "Do you want me to go in to get her?"

"We should both go in."

Joshua turned off the engine, reached across Tad to the glove compartment, took out his 9 mm Beretta, and checked the cartridge. It was loaded.

When Joshua saw Tad's worried expression, he assured him, "It's legal. I picked it up at the sheriff's office with all the permits in proper order yesterday morning after my meeting with Wally."

"So you met our esteemed Sheriff Curt Sawyer?"

"Not yet. Every time I've stopped by his office to talk to him about Vicki, he's been out. I'm beginning to think he's avoiding me."

"Not necessarily. Sheriff Curtis Sawyer is a hands-on type of guy. He's more lawman than politician." Tad pointed at Joshua's gun as he warned him, "I don't want to get caught in any crossfire. I just want to get Beth out of there."

"I'm here because Vicki already tried to kill you. I don't want her to finish the job." Joshua tucked the gun into the front waistband of his jeans.

Seeing there was no arguing with his cousin, Tad sucked in his breath and climbed out of the car. The trailer seemed to throb with the rhythm of painfully-loud rap music blasting from inside. They walked up the metal steps to the door.

"I don't recall Beth having that taste in music."

"She doesn't." Tad knocked on the door. Getting no response, he rang the doorbell. They waited.

Joshua pressed his ear to the door. "I don't hear any movement inside."

When the lawyer put his hand on the doorknob, the door swung open as if an invisible being had opened it to invite the visitors inside. It was unlatched.

Expecting trouble, Joshua removed the gun from his waistband before stepping up into the trailer.

Tad cautiously followed.

On the other side of the threshold, Joshua and Tad found a kitchen overflowing with dirty pots, pans, and dishes in the sink. The smell of rotting food assaulted their sinuses.

Empty beer cans were stacked up to form an aluminum pyramid on the table. Pills in plastic bags littered the kitchen table. A large clear plastic bag filled with a white powder acted as the table's centerpiece.

Tad dipped a moist fingertip into the powder to taste it. "Cocaine. Good quality stuff, too." He observed the size of the bag. "Must be at least one kilo here." There was a box of small empty baggies and one baggie filled but not closed. "Looks like they were in the process of dividing it when they were interrupted."

Joshua observed the condition of housekeeping. It was hard to tell if there had been a struggle or if it was the normal state of affairs. Based on the garbage littering the trailer, his guess was the latter.

A cheap wooden computer desk against the wall between the kitchen and living area contained a desktop computer and a stack of computer games. Joshua paused to observe the type of games a drug dealer would play. The theme of each was either sexual or violent in nature.

While Joshua looked over the collection, his hand bumped the mouse. Abruptly, a woman's hysterical scream came from the computer's hard drive.

Both Joshua and Tad jumped at the sudden scream of terror and looked around them for the source until they noticed the image of a woman on the computer monitor.

After he saw that the scream was not real, Tad sighed with relief and resumed his search for any sign of where Beth had disappeared.

Joshua took a step back from the computer and peered at the image on the screen. The hysterical blond haired woman was handcuffed to a bed. She was completely naked. Her fear was directed at the unseen player of the game. As the player came towards her, she helplessly eyed the butcher knife in his hand.

Disgusted, Joshua turned away from the sight and crossed the obstacle course of discarded clothes and plates of half eaten food to the hallway leading back to the bedrooms. He kept his finger on the trigger of his gun.

"I don't think anyone is here," Joshua heard Tad yell from the kitchen. Disagreeing with his cousin's conclusion, he checked every bedroom along the length of the hallway to the back of the trailer. "Beth's car is here, and that truck belongs to someone."

The bedroom door was open at the end of the hall.

Joshua saw something black wedged under the door like a small animal crushed under a plank. It was a leather-driving glove. He considered picking it up until he saw what appeared to be splotches of blood on it.

Joshua's instinct that something was very wrong was confirmed.

"They must have gone somewhere," Tad called from the opposite end of the hall as Joshua stepped into the master bedroom.

A cold chill, not unlike a bucket of ice water dumped over his head, raced through Joshua's whole body.

It could have been Sarah's room. Clothes cluttered the floor and the bed was unmade. A poster of the girl's idol hung over her bed.

There the similarities to a typical teenager's bedroom ended.

Vicki's idol didn't play in any rock band. The poster over the unmade bed was of one of Satan's demons. A muscular, half-naked, horned and fanged beast grinned with bloodlust down at Joshua from over the bed. It wasn't until he stepped up to the bed that Joshua discovered that the blood splattered on the poster was real.

So was the body on the bed.

Vicki Rawlings could no longer torment Tad or anyone else. Looking like the angel she wasn't, she lay with her arms crossed over her chest. She was dressed in a black sleeveless shirt with no underwear or panties.

In her undressed state, Joshua could see the tattooed serpent in all his glory. The snake was wrapped around Vicki's right leg, up her hip, and across her stomach to her back. As Joshua stood over her, the tattoo seemed to come to life to strike at him in defense of the serpent's lifeless hostess.

A steel stake stood erect from the very center of the pentagram tattooed on her left breast.

"Did you find—?" Tad stopped speaking when he stepped into the bedroom and saw Vicki Rawlings. "Oh, Lord!" Always the doctor, Tad rushed to the girl.

"Don't touch her!" Joshua's order only made Tad slow down on his way around to the other side of the bed.

The sight waiting for the doctor on the other side of the bed stopped him. He didn't say a word. He halted, immobile, unable to speak his horror.

"What—?" was all Joshua got out before Tad put his hands to his mouth, and ran from the room and out the back door in the hall.

As he went around to the other side of the bed, Joshua could hear Tad vomiting from the open back door.

Beth's body was sprawled on the floor next to the Vicki's bed. The revolver was still clutched in her hand.

CHAPTER 11

▼

As if the victims could escape, Joshua stood guard in the bedroom doorway to dial 911 on his cell phone. He was still on the phone with the emergency operator when a headlight beam shone through the window to bathe the bedroom in light. The beam was coupled with the low roar of a van engine. After the van parked on the bare lawn, the lights and engine were extinguished.

Through the bathroom window, Joshua saw the news van with the satellite dish on the roof and "Channel 6" emblazoned on the side. Tess Bauer was climbing out of the passenger side.

Tad came back in from where he had leapt out the back door to throw up in the backyard.

"We have company," Joshua announced.

"Damn!" Tad cursed when he saw Tess Bauer giving instructions to the camera operator. "Who invited her?"

"You wait here," Joshua instructed his cousin before running to the front door to intercept Tess and the camera operator on the steps outside.

"What are you doing here?" Joshua greeted the journalist. He was further displeased to see the light on top of the camera glowing to signal that the operator was recording the encounter.

"Amber called. She told me that Vicki Rawlings had been murdered." Tess attempted to push her way inside, but the lawyer blocked her entrance.

While Joshua kept the journalist on the rickety front stoop, the camera operator did a balancing act on the unsteady step below her by juggling the camera hoisted with both hands onto his shoulder while keeping his footing.

Joshua accused the reporter, "So you come rushing over here with a camera crew and don't even bother calling the police?"

"First, I needed to check to see if Vicki had been murdered. It'd be pretty embarrassing if I called the police over here for a false alarm."

"Does that mean Amber has a history of lying?" Joshua shifted to block the camera's view into the trailer.

Tess stuck the microphone into Joshua's face. "Well, if you won't let us in, why don't you tell us who you are and what you are doing here? Do you work for the Rawlings?"

"If I did, I wouldn't be talking to you."

"Has Vicki Rawlings been murdered?"

"You'll get a statement from the police when they are ready to release one."

The sheriff's black and gold patrol car came up the driveway. The blue lights on top of the car lit up the dark enveloping the trailer's bare front yard.

Tess paused only long enough to note the arrival of the sheriff before resuming her interview. "Was Reverend Orville Rawlings here when you arrived? How long have you been here? What business do you have with Vicki Rawlings?"

"Go back to your van and wait for the sheriff's statement," Joshua ordered. "This is a crime scene."

Sheriff Curtis Sawyer stepped out of the passenger side of the car. His deputy got out of the driver's side.

Tess's camera operator whirled around to record them making their way across the yard.

"Get that camera out of my face!" Sheriff Sawyer ordered in a menacing tone.

When the lawman sprung threateningly in his direction, the camera operator jumped backwards and tripped over a rock. The acrobatic cameraman performed a strange-looking dance as he fought to regain his balance without dropping the expensive piece of equipment. The dance ended with him plopping down onto his rump on the ground with the undamaged camera held high up in the air.

The sheriff looked up at Joshua, who blocked his path through the door. "So you're Joshua Thornton, the guy who's been hounding my deputies for information about Vicki Rawlings?"

"It's nice to finally meet you, too, sheriff." Joshua offered the county's chief lawman his hand.

The sheriff reached out to clasp Joshua's hand into a firm grip.

"Sheriff Sawyer, is it true that Vicki Rawlings has been murdered?" Tess stuck her microphone into the sheriff's face as he sidestepped her to investigate the crime scene.

"I'll tell you what I know after I know it and not a minute sooner." Sheriff Sawyer stepped through the minimal amount of space that Joshua permitted to let him through the doorway while refusing entrance to the journalist.

The sheriff directed his first question to Joshua. "What have we got here?"

"Two bodies back in the bedroom," Joshua announced as he shut the door.

"Two bodies!" They both heard Tess shriek. She dropped the microphone with a loud clankity-clank onto the metal stoop right before the door snapped shut.

"You're a lawyer?" Curtis asked with the same tone as if he were inquiring if he were speaking to a leper. While he slipped on a pair of latex gloves, the sheriff studied Joshua as if to determine if he were friend or foe. "What are you doing here?"

Joshua studied Sheriff Curtis Sawyer just as closely. Like his predecessor, Charles Delaney, Curt Sawyer came from a military background. Joshua saw it stuck more with Sawyer who, while short and squat, was solid muscle. He stood straight with his shoulders back and his broad chest stuck out as if to proudly show off the shiny gold badge pinned on his navy blue sheriff's uniform. Joshua was a head taller and in good shape, but he quickly concluded that he did not want to get into a boxing match with this man.

Sheriff Sawyer noted the pills and cocaine on the kitchen table while Joshua answered his question. "Tad MacMillan asked me to come out here with him to look for Beth Davis after she left the hospital without being released this afternoon." As they spoke, Joshua indicated with a nod of his head the bedroom at the end of the hall in which the bodies were found.

The sheriff motioned for Joshua to lead the way. "Why was she in the hospital?"

"She fainted at Vicki Rawlings's hearing this morning." Joshua stopped at the bloody glove, already in a plastic evidence bag, which was still on the floor by the bedroom door. It had been photographed and the place marked. "I found this on my way in. When I saw there was blood on it, I left it there."

"Did you touch it?" Sheriff Sawyer squatted to study the glove.

Joshua swore he saw a look of recognition. "No, I didn't."

The sheriff was studying the carpet in the hallway.

Joshua knew what Sawyer was observing. "Judging by those drag marks, I think Vicki Rawlings was knocked out in some way, then dragged from the living room or kitchen into the bedroom where she was killed."

Sheriff Sawyer looked up at Joshua and gave him a small smirk. "Not bad, for a lawyer."

Joshua stepped back to let the sheriff into the scene of the murders.

"Why did she collapse?" Sheriff Sawyer asked as he passed him.

Joshua followed him into the room where the sheriff's deputy was already photographing the scene from every angle possible.

Part of the medical examiner's job was to examine the bodies at the crime scene before transporting them to East Liverpool Hospital for autopsies. Tad was in the process of bagging Beth's hands in paper bags held in place with rubber bands to protect any evidence that might be on them when the sheriff and his cousin came in.

Joshua noticed that Tad's latex-gloved hands trembled as he worked on the body of the woman for whom they both cared.

"Mr. Thornton?" Curtis Sawyer snapped.

Joshua started out of his thoughts. "Excuse me?"

The sheriff repeated his question. "Why did Ms. Davis collapse?"

"You'll have to ask her doctor about that. I left the courthouse as soon as the hearing was over to go to a meeting."

As he studied the scene on the bed, Sheriff Sawyer stepped around Vicki's body and knelt to examine Beth's. "How long ago did this happen, Doc?"

"Beth's been dead two hours." Tad stood up and nodded towards Vicki's body. "She's been dead four hours."

"You mean there's two hours difference between their times of death?" Sheriff Sawyer looked from one body to the other.

"At least."

Joshua was just as surprised. "That doesn't make sense. Why would Beth wait two hours after killing Vicki before offing herself?"

"Could you be wrong?" Sheriff Sawyer asked the medical examiner.

"Not by two hours." Tad shook his head. "According to her liver temperature, Vicki Rawlings died no less than four hours ago. Beth has been dead no more than two hours. They did not die at the same time."

Both Sheriff Sawyer and Joshua looked from one body to the other, then back again.

"You know," Joshua mumbled, "it doesn't make sense for Beth to kill Vicki with a stake through the heart, then take out a gun, and shoot herself. I mean, if I was going to kill someone, then kill myself, why not use the same weapon?"

Sheriff Sawyer agreed. "Yeah, why not just shoot Vicki Rawlings and then shoot herself? Why go to the trouble of bringing in a stake and driving it through her heart before blowing your brains out?" He turned his attention back to the medical examiner. "Any sexual activity?"

"No signs at all with Beth. Vicki's not wearing any underwear, but I don't see any bruising on her inner thighs. You'll have to wait for me to do the autopsy to find that out for certain," Tad told them.

The sheriff removed the bag covering Beth's hand with the gun still stuck in her hand. Her fingers clutched the gun in a death grip.

Tad explained why the dead woman was still clutching the gun. "Cadaver spasm. It happens when the brain shuts down instantly. I'll have to break her fingers to get the weapon for you."

"Awfully big gun for such a little girl," Sheriff Sawyer observed.

"I've known women in the military who were pretty handy with big guns. A female Marine major came right out and told me that size did matter." The men in the room chuckled at the meaning behind Joshua's off-color comment.

Joshua studied the gun stuck in Beth's hand. "Luger. Nine millimeter. Looks kind of old."

"You know something about guns, Mr. Thornton?" Sheriff Sawyer looked up at him.

"I am a Navy commander."

"You're a legal weenie," the sheriff snickered wickedly. "Most legal weenies I know don't know jack about guns."

Joshua retorted, "I know about a lot of things, sheriff."

Tad turned away from them while his cousin knelt down to study Beth's hand.

Joshua could feel the sheriff's gaze on him. "Look at these powder burns."

"I get the feeling you've done this before," Sheriff Sawyer noted as he motioned for his deputy to photograph Beth's hand.

"I didn't go straight into litigation from the Naval Academy."

"Just don't you be disturbing any evidence." The sheriff handed Joshua a pair of latex gloves and motioned for him to put them on in order to preserve the crime scene.

Joshua showed Beth's hand to Sheriff Sawyer.

The powder burns from the gun were evident, as was an outline over the top of her hand in which there was no powder burn. "If she fired this gun on her own, there should be a powder burn over the top of her hand," Joshua pointed out.

Sheriff Sawyer gave Joshua a hard glare as he took Beth's hand out of the lawyer's. "Like I said, it's a pretty big gun for such a little girl." The sheriff showed him Beth's grip on the gun. Her fingers barely got around the trigger. The grasp was awkward and clumsy. Without saying anything more, the sheriff put the bag back on Beth's hand and sealed it with the rubber band.

The sheriff then moved on to the next victim. "She doesn't appear to have put up much of a fight." Sheriff Sawyer observed the peaceful state of Vicki's death.

The closet door was open. Joshua casually peered inside.

Vicki favored black clothes. Her wardrobe consisted of a variety of black coats, pants and tops. Joshua noted that there was not one skirt or dress. Some of her clothes were hung up on hangers; others were in a pile on the floor. All of them were black in color.

For that reason, a blue-silver trench coat stood out amongst the collection.

Joshua examined the coat where it hung on a wire hanger in the closet.

"I certainly didn't expect her to go peacefully," Sheriff Sawyer was remarking about the murder victim stretched out on the bed. "What are you doing, Mr. Thornton? I told you not to go disturbing any evidence."

"All the clothes in this closet are black except for this trench coat." Joshua pulled the coat by the bottom hem out of the closet so it still hung on the hanger to display the front of it to the lawman. The front was splattered with blood and body tissue.

Sheriff Sawyer joined Joshua at the closet. "That's a man's trench coat." He examined the coat and its pockets. "We have more gloves." The sheriff removed a bloody leather glove from one of the pockets. After sniffing it, he held it out to Joshua for him to smell. "Carbon."

"Whoever wore these gloves fired a gun," Joshua observed. "And it's too big for either Beth or Vicki."

After replacing the glove in the pocket, Sheriff Sawyer told the deputy to get a picture of the coat and the closet.

Tad was making a note in his notepad when the sheriff questioned him. "Thornton said you came here looking for Beth Davis. Considering all the trouble Vicki's been causing you, I would have thought you would have stayed as far away from her as humanly possible."

"I had no choice. It was imperative to get Beth into detox as soon as possible," Tad said. "I didn't want to come here." He pointed to Joshua. "That's why I brought him with me."

"Why would you think Ms. Davis would be here?"

"Beth was on a binge. Vicki Rawlings is a drug dealer."

"Wasn't Ms. Davis a pharmacist?"

Joshua and Tad exchanged looks.

The lawyer wordlessly advised Tad that there was no hiding the truth anymore before answering the question himself. "Beth got fired from her job. There is speculation that she was supplying to Vicki Rawlings."

Sheriff Sawyer laughed. "Speculation? You damn well talk like a lawyer." He turned serious. "So Ms. Davis was afraid Vicki Rawlings was going to roll over on her to save her own neck?"

Joshua shrugged. "It's only speculation at this point."

As they were speaking, Tad couldn't take his eyes off Beth's body.

"What condition was she in the last time you saw her?" the sheriff asked Joshua.

"Unconscious," the lawyer answered simply. He turned to Tad as he spoke to the sheriff. "Dr. MacMillan was the last one to see her."

"No, a nurse at the emergency room was the last one to see her. She appeared to have taken an overdose of Valium and alcohol. The nurse left because another doctor needed her. When I came back, Beth was gone."

Sheriff Sawyer crossed his arms and studied Tad as he asked, "And what condition was she in when you left her with the nurse?"

"Conscious, but not strong enough to get up and run away. She didn't want to go into detox. She wanted me to just let her die."

"So she was suicidal?"

Tad's grief turned to anger. "Do you think Beth wanted this to happen? You think she decided back when she was a child that she wanted to grow up to be a drug supplier for a manipulative little bitch like Vicki Rawlings? Vicki was blackmailing Beth. Somehow, she found out that Beth had stolen drugs from the pharmacy inventory for her own use, and she threatened to tell Jan Martin if Beth didn't do as she told her. She knew what she was doing, but she felt like she had no control over the situation. That was her problem. She had no control. She lost it all and she didn't know what to do anymore!"

"So she decided to kill the little bitch who ruined her life and take her own." Sheriff Sawyer turned around and surveyed the scene while Tad waited by the door.

Joshua studied Vicki's position on the bed. If it weren't for the blood and the steel stake sticking out of her chest, one would have thought she was sleeping.

"If she was so high on Valium and alcohol, then Beth would not have been able to overcome Vicki," Joshua pointed out. "It took two men to drag her out of that courtroom this morning."

Sawyer agreed, "Vicki was a wildcat. I broke up a few bar fights with her." He took a deep breath. "She had to have been drugged, knocked out or something, and then brought back here. Then, it was just a matter of putting the gun to Beth's head—"

Tad was gone. He escaped the scene out the side door and into the barren backyard. He ran to the edge of the property, away from Beth's death, before dropping to his knees and throwing up again.

Tad jumped when he felt Joshua's hand on his shoulder. His cousin knelt next to him to offer him his handkerchief.

"She never got over you," Tad gasped while fighting to stop the churning in his stomach.

"I know," Joshua sighed. "Tad,—?" He wanted to ask his cousin if Beth had shown any signs of being suicidal in the past.

"Now is not a good time." Tad threw up again.

Joshua went for a walk. He rounded the corner of the mobile home to the driveway to find it illuminated with spotlights. Through the glare of the lights, he could make out Tess Bauer standing before the cameras.

"This is Tess Bauer at the home of Victoria Rawlings, whose murdered body has just been found in her bedroom. From what we've been told, for the granddaughter of the Reverend Orville Rawlings and daughter of Wallace Rawlings, life has ended as violently as she lived it. She was found murdered, apparently by Beth Davis, a pharmacist from nearby Chester. According to an unidentified source close to the investigation, allegedly Ms. Davis was believed to have been one of Ms. Rawlings's drug suppliers. It appears that after driving a steel stake through Ms. Rawlings's heart, Ms. Davis ended her own life with a single gunshot wound through the head…"

Joshua ducked into the shadows to return to the crime scene.

CHAPTER 12

▼

Joshua sighed and clutched the cushion to his chest. Even in his sleep, he was aware of a presence coming into his office. With effort, he forced himself awake, opened his eyes, and, as his vision cleared, made out the feminine form standing over him.

"What—?" Joshua mouthed before he remembered where he was. He started and sat up on the sofa on which he had stretched out for a nap while packing up Dr. Wilson's library.

"That's okay," Marjorie Greene stepped back from the sofa to let him up. "I fall asleep in my office, too. It's just that the voters don't know it."

Joshua shook the sleep out of his head and looked around at the mess that failed to disappear while he was napping. There were still boxes and piles of musty books and journals on every available surface, including the floor.

Marjorie stood in the center of the mess while Joshua hurriedly made himself as presentable as he could in his dirty work shirt, faded jeans with holes in both knees, and bare feet. He was a stark contrast to Marjorie's polished suit with matching pumps.

"I'm sorry. You caught me." He offered her a seat on the sofa. "I'm not really open for business yet. I thought when I started my own practice that I would have time to set up before getting any work. Here, I'm still clearing Doc Wilson's junk out, and clients are coming out of the woodwork...unless this is a social call." He sat on the sofa next to Marjorie.

"No, this is business." With a critical eye on the cluttered office and disheveled appearance of her colleague, Marjorie shifted in her seat. Her eyes fell to Joshua's bare feet.

Joshua's eyes followed hers. "Oh," he smiled and slipped the pair of worn dock shoes he had kicked off back onto his feet. "I guess my roots are showing. My shoes seem to come off as soon as I cross the state line."

Marjorie failed to see Joshua's attempt at humor. "I'm from West Virginia and I don't go barefoot."

Joshua cleared his throat and took on a professional demeanor. "What can I do for you, Ms. Greene?"

"I'm going back to Charleston. I was working on a case down there that had been continued, and now, with Victoria Rawlings's murder, it is apparent that this case will be more involved than the attorney general had anticipated. He wants to appoint someone who can spend more time on it, someone better equipped to sort out all the intricacies, and who already has the local citizens' trust."

Joshua caught her meaning. "Me? Special prosecutor?"

"The attorney general spoke to your former commanding officer and he is convinced you are the man to put Reverend Orville Rawlings out of business."

"Listen, I admit that Orville Rawlings is a pompous ass, but why is the attorney general so set on putting him out of business?"

"Have you kept up on the local news?"

"Are you talking about the Amber tapes?"

Marjorie was impressed with the phrase. "The Amber tapes. That's good."

"I came up with the name myself. Amber's not exactly a credible witness."

"She wasn't lying. Reverend Orville Rawlings is the valley's drug lord," Marjorie stated.

Joshua gazed at her, and then shook his head. "I must be naive. Reverend Rawlings has the biggest non-denominational church in the valley."

"Can you think of a better cover for a drug lord than as a church pastor?" Marjorie sat back and crossed her legs. "Unfortunately, every time we, or the feds, think that we are just about to get him, our witnesses end up dead or disappear off the face of the earth. When you called us about Vicki shooting at your cousin in a church full of witnesses and the evidence you had of her stalking him, we thought we finally got what we needed to get Vicki to roll over on her grandfather, but she ended up dead." Marjorie shrugged sarcastically. "Go figure."

"Whose turf is this? The attorney general's or the feds'?"

"Vicki was not an official witness, nor was she charged with drug trafficking. Officially, it is not their turf. But you have the feds' attention, and they will give you any help you need to get Rawlings."

"So what do you want me to do? Get Rawlings, or solve Vicki's and Beth Davis's murders? I'll find out who killed them, but I'm not going to set up Rawlings for their murders if he didn't do it."

"Who else would have killed them? Reverend Rawlings's glove was found at the scene."

"Was it his glove?"

Marjorie scoffed. "Everyone saw him with those gloves at the arraignment."

"I know," Joshua snickered. "Pretty sloppy move for such a smart man, don't you think? Don't you think a man as powerful as Rawlings would have ordered someone to kill them for him?" He shook his head. "No, the scenario of Reverend Rawlings carelessly dropping a glove that God and everyone had seen in his possession just hours before after driving a stake through his granddaughter's heart and shooting Beth Davis in the head just doesn't fit."

Annoyed by Joshua's consideration of Reverend Orville Rawlings's possible innocence, Marjorie stood up in preparation to leave. "What should I tell the attorney general?"

"Tell him I will look into the murders of Vicki Rawlings and Beth Davis. If Orville Rawlings is behind them, then I'll get his man. If not, I will get their killer. And if we are lucky, I'll get both."

*   *   *   *

"So this is where you've been hiding." Joshua found Tad in the basement of the East Liverpool Hospital, located across the river from Chester. Since the murders, after tending to live patients during his office hours, the medical examiner had been probing the two bodies to collect evidence that would identify and convict their killer.

Even though East Liverpool Hospital was in Ohio, another state and jurisdiction, the hospital permitted Hancock County's medical examiner to use their morgue for his autopsies. He sent the physical evidence that needed to be evaluated down the river to a state lab in Weirton, West Virginia.

Tad was peering through a microscope when Joshua, freshly showered and dressed for business in slacks, shirt, and shoes after his meeting with Marjorie Greene, came through the swinging doors to startle his cousin in the deathly quiet of the morgue.

Tad contrasted Joshua's appearance in his old jeans and a wrinkled shirt that he wore under his lab coat. The lack of sleep was evident by his unshaven face and the dark circles under his eyes.

"What are you doing here?" Tad asked even though he knew the answer.

"I'm here to learn what you found in Beth's and Vicki's autopsies?"

Tad returned to peering through the microscope. "Is this professional interest or are you just being nosy?"

"Why would it be professional interest?"

Tad grinned knowingly. "It's a small town."

While the medical examiner studied his microscopic specimen, Joshua made himself at home by reading the reports on Tad's desk. "What do you know about Orville Rawlings being the valley's drug lord?"

"Is it fact or fiction?"

"Fact?"

"I already told you. Fact. Get your nose out of my desk."

Joshua put down the report he was scanning. "Was he trafficking drugs in the valley when you were using?"

"Yep." Satisfied with what he saw, Tad made a note on his clipboard and turned off the light under the microscope.

"Why didn't you ever say anything to me about it?"

"I figured that in this case the less you knew, the better." Tad turned around on his stool to face Joshua, who was leaning against his desk. "I got involved in drugs back in the sixties when it was the in thing. Lulu Jefferson introduced me to pot."

"Did she introduce you to heroin?"

"Do you mean the stuff that killed her?"

Joshua nodded.

Tad shook his head. "Heroin never turned me on, never turned Lulu on either. All she did was drink and smoke pot and cigarettes. She did nothing that involved needles, neither did I."

"Who killed her?"

"Why are you asking me that? You were appointed to find Beth's and Vicki's killer."

"You know everything that goes on in this valley. Did Reverend Rawlings kill Lulu Jefferson because she saw the picture of that John Doe in his office?"

Tad squinted questioningly. "What picture in what office?"

Joshua suddenly recalled that he had not said anything to Tad about Lulu's letter. He carefully chose every word in his response. "A source told me that on the day Lulu died she saw a picture in Reverend Rawlings's office of the same man whose body she and my folks found in that barn." He added firmly, "This information goes no further."

"I guess that means you aren't going to tell me the name of your source." When Joshua didn't answer his question, Tad told him, "I didn't even know Lulu was there with your folks until you told me." He chuckled. "Do you seriously think Reverend Rawlings would kill Lulu because she saw a picture years after seeing a dead body?"

Joshua responded with a smirk, "Depends on who the victim is and what connection he has to Rawlings. If the good reverend is a drug lord, then he would have access to the heroin to kill Lulu."

Tad's chuckle turned to laughter, after which he told Joshua the reason for his mirth. "Rawlings never has any contact with the drugs or the people involved in the dealing. That's one of the ways he keeps himself out of jail. He hires other people to do all the dirty work. He just gives orders and takes his cut."

"Smart man."

"He wouldn't have been in this business as long as he has if he wasn't."

"So he'd order someone to kill Lulu for him?"

"Right."

"And who would that someone be?"

Tad sighed and answered with reluctance. "Sheriff Delaney." His paternal feelings towards his younger cousin made him hate revealing the dark side of their hometown to him.

Joshua smiled. "So I was right. How long has Rawlings been involved in drug dealing?"

"He got in on the ground floor in the valley. From what I was told, he was in it back in the early sixties or late fifties, when pot first became hip around here."

"And who besides Delaney did the dirty work?"

"Bridgette was his dealer when she was in high school, when you were in school."

"I remember some of my friends buying from her," Joshua groaned, "but I had no idea that her father was behind it."

Tad went on, "Now Bridgette is the second in command, right below the reverend. She's the one the dealers deal with."

"But you said Vicki blackmailed Beth into working for her."

"Beth dealt with Vicki. Bridgette isn't stupid. She learned from her father that with each direct contact, there is the risk of being caught."

Joshua nodded thoughtfully. "What about Vicki's hatred for her family? Was that real? Or was it just an act to explain her immersion into the drug culture in the valley?"

"No, it was real. Vicki hated her family. She'd say wild things. Like, she swore that the reverend killed her grandmother. Yet, she liked the money and dealing supported her drug habit."

Tad yawned, stretched, and sat back in his chair. He propped his feet up on the corner of his desk next to where Joshua leaned and continued, "You see, Bridgette never got hooked. It was just business for her. Vicki got hooked and that is where all the trouble started. You know the old Navy saying?"

"Loose lips sink ships," Joshua responded.

Tad smirked. "Vicki has been airing a lot of dirty laundry about her family that never saw the light of day before."

"Dirty laundry without evidence doesn't lead to legal conviction."

"Well, it's coming," Tad made a clicking sound with his tongue that resembled the sound of a clock ticking. "She got the feds' attention. Maybe subconsciously she wanted to sink her grandfather, or maybe it was just plain stupidity. You see, when Bridgette was the dealer, those outside the inner circle never guessed her father was the lead man. Bridgette knew to keep her mouth shut."

"That's why all this is news to me now." Joshua smiled softly.

"You and everyone else from the outside looking in thought it was something Bridgette got involved in on her own. You know. Teenage rebellion stuff. If you don't know, you will." Tad snickered over the mental picture of Joshua trying to control his teenagers.

"I'm not worried. There's always military school."

"My dad preferred the woodshed. It was cheaper and more efficient."

The phone on the wall behind Joshua rang. Instantly, Tad propelled his stool across the room to grab the receiver.

Joshua resumed nosing around the lab while listening to the one-sided conversation.

"Hello." A wide grin crossed Tad's face. "No, you're not bothering me. I'm glad you called. I was worried. How are you doing?"

Out of the corner of his eye, Joshua could see by Tad's body language, and hear by his tone, that he was not just making conversation. He was sincere in his concern for the person on the other end of the phone line.

"Would you like me to come up?" When the caller tried to decline his offer, Tad insisted that it was no trouble. "No, I can be there tomorrow if you need me."

Suddenly reminded of Joshua's presence, Tad turned his back and lowered his voice. "Listen," he whispered, "I can't talk right now. I'll call you back in a few minutes." He added tenderly, "I love you."

Tad hung up and turned back to Joshua. "Maggie's first broken heart." He shifted the topic too quickly. "Now, where were we?"

Joshua reminded him, "Vicki's drug dealing."

Tad shook his head. "Things are a changin' for the Rawlings. Whereas, before it was always a known secret in the underground that Rawlings was the man in charge of the valley's drugs, no one outside ever knew, and those who did, knew to keep their mouths shut. Now, everyone knows."

"Amber made sure of that." Joshua cocked his head at Tad. "Who is this Amber?"

"I have no idea."

"Come on!"

"No, I don't." Tad smiled. "Listen, Josh, I stopped drinking and using over ten years ago. People, places, and things. I had to totally remove myself from all that. I don't hang out with the old gang anymore. You think I'm the fountain of information in this valley, but that is not true anymore. I'm out of the loop."

"Who do you think Amber is?"

"What does it matter what I think?" Tad laughed.

"Is she a fed?"

"You'd know that better than I would."

Joshua was speaking more to himself. "If she was a fed, she wouldn't have given that tape to a journalist."

"It wouldn't be the first time the feds decided to prosecute a man through the media when they couldn't get him in the courtroom," Tad muttered.

"You think she's a fed."

"It doesn't matter what I think." Tad got up from his stool, shooed Joshua from his desk, and sorted the stack of papers on it. "Listen, I know about flesh and blood and how fragile the human condition really is. When it comes right down to it, death doesn't give a shit about how rich or powerful we are."

"Then tell me what you do know." Joshua plopped down onto the stool the medical examiner had just vacated.

Tad referred to a report in a file. "The toxicology report says Vicki had been shot up with a muscle relaxant. She was also on a host of other recreational drugs. That was how the killer incapacitated her. The state lab is still trying to identify all the drugs in her system. The murder weapon was one of those camping spikes used to brace tent flaps. They found a couple more like them in Vicki's shed behind the trailer. No usable prints. It went right through her sternum into the heart. One strike, on target."

In his mind, Joshua used Tad's information to re-enact Vicki's murder. Mentally, he saw the camping spike plunge through her chest wall to impale her heart. "That means our killer was very strong, and or their blood was pumping with adrenaline to plunge that stake through her sternum and into her heart. That, or they used a hammer or something…"

Tad referred to the second report. "Beth was in a coma from the overdose when she was shot, which proves she didn't shoot herself. If the bullet through the brain hadn't have killed her, the Valium and booze would have. If she had stayed in the hospital I probably could have saved her."

"How did she get out of the hospital?"

"When she left, she was conscious enough to walk, with help."

"Do you know that for a fact?"

"Security has it on tape. They are sending it to Sheriff Sawyer and, I guess, you. Right after the nurse left, someone in a trench coat went into her room and helped her out. Beth was on her hind legs, barely. Trench Coat had to hold her up."

Joshua grinned at the lead. "Man or woman?"

Tad shook his head with a smile. "Can't tell. They knew the camera was there. They wore a man's fedora and kept their face from the camera."

Joshua groaned. "The trench coat. What do you know about that?"

"Most likely the same one you found in the closet." Tad continued, "When he or she pulled the trigger, the killer left a perfect print on Beth's fingernail. Her clothes aren't going to be much help, though."

"Why not?"

Tad frowned. "Beth had been wearing them for days and had been all over. You know how physical evidence works. Every time you come in contact with someone or someplace, you leave a piece of yourself behind, and take a piece of where you have been with you. Beth was on a major binge and hadn't bathed or changed her clothes in that time. She had three days worth of DNA on her, at least, including yours and mine."

"Is there anything you can tell for certain from her clothes?"

"Judging by the carpet fibers we found, Beth was the one dragged down the hall. Vicki was killed on the bed according to the blood splatters at the scene."

Joshua nodded thoughtfully. "Her being dragged down the hall makes sense if Beth was in a coma when she was killed."

Tad continued, "I also got a lock of hair off the gun that wasn't Beth's. It was caught in the chamber. Beth was a strawberry blond and this one was a darker shade."

"Red hair," Joshua remarked. "It could have been Vicki's."

"It could have, but Vicki was killed two hours before Beth. I sent the hair to the lab."

"What about the blood on the coat? Does it match either of our victims?"

"Shouldn't you be talking to state forensics about that? I only deal with the bodies."

"But you two compare information all the time. You compare the evidence you get off the bodies with the evidence they get at the scene, and they compare what they have with what you get, and then both of you will send your reports to me. Tell me what have you learned while comparing notes."

Tad relented. "It was Beth's blood and body tissue on the coat. The killer was kneeling in front of Beth when he or she pulled the trigger and the blood splattered across the front of the coat when the bullet went through her head. They also found hairs around the collar and on the shoulders of the coat. Some short ones and some long ones. The long ones had red hair coloring, just like the hair I found on the gun."

"A woman," Joshua noted.

"Some men color their hair," Tad argued before continuing, "It was also Beth's blood on the gloves in the coat's pockets. None of Vicki's blood was on the coat, but her blood was on the leather driving glove that was found by the bedroom door. None of Beth's blood was on that."

"That's weird." Joshua mused, "Whoever killed Vicki had to get blood on him or her."

Tad agreed. "When that spike punctured Vicki's heart, it was like bursting a water balloon."

"The killer wasn't wearing the coat when they killed Vicki."

"Nope."

"So who killed them?"

✷   ✷   ✷   ✷

"I certainly appreciate you coming over here to personally give us a status report on your investigation," Wallace Rawlings told Sheriff Curtis Sawyer as their maid, the sheriff's mother, poured her son's coffee into a china cup from a silver pot.

"Well, sir, you are a taxpayer and I am your servant." Curtis greeted his mother with a nod of his head.

Nadine Sawyer placed the pot on the serving tray and left the parlor. On her way out, she closed the double doors so the Rawlings family could have an audience with her son in private.

Bridgette Poole sat on the sofa next to her husband. Wallace sat in a leather wing-backed chair across from the sheriff. It was one of those chairs that looks elegant but is uncomfortable to sit in. That was the case with the whole mansion built on a hill overlooking the Ohio River between Chester and Newell. The estate was more for show than comfort.

In the chair of honor, a large leather wing-backed chair in the center of the room, sat the imposing bulk of the Reverend Orville Rawlings. As was usual, he was dressed all in black. His diamond and gold jewelry flashed at the sheriff as it caught the sun.

"My granddaughter was killed three days ago. We want to know why her body has not been released for burial yet," the reverend stated rather than asked.

"Well, sir," the sheriff drawled, "with all due respect, there are still a few questions I have that came up during the autopsy—"

"I must say," Orville Rawlings shifted his great frame in the chair, "I was quite disturbed to discover that Dr. Tad MacMillan did the autopsy on Victoria. Wouldn't you say there was an obvious conflict of interest?"

"Not really. I was there for the whole exam and I have had no problems with Dr. MacMillan in the past. He behaved in nothing but a professional manner."

"So there are not going to be any problems?" Hal Poole sighed with relief.

"Oh, no, I'm afraid there are going to be lots of problems." Sheriff Sawyer heard a collective gasp in the room.

The family turned to their leader, who glowered at the sheriff. "What kind of problems?"

"Well, you see, I have questions about what happened and so do other people."

"What other people?" Wallace asked. "Joshua Thornton?"

"The state attorney general did appoint him special prosecutor."

Bridgette shrieked and covered her mouth. She turned to Wallace, whose eyes narrowed to thin slits.

"You weren't aware of that?" Sheriff Sawyer asked as if he didn't know that they weren't aware of the appointment.

"No," the pastor responded.

"Why Joshua Thornton?" Bridgette's voice was an octave higher than usual.

The sheriff shrugged. "It turns out Joshua Thornton did investigative work for the Judge Advocate General. He was one of their top lawyers. He's a Naval Academy graduate and so is the state attorney general—"

"He has friends in high places," Wallace sneered.

"He's very sharp," Sheriff Sawyer warned. "He found evidence that Beth Davis did not pull the trigger."

"But the gun was in her hand," Hal Poole objected.

"There is evidence that suggests someone else's hand was holding hers when the trigger was pulled. I wonder about your niece's death."

"We already know she was murdered," Wallace scoffed.

"Yes, but by whom? Dr. MacMillan found a muscle relaxant in Vicki's blood."

Wallace sneered mockingly. "Duh! She was a drug addict!"

"The muscle relaxant incapacitated her."

"That's how Beth Davis killed her," Bridgette said. "She stole the muscle relaxants from the hospital after she faked fainting at the courthouse. She stole drugs from the pharmacy where she worked, and she's a pharmacist, so she knew what to take. Then, she went back to Vicki's, drugged her, and killed her."

"But she was comatose when she was shot," Sheriff Sawyer informed her.

"According to a drunken medical examiner," Wallace reminded the sheriff of Tad's past.

"Another problem is there didn't seem to be any of Vicki's blood on Ms. Davis. Dr. MacMillan said that when that stake went through your daughter's heart, it had to have squirted all over the killer. It was on the bed and went up onto the wall but none was splattered on Ms. Davis. She wasn't in that room at all when Vicki was killed."

Sheriff Sawyer shook his head, as he said politely, "No, I'm afraid we can't dismiss this as a simple murder-suicide. As much as I would like to help you out, I can't explain it away. I can assure you that Joshua Thornton won't let it go. He and Ms. Davis used to be very close. Not only that, but Tess Bauer has been buzzing around us like a mosquito looking for blood."

"The little bitch," Orville Rawlings breathed.

"Do you own a gun, reverend?"

"What did you just ask me, sheriff?"

The sheriff appeared unintimidated by the reverend's threatening tone. "Do you own a gun? Ms. Davis was shot in the head with a German Luger. It was very old and is not registered. It's a distinctive gun, not unlike the kind the Nazis used during World War II."

"No one in this house has any guns. Never had, never will," Rawlings stated firmly.

"How about a trench coat?"

"We all own trench coats," Wallace answered with annoyance. "So do half the men in this valley—as I'm sure Joshua Thornton does, too."

"The question is who is missing one? One with Beth Davis's blood splattered on it was found in Vicki's closet."

"None in this house are missing." Reverend Rawlings dared the sheriff to challenge the truth of his statement.

"You certainly aren't suggesting that we committed these murders, are you?" Bridgette asked in her most offended tone.

"Oh, no." Sheriff Sawyer shook his head adamantly. "I would never even think that any of you would do something so horrific. Murder is such an un-Christian thing, and you and your whole family are the embodiment of Christianity."

"I'm glad you see that." The reverend bestowed a small smile on the sheriff. "So many of our enemies have tried to soil our name with accusations to the contrary."

"I would never think of making unsubstantiated claims." Sheriff Sawyer scratched the side of his head and grinned self-consciously at the Rawlings family leader. "By the way, sir, do you mind if I ask if you have a pair of black leather driving gloves?"

"I have several pairs," Orville Rawlings directed his black eyes at the sheriff. His unspoken warning was unmistakable.

The sheriff ignored the warning. "Are you missing a pair?"

"That would be hard to say. I have so many." The reverend held up his clean, smooth, manicured hands. "You see, these hands do the work of the Lord. I must care for them if they are to serve our savior well. We would not want anything to prevent me from doing the Lord's work, would we, Sheriff Sawyer?"

"I'm sure the Lord doesn't like anything preventing His will from being done here."

"You sound like a good man, sheriff." Hal Poole's eyes were so wide that they looked as if you could shine a light through them to the back of his head. "There are so few good men today and there is so much evil. Do you believe in evil, sir?"

"You have to in my line of work."

"I've seen evil. I've seen the personification of Satan's evil, and I've prayed to God to kill it. The reverend says God can do that. He says God has twice as many angels as Satan, but He still needs our help to defeat him."

"Shut up, Hal," Bridgette snapped.

Like an obedient dog, Hal stopped speaking.

Realizing her sharpness in front of their visitor, Bridgette smiled widely and laid a hand on her husband's knee. She turned her attention to her father. "What are we going to do about this situation, Father?"

"Cross your fingers that I don't have to arrest you." Sheriff Sawyer answered for their leader. "With Joshua Thornton involved, you can be sure that every move will be closely scrutinized."

Sheriff Sawyer drained his cup of coffee and set it on the coffee table. He stood up and bowed slightly to them. "I'm sorry I could not be of more help to you." He turned to leave, but hesitated and turned back to them. "If there is anything I can do to help you during this traumatic time, just let me know." Sheriff Sawyer smiled reassuringly before leaving them to discuss their problem.

The sheriff was making his way to the front door when Bridgette's voice stopped him.

"Sheriff Sawyer," Bridgette whispered in a loud tone. She had closed the parlor doors behind her. "I need to talk to you."

After grabbing a duffel bag from a table in the foyer and slinging it over her shoulder, Bridgette led the sheriff out the front door. She looked anxiously about while she walked him to his car.

"I really shouldn't be telling you this, but my father raised me to always do the right thing."

"I'm sure he has," Sheriff Sawyer said with a note of sarcasm. "Did I make you late for your appointment with your trainer?" He indicated the duffel bag.

Bridgette giggled. "No. Once a month I go away to our retreat in Raccoon for a couple of days to meditate. Do you meditate, sheriff?"

"No, I don't," the sheriff scowled. "What was it you wanted to talk to me about, Mrs. Poole?"

The grin dropped from Bridgette's face. "It's my brother. Wally had a German Luger just like the one you described. It was a gift from his late father-in-law. He had taken it off a dead German soldier during World War II. He had no sons, so he gave it to Wally."

"Where is it now?"

Bridgette shrugged. "He kept it in the safe in his room. Wally collects guns. He has over two dozen. It's not common knowledge. If some of our members knew we had or did anything that would be controversial—Well, you know." She smiled sweetly. "Do you want me to check to see if it is still there?"

"Do. And let me know."

"I will. If he killed Vicki, why my father would be heartbroken, just heartbroken." Bridgette put a handkerchief to her face and, with a squeaky sob, not unlike that of a mouse, rushed to her sports car, climbed in, and roared down the driveway to the main road.

Once he got into his patrol car, Sheriff Sawyer took a small tape recorder out of his jacket pocket. He held it low in his lap, out of sight of prying eyes. He rewound it, and then hit the play button. Bridgette's voice came from the tape, "If he killed Vicki, why my father would be heartbroken, just heartbroken."

Pleased with himself, Sheriff Curtis Sawyer slipped the tape into his breast pocket. He then turned the key in the ignition, put the patrol car into gear, and pulled out onto the main road to head in the same direction in which Bridgette had just raced.

CHAPTER 13

▼

"I am unable to comment on the specifics involving the current investigation into the deaths of Victoria Rawlings and Elizabeth Davis," Joshua Thornton read from the statement he had prepared for the journalists gathered in a conference room in the county courthouse.

Tess Bauer and the rest of the media had been hounding Joshua since Marjorie Greene announced that the former JAG officer was appointed special prosecutor in charge of the case.

The new special prosecutor was expected to make a statement about the status of his investigation. Therefore, Joshua felt he had no choice but to oblige. He intended to say nothing.

So, Joshua dressed up and went to the courthouse to face the local media head on. He was surprised to see how much the local media had grown in twenty years.

The double murder was big news. It isn't every day the Satan-worshipping granddaughter of a prominent church pastor gets killed after being arraigned for attempting murder during a Sunday church service.

Joshua handled the pictures and questions with the poise and charm that made him a commander ahead of his time.

The Thornton children were put out with their father for not taking them with him. While the appointment of special prosecutor was an honor, Joshua learned early in his career to shield his family from the media. His heart still ached for a fellow JAG officer whose wife was raped and murdered by a vengeful enlisted man the lawyer had convicted. She became a target only after her picture appeared on a newspaper's society page.

Joshua had already lost his wife. He wasn't going to risk losing his kids.

The special prosecutor's statement was simple. He announced that he was doing all he could to get the evidence he needed to convict Vicki Rawlings's and Beth Davis's killer. Then, he said he would take a couple of questions.

Tess Bauer shot the first question at the prosecutor. "Mr. Thornton, have you questioned Reverend Orville Rawlings?"

Prepared for that exact question, Joshua grinned broadly. "I just said that I would be unable to answer any questions on the specifics of the case. I can tell you that everyone is a suspect and all suspects will be interviewed, if they haven't already."

"Are you going to ask him about the glove?"

Joshua's smile dropped.

Tess pressed on. "The reverend's driving glove was found on the scene, wasn't it?"

The other journalists in the room, unaware of a bloody glove found at the scene, began questioning Tess.

Joshua turned to Sheriff Curtis Sawyer, who waited out of camera range off the small stage.

In response to the prosecutor's silent question, the sheriff glared at Tess, and then shook his head.

Joshua turned back to the microphones. "I'm not able to comment on that."

"Mr. Thornton, you were the first official on the scene of the murders that night," Tess announced. "You were there even before the police. Can you tell us exactly what your connection is to the Rawlings?"

"Ms. Bauer, I'm much too busy to have time to banter around insinuations. If you have any accusations to make about my credibility, then come right out and say them. Otherwise, let me do my job."

There was a hush in the room.

Tess took a second to regain her resolve. "Do you intend to seriously consider Reverend Orville Rawlings a suspect?"

"He is already seriously considered a suspect, as are several other people who I will not name."

"So you did identify the blood-covered glove at the scene as belonging to him?"

"Ms. Bauer," Joshua said with a forced smile, "a glove does not make for a conviction and I will not waste my time, or the taxpayers' money, arresting someone for a crime unless I can get a conviction. Do you know what 'circumstantial evidence' is?"

Joshua waited for her answer, which did not come, before answering his own question. "It is evidence that is based on circumstances. It is Reverend Rawlings's glove, so we are to arrest him? Anybody could have taken that glove and placed it at the scene. It was his granddaughter's home. He could have dropped it there while visiting her days or weeks before. I look for real evidence, such as a murder weapon with his fingerprints on it, or a witness who saw him at the scene at the time of the murder."

Then, Joshua challenged the journalist, "You bring me a witness who saw Reverend Orville Rawlings at the scene committing the murders, and I'll get the arrest warrant."

The lawyer nodded at the stunned media, momentarily unnerved by his candor, and smiled charmingly. "Thank you." Then, he stepped down from the podium and left the room before they could regain their composure to ask him more questions.

*   *   *   *

"I don't think anyone has ever laid into Tess Bauer like that before," Sheriff Curt Sawyer chuckled as he flipped through the pages of his notepad for his notes from his interview with the Rawlings.

The sheriff and special prosecutor had returned to the scene of the crime.

Joshua studied the pictures and report from the state forensics team. His meeting with them did not turn up anything he had not already learned from Tad.

"She is sharp." Joshua's attention turned to the bloodstained bed and floor where he and Tad had found the two bodies.

"You're right there. She could have gone to New York a couple of years ago. She had a job all lined up with the network."

"Why didn't she?" Joshua went to the other side of the bed to examine the blood-splattered wall with a hole cut out of it. Forensics had cut out a portion of the wall to take to the lab to remove the slug that embedded itself there after going through Beth's head.

"After her little sister died, Tess vowed to get the Rawlings for selling her the drugs that killed her."

Joshua looked down at where Vicki's body was found on the bed. He dug through the crime pictures for the ones of her body. "Any line on who that coat belongs to yet?"

"I think it's one of the Rawlings."

"But not the reverend?"

Sheriff Sawyer shook his head. "Not big enough."

"Why do you think it belongs to the Rawlings?" Joshua laid out the pictures on the bed.

"Because Wally made a big deal about how many people in the valley own trench coats." Sheriff Sawyer smiled. "He even pointed out that you probably own one."

Joshua snickered. "He's right."

"When did you last see it?"

"This morning. In my closet. Do you want to see it?"

Joshua recalled that Tad had said that he didn't think Beth was able to drive when she left the hospital. The security video showed someone escorting her out of the emergency room. "Where's Beth's car?"

"We impounded it. It's at a garage out on Route 8."

"Did anyone examine it?"

Sawyer nodded his head. "I had one of the crime scene investigators go over it. I heard Tad when he said that he didn't think Beth could drive. The thing was a mess. It looked like she had been living in it. We picked up some prints. There's no ID on them, but we got them."

"Good." Joshua squinted at the bed.

"What are you looking at?"

"How did Vicki end up on this bed?" Joshua referred to the forensics report. "Carpet fibers on Beth's clothes and shoes confirmed that she was dragged across the living room and down the hall to be put on the floor next to the bed. There are no carpet fibers on Vicki's clothes. She was killed on the bed."

Joshua studied the picture of Vicki's body. He cringed at the sight of the snake that had entangled itself around her body. He reminded himself that Vicki was only seventeen years old. She was still a minor. Legally, she was just a child. "Who gave her the tattoo?"

Sheriff Sawyer shrugged with a shake of his head. "Don't know."

"Valerie had to go with Tracy and sign a permission slip in order for her to get her ears pierced. I don't see any of the Rawlings giving permission for Vicki to get this tattoo."

"I don't either. Personally, I think it was an underground job. Vicki was deep into the drug underground and everything connected with it. It wouldn't have been hard for her to find someone to do the job for her."

Joshua forced himself to look beyond the snake tattoo to observe the body and the scene of her death. "She wasn't wearing any underwear, but there was no sexual activity, no semen in or on her. She was completely exposed. The killer didn't bother covering her up. That means either he didn't know her, or at least, if he did, he didn't care enough about her to cover up her body. If he cared, he would have pulled down her shirt or put a sheet over her."

Sheriff Sawyer noted, "Some girls don't wear underwear, and Vicki was the sort who wouldn't. She may not have been in here for fun and games. She could have been taking a nap."

"I knew I read it here somewhere." Joshua handed the autopsy report to the sheriff and pointed to the information that caught his attention. He studied the scene while the sheriff read.

"There was a puncture mark on the left side of her genital ridge." The sheriff translated, "She got a shot in the crotch."

"Tad said she was shot up with a muscle relaxant to incapacitate her so the killer could plunge the spike through her heart. She let him shoot her up in her groin."

Joshua nodded as he imagined the scene that had taken place on the bed. "She and the killer were having foreplay. That's why she wasn't wearing panties. The killer shot her up. She probably thought it was a stimulant to enhance sex, but instead it made her unable to defend herself. Then, she had to lie there and watch him ram the stake through her heart."

"What a way to go," Sheriff Sawyer breathed.

"Well, we know one thing about the killer," Joshua muttered. "It was someone Vicki Rawlings trusted, who didn't give a damn about her."

CHAPTER 14

▼

It was unseasonably cool. The threat of rain loomed in the air. Thunderclaps warned of the summer storm's imminent arrival.

Tad didn't notice that the living room light was on when he tossed his motorcycle helmet onto the kitchen table. He turned on the light over the kitchen sink before taking milk out of the refrigerator and gulping it straight from the carton.

"You could have called."

Tad started and whirled around to find Joshua standing in the living room doorway. "I thought we had agreed to see other people," he cracked before gulping more of the milk. Tad closed the refrigerator door, but kept the milk out to finish for his lunch.

"I was worried. Where have you been for the last two days?"

At the sound of his master's voice, Dog scurried in from where he was lounging on the bed in the bedroom. He welcomed his master by jumping up onto Tad, who returned the greeting before easing his front paws back down to the floor.

"I went to see Maggie." Tad stepped around Joshua to go into the living room, where he took off his leather jacket and tossed it across the arm of the sofa. After plopping down onto the sofa, the doctor placed the top of the milk carton between his teeth in order to free his hands to remove his boots. He let out a sigh after the cool air hit his sweaty feet.

Tad was so focused on getting nourishment into his body and removing his boots that he didn't notice the crates of books stacked up along the wall under the picture window three feet from him.

"How is she?" Joshua asked from the doorway.

"She's been better."

"That must have been some romance. I mean when she was up here—"

"What do you want?" Tad's abrupt tone startled Joshua.

"I was worried. You took off so fast, and no one knew where you went."

"I told Reverend Andrews I was going away for a few days when I asked him to take care of Dog."

"But you didn't say where you were going," Joshua countered.

"I'm a grown man. I can come and go as I please."

Joshua softened his tone. "I know. I'm sorry. I was worried. I was afraid—"

"Do I look like I was drinking?"

Realizing he was overreacting to Tad's sudden absence, Joshua shook his head with a frown.

Tad sat back and put his feet up on the coffee table. "Well, now you know I'm alive and well and sober. Feel better?"

"You could have called someone."

"I had other things on my mind. Can't a guy have things on his mind without being interrogated like a murder suspect?"

"I'm not interrogating you. Should I?" Joshua could see that Tad had not slept in a long time and, he theorized, hadn't eaten either. Tad never had regular eating habits. "What's going on?"

"My daughter is in pain, and there is nothing I can do to help her."

"I know what that's like," Joshua responded softly.

Tad took another gulp of the milk. "Did Sawyer tell you?"

"Tell me what?" Joshua sat on the arm of the recliner across from him. "Did the results from the DNA tests come back yet?"

"Nah!" Tad emitted a hollow laugh. "It's still going to be a couple of weeks for that." He laid his head back and shut his eyes.

Joshua wondered if his cousin was going to fall asleep in mid-conversation. "I guess I'm going to have to make a couple of phone calls to get our case pushed up at the lab."

"They got a match on the fingerprint off Beth's fingernail," Tad told him with his eyes closed. "You'll never guess whose it is."

"Reverend Rawlings?"

"Close. Wally. They got the match when they ran it through the state records. You get fingerprinted when you take the bar exam."

"I know."

"There's only one problem with that fingerprint."

"What?"

"It's upside down."

"Upside down?"

"It's the right index finger and it's upside down."

With an exhausted groan, Tad pulled himself up off the sofa and picked up a pair of scissors from a stack of magazines. "Let me show you. You're Beth. I put the gun in your hand and I put my hand over yours to pull the trigger. I would have to wrap my hand around yours and press the gun to your head to pull the trigger."

As he explained, Tad gently pressed the point of the scissors to Joshua's temple with his hand over his cousin's. He had his index finger over Joshua's. Tad brought his hand around to show Joshua the position of his index finger.

"Now, my index finger is right over your fingernail and when I pull the finger that is the position my fingerprint would end up, with the gunpowder over the ridges of my print. Right?"

"Right."

"That is not how the fingerprint is on Beth's fingernail."

"It was upside down?"

"Plus, the powder over the ridges of the print are not gunpowder but copier ink."

"The print was planted," Joshua stated.

Tad nodded and plopped back down onto the sofa.

Joshua speculated, "So someone tried to frame Wally."

"Or," Tad suggested, "Wally planted the fingerprint knowing that we would know it was planted, figuring that you would eliminate him as a suspect." He took another gulp of the milk before laying his head back against the back of the sofa and closing his eyes again. "What do you think of our Sheriff Curtis Sawyer?"

"He's on the ball. Kind of young."

"He ran unopposed after Patterson was elected to Congress. He was military police just like Delaney. His father died when Curt was just a baby. He and his mom lived in a trailer on the outskirts of New Manchester. He came back here to take care of her after she got divorced from a jerk."

"Good guy or bad?"

Tad sighed deeply, lifted his head again, and opened his eyes into a thoughtful squint. "I haven't decided yet. His mother is the reverend's maid, and he had Rawlings's support in his campaign. Yet, some of the things he does are completely contrary to what Delaney would do."

"What type of things?"

"Like one night, Vicki broke in here while I was out on a call. I came home and found him in here arresting her. She had slashed up my bed with a butcher knife. Sawyer said he was driving by and saw the broken window in my kitchen door. She had a knife and was flipping out on something. He still overpowered her and hauled her to jail. The way Wally feels about me, if it was Delaney, he would have let her kill me, and then frame someone who pissed him off for it."

"Why didn't he ever arrest her?"

"Sawyer claims he was doing all he could about Vicki. I think he was sincere. Before and after Vicki broke in here, I would see him out my window checking things out to make sure I was okay." Tad sighed and shifted gears. "But he never got her off my back."

"There's only so much the law can do, especially when the prosecuting attorney is refusing to enforce the law."

"That was what Sawyer told me."

Joshua acted casual as he asked, "Why was Vicki threatening you?"

"I don't know. Suddenly, out of the blue she was telling me that I was responsible for her mother dying, and that I was not going to take a breath or make a move without her being there."

Joshua cocked his head and furrowed his brows. "You were responsible for her mother's death? Was Cindy one of your patients?"

Sadness filled Tad's face as he shook his head. He went to the crate of books and dropped to his knees. With his back to Joshua, Tad fingered the old volumes of medical textbooks in the crates.

Joshua had seen the look in Tad's eyes in his own reflection in the mirror just eight months earlier when his wife died.

Cindy Welch was a girl Joshua had not thought about in years. A sweet girl with the voice and face of an angel, a complete contrast to her only daughter, Joshua could see how Tad fell in love with Cindy.

The Welch family was the model of middle-class domesticity. They didn't smoke, drink, or swear. Cindy's father worked in the steel mill, and her mother baked cookies for the PTA. The family lived in a brick ranch-style home with two deer statues in their manicured front lawn along Route 8. They attended Reverend Orville Rawlings's church every Sunday.

Cindy Welch was a winner with her honey blond hair, deep blue eyes, and warm smile. She entered and won all the beauty pageants, which climaxed with Miss West Virginia Junior Miss. She was clearly out of the motorcycle-riding, beer-swilling, and pot-smoking Tad MacMillan's league.

Things aren't always what they seemed.

Joshua recalled gently, "Back in high school, there was talk about you and Cindy Welch. Some people thought you two were a couple."

His back still to Joshua, Tad snickered. "Talk about the odd couple. The rebel and the virgin."

"You two did spend time together. I mean, I remember you and her being over at our house, lying together on the floor and watching television together."

Tad turned to Joshua. He held a thick textbook in his hands. "I was Cindy's project. She was going to save me from myself." He looked down at the book in his hand and fingered the exposed end of a slip of paper sticking out of the volume as he recounted, "I still can see her that first day I laid eyes on her. It was the last month I had of freedom before starting my residency and adulthood. I was at Tomlinson Run Park, sitting on my bike by the creek, smoking a cigarette and talking to Crazy Horse. There she was, playing on the teeter-totter with this fat girl. Cindy laughed and threw back her head, and all this blond hair fell down her back. She was the most beautiful girl I ever saw."

"Cindy was beautiful," Joshua agreed.

Tad smiled. "So I tossed aside my cigarette and went over and said, 'I'm a doctor. Will you marry me?'"

"Did you really say that?" Joshua laughed

Tad chuckled as he recalled a turning moment in his life. "Do you think I would have stood a chance with her if I wasn't a doctor?"

"I think it was pretty much already decided that she was going to marry Wally."

Tad's smile faded. "Yeah."

"What did Cindy say when you said that?"

"She laughed. Her fat friend told me to get lost. I didn't. By the time I was through, I knew her name and kept bugging her ever since. Since she laughed, I figured I did have a chance. I did, but—" Tad's eyes reflected regret, "I never got what I was looking for."

"You did love her," Joshua stated rather that asked.

"Now you know." Tad opened the book and glanced at the sheet of paper in between the pages.

"No, I don't. There's a lot you are not telling me." Joshua was about to ask about Vicki's e-mails when he saw that Tad had stopped listening to him.

As he studied the sheet of paper in his hand, Tad's eyebrows came together and met between his eyes. He read and reread the paper in his hand. Then, he studied the page the paper had been marking.

"What's wrong?" Joshua asked.

Tad laid the book aside, took another book out of the box, and fanned the pages. After dropping that one to the floor, he moved on to another, and then another.

"What are you looking for?"

"The rest of this." Tad handed the paper and medical book to Joshua before resuming his search of the books in the crate.

Joshua read the paper in his hand. He had seen this paper before: not this specific piece of paper, but this type. It said clearly what it was.

It was a death certificate.

Joshua recognized his scrawled illegible signature.

Dr. Russell Wilson had signed it as the medical examiner appointed by Hancock County.

The name typed on it read in clear letters: "Cynthia Anne Rawlings. Maiden name: Welch."

Below her name was the information prompting Tad's manic search. "Cause of Death: Homicide."

CHAPTER 15

▼

"What did you do with the rest of Doc's books?" Tad asked.

"They're still in my office," Joshua answered. "The kids are going through them."

"They didn't throw anything out, did they?"

"No. Why would Doc put a death certificate in a medical textbook?"

Tad reopened the book and stuck it under Joshua's nose. "Look at it. It's a textbook about poisons. Look at the page he put it in. It's a section on arsenic. He knew what was going on."

"Which is that anyone who gets close to the Rawlings ends up dying a premature death," Joshua stated with distaste.

"In Cindy's case it was a slow painful death over the course of a year." Tad picked up a crate, turned it upside down, and dumped the books to the floor. He dug through them like a miner digging for gold after finding a single nugget. "I need to find that autopsy report."

Joshua leafed through a couple of the books before he told Tad, "It's not here. It has to be at my office."

Tad yanked his boots back onto his feet and practically crawled on his hands and knees for the door in his haste to get to Dr. Wilson's former office.

Joshua followed Tad out the back door and down the steps. "That is what you've been looking for. Patient files were just an excuse. You've known all along that Cindy was murdered."

The clouds hung in the sky like a thick blanket threatening to drop onto them any second. The thunder rolled insistently.

Tad told his story while his younger and more athletic cousin rushed to keep up with the doctor's pace. "Doc laughed at me when I told him Cindy was murdered. When I asked to read the autopsy report he wouldn't let me see it. I had no authority to request it, nor did I have any proof that Cindy was killed. Doc said it was hemorrhaging from a bleeding ulcer."

As they turned the corner onto Carolina Avenue at the bottom of the hill, Joshua caught up to Tad, and they walked together. "I thought you two stopped seeing each other after she married Wally. That was at least ten years before she died."

"We didn't even talk to each other," Tad confirmed his cousin's assumption. "You see, in the beginning, Cindy was the virgin ground I wanted to tread and, I think for her, I was the guy she couldn't bring home to mother, sort of James Dean to her Natalie Wood: Rebellious, yet sensitive. Dangerous enough to be interesting, but not threatening."

"Then something happened," Joshua prodded him to continue.

"We got to know each other. She kept saying no, but I stuck around. At first, I had hopes that eventually she'd say yes. Then, after awhile I didn't care so much if she let me get into her panties. I wanted to be in her life…and, she saw that I had a problem that was going to kill me if I didn't do something about it. She set out to save me and I think—I know—she fell in love with me."

"But she married Wally."

"Because she didn't have the guts to stand up to her parents. Wally was the guy any nice churchgoing parents would want their daughter to marry. They were too blind in their faith to see that underneath it all he was a hypocrite."

"What happened between you two?" Joshua blinked against the droplets warning of the oncoming downpour.

"The last time Cindy and I were together was the night before she married Wally. She didn't want to marry him, but she didn't want to disappoint her parents, who had planned the valley's version of the royal wedding. She concluded that the only thing making her sneak around with me was her hormones."

"So you two did sleep together!" Joshua accused Tad.

"No!" Tad stopped trotting to face Joshua so he could see the conviction in his green eyes. "Cindy was a virgin on her wedding night. That was important to her. Can you believe it? This was the eighties and Cindy Welch wanted to wait until her wedding night for the right man. Unfortunately, she chose Wally Rawlings for that man."

Tad started trotting again. "She came to my apartment. Back then, I lived in that little efficiency over the garage on Second back behind the church. She did not look like an excited bride. She was scared to death. She came right out and asked me if she was doing the right thing. I was drunk because I was sick about her marrying Wally. We started kissing, and that night we went further than we ever had. I thought we were finally going to consummate this little love affair we were having, but then, she suddenly got scared. I got mad. She cried. Then, she left. The next day, she got married, and I got drunk."

Tad stopped in front of Joshua's law office. While he waited for his cousin to unlock the door, he pawed the ground like a racehorse ready to bolt when the gate was opened.

"A couple of weeks later, when they got back from the honeymoon, Cindy called me. She had told Wally everything, and he forbade her from ever seeing me again." Tad glared at the memory. "Needless to say, she vowed to obey rather than cherish."

"It'd be hard for me to vow to cherish Wally," Joshua cracked while racing to beat the storm in unlocking the door.

"I told her, 'No problem.' Like I was going to hang around as her toy boy! She burst out crying and hung up. Some happy bride."

"Was that the end of it?" Joshua opened the door and Tad stepped in ahead of him.

"For a while. That was the worst of my illness." Tad waited for Joshua to close the door and turn on the lights before leading him up the stairs to where the books waited. "I'd see Cindy around. This is a small town. We'd make eye contact but nothing more."

"She had Vicki not long after they got married," Joshua added casually on his way up the stairs. "I recall hearing talk that maybe Vicki was yours."

"We never completed the act," Tad asserted.

He passed Joshua at the top of the stairs and went into the office. When he turned on the lights, Tad, overwhelmed by the volumes of books that lay before him, halted.

Joshua came in behind the doctor and sighed. "I think I better call for reinforcements."

*   *   *   *

In the reception area, Joshua poured Tad a fresh cup of coffee while they waited for his children.

The clouds burst. Rain beat on the old roof above them.

As he warmed his hands on the coffee mug, Tad recalled his unrequited love. "I was mad at Cindy. I told myself and everyone else that she was a gold-digging bitch."

His cousin consoled him with, "You were hurt."

"I was an idiot, that's what I was."

"So you two stopped seeing each other—" Joshua urged Tad to continue.

"She was not allowed to even talk to me," Tad scowled, "and I didn't want to talk to her." He sipped the hot coffee.

"Then," the doctor sighed, "I got sober. I found God. I learned to love myself. I grew up." He sighed again. "I wasted so many years with my daughter because of my stupidity."

"You weren't the boy who had worked so hard to get into Cindy's pants anymore," Joshua observed with a small smile.

Tad scoffed. Shaking his head, he got up and crossed over to the picture windows looking out onto the rain soaked street.

"It was raining like this the last time I saw her," Tad recalled. "I had my office on Indiana for about a year. I did okay. Most everyone went to Doc Wilson, but my practice did grow steadily. I saw her outside my back window when I went up to the apartment for lunch. It was pouring rain, and she was standing there under an umbrella looking at my back door like she wanted to come up. I decided to go down and talk to her. One of the twelve steps in AA is to apologize to those you hurt, and I did owe Cindy an apology."

As if turning his back on the memory, Tad turned around and leaned against the windowsill. He recounted their last meeting. "I didn't even bother getting my umbrella. I got soaked, but I didn't care. I came down with a terrible cold afterwards." He laughed, "Funny, how you remember things like that."

Tad's smile dropped. "She looked so frail, more delicate than I had ever remembered her being. She told me I looked good and she was happy that I had been saved. I don't know if she meant that physically, medically, or spiritually. I asked her to come in, but she said she couldn't. Then, I saw that she did not look well at all. She was so thin and her color wasn't right. I asked her if she was all right, and she said that God was punishing her for her sins."

"God was what?" Joshua gasped.

"Punishing her for her sins."

Tad's voice raised an octave as he spoke to Joshua across the reception area. "That's what Reverend Rawlings preaches. He tells these people in his church that God punishes us for our sins. If we get sick, if we lose our job, or if a kid of ours turns out bad; then that is God punishing us for something we had done." He asked, "Do you remember Tony Carson?"

Unable to place a face with the name, Joshua shrugged. "Barely."

"He lost his job at the trucking company. He was convinced it was because he had too much to drink one night when he and his wife were celebrating their anniversary." Tad whispered in a mocking tone. "Alcohol is a sin, you know."

"So I heard."

"So, that was why Tony lost his job, because he drank too much that one night. He didn't go into work drunk, mind you. He was just having a good time celebrating his anniversary at home and had too much to drink, so God punished him for having a too good of a time that one night by making business bad and he got laid off. He was telling me this in my office after his wife dragged him there to see me. She is not a believer. He was having headaches. I did tests with him telling me the whole time I could not help him. It was prayer and fasting that would make everything right. So I ask him, I say, 'You lost your job because you drank too much one night. What did you do to deserve these headaches?' which I diagnosed as high blood pressure. Do you know what he said caused them?"

"What?"

"Having oral sex with his wife."

Joshua laughed. "Was it against her will?"

Tad responded, "She told me to my face, right in front of him, that she asked for it."

"He told you that oral sex with his consenting wife caused his high blood pressure?" Joshua rolled his eyes in disbelief.

Tad nodded. "Tony refused to take the medication. He said the answer was to stop the sinning. So, he refused to have sex with his wife anymore because of her lurid desires. He said as long as he kept sinning, his blood pressure would not go down. It didn't go down because he wouldn't take his medication because he said God was the answer. She ended up taking the kids and leaving. Then, he said that was God further punishing him for having sinful thoughts of oral sex with his wife. He ended up having a stroke and dying. Now, she blames herself for his dying, because she left him." Tad shrugged and scoffed. "People are buying the crap Rawlings is selling them and paying a high price for it."

"What was Cindy's sin?" Joshua asked with scorn.

"Loving me." Tad's disgust was still evident in spite of the passage of time. "She said that even though she had confessed to her husband her sin of lusting after me, she had not stopped loving me. She had to pay for her sins. Unfortunately, even though she was paying penance, she couldn't get me out of her mind and her heart. So, God continued punishing her. That was why she was unable to eat anything."

Tad snarled and shook his head. "I was so angry! I grabbed her and literally tried to shake sense into her. It is not a sin to love anyone! As for lust, we never did anything! How could God be making her sick? She said there was only one other explanation for why she was so sick."

"Which was?"

Tad answered in a soft voice. "She was being poisoned."

"She said that?" Joshua gasped.

Tad nodded. "She said she had no proof, but for over a year she had been getting sick every time she ate. The way she described it, it sounded like gastrointestinal illness. Doc Wilson was treating her." Tad indicated Joshua's office, the town doctor's former office. "She believed he knew Wally was poisoning her and wasn't going to do anything to stop it."

"Did you examine her?"

"I offered to. I told her to order Doc to send me copies of the blood tests so I could take over the case. She was afraid to do that, because she really believed in this obeying your husband crap. I told her that Doc would not send me the test results without her permission."

"And going to Sheriff Delaney was out of the question."

"That's right."

"How did you leave it?"

Tad sighed. "I told her to tell Doc that she had come to me and to send me the results from the blood tests. I said that would give him a warning that someone else knew what was going on and, I figured, without telling her this, that that might be enough to make it stop. We shook hands, and I took a chance and gave her one last kiss, and she got into her car and gave me this smile before leaving."

"I guess the poisoning didn't stop."

"She died that night."

Tad turned back around to look out the window. He continued with his back to his cousin. "I came to see Dr. Wilson and told him about Cindy's visit. He literally laughed at me and said that I had to have been on drugs again. Nothing ever happened, but I knew Cindy had been poisoned. I just never had the authority to get the evidence to prove it."

Tad turned back to Joshua. "Now, you know why I never married."

CHAPTER 16

▼

Joshua went back home to his study to dive into the web of intrigue that lay before him.

At first, the Thornton children refused to spend any more of their time searching through musty books that they had already been through. Then, Tad removed a handful of twenty-dollar bills, a hundred dollars total, from his billfold and offered it to the one who found the autopsy report he so desperately wanted to find.

With that, Dr. Tad MacMillan obtained his search party.

Tad's account of how Cindy Welch, one of the sweetest girls Joshua had ever known, died, gave the prosecutor tasked with bringing Orville Rawlings to justice a new sense of determination to fulfill his mission.

Joshua decided the best place to start would be with John Doe's missing body.

The criminal lawyer told his children the truth when he said that it would be almost impossible to prove Orville Rawlings had anything to do with the body found in the barn. The only thing that linked the body to Orville Rawlings was Lulu Jefferson's written statement that she saw a picture of the victim with Rawlings. That didn't mean the reverend killed John Doe, nor had any reason to kill him. It only proved Rawlings knew the victim.

Even if the letter could get entered into evidence in a trial, any half-decent defense attorney could cast reasonable doubt to a jury that Lulu was accurate in her identification of the John Doe in the barn as the same man she saw in the picture. Only one person who saw the body was still alive, and it was almost forty years since he saw it in a dark barn. That made Rick Pendleton unreliable as a witness.

Without the body to examine, there was no physical evidence to connect Rawlings to it. Without John Doe's body, it would be impossible to prove that there actually was a murder. The victim could have died in an accident or from natural causes.

Even if murder could be proven, how could they prove Orville Rawlings committed the act?

The killer could very well have been Sheriff Charles Delaney.

Joshua suspected this was the case. He had heard more than once from more than one person about the sheriff being Rawlings's man.

If Delaney killed John Doe on Reverend Rawlings's orders, they would be wasting their time pursuing John Doe's murder because the former sheriff was dead and unable to testify against Orville Rawlings.

Just because it was impossible didn't mean it couldn't be done.

Joshua Thornton's commanding officer told the young lieutenant commander that it would be impossible to convict a three-star admiral of murder, but he did it.

The best way to go after Reverend Orville Rawlings was to attack him from the rear. As long as the powerful pastor did not know about the letter Joshua kept securely locked up in the wall safe in the Thornton study, he believed he could do it.

As he reread the letter, Joshua snickered when he found Orville Rawlings's vulnerable spot. It was right there in the letter. Joshua picked up the phone on his desk and placed a call.

At his desk in the Judge Advocate General's office in Washington, D.C., Lieutenant Bruce Crawford answered on the third ring.

"You're getting slow in your old age," Joshua announced after his former assistant informed him that he was calling the Judge Advocate General's office.

"Commander!" Bruce yelled and sat back to enjoy a personal phone call from an old friend. "How are things in West-By-God-Virginia?"

"I'm a civilian now," Joshua reminded him.

"But you are still in the reserves."

"That's right." After a few minutes of talking about their families and gossip about the office, Joshua eased into the reason for his call. "Hey, Bruce, I need a favor, when you get a chance."

"I'll see what I can do. What is it, sir?"

"I need a list from the VA of all the men in a unit that served in the army during the Korean War. I don't know specifically what year or unit."

"That will make it tough."

"The person I am looking for is an army chaplain. His name is Orville Alexander Rawlings. I need to know who served with him in his unit and what happened to each of them."

Bruce squawked, "What happened to each of them?"

"Who is dead? Who is alive? Those who are dead, how did they die? Those who are alive, where are they now?"

"What is this for? What are you looking for?"

"A murder victim."

*   *   *   *

Jan was ready to quit and go home, except she couldn't because her mother owned the place and if she left no one would be in charge.

The pharmacy had been in total chaos ever since Beth was fired. Now that she was dead, Jan hadn't had any time to mourn the loss of her friend. She was too busy training the new pharmacist, a kid right out of college, while trying to keep her customers from deserting her for the bigger, more modern pharmacy across the river in Calcutta.

Jan had just escorted a new mother, upset about how long it took the druggist to fill a prescription called in four hours earlier, out the door so that she could lock it behind her when Joshua turned the corner and thrust his foot across the threshold.

"What do you want?" Jan snapped.

"Good day to you, too," Joshua greeted her with sarcasm.

Jan sighed and caught her breath. "Sorry. It's been a long day." She held the door open to permit Joshua to come in before closing the door and locking it.

As they walked down the aisle towards her office, Joshua reminded Jan that she had left a message with J.J. for him to call her.

"Sheriff Sawyer has been coming around," Jan announced another source of annoyance.

"That's natural. According to your inventory, Beth was dealing drugs out of your store. He's going to want to know if you knew about it. For all we know, you were in charge of the whole thing."

"That's why I need a lawyer."

Joshua frowned teasingly. "Were you involved?"

Jan was insulted. "No! I didn't know about any of it. Beth was in charge of the pharmacy's inventory." She added firmly, "A mistake I will not make again. I need you to make sure I don't get railroaded into anything."

Joshua nodded. "I understand. Don't talk to the sheriff again unless I'm with you. If he calls you, tell him to call me."

"I don't trust Curt Sawyer. He's too tight with the Rawlings."

"Well," Joshua shrugged, "they are politically powerful. He has to stay on their good side or risk being upset in the next election by someone they hand select."

"How do you think he got to be sheriff? That's why I don't trust him."

"Don't worry. I can take care of him."

"I'm sure you can. Anyone who can bypass Wally to get Vicki Rawlings arraigned for anything in this town has to have something on the ball." Jan nodded her head towards the street outside. "I saw Tad go by on his bike earlier. Have you talked to him?" After Joshua told her he had, she asked, "Has he been—?" The rest of her question was unspoken.

"He was sober. He went to visit Maggie. She had broken up with some guy or something like that, and he went to play daddy." Joshua saw a look of concern cross Jan's face as she silently recalled the scene in the emergency room. It was just a flicker, but he detected it. "What's wrong?"

"Nothing," Jan lied. "I was just remembering Beth. We had our differences, but she was my friend."

"That's right. You went to the hospital when she collapsed in the courtroom?" he muttered slowly in a questioning tone.

Unsure of why Joshua was asking her a question to which he already knew the answer, Jan chose her words carefully as she responded, "Yeah. She took off while Tad was on the phone with Glenbeigh."

"Did you drive her car to the hospital?"

"No, I drove my own car."

"Where was Beth's car?"

Jan shrugged thoughtfully.

Preoccupied with his question, Joshua shook his head, turned away, and started up the aisle.

"Josh, what's wrong?" Jan turned him around by the arm. "What are you thinking?"

Joshua's eyes met Jan's. "Tad said Beth couldn't drive in the condition she was in when he left her."

"I thought the hospital video tape showed someone helping her out of the hospital. They drove her. That's how Beth's car got to Vicki's place. I thought the sheriff impounded Beth's car."

Joshua agreed that he knew that. "They found a set of fingerprints that weren't Beth's, but there's no match in the database for them." He cocked his head at her. "How did the killer leave the crime scene?"

Jan guessed. "Drove his car."

"The killer had to drive Beth's car to Vicki's. Otherwise, how did it get there? Beth was in no condition to drive it there." Abruptly, Joshua announced, "Vicki bought a new truck."

Jan scoffed, "So?"

"It was in front of her trailer. It was a sweet new Ford. Sawyer found the dealer she bought it from a week ago. She gave the dealer a check for forty thousand dollars, and it cleared the bank." Joshua mused thoughtfully. "The killer drove Beth's car to Vicki's to kill her, then went to the hospital to get Beth and take her back to Vicki's to make it look like a murder-suicide. But then, how did he or she get away. There has to be another vehicle. Couldn't walk."

Jan agreed. "Vicki's place is in the middle of nowhere."

Joshua didn't seem to hear her. "There had to be another vehicle. Or…someone went to Vicki's and killed her, while their accomplice drove Beth's car to the hospital to get her, and brought her back to Vicki's. That would explain the two different methods of murder and the time difference. The first killer waited for the second, and the two left together." Joshua grinned with pride.

Jan asked him. "But who are the two killers?"

Joshua's grin turned to a frown. "I'm still working on that."

"Is Tad on your list of suspects?" Jan wondered gently.

"Why would he be? You're thinking something. What is it, Jan?"

"Just something I saw." Jan mumbled, "But Tad would never—"

"Never what?"

Jan sighed, "Just something I saw at the emergency room. Beth was crazy. She told Tad that she hated him."

Joshua scoffed. "Remember when Tad got high? He'd say things—"

"Beth told him that she was going to tell Maggie everything, and she was going to hate him. Then, Tad got this look in his eyes; I swear he was going—" Jan stopped just short of saying "kill her". Instead she said, "He grabbed her by the throat and shoved her down onto the table." She added ominously, "That was the last time I saw Beth."

Joshua laughed. "Tad did not kill Beth!"

"I can't believe he would do it either, but you yourself just said that Beth did not leave that hospital on her own. And the last one to see her alive was Tad, who had his hands around her throat."

"The last one to see her alive was Trench Coat. The security tape proves it."

"Tad could have been Trench Coat. Anyone can get a trench coat."

Aware of Joshua's close relationship to her chief suspect, Jan's conviction softened. "I'm sorry. I didn't say anything to Sheriff Sawyer, but I think you should know."

Joshua chuckled, "Even if Tad had a trench coat, which he doesn't, there's a logistical problem with your theory."

Jan was offended. "What? You just said that there had to be two killers and they left together. You just reminded me of Tad's wild days. He knows everyone. All he had to do was call up one of his old drinking buddies from the underbelly of society and set it up for him to kill Vicki who was clearly going to get off for making his life hell, and then meet this guy outside the hospital in Beth's car, and take her over to Vicki's to get rid of her because of this secret she knew about him that would make Maggie hate him. He killed two birds with one stone."

"Come on, Jan! Do you really believe Tad is capable of murder, let alone a double murder?" Joshua laughed out loud, which annoyed his old friend.

"Anyone is capable of murder in the right circumstances." Jan stomped a foot and slapped Joshua's arm with a discarded newspaper left on the checkout counter. "Stop laughing! If he wasn't your cousin you'd be taking me seriously."

Joshua threw up his hands and leaned against the pharmacy counter with his arms crossed. "Okay! So, Tad got a couple of his old party buddies to kill both Vicki and Beth, while he was setting up an alibi by looking for Beth in all the bars within walking distance of the hospital."

"Tad has a lot of friends," Jan sniffed. "He got two of them to do it for him. One drove Beth's car. The other drove the getaway car."

Joshua frowned. A jury could buy Jan's theory, but he refused to believe it.

"What do you think?" Jan asked him.

"I'll look into it."

"No, you won't."

Joshua replied, "Yes, I will."

"No, you won't. Because it's Tad."

"I said I would question all suspects, and that includes Tad, if he has a motive for killing Beth, which I don't believe he does. But I'll find out if he does, and then I'll find out if he did it."

*   *   *   *

Books were everywhere when Joshua returned to his office with a boxed dinner from the diner next door. Joshua's family had searched every book for the missing report and found nothing.

Starved and grateful for the break, the children pounced on the burgers, fries and milkshakes like a pack of wolves dividing a kill. Defeated in his quest, Tad wouldn't touch any of the food.

After snatching a burger for himself, Joshua opened the textbook in which Tad had found the death certificate, which he had stopped at his cousin's apartment to pick up on his way back to his office, and sat on the floor with his children, who ate picnic style around the box of food. He studied the page still marked with the death certificate.

At the back of the office, Tad continued to search through a hip high stack of Smithsonian magazines that were now collectors' items.

"You know," Joshua said thoughtfully. "I've been thinking about this theory of yours that Doc Wilson hid the actual autopsy report in a book. Why hide it?"

"It makes sense when you think about it," Tad argued. "If Wilson was blackmailing Wally, knowing that the man was capable of murder, Doc would have hidden the report. Look at all these books! It's like looking for a needle in a haystack.

"That's for sure," Donny grumbled.

"All the better to keep Wally from breaking in here and getting it."

"Or anyone else." Sarah laid down flat on her back on the floor while she ate her burger.

"Do you really think Doc was capable of blackmail?" Joshua wondered.

Tad shrugged. "Why else would he not make the official cause of death murder and have Wally arrested? Because he thought Wally was such a great guy?"

"From the looks of this building," Murphy observed, "Dr. Wilson was not a rich guy."

"I agree he would blackmail Wally Rawlings," Joshua mused, "but not for money."

"For what then?" Sarah wondered.

"For something more important."

"What is more important than money?" Donny asked.

"The greater good," Joshua answered. "Doc Wilson was a man of principle. Reverend Rawlings groomed Wally since he was a baby to be president. Yet, here he is, almost forty, and Wally is a county prosecutor in West Virginia. His office is in a school basement."

Tad was suddenly aware that Joshua was right. "He could have run for county prosecutor right after he graduated from law school, but he didn't until three years ago."

Joshua noted, "Doc died four years ago. Wally didn't get into politics until after Wilson was dead."

Tracy got her father's point. "Are you saying that you think the doctor held the report over Wallace Rawlings's head to keep him out of politics?"

"I remember Doc Wilson. He delivered me." Joshua gestured towards his cousin. "He delivered Tad. He also delivered our parents."

"He was the only doctor in the area." His hands on his hips, Tad surveyed the top shelf of the bookcase before him to see if he missed anything.

Joshua recalled, "I had to come see him every year for my annual physical for the football team. He knew everyone and everything, without checking any chart. He remembered every blood type right off the top of his head. Every one of his patients was his kid. One year, when he was filling out my form for football, he asked me if I smoked, fully expecting me to say no. Well, he knew I was lying when I said I didn't."

"You never were a good liar," Tad called out from behind the desk.

"Maybe that's it. Anyway, Doc Wilson read me the riot act, up one end and down the other. It wasn't a lecture from a doctor to a patient, it was a lecture from a wise old man to someone he cared about."

Tad explained, "There's a connection that happens between a doctor and a baby when he brings it into the world."

"If Doc had evidence that Wally was a killer, he would know that Wally would be dangerous in a position of power. In that case, Doc would make damn sure that something was done about it," Joshua told the group gathered on the floor.

Sarah didn't understand. "Why not take it to the police and have him arrested?"

Murphy answered, "Because the sheriff worked for the killer's father."

Joshua agreed. "An autopsy report only proves someone was murdered. It doesn't say who did it."

"Cindy told me Wally was doing it," Tad told his cousin.

Joshua turned around to Tad. "That's hearsay. She lived in that house with Wally, as well as his father, and his sister and her husband, plus a maid who cooked their meals. Any of them could have been poisoning her. She could have been mistaken."

"But," Donny objected, "if the report doesn't prove anything, then what are we doing here looking for it?"

"Oh, but it can be very harmful, son," Joshua corrected him. "All of those people, except the maid, are part of a powerful and influential family. A report of Wally's dear sweet wife being poisoned in their home would be very scandalous. It would kill his political career forever."

"Plus, it would shake up the reverend's church," Tad pointed out.

Finished with her burger, Tracy shook her head while she wiped her hands on a paper napkin. "If you are saying that Doc Wilson put the report away to keep Rawlings out of office, then why did he not make sure it got into the right hands after he died?"

"I can answer that," Tad responded. "Doc was one of those people who never thought he would die. He never retired. He never wrote a will. He simply refused to admit he was mortal." He tossed down the magazine he held and sat next to Joshua with a sigh of disgust. "That's it. I don't know where else to look. That man was a nut case."

Joshua was studying the binding of the textbook on deadly poisons. He spoke in a steady easy tone as he carefully eyed the volume. "Nah, Tad, I disagree. Doc was a very clever man. He knew what he was doing. He knew that even though he could prove Cindy was murdered, he could not prove who did it. But he did have enough to keep Wally in line. He also knew that if he made that report easy to find, then he might as well write his will and kiss his butt good-bye."

While he continued, Joshua turned the book around so that the spine faced him and, starting at the bottom, he rubbed the spine with fingertip over fingertip from the bottom and worked his way up along the binding.

"That was why Doc made it so hard to find the autopsy report. So an idiot like Wally would never find it. Doc was also very clever. He didn't want the autopsy report to be impossible to find for a smart man—"

Everyone gasped when a small silver key popped out from the top of the spine of the book.

"—like yours truly."

Joshua took the key out of the book and offered it to his cousin. When Tad reached for it, Joshua snapped it back. "I believe you owe me a hundred dollars."

CHAPTER 17

▼

"Somebody get that!" Joshua covered the phone's mouthpiece with his hand to yell at anybody in the house who happened to be within the sound of his voice.

After apologizing for the interruption to the moving company clerk on the other end of the line, Joshua resumed chastising her. "Listen, I have been very patient. It has been three weeks. All of our family's legal documents, not to mention our family memories are in those boxes. None of it can be replaced!"

The doorbell rang again.

"I don't want any more apologies. I want my wife's picture back!"

The doorbell rang once more while the clerk responded in an indifferent tone.

Joshua gritted his teeth. He did not want to chew out the clerk, who surely was not personally responsible for losing their belongings. "Just a minute."

Cursing under his breath, Joshua pressed the hold button and hurried to the front foyer while searching for any sign of his children. "Five kids and not one to answer the door," he muttered as he threw open the door to find Ken Howard standing before him.

Startled by Joshua's obviously angry expression, the teenager from across the street stood frozen in the doorway.

Unaware of his threatening appearance, Joshua barked at the young man. "What?"

"Uh-Hello, sir," Ken stammered. "Is Tracy home?"

As if Ken was an enlisted man needing an inspection from a superior officer, Joshua looked the young man up and down. His clothes were clean, his appearance was neat, and Joshua saw no sign of body piercings or offensive tattoos.

Ken smiled nervously at his intended girlfriend's father.

"I'll see." Joshua left Ken on the doorstep and closed the door while he yelled for Tracy.

Carrying a basket filled with freshly washed clothes in need of folding, Tracy came up the stairs from the laundry room in the basement.

"There's someone at the door for you." Joshua followed her and the clothes-basket into the living room.

An old Humphrey Bogart movie played on the television set kept in an entertainment center in the corner of the living room. A pile of laundry waiting to be folded was piled up on the sofa.

"Who?" Tracy inquired.

"The boy who lives across the street. He keeps calling and coming over. If you don't like him—"

"I like Ken. It's just that he keeps asking me out when I have things I have to do. Right now, I need to fold these clothes."

"I'll get rid of him then." Joshua stepped for the foyer, but his daughter stopped him.

"I don't want to get rid of him. He's really nice."

Laughing and talking amongst themselves, Murphy and J.J. came through the front door with Ken between them. Upon seeing the senior Thornton, Ken lowered his eyes to the floor.

"Hey, Tracy, look who we found," J.J. announced.

"And guess what he's got." In his next breath, Murphy answered his own challenge. "Tickets to see the Pittsburgh Pirates. They're playing today."

"A major league game. How about that?" J.J. told Ken, "Tracy used to play second base on the softball team back home."

"Really?" Ken grinned at her. "I play second base on our team. Would you like to go with me to see the game?"

"Now?" Tracy was torn between the chores she took it upon herself to take on when her mother died, and what promised to be a good time for the teenaged girl.

"Well, I would have asked you sooner, but my brother just gave me—"

"Today is laundry day."

"Every day is laundry day in this family," Joshua explained. "I'll take care of the clothes."

Tracy laughed. "Dad? You? The last time you did your own laundry, Mom ended up giving all your sweaters to Goodwill."

"That was a long time ago."

Murphy reminded him, "That was a year ago."

Joshua ordered his daughter, "Go. It isn't every day a nice guy offers to take you to see the Pirates."

Relieved, Ken smiled. "You think I'm a nice guy, sir?"

Joshua stated in a deadpan tone, "Don't disappoint me. You don't want to see me disappointed."

Tracy dropped the sheet she was folding and smoothed her clothes. "Just give me a minute, Ken. I need to go comb my hair." She turned to her father. "Now, there's a load in the dryer and the washer. Take the clothes out of the dryer as soon as they are done and fold them. They're your shirts, and if they aren't folded, then they'll wrinkle, and then I'll have to iron them. Put the clothes that are in the washer in the dryer, and dry them for an hour. Don't forget to clean the lint trap first."

Joshua gestured for her to go on up upstairs. "It's as good as done. Just go."

After smiling shyly at Ken, Tracy ran upstairs.

Joshua turned to Murphy and J.J., who were watching *Key Largo*. "Take care of that." He pointed to the pile of clothes on the sofa.

On his way back to the study, Joshua discovered that the moving company had hung up. With a disgusted sigh, he sat down at his desk to reread the police and Tad's autopsy reports for Vicki Rawlings and Beth Davis.

The killer had given Vicki Rawlings a shot in the crotch. A girl doesn't just let anyone give her a shot in that area unless she trusts him. However, judging from what he observed, Joshua felt it was safe to assume Vicki would have intercourse with anyone, in which case it could have been anyone.

The killer could even be a total stranger with no motive, except the thrill of killing.

"Can't discount that possibility," Joshua groaned to himself.

"Dad!"

Joshua dropped the report he was reading onto the desk.

"Come here! Quick!" Murphy was yelling.

Donny intercepted his father at the study door. "Dad! Come on!"

Joshua's youngest son led the way back to the living room where the rest of his kids were folding clothes. All of them were pointing to the television.

Amber was on the news.

"I think you're going to want to see this!" Murphy told his father while J.J. turned up the sound.

"Hello, this is Morgan Lucas," the perky young news reporter on the screen was saying, "with a Channel 6 News Special Report. With me now is Amber, who recently consented to be interviewed by reporter Tess Bauer about the drug trafficking in the Ohio Valley. Today, Amber is in our studio live to tell our audience what she witnessed the night Victoria Rawlings and Elizabeth Davis were murdered."

Amber appeared on the screen. She looked the same as when Joshua had seen her in the interviews with Tess Bauer, except this time the studio backdrop was behind her. She had the same blood red crew cut, black makeup, and assorted black necklaces and bracelets and rings. Her scanty black clothes revealed her pale flesh.

A young beauty with long chestnut hair and striking blue eyes, Morgan Lucas starkly contrasted to the subject of her interview. Her royal blue blouse matched her eyes. Diamond and gold jewelry completed her ensemble.

"Ms. Amber, you came into our studio to tell us the truth about what happened that day in the home of Victoria Rawlings. How is it that you know what happened?"

"Because I was there," Amber said with a deep sigh. "Vicki and I are—were—best friends. I was hanging with her and I saw everything."

"You saw her killer?" Morgan said with wide eyes framed with lush lashes.

"Yeah, I saw the whole thing, beginning to end. I was hiding in the closet."

"Tell us what happened, Amber."

"We were partying. She had just gotten a shipment of cocaine and she was splitting it up when there was this knock on the door. I looked out the window and I saw him. Well, I didn't want no hassle, but I wasn't ready to go yet, either. So Vicki told me to hide in the closet. I knew it was going to be a messy scene, man."

The interviewer inquired, "So you hid?"

"In the closet in the bedroom in the back." Amber paused to take in a shuddering breath. "I heard this fight, and then he took her back there. He had her by the wrist, and they were arguing."

"What about?"

"About her keeping her mouth shut. She said she would keep her mouth shut, but then he said she had already said too much. I heard Vicki screaming at her old man! I could hear her fighting him. Then suddenly, it was quiet, and that was worse than the screaming because I couldn't tell what was happening. Then—Oh, God!" Amber covered her face with her hands.

There was silence in the studio.

Morgan regained her composure to ask about Beth's murder.

"Well," Amber responded to Morgan's question, "I was stuck in that closet and afraid to try to leave, because I thought he would kill me. I mean, he's crazy.

So, I had to watch him carry her in. He laid her down next to the bed, and he put this gun to her head and blew her brains out."

"Amber," Morgan asked dramatically, "who did you see kill Victoria Rawlings and Elizabeth Davis?"

"Vicki's grandfather. Reverend Orville Rawlings."

Joshua stood up. "I'm going to the studio."

$$* \qquad * \qquad * \qquad *$$

Pittsburgh's roads hadn't changed much in twenty years. Joshua never did like the city's freeways and one-way side streets. He always seemed to be heading away from where he wanted to be.

By the time Joshua found the television studio, Morgan Lucas was in the newsroom surrounded by fellow journalists giving and getting high fives over their scooping their competition by breaking the Rawlings and Davis murder case with an eyewitness about whom the police didn't even know.

The anchor and her colleagues immediately recognized the special prosecutor assigned to investigate the case.

Upon seeing the local celebrity, Morgan seized the opportunity for another exclusive interview. With her most charming smile, she cocked her head, tucked a lock of hair behind her ear, and offered Joshua a slender hand with long fingers. "I'm Morgan Lucas, the anchor for the evening news, and you are Commander Joshua Thornton. It is a pleasure to meet you. I followed the Admiral Thompson case when I was in college. I'm a fan."

Joshua shook her hand firmly. "Lawyers don't have fans. Where is Amber?"

"Are you asking the media to give you the witness you should have found in the first place?" a young reporter wearing ill-fitting clothes lingering within earshot giggled with a cocky attitude.

Joshua responded to the upstart with a glare that caused him to suddenly recall a deadline that he had to rush off to meet.

Morgan was more helpful. "Amber left a half an hour ago. Listen, I told her to go see you before I interviewed her on the air, but she was afraid."

"Afraid?" Joshua scoffed. "If she was so afraid, why did she just tell the whole Ohio Valley that she saw two murders?"

"She's afraid of Reverend Rawlings. She should be. He killed his own granddaughter. She thought if she publicly told her story that he would know that if anything happened to her, then he wouldn't get away with it."

"That's not very smart thinking."

"Hey, she came to us! She walked in here of her own free will with her story."

"Morgan Lucas! I want to talk to you!" Tess's usually refined voice carried across the newsroom.

Morgan's charm evaporated as she went on the defensive.

Dressed in a pale blue, loose-fitting, pantsuit, Tess charged across the newsroom. Her hair was brushed into loose waves down to her shoulders. Her shoulder bag, filled to bulging, bounced clumsily from where it was slung across her shoulder.

From his vantage point between the two women, Joshua observed that the anchor was more petite and at least five years younger than Tess. Morgan Lucas clearly had more charisma than the more seasoned journalist did. He guessed that it was Morgan's looks and charm, not her expertise, that won her the anchor position.

"Who do you think you are interviewing my source on the air?" Tess pointed an accusing finger at the offending young star.

Joshua ducked just in time to keep from being stabbed in the crossfire by a lethally-long, magenta-colored fingernail.

Morgan studied the threatening finger aimed between her eyes. Her eyes narrowed to slits. After a beat, she launched her defense. "You weren't here and I was."

With her hands on her hips in the stance of a seasoned professional going up against an inexperienced underling, Tess sneered. "I was following a lead. I was doing real news journalism, not just playing a talking head."

"It's not my fault. Ask Richards. She was here. Amber came in looking for you, and we tried to find you. You didn't answer your cell phone."

"The battery had run low."

"That's your tough luck. It was either we run with the story or lose it completely. Richards made the decision to go with it. If you don't like it, talk to the producer." In a gesture of farewell, Morgan nodded her head politely at Joshua before walking away with an air of justification.

At her desk, Tess hurled her shoulder bag to the floor.

When the shoulder bag dropped open, Joshua caught a glimpse of a pair of black panties and cosmetics case. Maybe it wasn't a lead she was following, he thought.

"Sorry about that," Tess shot him over her shoulder while she hurriedly repacked the bag. "In this business, you have to protect your stories or the vultures will steal them right out from under you."

"It is the same way in law." Joshua asked her, "Did you know Amber witnessed the murders?"

"If I had I would have told you." Tess stood up. "I'd give my right arm to have that monster put away."

With a hand on his elbow, Tess guided the prosecutor towards a small kitchenette out of earshot of her colleagues and competition. In the tiny room, a coffee maker contained a carafe half-filled with hours old coffee.

As she poured herself a cup of coffee, Tess told Joshua in a low voice, "Did you know that Rawlings killed my sister? Not him, but his drugs did."

"What's Amber's last name?"

"I can't tell you."

Joshua cocked his head at her. "You just said that you'd give your right arm to get Rawlings. Now, you have a source with the power to get him, but you won't tell me where I can find her?"

"Amber is up to her eyeballs in the drug underground, and she is obviously running for her life. She saw Rawlings kill two people, including his own granddaughter. I think that gives her reason to be scared."

"We can protect her."

"Yeah. Right." Tess sipped the overcooked coffee and grimaced.

"Where can I find her?"

"I don't know."

Joshua glared at her.

"Really! I don't know. She finds me." Tess dumped the coffee into the sink next to the coffeemaker.

"But she didn't find you today."

"I was following a lead on another story."

"Well, the next time she finds you, if you are serious about getting Rawlings, you'll convince her to call me. That little show she just gave for the valley is not going to be enough to convict Rawlings. There is a thing that is guaranteed in the constitution. That is the right to face your accuser. If she thinks she can give her statement to the media and not show her face in court, then Rawlings will never spend one day in jail no matter how good a show she gives for the cameras. She has to come forward and testify in court if she wants to get Rawlings to pay for what he's done. Got that, Ms. Bauer?"

Tess glared back at him. "Got it, Mr. Thornton."

CHAPTER 18

▼

"Why so glum?" Murphy leaned in Joshua's study doorway.

J.J. sat down in the chair across from their father's desk.

"I'm thinking," Joshua answered Murphy's question.

The prosecutor was brooding over Amber's interview, which was flawed. She was lying. That was clear to Joshua. Amber said repeatedly that she was in the closet. If Rawlings killed Vicki and Beth, then how could he have hidden the trench coat in the closet without finding the witness?

Why would she tell such a blatant lie?

Yet, Amber did know about Vicki being incapacitated before her murder. She described Vicki's frightening silence that must have occurred after the injection that rendered her incapable of defending herself against the killer. That was information that only the killer could have known.

He had to talk to Amber.

Joshua leaned back in his chair and stared up at the ceiling. He pretended not to see the crack in the plaster above his head.

J.J. tried to appear casual as he asked about what his father was thinking.

"I'm trying to figure out why Amber would want to kill Vicki Rawlings."

Murphy laughed. "She just told the whole world that Reverend Rawlings did it."

"She's not telling the truth. She's telling some of it, but not all of it."

"According to the word around town, this wouldn't be the first murder Reverend Rawlings committed," J.J. scoffed.

"What word around what town?"

Murphy told him, "We've been playing basketball at the junior high and met some of the kids. We threw Vicki's name out to see what reaction we'd get. There was nothing she didn't deal in: pills, cocaine, and heroin, too."

"She'd sell her grandmother for a buck was what we heard," J.J. interjected.

"And she learned that from her grandfather," Murphy finished.

"I believe that." Joshua shrugged with his eyes still on the ceiling. The crack was starting to annoy him.

"No, seriously," Murphy said. "One of the kids said that he heard from some-one who was tight with Vicki that she said Reverend Rawlings killed her grand-mother." He clarified by adding, "His own wife."

"I heard that, too." Joshua sat up and slumped over his desk. After a deep sigh, he added, "I think your source was confused."

"Why is that?"

"Because it was her mother who was murdered."

"Yeah," J.J. agreed. "Tad says Wally did it."

"And if Tad is right," Joshua pointed out, "then that will be Vicki's father who killed her mother." He chuckled, "This is a textbook case of a rumor going hog wild. Most likely, Vicki told someone that her father killed her mother. Her statement was then repeated over and over again, each time, splitting, dividing, and multiplying. That's what happens with gossip."

"Or maybe it didn't." J.J. stated what Joshua was afraid to seriously consider. "If the Walkers could be a family of spies, why can't the Rawlings be a family of killers?"

✳   ✳   ✳   ✳

Tad rested his head on his folded arms on the tabletop in the corner booth at Allison's Restaurant. Inches away, the silver key taunted him from the center of the table.

In her seat across from him, Jan buttered the roll that came with her dinner of meat loaf, mashed potatoes and gravy, and sweet peas. "Do you think that if you stare at it hard enough it might just speak to you?" She dipped her roll into the gravy pooled in the center of her mashed potatoes before taking a bite of it.

On the corner, one block up from Joshua Thornton's new legal office, Allison's Restaurant, like the other businesses in Chester, was short on sophistication, but long on quality. The food was good and inexpensive, like the decor.

When they spotted the two diners through the restaurant's front window, Joshua and his twin sons waved to Jan and Tad before joining them inside.

"Just the guy I was looking for." Joshua slapped Tad on the back before sitting next to him. J.J. sat next to Jan, and Murphy pulled up a chair to the end of the booth.

Too disgusted to sit up, Tad continued to slump over the table. "I don't want to talk to you unless you can tell me where this key goes."

Joshua greeted Jan with a smile, followed by a quizzical frown. "You look different."

"Do I?" Jan responded coyly.

Before taking her dinner break, Jan put on the wildest earrings she could find at the pharmacy and tied her hair back with the most colorful scarf in stock.

"What did you do?" Joshua tried to determine what was different about her.

"She's wearing makeup," Tad told him.

"Nah, that's not it. She was wearing makeup last week." Giving up, Joshua turned to Tad. "You still owe me a hundred dollars."

"So sue me."

Jan told Joshua, "He's been to every bank in the valley, and that key doesn't belong to any of their safety deposit boxes."

"I could have told you that." Joshua observed, "It's too small."

"Why didn't you?" Tad sat up.

"You didn't ask me."

"Could it be a post office box?" Murphy wondered.

"Nah," Joshua disagreed. "Post office keys have USPS stamped on them."

"Bus station locker," J.J. suggested.

"Not the right shape and too big," Tad responded.

"Looks like a padlock key to me," Jan told them before eating the last bite of her meatloaf.

The waitress, Madge, an older plump woman with a bleached blond beehive and long red acrylic fingernails, handed Joshua a typewritten menu stuffed inside a scuffed up plastic cover. "Coffee anyone?"

Joshua didn't have to read the menu. He handed it back to Madge and ordered for himself and his sons. "We'll have three apple pies a la mode."

"Make that four," Jan chimed in.

Madge smiled becomingly at Joshua as she retrieved the unused menu and went to get the pies. The twins chuckled to each other about the waitress's obvious attraction to their father.

"Did you see the news?" Jan anxiously asked Joshua.

"Yes, I did." Curious for his cousin's reaction, Joshua turned and laid his arm across the back of the booth behind Tad's shoulders. "Did you see Amber on the news?"

Tad sighed heavily and rested his head in a hand he had propped up against the windowsill. Seemingly unaware that all eyes were on him, he continued fingering the key that was the source of his frustration. "She's lying through her rotten little teeth," he finally declared.

Satisfied that Tad confirmed his conclusion, Joshua grinned.

"Why are you protecting Reverend Rawlings?" Jan accused the doctor.

"I'm going by the evidence and what I know about the man. He doesn't kill people. He orders people to do it for him. Besides, Amber's story contradicts the evidence. She said Vicki was fighting him when he gave her the shot." Tad shook his head. "She didn't put up a fight. The only evidence of any fight was a days old bruise right below the left temple where a certain someone—" he pointed a thumb in Joshua's direction, "slugged her alongside the head."

Joshua agreed. "She also said Reverend Rawlings carried Beth into the bedroom, then shot her. Beth was dragged in, not carried."

They stopped talking while Madge served their pies.

After the waitress left with Jan's dinner plate, Tad sighed with disgust once more, laid the key flat in the middle of the table, and sat back. "What else do you want to know?" he asked Joshua.

"J.J. and Murphy tell me that the word on the streets is that Reverend Rawlings killed his wife."

"Oh, yeah," Jan responded, "I had forgotten all about that."

"That's old news," Tad scoffed.

"He killed his wife?" Joshua uttered a whispered gasp. "I don't believe it."

"If it was true, then that would explain where Wally learned to kill Cindy."

"That's what we said." Murphy was proud that Tad and he were on the same wavelength.

"How did the reverend kill her?" J.J. asked.

Jan squinted at the doctor. "Her death was ruled accidental, wasn't it?"

"She drowned in the bathtub. They said she fell, hit her head, knocked herself out, and then drowned." Abruptly, the doctor chuckled. "Let's not forget Doc Wilson was the medical examiner. He's the same one who said Cindy's death was natural causes." He sorted out the long unused data in his mind as he said slowly, "Vicki Rawlings was just a little kid when her grandmother died. I think she was maybe five. It was before she started school."

"Why would Reverend Rawlings kill his wife?" Joshua inquired.

"Why else? He was sick of her. You remember who the reverend was married to, don't you, Josh?"

Unable to remember anything significant, Joshua shrugged, and then shook his head. "Her name was Eleanor. She never did strike me as quite right. I remember once at the Hookstown Fair, Grandmomma and I ended up sitting at the same picnic table as the Rawlings. That was the only time I remember ever seeing her up close. She had this weird look like—"

"I remember that look," Jan interjected. "She had bad vibes. She always seemed scared or spaced out or something."

"She never said anything," Joshua agreed. "I don't recall her ever saying a word."

Engrossed by the exchange, J.J. and Murphy ate their desserts in silence while the elder family members recalled the history of the Rawlings clan.

"Do you know who her father was?" Tad asked Joshua and Jan.

With the excuse that Eleanor Rawlings's father died before he was born, Joshua confessed that he didn't know.

"Sam Fletcher," Tad told his audience. "He owned the land that Rawlings's church is built on. He also owned all that land that Rawlings Meadows, that big subdivision out by the high school, was built on. And that big shopping center out in Calcutta? Rawlings sold them the land for that. All inherited from Sam Fletcher."

Tad smiled fondly. "Sam Fletcher. Now, he was the original Jeb Clampett. Did not look like he had a dime. Always wore old blue jeans overalls with patches all over them and this beat-up straw hat. He drove the same old pickup truck as long as I knew him. Every single day, he'd get up at the crack of dawn to milk the cows. He had this dairy farm out towards the state line, and was as tight with a dime as they come."

"Doesn't sound like he would be friends with *the* Reverend Orville Rawlings," Joshua commented.

Tad agreed. "Most likely not. Eleanor was a WAC. She joined the women's army corps right out of high school. Her folks never even saw Pittsburgh. She went off to see the world and brought back the reverend. They lived with Sam at the farm, until after he died. By that time, Reverend Rawlings had a small following. He preached in this old abandoned theater in East Liverpool. He sold the farm before Sam's body was even cold and built that church of his. The rest is history."

"So Reverend Rawlings would never have been who he is today if it weren't for his father-in-law's money," Murphy pointed out.

Also suspicious, J.J. asked his cousin, "How did Sam Fletcher die?"

"Now, there is a story!" Tad grinned at what he knew J.J. was thinking. "He went nuts."

"Nuts?"

"He had a nervous breakdown. One day, my dad went out to see him about buying this milk cow Sam had for sale and found him up on the roof of his barn. He was ranting and raving about snakes, tearing at his clothes, and screaming for Dad to get the snakes off of him. Scared Dad to death! He never saw anything like it." Tad shook his head with sadness. "Sam was the sanest man you ever would have met. Suddenly, he just lost it."

Tad mused with a note of sadness, "Eleanor tried to control him. They locked him up in the house. One night, he escaped. A couple of days later, they fished him out of the Ohio River. He must have jumped from one of the bridges. When he died, he left it all to Eleanor, and Rawlings did very well with it."

J.J. and Murphy were more suspicious.

"So, Rawlings would not have been as successful as he had been, if it weren't for Sam Fletcher dying when he did?" Murphy looked to his father whose brow was furrowed in deep thought.

Joshua asked, "When did Cindy die?"

"Nine years ago," Tad answered.

"When did Wally's mother die?"

Jan answered, "If Vicki was five, then that was twelve years ago."

"Why didn't Wally run for prosecutor as soon as he was eligible, which would have been as soon as he graduated from law school…about twelve or thirteen years ago?"

"Well, he started to," Jan responded while looking at Tad to confirm her answer. "He did announce his candidacy."

"That's right," Tad breathed. "I forgot all about that. Wally held a big press conference in the church to announce it."

"Then what happened?" Joshua asked.

Jan told him, "His mother died, and he said that he felt it was best to withdraw from the election for personal reasons. Everyone figured he was distraught over her death."

Joshua looked at Tad with raised eyebrows. "Or Dr. Wilson told him he had better withdraw or go to jail for murder."

"Kill his own mother?" Tad scoffed. "Nah! I'd rather believe the reverend did it."

"Either way," Joshua picked up the key and examined it, "we need to find out what this key goes to if we want to stop speculating and end this killing spree."

＊　　＊　　＊　　＊

"I had a great time," Tracy told Ken as he walked her across the front porch to the door.

She wasn't thinking about the ball game or the dinner her date bought her on the way home. The girl was wondering if she should kiss him good night. She wasn't sure if she wanted to kiss him. She did have a good time, and he was a nice guy and even cute, but…She didn't know what the 'but' was, but there was one.

At the door, Ken gave her that look that said he wanted to kiss her, but he was going to wait for a green light from her.

"I had a great time, too." In an effort to appear casual, he leaned against the doorway. "Maybe tomorrow I can show you around and—"

Joshua yanked open the front door. Ken jumped to his feet and stood at attention while his date's father, dressed in his pajamas and bathrobe, glared at the two startled teenagers.

"Dad!" Tracy shrieked.

"Someone rang the doorbell," Joshua told them.

"I'm sorry, sir," Ken stammered. His face reddened when he realized that he had leaned on the doorbell.

"As you were," Joshua responded before closing the door.

Ken took a deep breath and looked at his date for her answer to his invitation. Tracy was too busy giggling to tell him.

In front of the fireplace, Joshua sat back in his recliner with his feet propped up. Admiral was asleep under the footrest. Joshua was in the midst of re-reading a police report when his daughter came in.

"It's okay. He's gone," Tracy announced.

"I'm sorry I interrupted you guys."

Admiral grunted with displeasure after being rousted from his sleep when the footrest dropped on top of him as his master sat up in his chair. The dog crawled out from under the furniture and left the room to find a safer place to spend the night.

Tracy waved off her father's apology and sat at his elbow on the arm of the chair. "He asked me out again, even though you scared the tar out of him."

"Fear is a good thing in a daughter's boyfriend."

"He's not my boyfriend. He offered to show me the town tomorrow."

"Well, that should take all of five minutes. Then what does he have planned for you?"

Tracy giggled playfully. "How do you know I might not plan something for him?" Before her shocked father could respond, Tracy kissed him on the cheek and raced up the stairs to her room.

Joshua was still wondering if Tracy was serious and, if she was, was she too old to lock in her room, when the doorbell rang. Noting the late hour of eleven o'clock, he answered the door to find Jan on his doorstep.

"Looking for a cup of tea?" Joshua asked his old friend after inviting her inside.

"No, I just had to talk to you, and I had to do it now while I had my nerve up."

Joshua took note of Jan's appearance and wondered again why she looked different. "Did you do something to your hair?"

"No," Jan lied. The truth was that she had had it highlighted that evening after dinner. Her hairdresser told her that it would be so subtle that no one would notice. The last thing she wanted was to give Joshua Thornton ammunition for teasing her.

Joshua responded to her lie by raising an eyebrow and smirking. He knew she was lying.

Jan snorted. Nonverbally, she dared him to challenge her.

"I was just going to make some tea," Joshua announced by way of invitation before leading her to the kitchen.

Jan watched Joshua fill the teakettle from her seat at the kitchen table. She tried to appear casual with her questions. "Have you given any more thought to Doc Wilson's key?"

"Yeah, but I can't come up with anything."

"What do you expect to find when you do find what the key goes to?"

"Well, I have to admit that it is a conclusion that Tad and I are jumping to, but we believe that we'll find Cindy Rawlings's autopsy report." Joshua put the kettle on the stove before searching the cabinets for their mugs.

"Why can't the death certificate be enough to make Sheriff Sawyer reopen the case?"

"In most cases, it would be." Joshua closed one cabinet door, and then opened another in his search for the cups. "But both you and Tad think Sheriff Sawyer is crooked."

"Don't you?"

"I haven't decided yet."

"I told you that he's real tight with the Rawlings."

"That would make me nervous, too, except for one thing."

"What?"

"Ah, there you are," Joshua sighed upon finding the mugs and set two on the counter. "There's an old saying that I've learned is very true. 'If you want to know what your enemy is up to, keep him close, where you can keep an eye on him.' I watched Sawyer while he was examining the crime scene at Vicki's trailer. If he was covering anything up, I didn't see it."

"If you trust him, why haven't you gone to him with the death certificate?"

"Because all the death certificate says is that Doc ruled Cindy's death a homicide. It doesn't say how. It doesn't say by whom. It doesn't give specifics. If the Rawlings are involved, you can bet they'll get a Philadelphia lawyer like Mannings who will get them off like that." Joshua snapped his fingers. "Then, because of double jeopardy, no one will ever be able to touch them again. It's better to take our time, keep everything close to the vest, gather our evidence, and then attack."

The teakettle whistled.

C H A P T E R   19

▼

As soon as Amber's latest news hit the air, Reverend Orville Rawlings called Clarence Mannings in Philadelphia to return to Chester to act as his intermediary with the authorities. Even though no formal charges had been filed against the noted pastor, he was not one bit ashamed to "lawyer up" early.

As if to add insult to the injury of Amber's public statement, Joshua Thornton requested that the Rawlings family, all of them, come down to his dingy office in Chester to answer questions.

There was a power struggle for a full week. It was a matter of home field advantage. The Rawlings insisted that Joshua Thornton come to see them at their estate. Refusing to show any fear of the Rawlings and their politically influential friends, the special prosecutor countered with an invitation to come to his office voluntarily, or be served subpoenas and brought to the courthouse in the sheriff's patrol car to answer his questions in front of a judge, which would not look good for the reverend on the evening news.

In the end, Joshua won when he suggested that they meet across the street from his office at the Chester police chief's office on the second floor above the volunteer fire department. It was neutral territory.

As expected, Clarence Mannings did the talking while the Rawlings family leader, looking cocky and bored, sat at the head of the table in the tiny conference room.

The reverend noticed Joshua displayed not even a hint of intimidation as he looked him straight in the eye and asked where he was between four and six o'clock on the day his granddaughter was killed.

"My client was in meditation," the lawyer answered while Reverend Rawlings chuckled.

"From four o'clock to six?" Joshua looked at the reverend with a raised eyebrow to show his doubt.

The reverend snickered.

"He has been quite distressed about the soul of his granddaughter. He has been praying unceasingly ever since this whole thing started."

"I see," Joshua replied sarcastically and sat back in his chair.

The pastor laughed with a broad grin at the special prosecutor, who responded to his laughter with "Thank you for coming down."

After a week of negotiations to set up the interview, Clarence Mannings was startled by the short duration of the meeting. "What?"

"I said thank you. That will be all for now." Dismissing the high-priced lawyer and his client, Joshua made cryptic notations on his notepad.

"You mean you called us all the way down here for that one question?" Clarence Mannings didn't know whether to be relieved, outraged, or worried.

"Yes. Good day."

"Aren't you even going to ask us about this Amber's statement on the news?"

Touché, Joshua thought. "I thought you wouldn't want her statements dignified by being asked to comment on them."

Clarence Mannings snorted through his mustache. He had been had.

If Amber was lying, then the Rawlings wouldn't be so concerned about the authorities looking into her statement. The prosecutor would surely discover that she was lying. Therefore, why would they even wish to discuss Amber's public statement?

"Since you opened the door—" Joshua smirked at Mannings.

"All we have to say about Amber is that as soon as our people find her, she will be slapped with a gigantic lawsuit."

"If not something more lethal?" Joshua's smile dropped. "I'll be in touch with you and your client."

With a look of concern, the older lawyer led his client out the door. "We have our work cut out for us," he warned the pastor once they were out of earshot.

"That peasant doesn't know anything."

"Commander Thornton is clever, very clever."

"Commander?" Rawlings stopped and peered down from his great height at his lawyer.

"Commander. Thornton was promoted to commander after he convicted a Navy admiral I was defending of murder." Aware that he revealed that he was less than invincible, Mannings attempted to console his client. "But in this case, he has nothing but circumstantial evidence and a less than credible witness that no one can find."

"Thornton was a JAG lawyer before he came here?" Rawlings asked. "Does he still have military connections?"

"He's still in the reserves," Mannings told him. "Thornton was on the fast track before he quit. He's very methodical and he never makes a move without there being a reason behind it. If you have something to hide, you can bet your bottom dollar he'll find it. But you don't have to worry. If you did, you'd still be up there answering questions."

The rest of the Rawlings family was no further help.

Bridgette was in a tanning booth in East Liverpool from four o'clock to four-thirty. Joshua noted that while Bridgette supplied her signature on the sign-in sheet, there was no checkout time. He also noted the salon was only a few blocks from the hospital and Bridgette was alone the whole time she was in the tanning booth.

Hal Poole was in a meeting at the church in New Cumberland, but no one saw him between two and five o'clock.

Cockiness prevented Wallace Rawlings, the last to be interviewed, from having a lawyer present. He refused to shake Joshua's offered hand, plopped down into the chair at the head of the conference table, and glared at his rival.

"Let's get on with this. I have a very busy schedule. From here, I have a meeting with New Cumberland's mayor, and after that the county commissioner. Then tonight, I have a dinner engagement at Senator Brunswick's home."

"I'm impressed," Joshua told him as he slid into the chair across from Wallace. "Not terribly, but I am impressed. I am glad to see that you can keep up such a busy social schedule with your only daughter being murdered and all. I know I couldn't possibly do it if I were in your shoes. I guess you aren't into this mourning thing."

"Victoria and I were not that close."

"That's right," Joshua breathed. "She wasn't your daughter. At least, that's what I heard."

"That's correct," Wallace said without emotion. "Tad MacMillan was her father. I assume, since you're investigating this case, he's not a suspect."

Joshua ignored Wallace's question. Instead, he responded with his own question. "Did you tell Victoria that Tad was her biological father?"

Wallace's round face reddened with rage. "If I could have given him custody of his demon child, I would have!"

"How could you hurt her like that?" Momentarily, Joshua forgot about the reason for his interview. "She was a child. First, she loses her mother, and then, you tell her that you're not her father. No wonder she turned out the way she did."

Wallace's tone was void of emotion. "She was the product of sin. The only reason we let her stay under our roof as long as we did was because my father ordered us to let her stay and to tell no one what she really was! Fortunately, God drove her out."

Joshua shook his head. "Even if Tad had slept with Cindy, which he says he didn't, what makes you so certain Vicki wasn't your daughter? Cindy was your wife, after all."

"Because I would never take to my bed a woman who smells of another man. I knew even before she confessed her sins on our wedding night that she had been with Tad MacMillan. She reeked of him right up to the day she died!"

"It sounds like your marriage got off on the wrong foot."

"Cindy was a slut."

"So why did you marry her?"

"Because my father ordered that I marry her. 'Obey thy father and thy mother.'"

"Actually, it is 'respect your father and your mother,'" Joshua corrected him.

Insulted by the correction, Wallace glared.

Joshua could not resist continuing, "It is the fifth of the ten commandments that Moses brought down from Mount Sinai. In the Contemporary English version, it translates to 'Respect your father and your mother, and you will live a long time in the land I am giving you.' You can disobey someone and still respect them. My father disobeyed by grandmother by marrying my mother and enlisting in the Navy instead of joining the academy, but he still respected her."

Wallace asked curtly, "What other questions do you have?"

"So you married this woman and she has this baby, who you swear is not yours. You must have hated your wife."

"I despised her."

"Enough to kill her?"

"I resent that question!"

Joshua was as unfazed as Wallace was infuriated. "Vicki must have been a constant reminder of your wife's infidelity. How that must have made you hate her, especially with all the dirty laundry she was airing. And then, with her arrest and pending trial—"

"There would have been no trial. You do know Clarence Mannings, don't you?"

"Yes. I beat him before."

"But you weren't the prosecutor on Vicki's case. He was enough to scare Marjorie Greene." Wallace's cocky attitude returned. "She was talking deal."

"What kind of deal?"

"It doesn't matter now. That troublemaker is dead, and I was in a meeting with Marjorie Greene and Clarence Mannings at her temporary office in the courthouse in New Cumberland at four o'clock in the afternoon until five." Wallace smiled broadly. "I understand Victoria was killed at about four o'clock. I have an alibi."

"Yes, you do...for Vicki's murder, but not for Beth Davis's murder at six o'clock." Joshua grinned. "Tell me, are you missing a trench coat by any chance?"

Wallace's smug grin disappeared and his glare returned.

*   *   *   *

That evening, Orville Rawlings was seated in his recliner in his private study in their mansion when his son reported to him. Even though the hour was late, no one at the estate was asleep. Joshua's interrogations took care of that.

"You wanted to see me, Father?" Wallace asked from across the room.

Dressed in his silk pajamas and robe, Orville Rawlings marked his place in the latest Stephen King book he was reading and closed it. He took a single gulp of his scotch before placing his pipe between his lips and puffing it.

For a long moment, Rawlings studied his only son, who stood before him. Finally, the church leader removed the pipe from his lips. He studied the smoldering tobacco in the bowl as he stated the reason he had demanded his son to come see him. "Why is Joshua Thornton causing trouble for this family?"

Wallace didn't have an answer.

"Take care of him," the reverend ordered and then took another gulp of his drink.

"That won't end the murder investigation, Father. The attorney general will just send another special prosecutor."

"This valley needs to be reminded who is supreme. Joshua Thornton has defied me. We can't let that go unpunished." The reverend looked at his son. "Talk to Sheriff Sawyer. He is a reasonable man. He respects my authority. Tell him to take care of this problem."

"But Thornton has five kids."

"For some reason, you keep bringing trouble onto this family and I keep having to fix it. It is time you start taking responsibilities for the problems you cause."

"Me?" Wallace squawked. "I didn't bring Thornton back to Chester."

"It was your daughter—"

"Victoria was not mine! She was the product of Tad MacMillan's loins!"

"And that woman in Steubenville? Did Tad MacMillan's loins have anything to do with that?"

Wallace was struck speechless, as he always was when his father reminded him of Steubenville.

Pleased with his son's compliance, Orville Rawlings chuckled. He resumed with his instructions in a low steady tone. "Make sure Sawyer is well paid."

His order issued, the Reverend Orville Rawlings resumed reading about a small town invaded by an evil force from hell.

Wallace waited for his father to say something more on the subject. When it became apparent that the reverend had no further orders, the son responded, "Yes, Father."

*   *   *   *

Joshua Thornton didn't realize how much he missed silence.

At some point while traveling all over the world and having a family, Joshua had forgotten about the peaceful solitude back home. The fond memory came back to him shortly after his homecoming.

On the summer evenings, Joshua would sit on the porch steps and play the guitar for his grandmother, who would listen from her rocking chair until after the last porch light on their street went out. The Thorntons weren't the only ones who spent their evenings on the front porch. That was the routine all the way up and down the cobblestone streets in Chester.

Decades later, the neighbors and customs had changed.

Most of Joshua's childhood friends from the neighborhood had moved on to one of the surrounding cities. Some of the older neighbors died off and left their homes to their children, who quickly sold them to young families.

While the new generation residing on Rock Springs Boulevard may have sought the solitude of small town life, it was apparent by how few of them sat on their porches that they were too busy or sophisticated for guitar music and neighborly conversation.

After spending the day untangling homicidal chaos, Joshua fell right back into enjoying the peace and quiet on his front porch after dinner.

The children went their separate ways. Sarah had already made a couple of friends on the middle-high basketball team. They went to the school playground for her to show off her athletic talent. Tracy was stenciling a border in her room. Murphy and J.J. were surfing the Internet. Donny was reading in his room.

The contractor Tad had recommended for adding two bathrooms to the house never showed to give an estimate. Joshua claimed that was sufficient grounds to not hire him. Tad swore it was par for the course. Contractors never show and, Tad insisted, Joshua should have known and accepted that as a fact of life.

The twins found their father's old guitar in the attic. Joshua was pleased to discover as he tuned it, that his musical talent was coming back to him. He had just broken into a chorus of *Puff the Magic Dragon*, one of the first songs Tad had taught him, when a shadow fell across the steps where he sat.

"Don't stop on my account." Tess Bauer was standing before him. For her, she was dressed casually in jeans with a sports jacket over a crisp blue blouse. Her honey-colored hair fell to her shoulders in one soft wave. Joshua continued to strum while she sat on the step next to him. "I came to call a truce."

"I didn't know we were at war." Joshua cringed when he hit a sour cord. Not wanting to embarrass himself further, he set the guitar aside. "Did you bring me a peace offering?"

"What do you want?"

When Tess smiled becomingly at him, Joshua realized the reporter didn't smile during her news reports. Her smile looked out of place on her face.

"Amber," Joshua answered her question.

"She's afraid."

"She'll get protection."

Tess laughed. "That's what they always say. Every time anyone gets someone to testify against Rawlings, they disappear off the face of the earth."

"So Amber thinks it would be better to disappear before that happens and leave it to someone else to get rid of Rawlings. Tell her that now, not only is she running from Rawlings, she's running from the police. There is a warrant out for her."

"Amber didn't do anything."

"She's a material witness," Joshua told the journalist. "You should know that."

"I do. I just thought you would understand."

"I do, but there is nothing I can do. Amber knows things about the Rawlings and Davis murders, and I need to question her. Where can I find her?"

"You can't."

"Where did you find her?"

"She found me. After Diana died, I vowed that I was going to get whoever was behind the drugs that killed her. It wasn't hard to find a lot of people who could tell me that Reverend Orville Rawlings was the valley's drug lord. Unfortunately, I could find no one who would talk on camera."

"Until you met Amber."

"Amber showed up at my apartment one night." Tess nodded up the street to the rise in the hill over Chester. "I rent a little two-bedroom on Nevada. She wouldn't even go into the studio. I had to record the interviews by myself at home because she was so afraid."

"If she was so afraid, why'd she consent to the interviews?"

"She and Vicki Rawlings were very close. She wanted to help her."

"Best friends?"

Tess grinned. "Closer than that."

Joshua cocked his head and raised an eyebrow. "Really?"

"Shocked?"

"Lady, I've been all over the world and back."

"So I heard." Tess hugged her knees to her chest.

Joshua observed that Tess had trimmed her fingernails to a normal length and replaced the dark color with a delicate French manicure more in keeping with her conservative manner.

The journalist gazed up at the stars just starting to peek at them from above. "Chester must seem awfully boring after living in the likes of Hawaii and San Francisco."

"And Naples and London." Joshua laughed, "Nah, I haven't had time to be bored."

"Dad, who are you talking to?" Tracy stepped out onto the porch. She had Admiral on his leash.

"Hey, kiddo. It's Tess Bauer. She came by to offer me an olive branch." Joshua introduced his older daughter to the news journalist.

"Hello, Tracy." Tess twisted where she sat on the step to look up at the girl above her on the porch.

Tracy greeted the reporter and complimented her on her work before telling her father that she was taking the dog for a walk.

"If you can wait a minute, I'll come with you." Joshua started to stand up.

Tracy shook her head at his offer. "That's okay. I'm meeting Ken."

Joshua chuckled. "Aw, so this isn't a humanitarian trip to give Admiral some exercise. It's a date."

"And Admiral is my unwilling chaperone," Tracy confessed.

Joshua returned to his seat on the step next to Tess. When Tracy stepped around him with the huge dog, Joshua leaned to the side to make room for them to descend to the driveway. As he did so, Joshua's thigh brushed up against Tess Bauer's leg.

"Who do you think you are?" Tess shrieked. In an instant, she was on her feet.

Startled by the outburst, Tracy stopped to watch while Tess glared down at where Joshua sat. The reporter's fury was so abrupt that the dog hid behind his mistress's legs as if they were big enough to conceal him.

"You think that you can have any woman you want! You think that women will fall all over themselves and degrade themselves by putting up with your sick fantasies in hopes that you will honor them by choosing them to be with you!"

Joshua's expression was one of confusion while he mentally replayed the moments before Tess's explosion in his search for the action that motivated it.

Meanwhile, Tess continued ranting, "Well, I'm not like those other women! I'm independent and do you know what independent is?"

"Of course, I do," Joshua muttered meekly.

"It means I don't need you. I don't have to put up with any of your shit!"

Both Joshua and Tracy sensed that the man on the porch step was no longer the source of Tess's fury.

"You can't make a fool out of me! I'm in control here and do you know what it means when you're in control?"

"What?" Joshua watched her closely.

"You're free! You're free to walk away at any time or, better yet, to stand up for yourself. If you don't stand up for yourself, then they will think that they can get away with humiliating you because you are unable to walk away."

Tess laughed loudly, "Not only can I walk away! But I can also fight back!"

Joshua cautiously rose from where he had been sitting on the porch so peacefully just moments before. "I'm sorry if I offended you."

Tess responded to the apology with a slap across his face.

Without another word, Tess turned, shoved Tracy aside, and stormed out the driveway and up the road.

The father and daughter gazed questioningly at each other. Unable to come up with what he had done to offend the journalist, they both shrugged.

"I see you still have a way with the ladies." Jan was coming up the driveway with a wide grin on her face. Joshua and his daughter were so enthralled by Tess's wrath that they had not noticed their audience.

When she saw Ken waiting for her across the street, Tracy greeted and bid farewell to Jan in one breath before rushing off with Admiral to meet her date.

"What was that all about?" Jan's amusement at Joshua's expense was evident.

"I have no idea," Joshua muttered.

After they sat back down on the same step where Joshua had been enjoying the quiet of the summer evening, Jan handed him a small green tin. "I brought you some more of that tea you like."

"You don't have to keep bringing me tea," Joshua told her. "Let me pay for it."

"You don't have to pay me." Jan cocked her head to one side. "However, if you do want to repay me, there is something you can do for me."

"What? Is it legal?"

"I want in."

"In? On what?"

"On your murder investigation. This is my chance. I never got to pursue my dream to be a writer because I had no story. Now, if you bring down the Reverend Rawlings for a double murder, then there will be a big story. If you let me have an exclusive, then I'll finally be able to do what I want to do with my life instead of running that little drug store in this small town."

"What if it isn't Rawlings? Then, you have no story and wasted your time."

"Who else could it be?"

"I thought you said it was a murder for hire and Tad was behind it," Joshua reminded her.

Jan snorted. "Have you even tried to pursue that? Have you talked to Tad about it?"

"I know Tad too well." Joshua shook his head as he recalled Tad's nausea upon finding Beth's body. "He took Beth's death very hard. I was there when we found her."

Jan reluctantly agreed. "Tad is no killer. But I still want to know what Beth meant when she told him she was going to make Maggie hate him."

Joshua chuckled. "You still haven't figured that out?"

"I wouldn't have to figure it out if you'd tell me."

"I haven't confirmed it, but I think I know and you would, too, if you think about it. What could Beth know that would make Maggie hate Tad?"

Jan sighed with disgust and looked at Joshua. Feeling stupid, she shook her head. "I give up. Tell me."

Pleased with himself for his deduction, Joshua grinned. "Beth was Maggie's mother."

"No." It was a statement.

"Yes," Joshua asserted. "Tad never told anyone who Maggie's mother was for a reason. Beth and I used to go together. After I left her for Valerie, she started partying with Tad and got pregnant. Tad never said she was Maggie's mother because he was afraid I would be offended that he slept with my old flame."

"No," Jan stated again. This time her tone was firm. "Beth never slept with Tad. If she had she would have told me, if only for bragging rights. Yes, she got wild after you dumped her. She was even fooling around with Wally."

Joshua's head snapped up to look at Jan's profile in silhouette. His gasp was audible. "Wally Rawlings?"

Vigorously, Jan nodded her head. "Right after you dumped her. She claimed she was in love. I told her that she was subconsciously trying to get even with you."

"Beth hated Wally."

"But she hated you more for dumping her." Jan told him, "Beth didn't have any baby. I certainly would have known about that."

Aware that Jan had just confessed to looking for a story about which to write, the lawyer refrained from countering her assertion with information that Tad had noted in Beth's autopsy report, but neglected to call to anyone's attention. In a section on the form, the medical examiner had checked off that Beth's body showed evidence that she had given birth at some point during her life.

Upon seeing the simple check mark, suddenly Beth and Tad's relationship became clear to Joshua. It also explained Tad's resistance to naming Maggie's mother.

Instead of revealing the indisputable evidence of the autopsy report to Jan, Joshua argued, "Didn't Beth leave town to go to school at West Liberty?"

Jan agreed that Beth had gone away to college.

"Wasn't she gone for several months? Like long enough to have a baby?"

Jan reluctantly admitted that she had, but she still shook her head at Joshua's conclusion about Beth being Maggie's mother. "Beth and Tad never slept together. There's no way Maggie could be their daughter."

"Then who is Maggie's mother?" Joshua asked. "What else could Beth threaten to tell Maggie that would make her hate Tad?"

"I don't know. I guess we need to ask Tad that."

"I guess so." Joshua didn't relish that interrogation.

"Who are your other suspects?" Jan inquired with enthusiasm that matched Joshua's dread.

"You."

Jan hesitated before laughing at what had to be a joke. "Why would I kill Beth? She was my friend since high school."

Joshua's tone told Jan that he was indeed serious. "You were always jealous of Beth. She just about ruined you. She stole drugs from your store. The Frosts were suing you because of her negligence. You're lucky I convinced them to accept the insurance company's settlement, instead of dragging your butt into court. As it is, your insurance premiums will be raised and the store's reputation is ruined. You can thank Beth for that."

"Thanks a lot." Jan stood up and stepped down off the porch.

Joshua stopped her. "That's how a murder investigation really works. You ask questions, accuse people, sometimes your friends, and they get offended. It's one confrontation after another. It's not fun and games."

Jan came back to where Joshua remained seated on the steps. "You don't really think I'd kill Beth, do you?"

"You two weren't the best of friends. I saw that the first day I saw you at the drug store. There was tension, slight, but it was there."

Jan stood over Joshua with one foot propped up on the step next to his thigh. "I knew Beth was having problems. I was afraid she was going to make a mistake just like the one she made. But she was my friend, and I didn't want to hurt her. That was my mistake. I let our friendship get in the way of business." She hung her head.

Joshua could see even in the dark that she was sad.

Jan went on with her confession. "You're right. I was jealous of Beth. Men always came so easy for her. She'd go through one guy after another, especially after Wally. That was one dumb relationship, and I told her that from the start. Beth had this insane idea that Wally was going to dump Cindy Welch and marry her. Then, she was going to go off and live at the Rawlings estate, and you were going to kick yourself for dumping her. Of course, that didn't happen."

Joshua murmured as he asked, "Are you saying Wally was fooling around with Beth right up to when he married Cindy?"

"And afterwards. It was months before Beth got it through her head that she was just the other woman and not some soap opera vixen. Then, she went off to school and it was over."

Jan snickered at Joshua's surprise. "Tad knew all about it. Didn't he tell you?"

CHAPTER 20

▼

"Why do I have to get a shot?" Eight-year-old Mitch DeLong eyed the syringe Tad was preparing for the tetanus injection.

"Because you stepped on a rusty nail. You don't want to get lockjaw, do you?" Tad pulled the needle out of the vial and turned to the boy with a dirty face that his mother had unsuccessfully attempted to wash before rushing him to the doctor's office. The child's pants were torn and his shirt was covered with food, dirt, and grass stains.

"Depends on which hurts more." From where his mother held him still on the examination table, the patient eyed the doctor defiantly.

"Lockjaw hurts more." Without any hesitation, Tad grabbed the boy's arm, shoved the needle into his bicep, pushed the plunger, and dispensed the medication.

Mitch yelled.

Tad yanked the needle from out of the boy's flesh and turned around to drop the used syringe into the hazardous material bin. "There. That didn't hurt that much, did it?" Unexpectedly, he felt a sharp pain in his upper arm.

Mitch had grabbed and twisted the flesh of Tad's bicep, concealed under the cotton material of his white lab coat, into a painful pinch.

The doctor yelled. He grabbed his arm and whirled around to Mitch, who scowled up at him.

"It hurt that much!" the boy announced.

The apologetic mother was already helping her son down from the examination table.

Tad forced himself to grin pleasantly at Mrs. Delong. "I think we are done here." He handed Mitch's medical chart to his mother. "You can give this to the receptionist."

Before Tad MacMillan's office was a place of business, the lab was an elderly spinster's kitchen. The cabinets, counters, and appliances survived the renovations.

After dealing with Mitch, who had been a handful since the day Tad delivered him, the doctor went to the lab in the back of his medical office. He removed a bottle of water from the refrigerator and took a couple gulps before he noticed Joshua sitting at the break table. "What are you doing here?"

"Why didn't you tell me Beth slept with Wally?" Joshua could be direct with Tad.

Tad gulped another mouthful of water, and then leaned against the counter. "I only have fifteen minutes before my next appointment. I do have to make a living. I have a mother and a daughter to support."

"Answer my question. My back is killing me and I'm short on patience."

Tad put the water back into the refrigerator and stepped behind Joshua. Even though they were arguing, the doctor examined his cousin's aching back. "Beth slept with Wally a long time ago. This has nothing to do with her murder."

"You don't know that. I need to know everything in order to invest—" Joshua screamed when Tad snapped one of his vertebrae back into place. The pain subsided as abruptly as it erupted. Instantly, Joshua was overcome with relief from the sharp ache to which he had awakened that morning.

Tad continued to massage Joshua's back while prescribing the solution to his pain. "You're too tense, Josh. You need to learn how to walk away from this case at the end of the day."

"I can't walk away from it. I may not have married Beth, but I did care about her. I almost married her. I need to find out who killed her and, in order to do that, I have to learn her secrets, secrets you seem to know."

"Are you sure you really want to know all of Beth's secrets?" Tad shot him a naughty grin as he took the chair across from him.

"I'm a man. I can take it."

"Can you? Am I a suspect?"

"I didn't say you were a suspect."

"If I'm not, I should be. Vicki was making my life hell. Beth endangered one of my patient's lives, and I know Jan heard her threaten Maggie. She had to have told you. Plus," Tad added with a grin, "I have no clear alibi."

"I checked with the bars around the hospital. They confirm that you were making the rounds looking for Beth at the time of her murder, and the hospital confirms you were treating her when Vicki was killed."

"So I have an alibi. It could have been a murder for hire."

"Are you confessing to killing Beth?"

"I'm only confessing that our relationship can bring your integrity into question." Tad chuckled, "How can you be so sure that I have an alibi for the times of the murders?"

"Because you have dozens of witnesses that can account for where you were," Joshua said.

"According to times of death supplied to you by me," Tad told him with a wicked grin.

Joshua looked his cousin in the eye. He couldn't tell if Tad was joking or serious about giving the special prosecutor false information. It was hard for him not to trust his closest friend and confidante. Both Jan and Tad were right. It was impossible for him to be objective about Tad's possible guilt in this case.

Joshua had no choice but to go with his gut. "Whoever killed Beth had to have driven her car from the New Cumberland courthouse to Vicki's place, and probably picked her up from the hospital before taking her to Vicki's place. Forensics picked up some fingerprints in the car, but they don't have a match for them."

Tad nodded thoughtfully. "Beth didn't usually lock her car. More than once, she left her keys in the ignition. Anyone could have taken it."

"How could Beth make Maggie hate you?" Joshua shot Tad the question weighing on his mind.

Tad sat back in his chair. "A smart man like you—" He stopped chuckling to ask, "What do you think Beth was talking about?"

"About that check mark you put on her autopsy report that says she gave birth." Joshua paused. "Did you flip a coin to decide if you were going to neglect to mention the distended uterus?"

"I never lie. You know that. As medical examiner, I am obligated to put those things in the report."

"But you neglected to go out of your way to call it to my attention."

"Because it is not relevant to your case."

Joshua shook his head. "Until this case is solved, everything is relevant until I say it's not." He held Tad's gaze. "Tell me your little secret about Beth."

Tad broke the gaze and sat back in his seat. He challenged him. "If you're so smart, you tell me." He smirked. "To show you that I'm a good guy, I'll even fill in the blanks when you're through."

Joshua accepted the challenge. "I thought that Beth was Maggie's mother, but Jan swears that if Beth slept with you that she would have told her. If Jan is right, then you didn't sleep with Beth. Therefore, she could not be Maggie's mother. However, according to your autopsy report, Beth did have a baby. Yet, for some reason, you don't want anyone to know anything about it. Why?"

"She wasn't married," Tad scoffed.

"That's not it."

"Why do you assume that I even knew about her pregnancy before the autopsy? I was gone for years while I was in medical school and doing my residency, and Beth had gone away to school herself."

"If you had been surprised by those findings during Beth's autopsy, you would have told me that she had given birth. Plus," Joshua grinned at his excellent deduction, "if you don't know the circumstances behind that birth, then how can you be so sure that Beth's pregnancy is irrelevant to her murder?"

"You are good," Tad admitted with a smile. He then drawled, "Now, don't tell me that the thought has not crossed your mind that maybe you might be the father of that baby. My exam did not reveal any evidence of when Beth gave birth."

"You can't determine that information from an autopsy. You can only determine if it was recently or not."

Tad agreed. "So, for all you know, she was pregnant with your baby when you ended your relationship with her."

Joshua ordered without humor, "Fill in the blanks."

Tad's only response was a wide grin.

Joshua asked in a low voice, "What did Beth mean when she said she was going to tell Maggie the truth? What did she threaten to reveal that made you so angry?"

"Beth was out of her mind."

"I want to eliminate you as a suspect."

"I didn't have the means to get to the murder scene to commit the crime. Beth's car was in New Cumberland. My bike was here, home. You drove me to the courthouse for the hearing, and I rode to the hospital in the ambulance with Beth. The only way I got home to get Dog and walk to your place to get you to drive me to Vicki's place was by hitching a ride with a nurse." Tad gestured with both hands, not unlike the gesture of a magician who had just performed a magnificent illusion. "That eliminates me as a suspect."

"Unless you lied about the times of death, or it was a murder for hire." Joshua pleaded, "Help me, Tad. Please."

Tad eyed Joshua a long moment while he considered his options. He sighed deeply before giving in. "Both you and Jan are right."

This only confused Joshua more. "How?"

"Beth was Maggie's mother, but I never slept with Beth. I couldn't." Tad cringed. "That would be like sleeping with my sister. I just couldn't think of her like that, no matter how drunk I got."

Joshua sorted the information in his mind. "Beth was Maggie's mother. That's why you took off like that to see Maggie after Beth was killed. It wasn't because some guy dumped her. Her mother died. Maggie knew?"

"I told her years ago. Beth never acknowledged her, though. She was furious with me for telling Maggie. Beth thought she had been adopted and sent far away from here."

"But you weren't Maggie's biological father?" Joshua gasped. "I never would have imagined. I must be losing my touch."

Tad smiled proudly. "I am her father. She was the first baby I delivered. I took care of her. I supported her financially and emotionally. No one can say I'm not her father. I just didn't sleep with her mother."

"Then who—? Don't tell me Wally—"

Tad was already nodding his head. "He never knew," he quickly shrugged, "that I know of."

Joshua was taking it all in. "How?"

Tad laughed, "You have five kids!"

"How did you end up with Maggie when Beth thought she had been adopted? Why did you tell everyone, including your own mother, that she was your daughter?"

Tad started his confession with a deep sigh. "After Wally married Cindy, I went back to Morgantown to finish my residency. Suddenly, one day, Beth shows up on my doorstep. She and Wally had ended it, but then she found out she was pregnant. She was afraid to tell her mother. You remember how her mother was?"

After confirming that he recalled that Beth's mother was a perfectionist, intolerant of any behavior that was less than perfect from her children, Joshua gestured for Tad to continue.

Tad took another deep breath. "Beth thought that because of our past, my being your cousin and all, that I would get rid of it," he held up his fingers in quotation marks as he said, "get rid of it", "and no one would ever know."

"She wanted an abortion," Joshua clarified.

Tad shook his head slowly. "I couldn't do it. Beth went nuts. She was so afraid that someone would find out, Wally, in particular. She was terrified of him until the day she died. She said flat out that if he found out she was pregnant he'd kill her."

He paused before resuming his story. "No one in Morgantown knew Beth. So, I made her an offer. She could stay with me, take a year off school, have the baby, and I'd arrange for it to be adopted. I'd even put my name on the birth certificate, so there would be no record of Wally being the father."

"So Maggie was supposed to be adopted?"

Tad said she was. "I got a lawyer friend of mine to arrange for a private adoption. He found a couple who were very anxious to take her."

"So how did you end up with her?"

"Beth was already on her way to being an alcoholic. She agreed to the arrangement until she started showing, and then she couldn't stand it. By then, it was too late. I couldn't keep her sober." Tad laughed, "Hell, I couldn't stay sober myself."

His laughter subsided. "Beth ended up having Maggie on my living room floor two months early. I delivered her. On top of weighing only a couple of pounds, Maggie had a hole in her heart. Her adopted parents got their lawyer to point out a clause in our agreement that the baby was to be healthy. So they got out of it. Beth never even looked at her. She was gone as soon as they released her from the hospital."

Tad shrugged as he said softly, "That left only me. I was all Maggie had."

Joshua added, "And your name was on the birth certificate, so you were legally responsible for her."

Tad chuckled. "First responsible thing I ever did in my life."

"For a baby that wasn't even yours."

Tad disagreed. "I never once, for an instant, felt like she wasn't mine. I fed her. I changed her. I got a doctor friend of mine in cardiology to fix her heart. By the time the lawyer found a couple willing to adopt a baby who was in need of a lot of medical care, I couldn't give her up. I knew I was too sick to care for her, but I couldn't let her out of my life. So I called Mom, told her she was a grandmother, and she gladly took her. She was thrilled. She always wanted a daughter."

"Does Maggie know all this?"

"I told her everything after I sobered up. I neglected her while I was drinking, and I've been trying to make it up to her ever since. She wanted to know about her mother, so I told her. She had the right to know."

"Did you tell her about Rawlings?"

Tad nodded his head. "Hardest thing I ever did in my life, telling her that part of it."

"How did she take it?"

"Wally Rawlings is just a man to her. Maggie tried to make a relationship with Beth, but her mother was too emotionally weak to be a parent. Maggie understood Beth's problem because of being in Al-Anon because of me. But understanding didn't take away her hope that one day her and Beth could have a relationship."

"So, if Maggie knew everything, then what did Beth mean when she said she was going to tell Maggie the whole truth and make her hate you?"

"Beth was higher than a kite. She knew Maggie knew everything. It terrified her. She was convinced that Wally Rawlings was going to kill both of them."

"If she didn't know anything that could hurt Maggie, why were you angry?"

"Because she was Maggie's mother, and I wanted her to sober up and get well. Every time Maggie came to town Beth would go on a binge. It hurt Maggie. That—" Tad held up a finger to make his point, "That frustrated me, because I was helpless in helping Beth." He muttered as he added, "Now, I know how you and Mom felt when I drank."

Tad checked his watch. "I have a patient waiting. I've got to go."

Joshua blocked the doctor's escape from the room when he headed for the door. "Did Wally and Cindy know the truth about Maggie?"

"I told you already. Not that I know of."

"Did Cindy know about Wally and Beth's affair?"

Tad crossed his arms and looked Joshua in the eye. "I told her, not because I was noble. I thought it would convince Cindy not to marry Wally, but she did anyway."

Joshua's jealousy about Beth and Wallace was replaced with sympathy for his cousin and friend. "So Cindy went ahead and married Wally. Wally continued seeing Beth on the side and got her pregnant. Then, you ended up raising his baby."

Abruptly, Joshua's sympathy turned to horror.

His mind pieced together the picture of what he had just observed as an irony with fresh information received from a report he had read that morning during his breakfast. The DNA report from the state lab was hand delivered to his home by courier. As his mind put the facts of the report together with Tad's revelation, the color drained from Joshua's face.

"What?" Tad cocked his head and looked questioning into Joshua's glazed eyes. "What's wrong?"

The touch of Tad's hands on his shoulders started Joshua out of his sickening observation. "Maggie is Vicki's half sister."

Unsure of where Joshua was going, Tad cautiously nodded his head. He wanted to deny it, but in light of what he had just told his cousin, he had to admit to the relationship between his beloved daughter and the girl who had been terrorizing him for the past three years.

Joshua's tongue felt heavy as he told Tad, "I got the result of the DNA tests this morning."

"What about them?"

"The red hair that was found in the collar of the trench coat and the gun chamber of the murder weapon," Joshua swallowed. "When the lab compared the DNA tests, they found a relationship between whoever the hair came from and Vicki. There were enough common markers between them for them to share a parent. They're half siblings."

Sickened by the news, Tad dropped down into the chair at the table.

"You just admitted that Wally is Maggie's birth father," Joshua said. "If you aren't Vicki's father, and Cindy never had an affair with anyone else, then Wally has to be Vicki's father. That makes them half sisters."

Tad glared up at the prosecutor. "Don't even go there, Josh."

"Maggie had motive. You just told me. She's Vicki's half sister and she has red hair."

"She has blond hair!"

"Strawberry blond! It's got red in it!"

"That hair was color treated! Maggie's hair is natural!" Tad blurted out. "Plus, Penn State is four hours away! Maggie doesn't even know where Vicki lives!"

"Beth rejected her! Vicki was terrorizing you!"

"Maggie was looking for a job when they were killed."

Joshua wished he wasn't having this conversation. "I'm going to have to have Sawyer talk to her and get her statement."

"You can't put my daughter through that!"

Joshua cursed himself for his curiosity. He wished he had never asked Tad to tell him about Beth and Wally Rawlings. "You yourself said that because of our relationship that the integrity of this investigation will be called into question. If I found out about Maggie's relationship to the victims, a defense attorney can find that out and when we find the real killers they'll go free because that attorney will make Maggie look like the killer. Hell! It turns out she is connected to both victims in this case!"

Tad gasped.

Joshua was almost frightened by the smile on his cousin's face and the finger he pointed at him. "What?"

"You just said that Maggie is connected to both victims."

Joshua nodded his head. "That's what you just told me," he reminded Tad. "Wally has to be Vicki's father and you also just told me that Beth and Wally are Maggie's birth—"

The finger Tad was pointing at Joshua started wagging. "That's right! Beth is Maggie's birth mother!" He rose from his chair with the wagging finger aimed at Joshua's face. "The lab compared the DNA from that hair to both Vicki's and Beth's DNA!"

Joshua sighed. "There was no indication in the DNA test to show any familial relationship between Beth and that hair."

"Which means that whoever that red hair came from is in no way related to Beth, but I saw Maggie come from Beth's womb." Overcome with relief, Tad's shoulders sagged. He slumped against the lab's counter.

"I'm sorry I put you through that," Joshua whispered as he laid a hand on his cousin's shoulder and squeezed it affectionately.

Tad signaled his acceptance of the apology by patting Joshua's hand. "You're just doing your job."

"I still have to have Sawyer get a statement from Maggie," Joshua told him, "if only to maintain the integrity of this investigation." He was relieved to hear Tad agree.

"Do you mind if I call her first so she doesn't get upset when he calls?"

Before Joshua could give Tad the permission he sought, Stella, the doctor's nurse, came into the lab. She carried a package the size of a shoebox. An older woman, Stella resembled the stereotype of a guard in a women's prison. She had the attitude of one, too.

The nurse thrust the package with postal markings that read "priority" into Tad's hands as she announced in a terse tone, "This came for you, and Mrs. Anderson has been waiting in examination room two for ten minutes." Before Tad could comment or thank her for the package, Stella left the lab to return to her duties.

"This is weird," Tad muttered while reading the package's mailing label. He removed a pair of scissors from a drawer next to him at the counter.

"What?" Joshua studied the package to see on what Tad was commenting. It was wrapped in plain brown paper.

"It's from New Cumberland. My pharmaceutical company is in Pittsburgh."

"You're not expecting anything?"

"No." With the scissors, Tad snipped the taped seal at the bottom of the package.

Overcome with a sense of dread, Joshua snatched the package out of Tad's hands. "Don't open it!"

"Why not?"

"This has no return address."

Tad laughed, "Aren't we getting a little paranoid?"

"If Beth had been a little more paranoid she might still be alive. And how about Cindy?"

Tad's smile faded.

They both stared at the package Joshua held gingerly in his hands. "Do you have an x-ray machine?"

Tad backed away from Joshua and the package. "No, I send my patients to radiology at the hospital."

"I'm sure the post office has something, especially since 9-11." Joshua gently put the package down on the table and backed up to where Tad stood by the door for a fast exit.

"Won't we look pretty silly if we take that to the post office and it's nothing?"

"You'll look worse if you open it, and it blows up in your face."

"The Rawlings have never used explosives in the past."

"From what I've seen, they vary their M.O." Joshua went back to the table and carefully picked up the package. "I'm going to take it to the post office and ask them to examine it."

Tad objected, "No, I'll take it."

"You go take care of your patient. We've made her wait way too long."

"It's meant for me. If it blows up on your way—"

"It's only three blocks. If it made it here in our government's postal service with all the tossing and bumping that goes on, then it will survive a three block walk." Joshua was going out the back door. "I'll be fine. Don't worry. I'll call you."

Wishing he could go with him, Tad watched through the screen door while Joshua made his way down Church Alley in the direction of Fifth Street.

*   *   *   *

"You don't recognize me, do you?" the postal worker asked Joshua.

Untouched, the package rest on the counter between them. While Joshua was very aware of it, the postal clerk with "Eric" embroidered in red on his breast pocket was more concerned with his customer.

Joshua looked the clerk up and down.

In appearance, the former naval officer starkly contrasted him. Joshua was tall, slender, and neatly dressed in a navy blue sports coat over freshly pressed slacks. The clerk was short and overweight. His long greasy hair looked like it hadn't been washed in weeks. His postal uniform was faded and wrinkled. His sour expression made him even less attractive.

Joshua was certain Eric mistook him for someone else.

When Eric once again opened his mouth to speak Joshua recognized the whine that was as much a part of his speech pattern as an accent. "Never thought I'd see you come back to this burg."

"Eric Connally, how are you doing?" Joshua forced himself to remain pleasant.

"Fine," Eric lied. "Been working here for twenty years. I have my own house out in Birch Hollow. Not bad for a guy voted most-likely-to-fail."

Joshua cringed.

Eric Connally was a pathological liar. In school, the boy claimed that Farrah Fawcett, during the height of the actress's fame, was his illegitimate sister.

Realizing that the outcast was lying for attention, Joshua had felt sorry for Eric.

Their peers weren't as sympathetic. At the end of their senior year, the student body cruelly voted Eric most-likely-to-fail.

Eric retaliated by using his car keys to scratch the paint of his classmates' cars.

Joshua had the misfortune of witnessing the vandalism when he arrived at school late after a dental appointment and turned Eric in to the principal. Eric, perceiving Joshua Thornton's action as betrayal, blamed the attractive and popular student voted most-likely-to-succeed for every misfortune he suffered from that moment onward.

While Eric directed his wrath over the world's injustices at the embodiment of success now standing before him, Joshua wondered how the post office ever came to hire someone so obviously unbalanced.

"Heard you left the Navy…Left or was kicked out?" He snickered wickedly as he added, "For treason, maybe?"

Insulted by the insinuation, Joshua defended himself, "Not that it is any of your business, Eric, but I lost three friends at the Pentagon on September 11. I would love to personally pull the trigger on Bin Laden; but I also care about my children, and it is hard to raise five children by yourself when people are shooting at you. That's why I had to quit JAG."

"JAG?" Eric's face screwed up at the unfamiliar milspeak term.

"Judge Advocate General Corps. I was—am—a lawyer."

"Lawyer?" Eric sneered. "So you never killed any towel head or anything like that?"

"I can kill a man, and I have. I learned how to do that with my bare hands at the Naval Academy." Joshua added with a wide, nasty looking grin, "And at Penn State Law School, I learned how to get off for it."

Eric glared at Joshua's threatening tone. "Why do you want this x-rayed?" The clerk indicated the package cluttering his counter.

"There's no return address and my cousin was not expecting anything from anyone in New Cumberland."

"Your cousin? Dr. MacMillan?"

"Yes. Dr. Tad MacMillan."

"Then it's probably a gift from one of his women." Eric forcibly shoved the package back at Joshua as a sign of dismissal.

Joshua gingerly slid the package back towards him. "As a taxpayer, I am requesting that this package be examined for any possible explosives or bacteria." He forced a note of courtesy in his voice. "Please."

"I'm too busy to be bothered with petty paranoia."

Joshua observed that he was the only one in the lobby. "May I speak to your supervisor?"

Eric glared. "I'm in charge here."

"I want to speak to the postmaster."

Eric grabbed up the package. "If you insist, then I guess I'll have to. This isn't Washington, you know! We don't have germ warfare here in Chester!" Eric stomped back behind the obstacle course of partitions making up cubicles to serve as offices.

Once Eric was out of sight, Joshua shook his head at how difficult the clerk had made it. If he had just run the package through the x-ray machine when Joshua first asked, he and the package, assuming it was nothing, would have been on their way back to Tad's office by now.

Joshua crossed to the brick wall next to the counter to study the faces of the FBI's most wanted displayed on the bulletin board. There was a separate list with the pictures of those identified to be the leaders of the Al Qaida terrorist network that had changed the lives of the Thornton family and many of his closest friends. He was refreshing his memory of their faces when all hell broke lose.

The explosion ripped through the partitions and postal packages in the bomb's path from the back, over the counter, and out the plate glass windows at the front of the post office looking out onto Carolina Avenue.

CHAPTER 21

▼

Instinctively, Joshua dropped to the floor behind the cover of the brick wall next to the counter and covered his head.

After the single shuddering blast faded to a thundering quiet, Joshua raised his head from where he was sheltering it under his arms to see bits of charred mail and wrapping paper floating down from the ceiling like a black snowfall. The smell of burnt flesh assaulted his nostrils.

Joshua did not entertain the thought that the burnt flesh he smelled could have been his own. His rushing adrenaline overtook any feeling of pain from the bits of brick and splintered wood that tore through the back shoulder of his sports jacket from the force of the explosion.

"Eric!"

Remembering the obstinate postal clerk, Joshua hurdled what was left of the counter and maneuvered the obstacle course of ruins that had once been packages, letters, and mail bags to the back of the post office.

Sirens announced the arrival of the fire truck from less than a block away. Calls from potential rescuers drifted in from the street.

"Is anybody in there?" a male voice yelled.

"Call an ambulance!" Joshua called back as he turned his attention to a pile of partitions, stacked one on top of another like a fallen house of cards. "Eric! Are you okay?" Joshua dug through partitions, wires, and twisted metal in search of the clerk.

At the front of the post office, the volunteer fire rescuers worked their way through the rubble. "Where are you?" one called out.

"Back here!" Joshua shouted over his shoulder after he reached the bottom of the pile.

Just as the rescuer reached him, Joshua pulled back the last partition to reveal his former classmate.

The volunteer fire worker looked over Joshua's shoulder at the disfigured body of the postal clerk. Overcome with nausea at the sight, he turned away.

"Is there anyone else here?" the firefighter's voice choked. Such gruesome deaths didn't occur in Chester.

"No." Joshua tossed the partition aside.

*   *   *   *

The Thornton children raced to the scene of the explosion as soon as they heard from Ken Howard, who heard from a friend whose father was a volunteer fire fighter, that the post office had been blown up and their father was seen going inside just moments before the blast.

The children's first thoughts turned to not long before when the father of one of their friends was killed while working at the Pentagon. His body was found still sitting behind his desk. He never stood a chance. Now, they wondered if the war had invaded the sanctuary of their obscure little hometown.

After discovering that their father was alive, the Thornton children didn't mind cooling their heels in Tad's waiting room.

The lack of pain convinced Joshua that he was uninjured. Therefore, he objected to Tad's examination, even while the doctor and nurse cleansed the soot from his body.

Tad chose not to tell his cousin how much agony he would suffer once his adrenaline subsided.

"If Eric had just x-rayed the package like I told him to," Joshua said for the tenth time since Tad found him at the burnt-out shell that had once been Chester's post office.

"Eric wasn't the smartest critter to come off the ark." Tad helped him to remove his sports coat.

Still unaware of his injuries, Joshua groaned, "Eric didn't deserve to die like that. No one deserves to die like that." He hoped Tad and Stella wouldn't notice how his fingers trembled as he fumbled with the buttons on his shirt in an effort to unbutton it.

Wordlessly, Tad waved Joshua's hands from the front of his shirt and went to work on the buttons himself. "Eric wasn't a bad person. He just had problems."

The patient observed his shredded sports coat tossed on the counter and grimaced.

A small smile crossed the doctor's face when he saw the pain seeping in as the adrenaline faded. After tossing the shirt on top of the sports coat, Tad took a syringe out of a drawer, a vial out of the medicine cabinet, and filled the syringe.

"Josh! Josh!"

The examination room door banged open.

Her eyes wide, Jan rushed in. When she saw Joshua, she threw her arms around him in an attempt at a hug. "Madge told me she saw you go into the post office just a few minutes before the explosion! When I heard someone was killed, I thought it was you!"

Joshua almost fell off the table when a sharp pain suddenly shot through his arm and across his shoulders that made him sit up straight.

Tad injected him in his bicep.

Joshua shrieked and glared at his cousin. "You're not very good at that."

Tad removed the syringe and disposed of it. "I know. That's why I never did needles when I was using." The doctor directed Joshua to lie down on his stomach while the doctor went to work on his wounds.

Jan took a seat on the stool at the patient's head. With Joshua and his injuries being the center of attention, no one noticed her turn on the microcassette recorder in her purse. "What caused the explosion? Was it terrorists? Was it an old enemy from when you were in the Navy?"

"It was a mail bomb sent to Tad. I took it to the post office to have Eric Connally x-ray it, but I guess he chose to open it."

"So it was Eric Connally who…" Jan couldn't say the word. "Poor Eric. That guy never could get a break."

"If you ask me," Stella said, "he didn't know how to get a break."

"Don't speak ill of the dead," the doctor ordered his nurse before telling his patient, "You're in luck, Josh. You won't need any stitches. Looks like the explosion just grazed you."

Joshua told them, "I was behind the brick wall looking at the 'Most Wanted' poster when it happened."

"What luck," Jan breathed.

Tad continued examining Joshua's injuries, "You have quite a few splinters and minor cuts, but nothing major, nothing that will require stitches. You're going to feel some discomfort while I disinfect and bandage them. After I'm through cleaning you up, you can go get some sleep."

Tad directed Stella over Joshua's back, "Go tell Josh's kids to pack a bag for him. He's staying up at my place tonight."

Inside Joshua's head, Tad's words sound like tennis balls bouncing off padded walls. "I can go home," he objected with the strength he had left.

Tad continued working on his shoulder. "Not with your backache. You need a good night's sleep. Murphy and J.J. can keep an eye on the others for one night."

"Remember when Eric was arrested for vandalizing the post office?" Jan was asking Tad.

"He vandalized the post office?" Joshua lifted his head from where he had it resting in the crook of his arm. "Sounds like something he'd do."

"Lucky thing he didn't shoot up the place," Tad chuckled. "If Eric ever got his hands on a gun, he'd probably shoot himself in the foot."

"Let's not speak ill of the dead," Jan reminded him.

"When did he vandalize the post office?" Joshua winced when Tad removed a piece of shrapnel from his shoulder.

Jan spoke across Joshua's head to Tad. "When was that? It was a long time ago."

"It was around the millennium. I remember because it was the same week Doc Wilson had that stroke, and I was running around like a chicken with his head chopped off covering for him. The man was like a hundred and he still kept a full calendar. Here I was covering his patients and mine." Tad held a hunk of cotton soaked with antiseptic up in mid air. "That was the same week that the court-house was robbed."

Joshua struggled to stay awake while he listened to Jan and Tad talk between themselves.

"The crime editor at the paper was convinced those two break-ins were connected," Jan was saying.

"Nah!" Tad disagreed. "Computer equipment was stolen from the courthouse. All that was taken from the post office was a bunch of mail. There was no vandalism at the courthouse. All types of stuff at the post office were broken and graffiti was spray painted on the walls. Eric trashed the post office because he was mad about being passed over for promotion."

"A jury said he didn't do it."

"Who defended him?" Joshua's tongue felt like cotton.

"Wally," Tad answered. "That was the last case he defended before he ran for prosecuting attorney."

"Wally showed that there was a connection," Jan told them. "Both break-ins had the same M.O. Whoever did it knew his way around the security system."

"Which Eric, working at the post office, knew about," Tad interjected.

"Why would Eric break into courthouse?"

"This all happened four years ago?" Joshua yawned.

"About then." Tad gently patted Joshua on the shoulder that escaped the explosion. "I'm done. You can sit up and I'll get your kids to help you upstairs."

Even while Jan was helping Joshua to sit up, the patient couldn't decipher the revelation loitering at the edge of his mind. "Four years ago. What happened four years ago?"

Jan was unable to understand Joshua, whose drugged speech was slurred beyond understanding. "What did you say?"

Joshua repeated his question, but Jan still failed to understand him.

*   *   *   *

"Four years ago. What happened four years ago?"

As he drifted off to sleep, Joshua was aware of Tad setting a pitcher of ice water on the nightstand next to the bed. He rubbed his face into the pillow, but was so numb that he couldn't feel the cotton material against his skin. The scent of pizza drifted in from the kitchen in the small apartment. Dog slept on the floor next to the bed.

"What happened four years ago?" Joshua asked himself over and over again.

Unaware of the question weighing on his cousin's drugged mind, Tad turned off the light and tiptoed out of the room. He shut the door, and all seemed quiet, quieter than the father of five had experienced since he became a parent.

Joshua felt the bed shake, and the distinct feeling of four paws circling next to him until Dog laid down and groaned, as if to say that a dog's work is never done.

Outside his door, Joshua could hear Tad's voice. He wondered to whom his cousin was speaking, until he realized that it was a one-way conversation. Tad was on the phone.

"Honey," Joshua heard Tad say in a soothing tone, "you don't have to worry. The DNA didn't indicate any relationship between whoever the hair belonged to and your mother. That alone eliminates you as a suspect. The sheriff just needs to get your statement and verify your whereabouts at the time of the murder for the record."

Tad was warning Maggie about Sawyer's impending phone call.

Joshua groaned and sank deeper under the covers. He couldn't deny that he would do the same thing if it were one of his kids connected to the murder.

"Four years ago."

Joshua went to sleep asking himself what was the significance of four years ago. Tad had said it. Joshua heard him say it, but the drugs prevented his brain from making the connection.

*   *   *   *

Joshua Thornton was in high school again. It was the big game against Weirton High School and Oak Glen's rival was winning. Oak Glen had the ball with thirty seconds to go in the fourth quarter.

On the field, quarterback Joshua Thornton called the play. The ball was snapped. He faked a hand-off to Reggie Fields. When Weirton went after Fields, Joshua dropped back to send a long pass to Mickey Brewer.

"Josh! Look out for Norton!" Cheerleader Beth Davis called from the sidelines.

Somehow, Joshua heard her over the roar of the crowd.

Chad Norton was a Weirton senior who had a grudge against Oak Glen's quarterback ever since Beth dumped him for Joshua.

Out of the corner of his eye, Joshua saw the freight train racing towards him with hatred for its fuel, but he didn't have time to waste on Norton. Joshua let the ball go a split second before Norton knocked both of the quarterback's feet out from under him. Joshua flew into the air, turning head over heels, before landing on his head.

Everyone in the stadium felt the impact.

Oak Glen's star quarterback was unconscious when Brewer caught the pass, made the touchdown, and won the game.

Dr. Russell Wilson was standing over him when Joshua woke up in the hospital. "How are you feeling, Joshua?"

"I've had finer moments," Joshua muttered as it all came back to him: the faked hand-off, Norton's charging bulk, the long pass, and his flight through the air. "Am I going to live?"

"You got a concussion," the doctor reported. "We need to keep you here a couple of days to keep an eye on you."

"But I have to go to Charleston with the debating team in the morning. It's the state championship. Then, student council is meeting on Tuesday, and I have to prepare a presentation to the school board—"

"You take after your mother," Dr. Wilson stated as if it was an accepted fact. He was checking his patient's eyes with a penlight while he asked casually, "Tell me, Josh, have you ever experienced joy?"

Not knowing what to say, Joshua looked up at the doctor's kindly old face. Then, he heard a ringing in his ears. Joshua looked around the examination room for the source of the ringing.

It was the phone.

By the time Joshua found it in the dark by slapping the nightstand, Tad had run into the bedroom while ordering him not to answer the phone.

He was too late.

Joshua knocked over the pitcher and spilt water onto the floor.

Tad cursed the caller.

Joshua looked at his cousin's silhouette and blinked.

"I've got it." Joshua put the phone to his numb ear.

Tad rushed into the bathroom to get a towel to mop up the spill.

"Joshua? Joshua Thornton?" Joshua heard a voice inquire across the phone line.

Joshua felt like he was drifting on a soft fluffy cloud. "Who is this?" His mind was so muddled that he couldn't determine if the voice was man or woman.

Tad came back from the bathroom with towels. "Who is that?" He squatted to mop up the water.

"This is Amber," the voice said.

Tad sat up. "Josh, hang up and go to sleep."

"Amber?" Joshua muttered.

"Josh, are you still awake?" Before his patient could stop him, Tad grabbed the phone from out of his hand. "Who is this?" he asked into the receiver.

"Amber," Joshua reached for the phone but missed.

Tad hung up the phone.

"What did she say?" Joshua asked.

Tad shrugged. "Whoever it was, they hung up. Probably just a crank. Go back to sleep."

*   *   *   *

"Did you send a package to Dr. Tad MacMillan yesterday?" Sheriff Curtis Sawyer asked prosecutor Wallace Rawlings.

In contrast to his unimposing office in New Cumberland School's basement, Wallace had the same smug expression on his face that his father had when he met with his underlings.

The genetics between father and son was obvious.

"Why do you ask?" Wallace responded in an offended tone.

The sheriff drawled, "Well, it's a natural question." He slumped back in the chair across from the prosecutor. He fingered his police whistle. "You just offered me five thousand dollars to kill Josh Thornton and Doc MacMillan. This afternoon, a postal worker was blown up by a package mailed to MacMillan from New Cumberland yesterday. Obviously, you want MacMillan killed. Five thousand dollars' worth. It makes me wonder if maybe you already tried, but failed. Either that, or you have some competition out there?"

"It would be stupid for me to offer you five thousand dollars to do what I could do for free."

"And if the sheriff did it for you, you can be assured of getting away with it. Is that the arrangement you had with Sheriff Delaney?"

"Sheriff Delaney didn't work for me," Wallace clarified, "he worked for my father. This arrangement is between you and me." He shifted back to the subject of their meeting. "I want this done as soon as possible."

"A good killing takes time."

"How much time?"

"Why the hurry?"

"Thornton and MacMillan are troublemakers."

"Is this about your daughter and Beth Davis? Did you kill them?"

"I won't dignify that with an answer."

"If I'm going to do this, I have a right to know why I'm doing it. You have to admit Doc MacMillan collected substantial evidence against your daughter for stalking him. I warned you to keep Vicki away from him, but you did nothing. I wondered for a long time if you wanted her to kill him. This job offer proves I was right."

"No one could control that girl," Wallace said. "She was an embarrassment from the moment she was born."

"Well, she won't be embarrassing you anymore." Sheriff Sawyer eyed Wallace through narrow slits in his eyes. "It was your gun that killed Beth, and that was your trench coat Thornton found in the closet."

"Are you going to do this or aren't you?"

"If only MacMillan and Thornton hadn't happened on the scene and ruined the murder-suicide set up, then you and your family would not be under a microscope."

"Sheriff Delaney didn't ask so many questions," Wallace warned him.

"So you want them dead because they are troublemakers?"

Wallace leaned forward and spat out with conviction, "MacMillan takes any woman he wants, defiles another man's bed-He doesn't deserve to live."

Sheriff Curtis Sawyer shifted uncomfortably at the sight of genuine hatred in Wallace's face. He had seen hatred like that before. It was lethal.

Wallace demanded to know, "When can I count on this being done?"

"I need half up front. The rest when I finish the job. I'll have to have time to do it right. If I'm sloppy, like whoever killed Vicki and Beth, then you will find yourself having more trouble than eliminating it."

CHAPTER 22

▼

"Hello, Daddy. It's me again. Do you really think you can get rid of me? I think not. Your sins never go away. They stay with you forever—even in death."

Joshua could actually hear Vicki spitting out the words from the page on which her e-mail was printed.

"Hey, cuz! How are you feeling this morning?"

When Admiral refused to budge from his spot in the middle of the study floor, Tad stepped over the huge dog while telling him, "That's okay. Don't get up on my behalf."

He set his medical bag on the desk, opened it, and returned his attention to Joshua. "How late did you sleep? You were still snoring away when I left at eight."

"I don't snore," Tad's patient asserted. "I got up at nine when the kids couldn't take it any longer and came to wake me up to make sure I was still alive."

Joshua went on to read the next e-mail. "Are you really afraid of little old me? You don't know what fear is. I'm going to teach you fear, Daddy. Are you afraid, Daddy? You should be. Be very afraid."

Tad read the e-mail over Joshua's shoulder. "Sick girl." The doctor gestured for his cousin to sit sideways in the chair behind his desk. "I need to change your bandages."

Joshua turned to the next page, stood up, took off his shirt, and sat on the corner of his desk to permit the doctor to examine his shoulder.

"Hello, Daddy," the e-mail greeted the doctor. "It's me again. Why weren't you home last night, you bastard? Out screwing another one of your whores?"

The e-mail went on to inquire in detail about Tad's sexual practices. It concluded with a sexual innuendo about castrating him.

"Where are the kids?" Tad asked.

"They went out with some friends."

"They have friends already?"

"There was a whole van load of them. The boy across the street is showing them around. That package was mailed yesterday." Joshua corrected himself after checking his desk calendar, "The day before yesterday. I think it's safe to assume Vicki didn't mail it."

"I realize that."

The lawyer continued, "I re-read all these e-mails and noticed something. While in each one she addresses you as Daddy, Vicki doesn't ask you for anything or say anything about being your daughter. All she does is threaten you and assault your sinful ways."

"That's enough. No one likes to be threatened."

"Who else was threatening you?"

"Who else would be threatening me?" Tad picked up one of the e-mails and pointed to the address on the from-line. "See, it says right here that the e-mail came from Vicki Rawlings."

Joshua shook his head. "My kids send e-mails all over the country to their friends. As far as the server knows, the mail comes from Joshua Thornton, because they use my service, my user ID, and my password. Any one of those kids can go to any network anywhere, log onto our server using my ID and password, and send an e-mail, and it will have my name on it."

Tad realized what Joshua was saying. "So the person who sent these knew Vicki's ID and password, and sent them to make me think Vicki was threatening me."

Overwhelmed, Tad gave out a small gasp and lowered himself into the chair across from where Joshua sat on the corner of his desk. "So you are saying that someone else was framing Vicki for stalking me?" He answered his own question. "No, you're wrong. Vicki broke into my apartment. Sheriff Sawyer caught her red-handed. She stole drugs from my office."

Joshua wondered, "Did Vicki ever threaten you in person? Face-to-face?"

"She pulled that gun in the church."

Joshua dismissed Tad's reminder with a shake of his head. "She was higher than a kite when she did that. I'm not saying that she wasn't fixated on you. I just wonder if someone else was using her obsession. Where there any other incidents involving Vicki?"

Tad thought a moment before asking, "What makes you so certain that Vicki didn't send all these e-mails?"

"Satan considers sin a good thing. Yet, in these e-mails, Vicki refers to your lust and says how she is going to stop your sinning. Why stop lust if it is good?" Seeing that the doctor was finished redressing his wounds, Joshua put his shirt back on. "Can I have some of your DNA?"

If Tad was startled by the question, he covered it well. He grinned knowingly as he asked, "Why do you want my DNA?"

Joshua was relieved by Tad's lack of offense to his request. "Right now, I only have your word for it that Vicki and Maggie are not your biological daughters." He held up a handful of the e-mails. "Clearly, someone was of the belief that you were Vicki's father."

"Do you think I wanted to tell you that Maggie was not mine?"

"You yourself have told me that alcoholics are the world's best liars." Joshua softened. "Tad, I'd trust you with my life. But I'm not going to bust my butt to find Beth's killer only to have him or her get off because some defense attorney uses your reputation and known relationship with Cindy to convince a jury that there is reasonable doubt about you being Vicki's and Maggie's father, and me using my position to cover it up." He sighed. "Anyone who knows the two of us could testify that there is just too much history between us for me to be objective when it comes to you."

Joshua held his breath while he watched Tad consider his request.

Tad answered the prosecutor's request by reaching into his medical bag. He removed a cotton swab and an evidence envelope. Tad then licked the swab before dropping it into the envelope, sealing it, and handing it to Joshua. "I don't want whoever killed Maggie's mom to go free, either."

Reluctantly, Joshua took the envelope containing the swab. "Even so, it would be better if you go to the state lab and have one of the state forensics techs take it. I don't want even the appearance of a cover-up."

"Maggie has an alibi."

"I don't doubt that. Sawyer called her this morning. Maggie was ready with five names of people she was with during the day of the murders, including a bookstore manager who interviewed her for a job at three o'clock. There's no way she could have been here to commit either murder and gotten back to Penn State for the job interview before meeting three friends at the campus pub for dinner. So Maggie is cleared."

Admiral woke up from his nap and stretched before plopping back down on the carpet between the two men.

Joshua closely watched Tad's face for his reaction to his next question. "Assuming that you are telling the truth, there has to be another woman out there who is Vicki's half sister, who was on the scene when Beth was killed. Who could that be?"

Tad's lack of a response answered Joshua's question, which he repeated. "Who?"

"I guess it could be possible," Tad muttered.

"Anything is possible at this point."

"I thought about it last night, at three o'clock in the morning, while I was on the couch listening to you snore."

"I don't snore." Joshua prodded him, "You thought about what?"

Tad reached down to the floor to scratch the sleeping dog's ears. At Tad's touch, Admiral woke up with a dreamy expression.

"I was thinking about those DNA tests. The perp is Vicki's half sister, but is not related to Beth. There was only one suspect I could think of. Alexis Hitchcock."

Joshua squinted at the new name to add to his list of suspects. "Who is Alexis Hitchcock?"

"Wally's illegitimate daughter." Tad chuckled. "This one he knows about."

Joshua grinned with anticipation. "Tell me more."

Tad settled back in his seat. "When Cindy died, I was out for blood. It was either that or go on a binge. I decided to be constructive with my anger. So, I went in search of evidence to prove Wally had a motive for killing Cindy."

Joshua asked in a low voice, "And what did you find?"

"Nothing for a hell of a long time," Tad answered. "Then, one night, about five years ago, I ran into a guy who told me about a retired topless dancer named Trixie in Steubenville. She lived in a house in the 'burbs with her daughter and granddaughter. They all attended Wally's church, and they were all living on the church payroll."

"Child support?" Joshua asked.

"Some might call it that. Others might call it extortion or white slavery. I made it a point to get close to Monica, Alexis's mother." Tad paused to swallow. "We became very close." He averted his eyes to look pass Joshua and out the window behind him to the rolling back yard.

Joshua could see how close Tad had become to Monica Hitchcock.

"Wally scared her," Tad said softly.

"Why?"

"Monica was fifteen years old when Wally got her pregnant. Trixie met Wally while working at a strip joint and found out that he liked them real young. So, she introduced him to her pretty daughter and when he got her pregnant, Trixie thought they had hit the jackpot. Wally agreed to put the whole family up. I got the impression he cared for Monica as much as he could care for anyone. All three of them went to Reverend Rawlings's church every weekend and sat in the second row, right behind Wally. He supported them financially, while he was married to Cindy, and came by regularly, with the agreement that Monica would…" Tad searched for words to describe the situation delicately, "meet his needs as he saw fit."

He swallowed before he diagnosed the situation. "Monica was his personal prostitute and her mother was her pimp." Tad went on, "We got close enough that she called me after each one of his visits. He humiliated and degraded her. He wouldn't let her forget that he was paying for her and if she refused, that they would all end up on the streets. She was so young when her mother set her up with Wally, that she didn't know what a truly loving relationship with a man was like."

Joshua dreaded the answer to the question he asked, "Did you show her how loving a man could be?"

Tad's eyes met his. "Monica was a sweet kid. Through me, she came to realize that she was deserving of respect and her mother hated me for it."

Joshua plopped down into the chair behind his desk with a groan. He covered his face with his hands. "Do you know what you've done?"

Tad declared, "I never said I was going to give up everything."

Ticking off on his fingers, Joshua told him, "First, you made Cindy fall in love with you while she was engaged to marry Wally, to the point that she confesses to him on their wedding night that she is in love with you. Then, you hunt down his mistress, and you bed her. No wonder Wally hates you!"

Tad defended himself. "That wasn't my intention. I wanted to find out who killed Cindy. Monica said that Wally told her that he loved her. He could have killed Cindy so that he would be free to marry her."

"But he didn't!" Joshua pointed out, "He didn't marry Monica. Cindy died nine years ago, and you said you found Monica five years ago, and they weren't married." He laughed sarcastically. "Like Wally would have an open relationship with a whore, let alone marry her? Even if Wally wanted to marry her, the reverend would never permit it." He asked with a moan, "What happened to them?"

"One night, I was on duty at the ER. Things were really wild in my life back then. Doc Wilson had just died and I took over most of his patients. Things were so bad, I was mostly running on autopilot. Monica called me and she sounded scared. She said she needed to see me, but she wouldn't explain what happened. I had four hours left on duty. We agreed to meet at a bar in Steubenville at one o'clock in the morning. When she didn't show, I went looking for her, but she wasn't home and I couldn't find her."

"Any sign of foul play?"

Tad squinted angrily. "No real evidence. There was no sign of a struggle in the house. No one saw anything suspicious."

"So," Joshua observed slowly, "as far as anyone can prove, they left voluntarily."

"As far as the authorities are concerned, they are dead."

"Dead?"

Tad snarled at the memory. "I reported them missing to the Steubenville police. This police officer—I even remember his name—some cocky son of a bitch named Officer Scott Collins—acted like I was just a jilted boyfriend and went through the motions of reporting a missing person."

"He had to investigate. You filed a missing persons report. He had no choice but to investigate."

"He only did what he had to until that DC-10 plowed into the hillside after taking off from the Pittsburgh airport the next day. As soon as it hit the news about this grandmother, mother, and girl being missing, this witness calls up Collins and says that she dropped all three of them off at the Pittsburgh airport to take that same flight to Chicago."

Joshua chuckled. "Don't tell me that you think Wally Rawlings blew up an airplane with close to one hundred people on it."

"No, but I don't believe they were on that flight. I was looking for them at least twelve hours before that. Collins swears that he checked it out and they were on that plane and killed." Tad added with conviction, "I think they were all dead long before the crash."

"Why would Wally kill them?"

"Just weeks later, Wally announced his running for prosecuting attorney. If it came out that he had an illegitimate daughter and a mistress while he was married to Cindy, the valley's version of Princess Di, he never would have been elected. Last night, it occurred to me that maybe, somehow, Alexis escaped and that maybe, she saw what happened to her mother and grandmother and came back to avenge them."

Tad waited for Joshua to deliver his verdict of the doctor's theory. It was a long wait as Joshua stared at the wall behind his cousin. Tad had decided that

Joshua concluded it was all hogwash, before he heard him ask, "How old would Alexis be now?"

"She was twelve when she disappeared. She'd be seventeen or eighteen now."

"How old do you think Amber is?"

Tad shrugged. "It's hard to tell with all the make-up she wears in those interviews. Late teens, early to mid-twenties."

"But you don't know who Amber's family is."

Tad smiled. "And I know everyone."

Joshua chuckled. "I wonder who Amber's daddy is."

The two men were silent as each one became absorbed in his own thoughts about the murders.

Admiral sat up and put his head between Tad's knees in order to assist the doctor in the scratching of his ears. The dog was so large that he had to stoop down in order to rest his head in the man's lap.

Tad didn't seem to mind, or notice, that the dog's cold wet nose was pressed against his crotch. Lost in his thoughts about Monica and her young daughter, he scratched the dog's ears with more vigor.

Joshua interrupted the silence with a question. "Who knew about you and Cindy?"

"The whole valley." Tad rolled his eyes. "It wasn't exactly a state secret that I loved her."

"Did you tell anyone about you and Monica?"

Tad shook his head. "I'm not stupid. Wally would have killed me if he found out about that."

Joshua's eyes met Tad's. "How long was it after the Hitchcocks disappeared that the e-mails started coming?"

Tad looked away. "I don't remember exactly, but it was not long."

Joshua said thoughtfully, "Cindy died nine years ago. Why?"

"Because Wally killed her, and then when he thought they were going to kill his election chances he made his mistress and her family disappear."

"But what was his motive for killing Cindy? He had the money. She would never defy him, even for a platonic relationship with the man she loved. I doubt if she stood in the way of his little affair. He certainly didn't kill Cindy so he could marry Monica because five years later he still hadn't married her."

Tad shrugged. "Then you got me as to why he killed Cindy. I just don't have any doubt but that he did it."

Joshua paced while he worked out the puzzle in his mind. "Then, suddenly, out of the blue, four years ago, Vicki gets it in her head that you are her father. And that is in the same time period that this Alexis and her family disappeared."

"That motive is clear. Wally got rid of them so they wouldn't cause him any scandal."

"Don't you think it would have been a bigger scandal if Wally was dragged into a murder investigation?" Joshua was on a roll. "What I want to know is where Vicki got the idea about you being her father. Her whole life, no one saw you and Cindy together. You never even speak to her mother, but Vicki got it in her head that you are her father right after her half sister disappears. Where did she get that idea?"

"Someone told her that."

"Who would gain anything by Cindy's murder, or Vicki killing you out of an insane sense of vengeance?" Joshua answered, "Someone who was insanely jealous of you and Cindy."

"You're making it sound like Cindy and I had an affair."

"You did." Joshua tapped his chest. "It was an affair of the heart. You still loved her and she loved you. Damn! She confessed it to her husband on their wedding night. Wally forbade her from seeing you." Joshua gasped as a thought came to his mind. "When did you stop drinking?"

"You know the answer to that. You were the one who dragged me, kicking and screaming, up to Glenbeigh."

"Eleven years ago," Joshua responded. "Then, a year later, you come back home to set up your practice. You see Cindy around town, and she sees you. Imagine what it must have looked like. When you were a drunk, you were no threat. Wally was the prestigious lawyer from a good family. You were the town drunk. Now, here you are, sober, a doctor establishing himself as a solid respectable man. Then, over the course of a year, Cindy is slowly poisoned to death."

Tad was outraged. "Do you think Wally was poisoning her out of jealousy over my getting sober?"

"It won't be the first time a man killed his wife rather than see her leave him for another man. It was only a matter of time before the two of you would have gotten back together. Wally had to see that."

Overwhelmed by Joshua's theory, Tad sputtered out his next question, "What type of man tells his own daughter that another man is her father?"

"Wally Rawlings." Joshua reminded Tad, "Vicki was a child. We can't forget that. Wally is a lawyer. They teach manipulation in law school. As unbalanced as Vicki was to begin with, it would have been a cinch for Wally to manipulate her into terrorizing you." Joshua shrugged, "Who knows? Maybe he even intended to drive Vicki into killing you when he found out about you and Monica. He was jealous of you and Cindy to begin with. If he found out that his mistress was sleeping with you—" The lawyer chuckled, "So, Wally murders you using his insane daughter as a weapon."

"But Cindy and I weren't seeing each other, and no one knew about me and Monica!"

"But you did see Cindy—in that alley outside your practice the very afternoon before she died."

Tad was speechless as Joshua's summation hit home.

"The only problem is that we can't prove any of it until we find out what that key goes to." Joshua sighed. "If I could only remember what Doc Wilson told me."

"What did he tell you?"

Joshua sat down. "Last night, I had a dream. Do you remember that time Chad Norton tackled me and I landed on my head in that game between Oak Glen and Weirton?"

Tad cringed at the memory. "Do I? Everyone felt that impact."

"When I came to, Doc Wilson—He wanted me to stay in the hospital for two days, but I didn't want to. It was my senior year, and I had all these things I had to do."

"Spoken like a true overachiever," Tad cracked.

"Well, then Doc asked me if I had ever felt joy." Joshua shook his head as the memory failed to come back. "I can't remember the rest."

"You had a severe concussion. You drifted in and out of consciousness for two days."

"It was important. He said something, and it was important."

"Important to what? To prove that Wally killed Cindy, or the key, or—"

"I can't remember." Joshua shook his head sadly.

Tad shrugged just as sadly. "And you probably never will."

*   *   *   *

The Thornton children weren't as interested in seeing the valley as they were in seeing the former Bosley farm. After Tracy told Ken about the dead body her grandparents had discovered on their prom night, he and his friends were equally interested in showing the Thornton children where the Bosley barn used to be.

They were in luck. One of Oak Glen's basketball players lived on what had once been the Bosley farm.

Joshua's children didn't say anything to their father about where they were going on their excursion. They were afraid of his reaction upon hearing that word about the disappearing body had slipped out.

It didn't take long after word got around amongst Chester's younger generation before Ken Howard put together what looked like a tour group made up of his friends to check out the site of Chester's most infamous disappearing body.

Both J.J. and Murphy were taken with Samantha Marlowe, their unofficial tour guide of what was formerly the Bosley farm. A head taller than Tracy, athletically slender with long chestnut hair, olive skin, and big brown eyes, Samantha could pass for a cosmopolitan fashion model.

The Marlowe farm was nestled in a hollow behind Locust Hill Cemetery, a mile off Locust Hill Road, a country road twisting through a small valley.

On their way to the scene of their grandparents' adventure, Samantha recalled her reaction to Ken's tale about the dead body. "I asked my mother about it. She says that she doesn't remember anyone ever finding a body."

"That is something I wouldn't forget." Murphy shot her his most charming smile.

"I can show you where the old barn used to be. It's all overgrown." When they broke through the wooded pasture, Samantha asked Murphy to pull the van over next to the large white barn.

J.J. suppressed a gasp of pleasure when he saw another girl with blond hair jump down from where she sat on the top of the gate leading into the barnyard. A large shaggy dog lay at her feet.

Samantha and her younger sister Dora led the group across the lane to a pasture with a stream lined by a single row of tall oak trees. There was no sign of a building ever being there.

Locust Hill Cemetery loomed down on the teenagers from the top of the hill above them. J.J. looked up at the row upon row of tombstones peering down on them. "Was that cemetery there back in the early sixties?"

Amused, Dora answered in a soft voice, "That cemetery has always been there."

"How can you sleep at night with that right there?" Donny shuddered.

"I never thought about it," Dora replied.

"It's really cool to go walking through it at night," Samantha said in a sinister tone.

J.J. crossed his arms. He looked like his father as he squinted up at the tombstones. "The sheriff called someone he claimed was his deputy, which Dad says was probably a signal to the killer or accomplice to get rid of the body. Now, let's say the accomplice had a half an hour to get the body out of the barn and hide it. Where would you hide a body if you only had thirty minutes to get rid of it?"

Getting his meaning, all the teenagers looked up the hill to the cemetery.

*   *   *   *

"I've come to ask you when Vicki's body will be released," Hal announced before he took the seat Joshua offered him in his still cluttered office.

Hal Poole did not make the trip into the special prosecutor's office just to find out when they would get his niece's body, but to impress on Joshua Thornton the importance of not letting Satan win in his war against the Rawlings family.

Dr. Wilson's old leather chair creaked when Joshua sat behind the scarred up desk. "Dr. MacMillan is waiting for results from toxicology tests and, depending on those results, he may want to do some more work."

"Why would he want to do that?"

"Your niece was murdered, Mr. Poole." Joshua pressed his hands together to make a makeshift steeple with his fingers.

"Bridgette said you suspected us. She says that was why you had us dragged into town to answer your insane questions about our whereabouts at the time of the murders. She told me how you always hated the Rawlings. People who don't know the Lord hate us. That makes them vulnerable to Satan's will."

"This is not a spiritual matter, Mr. Poole. It's a criminal matter," Joshua said. "I am working from experience and statistics, not emotion. It has been proven that in a majority of murder cases, the perpetrator is someone the victim knows. I am also looking for this Amber, who has made herself—"

"Amber is a demon from hell sent to destroy us. The reverend says so. You will never find her!"

"I don't care if she is the devil herself. She knows a lot of details about these murders and has yet to make herself available for questioning."

"Of course she knows a lot of details. Satan knows everything about us. The reverend has preached about how that is one of his weapons he uses to destroy us. He uses our guilt and our lust for sin against us to tear us away from God. If you came to our church and heard the reverend preach you would know that."

Joshua could see by the insanity in Hal's eyes that he was not going to be much help. "Mr. Poole, I'm just trying to do my job. God gave us life, and it is wrong for anyone here on earth to take that life."

"If circumstances were different, I would agree. But this is a war against Satan and his evil, and in every war there are casualties."

"Hal," Joshua said gently, as if he were speaking to a child, "if you know who killed Vicki and Beth, you have to tell me. This is a murder investigation. Their killers have to be brought to justice."

Hal laughed. "You don't have the power to do that. The reverend says that only God can bring Satan to justice. You are a mere mortal man…and a sinful one at that. You have not only ignored the words of God's messenger, but you have naively fallen in with Satan's demons to conspire against Him."

Joshua ignored Hal's accusation and asked the question to which he already knew the answer. "Are you saying Satan killed Vicki and Beth?"

"Satan took Vicki's soul a long time ago!" Hal scoffed. "I saw him take her soul."

"You saw Satan come in and take her soul away?" Joshua was now amused with the course the conversation had taken.

"I didn't know what had happened. The reverend had to tell me. After he told me how she had been taken prisoner in our war against Satan, and how Satan defiled her body while brainwashing her to go to work for him, then I understood. Oh, how she must have fought him! He took her soul from us and devoured it so that there would be no getting it back. Then, when he was through, our Vicki was gone from us forever!"

Hal looked at Joshua with wide eyes. "Mr. Thornton, that body that was found in that trailer was not Vicki Rawlings. She was one of Satan's demons sent to destroy all that is good and pure. You can't punish one of God's soldiers for doing His work!"

CHAPTER 23

▼

Bridgette Poole always expected to be first. After all, she was a Rawlings. Unfortunately, Jan Martin's new pharmacist wasn't aware of that.

The store manager was in her office, trying to make sense of her new employee's records, when she heard Bridgette's customary outrage because the druggist had the gall to tell her he would be with her in a moment. Jan rolled her eyes before going out to once again douse the flames.

Dressed in a pair of Capri pants with a matching midriff top, Bridgette pounded the counter and shrieked in a high-pitched voice. "You don't know who you are dealing with! How dare you!"

Bridgette stopped pounding the pharmacy counter when Jan grabbed her hand and shot a forced smile at her. "What seems to be the problem?"

"He is the problem!" Bridgette pointed an accusatory finger at the employee behind the counter. "You need to send your people to a course in customer service."

The pharmacist was equally annoyed. "I told her I'd be right with her."

"Ten minutes ago!"

"That's okay, Ron," Jan sighed. "I'll take care of Mrs. Poole." Ron returned to his duties, and Jan stepped behind the counter. "What can I do for you today, Mrs. Poole?"

Bridgette presented Jan with a slip of paper. "I want all my prescription records sent to this pharmacy in Calcutta."

The news that Bridgette was taking her business elsewhere was the best Jan had heard all summer. "Okay. I'll do that right away."

Bridgette was displeased with Jan's compliance. "I won't be doing business with this store anymore," she announced harshly.

Meanwhile, Jan keyed the information into the computer to forward Bridgette's records to her competitor, for whom the store manager felt great sympathy. "That's completely understandable, Mrs. Poole. I think it is best under the circumstances."

"How could I do business with this place, knowing that you have drug dealers working for you? Everyone knows there is no way Beth could have supplied Vicki with drugs all these years without you knowing it. Now that the police say Beth didn't kill herself, but was murdered to make it look like a murder-suicide, I wonder who could have been the killer. You had a lot to lose if Beth and Vicki told the police who really was behind her drug and cocaine dealing."

Jan handed Bridgette the information to take on to her new drug store. "I'd say it was nice doing business with you, Mrs. Poole, but, being a Christian woman, it is against my principles to lie."

Bridgette snorted, snatched the paper out of Jan's hand, and strutted up the aisle. In her rush to leave, Bridgette didn't notice that it was Tad who she almost knocked over when he held the door open for her to go through before Joshua stepped in.

When Jan saw the two cousins make their way down the aisle to greet her, she smoothed her hair and put the confrontation with Bridgette out of her mind.

"You don't look bad for a man who almost got blown up yesterday," Jan told Joshua, who stepped up to the counter while Tad took a detour down the hardware aisle.

"I'll take that as a compliment." Joshua cocked his head towards the door through which Bridgette had just left. "What did you do to offend Bridgette now?"

"I didn't beg her for her business when she announced that she was taking it to another store on account of my killing her niece because I was afraid she'd tell the police about all my drug dealing."

"She came in here to tell you she wasn't doing business with you anymore?"

Jan snickered. "She could have called in to ask that her records be sent to the other pharmacist. One push of the button, and it would have gone over by computer. She was just looking for a fight, and I didn't give it to her."

"I thought good business was giving your customers what they want," Joshua joked.

"What are you two up to?"

"We're looking for Amber. She called me at Tad's yesterday after the explosion. Unfortunately, I was too drugged to question her before she hung up."

"How did she know you were at Tad's place?" Jan cocked her head.

Tad appeared next to his cousin with his selection of light bulbs and a new mop head. Hearing the question, the doctor answered, "Anyone could have found that out. Tess Bauer came into the office with her news crew to try to interview me while I was treating patients. Someone told her that Josh was upstairs, and she tried to get up there to wake him up and interview him. She backed down when Stella threatened to use her microphone to give her an enema. Then, about a dozen reporters called the office to ask about Josh's condition. Stella had a cow because she had to answer the phone."

Joshua and Jan were laughing along with the doctor about his less than courteous nurse when Ron announced from his workstation that Leo Walker's prescription was ready. "When does the delivery person come in?"

Jan, Joshua, and Tad looked at the young man printing a label for a prescription bottle.

"When did you start making home deliveries?" Tad smirked at Jan.

"I don't."

The fear on Jan's face was transferred to her druggist. "I didn't think you did, but when Mr. Walker called in to have his prescription refilled, he told me to have it delivered to his house. When I said you didn't have home delivery, he said you did it for him because he was housebound."

"That's a lie. I never had his prescriptions delivered."

"Did you tell him the prescription would be delivered?" Joshua interjected his question to Ron, who nodded.

"That should be worth a million-dollar lawsuit," Tad joked.

Before Jan could throttle the pharmacist, Joshua offered to deliver the prescription. "I'd like to take a look at Leo Walker."

"Don't get too close," Tad warned him. "Leo the Litigious gets cranky for the rest of the day if he doesn't sue someone before lunch."

*   *   *   *

Leo Walker's home was a simple white two-story house in Chester's first residential development, built along the river during the baby boom after World War II. The narrow houses were constructed so close together that two grown men had to navigate single file the sidewalks between the homes. In modern times, the homes would have been constructed as townhouses.

Leo called out that the door was open when Joshua rang the doorbell at the top of the stoop from which a wheelchair ramp had been erected.

Joshua and Tad found Leo in the kitchen in the back of the house.

At the tiny kitchen table, Leo Walker noisily sipped soup, spoonful by spoonful, while leaning over the bowl from his seat in his wheelchair. His eyes narrowed to slits when he saw the doctor. "Business so bad, MacMillan, that you gotta make deliveries for Martin?"

Tad scoffed, "Come off it, Walker. You know Jan never did make deliveries. You took advantage of her new pharmacist not knowing that."

Without a word of thanks, Leo snatched the prescription bag from Joshua's hand and peered inside it. "I needed this right away and was in too much pain to go get it. You don't know what it's like."

"I know what real nerve damage and back pain are like," Tad countered.

"You doctors are all alike. You think you know everything. Well, you don't. You can't possibly know what it's like to be in constant pain, without it ever letting up for a second, even one little bit. You don't know that unless you've been there."

While Leo ranted about how much pain he was in and how desperately he needed the painkillers, Joshua observed that he didn't take any of the pills they had delivered to him. The lawyer silently signaled Tad with a cock of his head, which only confirmed what the doctor already knew.

Leo Walker was faking his back injury.

"You'd think that Martin, if she cared any about her customers, would have an ounce of sympathy for how much pain I was in and have these pills delivered. Do you know what it's like to be bound to this wheelchair? It's a major ordeal to just leave the house."

"I can see that," Joshua said sympathetically.

Leo smirked. "Anyone with eyes should be able to see it. Rawlings's lawyer doesn't. He refuses to pay one penny for what that junkie kid did to me."

"Are they willing to settle the case now that Vicki is dead?"

Leo sat up straight in his chair. His eyes were bright with excitement. "Now that she's dead, with all the drugs they found in that trailer of hers, I have more of a case."

"Rawlings's lawyer will move to have that information ruled irrelevant in your civil case."

"She was higher than a kite when she crippled me!" Leo's jaw was set tight.

"What the police found in her trailer a year later has nothing to do with this," Joshua argued.

"She was on drugs. She was a drug dealer!"

"I'm just telling you what a judge might rule. I could be wrong," Joshua back-tracked politely. "We're sorry to disturb you. We'll be going now."

Joshua urged Tad to leave with him.

Leo wheeled his chair to the doorway leading down the tiny hallway into the living room and watched Tad and Joshua cross to the front door.

At the door, Joshua suddenly stopped and turned back to Leo, who was perched in his wheelchair across the room. "Oh, I almost forgot," he removed an envelope from his jacket pocket. "We ran into the postman on the way in, and he gave us your mail to give to you." Joshua studied the envelope. "Looks like a check from your insurance company." He laid it on top of the television by the door. "I'll leave it here for you to get after you finish your lunch. Good day." With a pleasant wave of his hand, Joshua followed Tad out the door, which they shut behind them.

Leo peered at the check like a pot of gold at the end of the rainbow. He leaned over in his chair to watch Joshua and Tad turn at the end of the sidewalk to go back into town. Then, too impatient to go to the trouble of wheeling across the living room, Leo jumped out of the chair and scurried over to seize the envelope.

Leo's smile dropped at the exact moment Joshua opened the door. He and Tad stepped back inside.

"Oh, I'm sorry," Joshua's voice oozed with false sympathy, "that's my electric bill." He retrieved the envelope out of Leo's hands. "Have a nice day, Leo."

Leo was still trying to comprehend what had just happened when Joshua and Tad closed the door behind them as they stepped back outside.

The two men waited until they had stepped down off the stoop onto the side-walk before they burst into gleeful laughter at the success of their con.

Tad observed, "I guess those pills are really potent. They worked without him even opening the bottle."

Joshua shook his head. "He must have hired a real shyster. Why didn't his lawyer tell him not to wear shoes that are scuffed on the bottom if you want to convince a jury that you can't walk? If he can't walk, how did he scuff his shoes?"

"His doctor isn't much better," Tad added, "Rawlings's lawyer is going to want Leo to explain why he doesn't have atrophy after not walking for a year. Even after a few weeks of not walking, the leg muscles start to deteriorate. Leo's legs are way too thick and muscular. Also, his upper body isn't muscular enough for a man who has had to use his arms and chest to do everything."

"I wonder if Vicki Rawlings found proof that he was faking." Joshua stopped on the corner and looked back at Leo's house.

Tad hoped that Joshua wasn't considering returning to Leo's house to question him. Leo Walker was not the type of man to question without his lawyer being in the room. "Do you consider Leo a viable suspect?"

"If Vicki found out about Leo's scam, then that would give him reason to kill her. Since he can walk, then he could have gotten into her trailer to do the job. With her dead, there is no longer any threat from her to his lawsuit."

"Or maybe," Tad theorized, "Vicki found out, but instead of using the evidence to make him drop the suit, she used it to blackmail him into splitting the award from her father with her. That was more her style." He gestured towards the house from which they had just left. "Are we going back?"

"It will be a waste of time. The harder we push him, the more he'll dig in." Joshua scoffed as he crossed the street toward the railroad tracks, "Besides, Walker didn't kill them."

"And you say that because—?" Tad caught up with his cousin.

"Leo Walker's personality doesn't match the murder scene. Whoever did it went to a lot of trouble to create just the right setting for Vicki's body to be found. He drugged her so that he could drive a stake through her heart. The killer was making a statement."

"They kill vampires by driving a wooden stake through the heart."

"Vampires are blood suckers." Joshua mused, "Maybe it was someone Vicki was blackmailing. Or," he stopped and turned thoughtfully to Tad, "it could be a religious thing. We can't forget her family." He continued, "But then, Beth's murder doesn't fit."

Joshua shook his head. "If Vicki was blackmailing Walker, he would have just killed her. He wouldn't have bothered with symbolism. That's not his style. Plus," the prosecutor added, "we can't forget that Vicki's killer was someone she trusted enough to let him give her a shot in the crotch. Vicki wouldn't have let a toad like Walker see her naked, let alone touch her privates. Unless we find out something about Vicki's sexual preferences that we don't already know, we might as well go back to the drawing board."

Tad groaned, "So I guess we're going to have to find Amber."

"Who could also be Alexis," Joshua suggested. "From what you have said, Alexis has an ax to grind with the Rawlings. Enough time has passed for her to come back masquerading as Amber to avenge the harm, imagined or otherwise, they did to her family."

"But where are we going to find Alexis and or Amber?"

"Amber is a party girl. Where do you usually go to find party girls?"

CHAPTER 24

▼

Tad directed Joshua's Corvette to the scenic overlook at the top of a hill over-looking the Ohio River. The lush greenery of the valley stretched out before them. The sun was low and the horizon was red where the hills met the sky.

After Joshua parked the convertible and turned off the engine, Tad sat up on top of his seat's headrest and propped his feet up on the dashboard to admire the landscape.

"So when is—What's his name?—going to get here?" Joshua checked his watch.

"Crazy Horse," Tad answered. "I only just called him an hour ago."

"I hope word doesn't get back to my friends in Washington about my meeting with a couple of drug dealers."

Tad laughed with amusement. "They're not dealers. No dealer in his right mind would have these guys work for him. They'd use it all up before it got to the buyer."

After rolling his eyes, Joshua double-checked the time on the car console.

"What? You got an appointment with the governor?" Tad snapped in a good-natured tone.

"No, I have something more important: Five kids who are basically raising themselves while I'm conducting this investigation. This is not what I bargained for when I gave up active duty."

"Are you complaining?"

"I have a feeling Val is. Get your feet off my dashboard."

Tad dropped back down into the seat. "Face it, Josh. You are not the type of guy to sit around the house in his underwear watching baseball and drinking beer. Val never would have married you if you were."

"There is a middle ground between neglecting your family to chase bad guys around the globe and sitting around in your underwear drinking beer, and I'm having a devil of a time finding it."

Tad gestured towards an old VW van that looked like it didn't belong on the road that rolled up beside the Corvette. "Here they are."

Two men got out of the van. It was impossible to tell by sight that they were of the same generation as Tad. Decades of substance abuse had ravaged their bodies to the point where they looked like old men. Wrinkled, leathery skin hung from their malnourished frames. The sight of their rotted yellow teeth made Joshua's own mouth ache.

Judging by their looks, Joshua wondered if his cousin's old friends were so lost in the drug-filled haze from their youth that they hadn't noticed that the psychedelic era of the sixties was over. They were dressed in baggy, soiled clothes. Their long, unkempt hair was tied up with rubber bands into ragged ponytails. One of them had a bushy, untrimmed beard. The other looked as if he hadn't shaved for days.

They admired the classic sports car as each one came up on either side of the vehicle.

The one with the bushy beard smiled at Tad from Joshua's side of the car. "Doc! Good to see you!" He reached across the car's owner to give Tad a high five, releasing a whiff of body odor into Joshua's face that provoked an involuntary cough from the car's driver. "I about passed out when you called! A blast from the past!" He knelt down and looked over the car. "Nice wheels! You really did join the establishment, didn't you?"

"This is Josh's." Tad nodded to the driver. "Crazy Horse, remember I used to tell you about my little cousin?—Josh, this is Crazy Horse."

"Little?" Crazy Horse shook Josh's hand with a dirt-encrusted palm.

Joshua resisted the temptation to wipe the grime off with his handkerchief.

Crazy Horse introduced his companion as Skeet, who greeted them with a high-pitched, squeaky giggle before he reminded Tad about the reason for their meeting. "You said you had some questions."

"About Amber," Tad told his old friends.

"Amber? Ah, the girl yakking on television to that TV reporter."

"The very same," Joshua said.

"Why do you want her?" Crazy Horse frowned. "To end our party? Like I'd help you, fed!" He turned to leave.

"I'm not a fed."

"You look like a fed."

"Yeah," Skeet agreed. "Only a fed would have wheels like these."

"I told you we should have come on my bike," Tad muttered to Joshua.

"I want to live to see my grandchildren," Joshua snapped back. "Is that so wrong?"

All hell broke loose.

Skeet suddenly shrieked and charged over the hill. Crazy Horse ran for the van, but Tad jumped out of the Corvette and tackled him to the ground.

Joshua went over the hill after Skeet. A scream for help came from underneath the tangled thickets and bushy hair.

"Help! Josh! Stop him!" Joshua recognized Jan's cries.

"I told you he was a fed!" Skeet yelled up at Crazy Horse. "I got me a lady agent right here!"

Joshua pulled Skeet off Jan, whose clothes were torn by a combination of the bushes and Skeet's attack, and helped his friend up the hill to the car. Eying both of them with suspicion, Skeet followed them. Jan examined her camera for damage that possibly occurred in the attack.

Joshua introduced his perspective informants to the spy. "This is Jan Martin, the owner of the drug store in Chester."

"I'm a writer," Jan asserted. "I'm covering Beth Davis's and Vicki Rawlings's murders."

"Jan," Tad demanded to know, "what are you doing here?"

"Josh promised me an exclusive on this story."

"I did no such thing!" the prosecutor objected.

"Yes, you did. The other day."

"I did not say I'd give you an exclusive."

"You didn't say you wouldn't."

While Joshua and Jan were arguing, Crazy Horse shook off Tad and opened the van door to climb in. "I don't have time to waste watching a lovers' quarrel. I got a party to go to. See ya later, Doc."

Tad pulled Crazy Horse out of the van by the arm. "Josh isn't a fed." His assertion took on a pleading tone. "Crazy Horse, you know I'd never set you up."

Memories of old times made Crazy Horse pause to hear his old friend out. "Then what is he?"

"I am the special prosecutor investigating Beth Davis's and Vicki Rawlings's murders. Amber said on the news that she witnessed the murders. We need to talk to her to catch their killers."

"Listen," Tad joined in, "you guys liked Beth."

Skeet laughed. "Yeah, we liked Beth. She was lots of fun."

"Well, Amber says she saw Reverend Rawlings kill Beth."

Crazy Horse squinted at them. "Amber's probably dead by now. Rawlings has had his people looking for her ever since the first time she showed up on television with that reporter."

"I'm surprised she lived long enough to see the murders," Skeet giggled, "let alone make a withdrawal."

"Withdrawal?" Jan asked.

"From the bank," Skeet smiled broadly to expose a mouthful of rotten teeth.

"What bank?" Joshua could see where the conversation was leading. Silently, he kicked himself for only now realizing that no cash was found in the known drug dealer's home after her murder.

"A little bird told me that Vicki picked up a big payment from one of her couriers on her way home from jail. That money is now gone," Crazy Horse said.

Jan's eyes grew wide at the thought of the mysterious witness on the run from the powerful drug lord after stealing his illegally obtained money. "Does Amber have it?"

"Don't know! One thing is certain, the Rawlings ain't got it, and whoever does have it is not long for this world if the reverend catches them with it."

"Do you know where Amber came from?" Tad wanted to know. "Did she ever talk about her family and where they were from?"

"Nah! She just showed up one day." Crazy Horse shrugged and wiped his runny nose on his sleeve.

"Yeah," Skeet agreed.

"At a party? She just showed up one day?" Tad inquired.

Skeet and Crazy Horse nodded.

"How'd she find out where the party was?"

The answer was a unison shrug.

Tad coaxed, "Crazy Horse, you know I'm cool."

"But I don't know about them." Crazy Horse pointed an accusing finger at Joshua and Jan.

"I'll vouch for them," Tad said. "Tell me what you know about Amber."

"I don't know nothing, man!" When Tad gave him a doubtful look, Crazy Horse snorted. "Listen, I'm being straight with you!"

Joshua asked, "When did Amber show up?"

"Does anybody know what time is?" Crazy Horse sang.

In disbelief, Joshua turned to Tad.

Smiling with amusement at the song, the doctor continued the interview. "So Amber shows up. Who brought her to the party?"

"Diana Bauer," Crazy Horse answered Tad.

"Diana Bauer? Tess Bauer's sister? Diana died a couple of years ago. You've known Amber all this time, but you don't know anything about her?"

Not seeing what they found so difficult to understand, both Crazy Horse and Skeet shrugged.

Crazy Horse told them, "What is there to know except that she was cool? They used to party together. Amber started coming around with Di. Then, Di died and Amber stopped coming around. I assumed she got herself clean." He sniffed and wiped his runny nose with the back of his hand. "It was just like when you got clean, Doc. One day, you were there. The next day, you were gone and went respectable on us."

Tad returned to the topic of their discussion. "And then Amber came back?"

"Suddenly, Amber was back. I figured she fell off the wagon. That happens, you know."

"Then she got tight with Vicki?"

"And then," Joshua observed, "Vicki gets killed."

Crazy Horse grinned at the joke he had previously failed to notice. "Ironic, ain't it?"

"Yeah, but she didn't off Vicki," Skeet laughed his high-pitched cackle.

"Why wouldn't she?" Jan wondered.

Skeet responded with another cackle.

Crazy Horse answered, "She and Vicki—man! It was like sparks flying when they got together."

"Yeah," Skeet agreed. "Sparks! Like the Fourth of July."

"What do you mean by sparks?" Jan inquired.

Skeet and Crazy Horse laughed at her innocence. "Sparks! Like in the movies, man!" Skeet shrieked with glee.

"It was love at first sight!" Crazy Horse chuckled. "Seeing those two together was better than any chick porno flick. It was like a live stage show."

Joshua raised an eyebrow at Tad, who displayed no surprise by the revelation.

*   *   *   *

Noting the dates on the tombstones, many of which dated back over a hundred years, the teenagers strolled through the cemetery.

"If they buried the body here over forty years ago, how can we possibly find the guy?" Ken was asking.

"He'd be the one without a tombstone," Donny joked.

Sarah stopped searching. "If the body wasn't put in a grave, then why are we here?"

"There's lots of places in these woods to hide a body that it would never be found," Samantha pitched in.

"But with all the dogs and wild animals, you run the risk of it being dug up," Dora countered. "You'd want to hide it where no animal could get to it and no one would ever find it, at least for a hundred years or so." The girl cocked her head and smiled. "Now, if I was going to hide a body around here, I know where I'd put it."

Samantha snickered, "Dora reads all the gruesome murder mysteries Mom will let her read, without turning into some sick psychopath, which I think has happened."

"Brains and looks. A good combination." J.J. smiled at Dora. "Where would you hide a body?"

Dora pointed to an above-ground crypt next to where they were standing. "There. Look at the date on that crypt."

April 1963.

"Isn't that about the time your grandparents saw that body?" Dora inquired. After they all agreed that the month and year seemed about right, she continued, "And the only reason anyone would look inside would be if they moved the graves."

Samantha scoffed, "It'd take a dozen guys to get the cover off that to see if the body was in there."

Murphy agreed. "If we were caught, we'd be arrested."

"Then we'll never see the light of day again," Tracy stated as a fact their fate if their father found out.

Dora told them, "Like we're going to get caught looking inside there in the middle of the night. This is a tiny cemetery out in the middle of nowhere. If it's not there, we'll seal it back up and no one will ever know."

It sounded dangerous and thrilling.

"Sure," Tracy said with a note of sarcasm. "Where are we going to get a dozen guys to open the crypt under the cover of darkness?"

Samantha grinned slyly. "I know just the guys who can do it."

*   *   *   *

Admiral sat at attention. His eyes were focused on the banana his master was slicing into a bowl filled with ice cream.

"We need to take advantage of this, boy," Joshua told his faithful companion. "It isn't every day we get the house to ourselves."

Joshua ladled several spoonfuls of the hot fudge sauce onto the ice cream, and then licked the remnants left on the spoon.

As a bribe to not beg for the delicacy, Joshua offered Admiral a rawhide chew, which the dog swallowed whole before following his master into the living room.

Joshua had just sat back in his recliner to devour his sundae when the doorbell rang. While muttering a curse, he got up, put the ice cream on the coffee table with an order to Admiral not to touch it, and answered the door.

There, leaning in the doorway, stood Amber. "I heard you were looking for me."

Joshua took in the witness.

Amber's eyes looked older than he had imagined from her television interviews. Before seeing her face-to-face, he thought she was little more than a teenager. Now, even under all the black makeup, Joshua saw that Amber was not a small-town teenager.

The mysterious witness was dressed in black, as she had been on television. Her buzz cut hair was magenta. The tattoo of a black widow spider was just visible on her right shoulder.

Her presence sent a chill, not unlike the one he experienced when he stepped into Vicki Rawlings's bedroom, down his spine.

"Come in." Joshua stepped back and opened the door to let her in.

"Tess said you wanted me."

Amber sauntered into the family home. She draped her long lean body across the end of the sofa and dropped the shoulder adorned by the spider to let the strap of her top drop down her arm to reveal the top of a breast. Even her fingernails, which were as long as daggers, were painted jet black.

"Is that true, Mr. Thornton?" she breathed in a sultry whisper. "Do you want me?"

"From what I hear, I'm not your type." Joshua picked up the sundae and excused himself to put his dessert into the freezer. "Have you lived in Chester your whole life, Amber?" he asked casually.

Amber followed closely behind him to the kitchen. "I'm not from Chester."

"Where are you from then?" When he turned around after closing the freezer door, Joshua was startled to find Amber's body close enough to press against his. Excusing himself for bumping into her, he gently pushed her back.

"No apology necessary," Amber purred up into his face. "To answer your question, I'm from nowhere and everywhere."

"I wanted to ask you some questions about the murders." Joshua extracted her hands from his arms and forced her down into a chair at the kitchen table.

"About what?" Amber licked her black lips like a predator at the sight of a tasty prey.

Joshua fought to remember the subject at hand. Amber frightened him. "About Vicki's murder. I heard that you two were very close."

"I loved Vicki."

"So, you would want to do everything you can to have her killer caught." Strategically placing the table between them, Joshua sat across from her.

"Vicki's dead." The corner of Amber's mouth curled.

"You don't seem unhappy about that."

"When you're dead, you're dead. There's nothing you can do about it. She's having a hell of a good time now."

"I'm sure she is."

Amber missed the sarcasm in Joshua's tone. "Do you believe in evil?"

Joshua did not want to go there. "Let's go back to the night of the murder. You said in your television interview that you were hiding in the closet from the reverend."

"Yes, I was."

"In the master bedroom?"

Amber nodded playfully.

"Was there a trench coat in the closet?"

"Should there have been?"

"You tell me. Was there a trench coat in the closet?"

Amber gazed at him. Her expression was no longer playful, but thoughtful. "Yes," she answered finally.

"What color was it?" Joshua asked her.

Amber continued to gaze at him. The corner of her mouth curled again. "Joshua, when was the last time you were with a real woman?"

"I'm asking the questions."

"Tess told me your wife died. What's it like to go all this time without having sex? Doesn't it make you just about burst wanting to thrust yourself into the soft warm folds of a woman who is wet for you?"

Suddenly, Joshua was aware of pressure on his crotch. "No!" He shot out of the chair, away from Amber's foot that she had pressed against him under the table.

Amber laughed girlishly. "I just wanted to remind you how to have some fun." She pounced on him. Her lips were on his.

Joshua shoved the witness away and grabbed her hands, which were tearing at the zipper of his pants.

"You need me now, Joshua." Amber groped for him. "I'll give it to you like you never had it before."

"No!"

Joshua's eyes met hers. He saw that Amber was not a teenager as she was portrayed in the interviews. She was a woman, a grown, mature woman.

"This interview is over." Joshua shoved her to the back door.

"Stop it!" Amber dropped to the floor, so that Joshua had to drag her to the door. "You can't turn me away! You said you'd protect me!"

"Get out!" Joshua pushed her through the doorway and slammed the screen door.

Amber hurled herself at the screen like a bloodthirsty creature. "How dare you turn me away? No one turns me away! No one!"

Joshua slammed the storm door in her face and locked it.

Amber wailed like an animal. "I'll get you for this, Joshua Thornton! Oh, yes, you'll come for me! You'll need me, and when you do, you'll pay!"

*   *   *   *

"I can feel us getting into trouble." Tracy's objections weren't noted. She was outnumbered twenty-five to one the last she counted.

It was the perfect night for breaking into a grave. The full moon caused eerie shadows to dance in the moonlight in the graveyard. Spooking each other while carrying out their caper, the teenagers shrieked with joy.

Samantha called the football team to remove the top to the crypt in order to look inside for the body Dora claimed would be in there if she was the one to hide it. Sensing a good time, they brought friends with them.

Tracy concluded the group was much too large and noisy to successfully commit a crime, even if it was under the cover of darkness. The guests at the impromptu party were having too good a time to listen to her. She wished she had a way home to escape the trouble she knew with certainty was coming their way.

The teenagers, armed with tire irons, under J.J. and Murphy's direction, went to work at breaking the seal around the lid of the crypt.

"Okay, I think we've got it," the most muscular of the boys declared when the lid gave way slightly.

"Great, Bull!" Dora was armed with a high-powered flashlight. "Now, everyone lift up at once, and then I'll look inside for the body."

All the boys gathered around the heavy granite cover and pressed their fingers underneath. There were so many, they had to squeeze together to make room for all of them to fit around it.

J.J. counted off from one to three, and the team grunted in unison as they hoisted the lid only inches from its resting-place and shifted it off to the side.

Dora pushed her way between J.J. and Bull to shine the flashlight into the dark crevice.

"Do you see anything?" J.J. grunted.

"I can't—" Dora started to say before she screamed. It wasn't a small scream. It was an abrupt, high-pitched utterance that sounded like a small animal nabbed by a predator in the still of the night.

Dora dropped the flashlight into the crypt. When she leapt away from the sight, she bumped into Bull, who lost his footing and fell against the fullback next to him. As a unit, the boys stumbled and dropped the granite slab to the ground.

The slab shattered into three large chunks and a whirling cloud of dust.

"Is now a good time to renew my objections?" Tracy called out to the group.

"Tracy,—" Murphy whirled around from where he sat on the cold hard ground to chastise his sister, but a bright flashlight beam blinded him.

"Everyone stay right where you are! Police!"

*   *   *   *

Joshua checked the time on his watch, and then looked up at his grandmother's old anniversary clock on the mantle. They both read the same time. It was midnight, and he didn't know where his children were.

"Time's up," Joshua announced to Admiral, who was stretched out on the cool slate in front of the fireplace. The dog was snoring so loud that he didn't hear his master.

Joshua had just picked up the phone to call the police when the doorbell rang. When he saw Tad's wicked grin, the worried father knew that his cousin knew the whereabouts of his offspring.

"What have my kids done now?"

CHAPTER 25

▼

The cemetery was lit up like a carnival.

On the back of Tad's motorcycle, Joshua rode up the twisting country road that led to Locust Hill Cemetery to pick up his children and the van. He found a mob of teenagers waiting for their parents behind the yellow police tape marking off the crime scene.

The medical examiner parked his motorcycle behind the morgue's van, at the end of the string of official vehicles woven throughout the graveyard. Tad whipped off his helmet, retrieved his medical examiner's bag out of the travel compartment of his bike, and scurried under the tape to examine the main attraction of the show, the open crypt.

The first voice Joshua heard when he took off his helmet was Donny's call from the mob. "There's Dad! Dad!"

"Dad, we can explain!" Murphy's voice rang out from amongst the group.

Joshua searched the sea of young faces for those of his offspring.

"Dad, wait until you hear what happened!" Sarah yelled over the others.

Donny's defense was simple. "They told me they were taking me to the park!"

"Quiet!" Joshua screamed at the top of his lungs.

Everyone instantly stopped speaking.

"I want everyone with the last name of Thornton to step forward. Now!"

The Thornton children waded through the bodies to carry out his command.

"What have you done?" Joshua asked in a dangerously low voice.

Spokesman J.J. took a deep breath. "Dad, you won't believe it."

"Try me."

"We found the body."

"You what?" Joshua gasped.

"The body Grandma and Grandpa found." Murphy rushed on, "It was Dora's idea to check the above-ground crypt, because it was sealed about the same time they saw the body, and no one would ever look inside there. So we looked and—Guess what! We found a body."

Joshua scoffed with sarcasm, "A body inside a crypt? What a novel idea."

J.J. nodded. "That was where he put it."

"That's what crypts are made for. Burying bodies. Of course, there's a body in there."

"Yeah, Dad," Murphy said, "but since when do they bury bodies on top of coffins?"

For the time being, the news of them finding the missing body overrode any trouble the children were in for their crime.

Joshua squinted through the darkness at the crypt. Now the center of a host of police spotlights, it looked like the center stage of a horror show.

Squatting on the top edge of the crypt, Tad shone a high-powered flashlight into the crevice.

"You kids wait here." Joshua took a couple of steps towards the crime scene, and then stopped to remind them that they were still in trouble. He ordered, "Don't any of you move."

He joined the doctor at the crypt.

"Cool!" Tad exclaimed as he rose to his feet to straddled the find while he focused his camera to photograph the body. Spotlights lit up the inside of the crypt so that he could photograph it for the record.

"Damnedest thing I ever saw," Joshua overheard an older deputy say to another.

Joshua asked the medical examiner as he approached, "What have you got?"

"A dead body." Tad snapped the first in a series of pictures of it.

"Damn!" Joshua breathed when he peered over the edge.

The body lay like a rag doll tossed aside by a careless child. It was sprawled across the top of the casket. The body's hair, which was still attached to his scalp, was short and black. He stared up at Joshua with sightless eyes. The eyeballs had decomposed decades ago. His face still contained all the facial features from his life.

As his flesh hardened into reddish brown leather in the mummification process it pulled his jawbone down to open his mouth into a silent scream. His expression looked like one of horror that seemed befitting his last moments of life, when he saw whatever it was that put the gaping hole in his chest.

It was such an unbelievable sight that Joshua found it impossible to tear his eyes away from the lifeless form. He had to remind himself that it had once been a living breathing man, just like himself.

"Ever seen a real live mummy before?" Tad asked between shots of the body with his camera. He admired the corpse with the enthusiasm of a child. "He's perfect. The conditions must have been perfect for mummification. If he was killed about the time Aunt Claire and Uncle Johnny found him, it was spring and probably warm for the whole season. This crypt was airtight. No humidity got in to cause decomposition. No bugs got in to eat away at his flesh. It was just like the pyramids in Egypt."

After he squeezed his slight frame into the crypt, Tad patted one of the granite walls with latex gloved hands. "This was built when they did things right. Yep, I'm going to have to get me one of these here babies for when I bite the big one."

Joshua found his voice. "Is there any way you are going to be able to tell when he was killed?"

"Shouldn't I be asking that question?"

Joshua started at the sound of Sheriff Curtis Sawyer's voice. He had come up to lean against the crypt next to Joshua.

"Is this going to be a common occurrence with your kids?" the sheriff asked the new resident.

"No, sir," Joshua stated with certainty.

"What interest do you have in when this body expired?" Sheriff Sawyer looked from Joshua to Tad while the two cousins exchanged glances.

Tad proceeded to search the man's suit pockets for identification.

"Just curiosity, sheriff," Joshua responded.

"No wallet or identification," Tad told them, "but I do have something." The medical examiner removed a folded up magazine clipping from the inside breast pocket of the man's suit and held it up to the flashlight beam. Tad slipped the article into an evidence envelope and wrote on the label before handing it to the sheriff.

Joshua read the headline over the sheriff's shoulder. "How interesting," he breathed.

It was an article, dated February 16, 1963, about the dedication of Reverend Orville Rawlings's new church in New Cumberland, West Virginia.

*   *   *   *

Joshua Thornton's children were lined up in straight back chairs against the wall in the hallway outside the sheriff's office, on the ground floor of the courthouse in New Cumberland. Their friends were sent home with their parents. Tad escorted the body to the state police forensics lab in Weirton to be examined by the state medical examiner, who was more adept at handling mummified bodies.

Meanwhile, Joshua Thornton's kids waited.

Their father was inside Sheriff Sawyer's office talking about what they could not be sure, but they guessed it was about them.

Inside the sheriff's office, which rivaled Wallace Rawlings's office in dinginess, Curtis Sawyer read the article found in the body's pocket and a copy of Lulu Jefferson's letter.

"The reason I didn't come to you with this sooner was because," Joshua explained from where he sat before the sheriff, "one, I knew Sheriff Delaney would have made no record of this body being found in April of '63. Two, there was no way to prove they did find a body because it disappeared before anyone else saw it. At the time, Delaney accused them of a false alarm."

"How can you prove that this is the same body your parents and Lulu Jefferson found? They're dead now."

"But Rick Pendleton is still alive," Joshua reminded him.

"I'm sure that body doesn't look anything like it did when Rick Pendleton saw it, even if it was well preserved."

"Circumstantial evidence is strong enough to suggest it was the same. That article is dated only two months before my parents and Lulu Jefferson and Rick Pendleton saw it. Pendleton said that the body had a chest wound. So does this body. This body was found only five hundred yards from where the old Bosley barn used to be, which is where the body in '63 was found. That crypt was sealed in April 1963. How much do you want to bet it was the day after my parents found the body? Generally, proms are on Fridays, and funerals are on Saturdays. The high school should have a record of when their prom was in 1963, and the funeral home should have a record of when that funeral was held. The killer probably hid the body in the barn with the intention of dumping him inside the crypt after the funeral, before it was sealed." Joshua raised an eyebrow. "Do you want me to go on?"

"No." Sheriff Sawyer placed both pieces of paper in a manila folder.

"Do you have any leads on the mail bomb sent to Tad?"

"No, but I will. The feds investigating the blast said that it was a simple bomb. Nothing complicated." Sheriff Sawyer sighed. "Whoever built it very well could have put the thing together by information gathered on the Internet. We're looking at anyone and everyone."

"Wally Rawlings is anyone and everyone."

Sheriff Sawyer smiled knowingly at his intended victim while Joshua explained, "Wally has no experience in the military or with explosives, but he is smart enough that he could build a bomb if he got good enough instructions."

"Why would he want to kill your cousin?"

Joshua refrained from mentioning Tad's affair with Wally's missing mistress. Instead, he answered the question with, "Because Wally's late wife was in love with him. She told Tad the very day she died that she believed Wally was poisoning her."

Sheriff Sawyer squinted, "But Doc Wilson ruled her death as natural causes, and that was a decade ago. Why would Rawlings care now?"

Joshua lost all train of thought at the very mention of Dr. Wilson and Wally Rawlings in the same breath. It suddenly occurred to him what happened four years ago. Now, it made sense.

"Thornton? Are you still on this planet?"

Joshua started. "Can you get me a copy of the police report on the post office break-in and the break-in here at the courthouse? Both occurred in the same week four years ago."

"I probably will have trouble with the post office break-in. We're talking federal territory there. They like to keep things close to the vest. I can get you our file. Can I ask why?"

"I'm working on a theory." Energized to see the pieces coming together in his head, he added, "I also need for you to get me any information you can from missing persons in Steubenville about two women and a girl, last name Hitchcock, who disappeared four years ago. The detective assigned to the case closed it as presumed dead."

"Who the hell are the Hitchcocks and what are you looking for?" the sheriff snorted.

"A source told me that Monica Hitchcock was Wally's mistress and that she had his baby. Then, suddenly, out of the blue, she disappears. A witness stated that they were on that plane to Chicago that crashed in Pittsburgh. I want to know if the Steubenville police have any proof that they were on that flight and are dead."

"I don't recall Wally Rawlings ever being a suspect in any murder or missing person's investigation."

"That isn't the only reason I want to know what the police have on this case." Joshua reminded him, "Did you hear me say that Monica Hitchcock had Wally's baby? Translation, that baby is Vicki's half sister."

The sheriff grinned. "And DNA says that the strand of red hair on the murder weapon came from Vicki's half sister."

"That's why I want proof that Alexis Hitchcock is dead, and, if that is not available, I want to know where she is and what she is doing now."

Sheriff Sawyer smirked and chuckled. "You're good, Thornton." The sheriff stood up and stuck out his chest as a sign of authority. He was through with this discussion. "You continue working on your theories. I'll get you what you want, but I hope you don't mind if I continue working on my own theories."

"You keep right on doing that." Joshua stood up and shook Sheriff Sawyer's hand. "I promise my children will not get in the way any more."

The sheriff warned Joshua, who waited with his hand on the door. "I hope not. I'd hate for them to get hurt. I consider curiosity a virtue. At least, it is in my business. But if it is not harnessed, it can get you into trouble."

"I'm aware of that."

"Maybe you might want to find something else to take their minds off these bodies that seem to keep turning up." Sheriff Sawyer stated in a stern tone. "I understand that you just recently lost your wife. I'd hate for you to lose one or more of your kids, too."

"Don't worry. I'll make sure no harm comes to them."

"I'm not the one who needs to worry."

*   *   *   *

It was as if a gate had been opened when Joshua recalled the significance of four years before. Dr. Wilson literally held the key to everything. Now, Tad MacMillan had that key, but until he found out to what, they would get nowhere.

Dr. Wilson's former patient had the answer. All he had to do was recall the specifics of the conversation he had with his doctor after he regained consciousness in the hospital after that football game.

Joshua's children thought their father's silence all the way home from New Cumberland was due to anger over their criminal act. In reality, he was preoccupied with what Dr. Wilson had told him.

Maybe he could remember it again in his dreams, Joshua prayed before he went to sleep.

It happened again. The football game. The charging Norton just as Joshua threw the long pass, and his sailing head over heels through the air and landing on his head.

"Tell me, Josh, have you ever experienced joy?" Dr. Wilson checked Joshua's eyes with a penlight.

"What are you talking about?"

"If you spend your whole life chasing after brass rings, then in the end you can find yourself with nothing but regrets for not taking the time to enjoy the treasures that God has already blessed you with."

"What treasures are you talking about?"

Dr. Wilson smiled mysteriously. "If you stop to look around you, then you will know what I am talking about." The doctor sighed. "Life is so valuable, but it is also so very fragile. I became a doctor because I value life. It is the most precious thing God has blessed us with. That is why it is the very thing Satan wants to take from us. When the devil offers us all we desire, it is our life that Satan wants in return."

"I thought it was our soul that Satan wanted?" Joshua countered.

Dr. Wilson nodded in agreement. "Without our soul, we are condemned to death. Eternal life is no longer an option."

Joshua shook his head in an effort to remain conscious. He was losing it, but he didn't want to end the conversation before he knew where Dr. Wilson was going. "What are we talking about here?"

"The story is real, Joshua."

"What story?"

"Faust. The man who made a deal with the devil in exchange for his soul. Ever since he made his pact, he has been ruining one life after another."

"Do you know someone like that?"

With a grim expression on his face, Dr. Russell Wilson nodded his head. "Only in Faust's story, the man regretted making his deal. This man has no regrets."

Joshua was fighting to remain conscious. His head spun even more in his confusion. "Why doesn't he have any regrets?"

"Because he is evil."

"Evil?"

"And you are good." Dr. Wilson laid his hand onto Joshua's forehead and eased his head back onto the pillow. His grim expression softened. "Josh, no matter what happens, don't ever lose your faith."

"I have faith." The teenager wondered if Dr. Wilson was going senile before his eyes.

"Good will always win over evil. God won't have it any other way. As long as you have faith in that, then you will win, because you'll always have God on your side."

"Doc, why are we having this conversation?"

Dr. Wilson smiled down at Joshua. "I'm sorry. You need to rest. You need to take some time off from chasing the brass ring. In November, I get away from it all and go stay in my hunting cabin in Raccoon County."

"You don't strike me as the hunting type."

"I don't hunt. I just go up to my cabin and spend a week by myself. I eat too much, drink too much, and sit with my feet up in front of the fire." He leaned in to Joshua and whispered, "Don't tell your cousin Tad that. He'll use that against me next time I tell him he drinks too much."

Dr. Wilson's laughter echoed through Joshua's dream until he woke up before the sun with the smile of realization on his face.

CHAPTER 26

▼

The stone house on Rock Springs Boulevard was quiet the morning after the cemetery incident. Even Admiral sensed that it would not be a good time to disturb Joshua Thornton by asking to go outside once too often.

When Tracy got up at six o'clock to prepare breakfast, her father was already behind his closed study door making one phone call after another. No one was brave enough to disturb him, not even to offer him coffee. The door did not open until well after seven when the children were gathered around the kitchen table for their breakfast of chocolate chip pancakes and bacon.

The children were apologetic when Joshua came in to refill his coffee mug.

"Good morning," the father greeted his children after taking a long thoughtful sip of the fresh coffee before sitting at the head of the table.

Tracy set a plate filled with pancakes and bacon in front of Joshua before taking her own seat on his left.

In his role as spokesman for his siblings, J.J. once again apologized for the previous night. "We thought we were helping."

"Trespassing into a cemetery and breaking into a crypt was helping?" Joshua asked. "I thought we raised you kids better than that."

"Dad, would you have been able to get a warrant to search that crypt if we had told you our suspicions?"

"That was not a suspicion. It was a guess. A wild crazy guess."

"But the body was there," Sarah argued.

"That was dumb luck. The dumbest luck I've ever seen in my whole career." Joshua dismissed any further continuance of the conversation with a wave of his hand. "It doesn't matter any more. Maybe you kids will be lucky and I'll cool off by the time you get back."

"Get back?" Murphy wondered. "Get back from where?"

"You're not sending us to military school, are you?" Donny shrieked.

"No, I'm sending you to the beach."

Joshua's announcement was met with silence.

"The beach?" Donny finally asked. "You mean you're punishing us by making us go on a family vacation?"

"No, I'm staying here. I talked to your Aunt Carol this morning. She and your cousins are staying at the beach house at the Outer Banks this month. You're going to go stay with them."

"Why are you sending us away?" Tracy asked softly.

"Isn't it clear?" Sarah scowled. "He doesn't want us around. We're too much trouble for him."

"When you are out breaking the law, yes," Joshua responded.

"But we just got here," Murphy pointed out, "and we just started making friends."

"Last night, I saw what you and your friends are capable of. Listen, this Sheriff Sawyer is not the type of guy you mess with. You were very lucky I managed to talk him out of locking you all up and putting last night on your records. Some time away from here might make him forget what you did. Plus, a cooling off period would do me some good. Look, I'm not locking all of you in your rooms. That's probably what has happened to your friends. You guys are going to be fishing, windsurfing, and scuba diving. Damn! I wish my grandmother had punished me like I'm punishing you. End of discussion. Go pack. You're leaving in the van tomorrow after church."

*   *   *   *

Jan Martin caught up with Joshua Thornton in the same spot where they had their first fight.

It was on the corner of Rock Springs and Sixth, just outside the Martin home, where the five-year-old girl told the boy from up the block to not step on her hopscotch board or she'd kill him. Being one to never turn away from a challenge, little Joshua Thornton stepped on little Jan Martin's chalk drawn squares and instantly received a bloody nose in her attempt to carry out her threat.

Thirty years later, Joshua stopped at the same corner to let a yellow Volkswagen pass before crossing the street on his way down the street to Tad's apartment.

Through her front window, Jan saw Joshua and literally ran out to confront him with the latest news. "So you found another body, huh?"

Joshua eyed the rolled up newspaper that Jan slapped into her open palm like she was preparing to train a naughty puppy, and realized he was in trouble. "Not me. My kids."

"And you didn't call me!"

"I didn't have the time, or the means, to call you. I didn't know about it until I was out at the cemetery at one o'clock this morning."

"Haven't you ever heard of a cell phone?"

"Yes, but I didn't take it with me."

Jan slapped him on the top of the head with the newspaper. "I thought we were friends."

The newspaper fell to the ground. While taking cover as Jan slapped him with her open palm, Joshua caught a glimpse of the headline. The body in the crypt, the source of Jan's rage, was on the front page.

It was the banner headline that caught the special prosecutor's attention: "Channel 6 Journalist Murdered".

Joshua picked up the newspaper and studied the picture under the headline. The dead reporter was Morgan Lucas, the anchorwoman who interviewed Amber about the murders.

"I'll bet you called Tess Bauer," Jan accused him.

"I called no one." Joshua held up the newspaper for Jan to read. "Did you see this?"

All Jan could see was the broken promise. "Yes!" she shrieked. "What do you think I'm yelling at you about?"

"I mean Morgan Lucas."

"What about her? Is she another one of your tootsies?"

"Hey, I have five kids! When would I have time for any tootsies?" Joshua pointed to the headline. "She was murdered. She was the reporter that interviewed Amber."

While Jan fumed at him, Joshua scanned the article. The popular news anchor was found in her Pittsburgh condo Friday afternoon when she failed to show up for work. She had been stabbed to death in her bedroom.

Jan was disgusted with Joshua's lack of remorse for not calling her. "Some friend!" she fired her final shot at him.

Joshua was startled out of his thoughts. "What did you say?" He folded up the paper to read in detail later, but he was too late. Jan was trotting up the steps to her porch.

"Why should I even care?" Joshua muttered to himself. "For twenty years, we didn't keep in touch. Why should it matter to me that Jan Martin is mad?" But it did matter to him. "Maybe," he thought, "if I had handled things differently, Beth wouldn't have died the way she did."

"I found out what the key goes to!" Joshua yelled to Jan.

Jan stopped on the top step.

"You can be there when we find it. I'll even give you an interview."

Jan turned around. This could be a trick. She squinted at him with eyes that Joshua noticed, for the first time in their whole lives, were both the shape and color of almonds.

"Can I interview Tad, too? It is Doctor Wilson's autopsy report. Tad is the medical examiner now. If the story is to be complete—Two lovers, who, due to circumstances beyond their control, are never able to be together. Then, years after her death, the boy avenges his true love's murder."

"Tad will let you interview him if I ask him to." Joshua had a sudden thought. "You haven't missed out completely on this story. That body in the cemetery was perfectly preserved. You can interview Tad for a feature about it, and why the body didn't decompose. That is an interesting story in itself."

Jan cocked her head while considering Joshua's suggestion.

Joshua offered her his hand. "Come on. I was on my way there now."

"Let me get my recorder." Jan rushed inside. She didn't see Joshua cross his fingers that Tad would be agreeable to keep the promise he made for him.

$$* \quad * \quad * \quad *$$

"It's all there."

Despite Wallace Rawlings's assurance, Sheriff Curtis Sawyer counted the money and placed it back into the big manila envelope. "Twenty-five hundred dollars on the nose." He shoved the envelope into his backpack.

The two conspirators met along a path deep in the woods in Tomlinson Run Park outside of Chester. Wallace Rawlings looked uncomfortable in the jeans and plaid shirt he wore so that no one would notice him.

To any potential witnesses, the lawyer and sheriff looked like two hikers who happened upon each other in the woods.

"I want it done ASAP," Wallace Rawlings reminded the lawman.

"Do you want it done right, or do you want it done fast?"

"I want it done right and right now. Thornton called the courthouse this morning and asked for a copy of the transcript for the Eric Connally trial."

"Why should that concern you?"

"It's none of your business."

Sheriff Sawyer held up his backpack with the money in it. "This makes it my business. I'm putting my butt on the line for your family, and I don't do that without knowing the particulars."

"Let's just say that there was more to that trial than met the eye, and Thornton is savvy enough to see it."

"Did you break into that post office?"

"Are you asking as the sheriff or an employee?"

"Am I wearing my badge?"

Cagey even though he didn't see the sheriff's badge on his chest, Wallace Rawlings scoffed. "No, I did not break into the post office."

"What about the bomb that was mailed to Doc MacMillan?"

"We already discussed that!" Wallace looked around. All that was around, as far as they could see, were trees and fallen logs. "It must have been someone else whose wife he's been sniffing around."

"Doc MacMillan and Miss Cindy? I don't believe it."

"It's true. She told me she was in love with MacMillan." Wallace added with unmistakable hatred, "Then, she had his baby."

"Wait a minute!" Sheriff Sawyer sounded like a schoolboy whose buddy just told him that he had bedded the school's prom queen. "You're telling me that Doc MacMillan was Vicki's father?"

"Well, I certainly was not!"

"She was your wife."

"No, she wasn't! I never touched her after MacMillan soiled her. Because of him, our marriage was never consummated."

"What about Vicki?"

"She was sin itself."

"I guess her death was no great loss to you."

Wallace sneered, "You're beginning to sound like a sheriff, Sawyer. When are you going to do it?"

Sheriff Curtis Sawyer slipped the backpack on across his broad shoulders. "I'll have to wait until they are alone. It's best if I do it at MacMillan's place. That way, it will look like they interrupted a couple of kids breaking in to steal drugs from his medical office."

Wallace smiled with approval. "Good idea! I knew I hired the right man for the job."

*   *   *   *

Dressed in a pair of worn sweat pants in lieu of pajamas, and no bathrobe, Tad was finishing his morning pot of coffee when Joshua and Jan knocked on his kitchen door.

Embarrassed to see Tad bare-chested, the reserved drug store manager tried not to stare at his well-formed chest and flat stomach. In all the years Jan had known the doctor, she never realized what he kept concealed under oversized shirts and sweats.

"I see you made it back from the state lab," Joshua observed while greeting Dog, who sniffed his clothes for Admiral's scent.

"Only a couple of hours ago." Tad gestured towards the coffee maker. "If you guys are going to have any coffee, make a fresh pot."

After pouring a mug of coffee for himself and another for Jan, Joshua polished off the pot by freshening Tad's mug before launching into making a fresh one.

While his cousin filled the decanter with water from the tap, Tad smiled with amusement at Joshua's back and winked at Jan. "Do you still have five kids?"

Joshua chuckled while he poured the water into the back of the coffee maker. "Yes, I let them live. They're going to the beach."

Tad and Jan were impressed. "Some punishment! I wish I had you for a father," the doctor muttered.

"Too many bodies are popping up in this town, and I want them to concentrate on something else right now." Joshua spooned the coffee grounds into the filter. "They're going to the Outer Banks to spend some time with Val's sister and her two kids."

"Tell me about the body," Jan demanded of Tad, who responded with a raised eyebrow.

"I promised her you'd give her a story," Joshua warned the medical examiner. He took a seat across the table from Tad. Now, it was Joshua's turn to get the raised eyebrow, followed by an "Hmmm" through eyes narrowed to slits.

Jan laid her recorder in the center of the table and leaned towards Tad. "What did you find out when you examined him?"

Tad looked at the recorder like it was a ticking bomb. "I didn't examine him. I watched the state medical examiner do a cursory examination. White male. Late thirties. Sucking chest wound."

"Did you find any ID?" Joshua wanted to know.

"No ID on him. The only thing on him was that article. But his fingerprints are in perfect condition so they are running them through the database."

"What article?" Jan glared at Joshua for holding back on her.

Tad answered, "It was an article written forty years ago about Reverend Orville Rawlings. Need I say more?"

"Newspaper article?"

"Looked liked a magazine article to me," the doctor told the reporter.

Tad held his coffee mug out to his cousin and gave a silent order for him to refill it as payment for keeping the lawyer's promise. Joshua got the message, refilled Tad's mug with hot coffee, and then freshened Jan's and his from the freshly brewed pot.

Meanwhile, Tad continued answering Jan's question about the article found on the body. "It was about Orville Rawlings and that church he built back in 1963. It even had his picture in it."

"Where is it now?" Jan was writing as fast as her hand could go.

Joshua plopped back down into his chair. "It's evidence. Sheriff Curtis Sawyer has it now." He leaned his chair back against the wall and put his feet up on the table.

Jan stopped writing and looked at the two cousins like they were stupid. "Well, we can kiss that evidence good-bye."

Tad defended himself. "I had to turn it over to Sawyer because he is the sheriff."

"Tad's right," Joshua noted. "If he hadn't given it to Sheriff Sawyer, then he could have been charged with withholding evidence."

"Sawyer works for Rawlings," Jan asserted.

Joshua changed the subject by asking Tad, "How did this John Doe die?"

"Shot in the chest. Once and only once. There were no powder burns on the clothes or speckling on the wound."

"What does that mean?" Jan paused in her writing.

Tad shot Joshua an annoyed glance, which caused the lawyer to chuckle while he answered, "That means he was shot from a distance. A contact wound is when the muzzle of the gun is pressed against the skin when the trigger is pulled. Since there is no distance for the gunshot residue that comes from the muzzle to scatter outside the wound, they are propelled into the victim. In that case, you will find no speckling around the outside of the wound. The wound will actually fan out inside the victim.

"If the victim is shot from close up, but it is not a contact wound, then there will be speckling of gunshot residue around the wound. How much there is will tell forensics how close the shooter was to the victim. If there is none outside or inside the wound, then the shot was from a distance."

"That appears to be the case here," Tad concluded Joshua's explanation.

The medical examiner illustrated on his own bare chest while he described their findings. "The slug hit its target in the chest and went right through the heart. It bounced off a rib in the back, and then was lodged in the sternum. The forensics pathologist wants to do more tests before she actually opens him up. It isn't every day you get a body that well preserved, and she's hesitant to damage the goods, so to speak."

"Can you tell me what kind of slug it was that killed him?" Joshua asked.

"Forty-five caliber." Tad shrugged. "It looked like that on the x-ray. We'll know more when they open him up." He told Jan, "I can't tell you any more than that."

While Jan was busily writing down what his cousin had just told her, Joshua saw a small smile creep to Tad's lips. Their eyes met. Tad directed Joshua's attention to his arm. In a gesture meant to look like nothing more than a morning stretch and scratch of his arm, Tad showed Joshua a small bruise on the inside of his elbow. He had blood drawn while at the state lab for the DNA comparison.

The investigative team had not told anyone, especially the media, about the red hair found in the murder weapon and the trench coat, nor the discovery that it had come from someone related to Vicki Rawlings.

When Jan lifted her head from her notepad and looked expectantly back at Tad for more information, the doctor smirked over the edge of his coffee mug and cocked his head in Joshua's direction. "What have you got for the lady?"

Joshua responded with exaggerated casualness, "I figured out what the key goes to."

Tad fought to keep from spitting his coffee upon hearing the news. "You did? What does it go to?"

"Do you remember that I told you that Doc Wilson was talking to me after I landed on my head at the end of the Weirton game?"

"You had a concussion." Tad shook his head.

"Doc told me that he had a hunting cabin in Raccoon."

"Doc wasn't a hunter." Jan frowned. Had she forgiven Joshua for nothing?

"No, he wasn't. But he would go up there in November and just put his feet up and drink."

"Doc would get drunk?" Tad smirked.

"He told me not to tell you. Anyway, I remember the conversation now. I was trying not to pass out and he was ranting about Faust—"

"Faust?" Jan squawked.

"Remember the old story about the man who sold his soul to the devil in exchange for everything he wanted?"

"What does that have to do with this?"

"Doc told me that he knew a man who did that, only he didn't regret their deal because he was evil."

"Are you using evil as a noun or an adjective?" Tad asked.

"Jeez!" Jan shook her head at Joshua. "You just had to say that."

"Say what?" Joshua was thrown off track by Tad's question and Jan's reaction.

"Is evil a thing or a description?" Tad clarified his question.

In his mind, Joshua replayed his conversation with Doc Wilson while Jan explained her disgust. "Tad started an argument in our Sunday school class. Two people walked out because he insisted that evil is an actual force from hell."

"They couldn't deal with the truth," Tad declared. "Evil is a thing that is capable of complete destruction."

"I assumed Doc was using the word as an adjective," Joshua concluded, "but he could have been using it as a noun."

"Does it really matter?" Jan asked.

Tad answered, "If Doc knew that what we were dealing with here was evil and not just someone who has issues because his mommy held him too much, then yes it does matter."

"Was Vicki evil? She shot up a church and worshipped Satan, who you think is the source of this dark force."

"Vicki clearly had issues. Just look at her family." Tad gestured for Joshua to refill his mug.

"Then, are you saying that the whole Rawlings family is evil?" Jan added with a grin, "And I'm using the word as a noun."

As he refilled the coffee mugs, Joshua interjected before Tad could respond to Jan's question, "Doc said that good will always win against evil. He wasn't talking about two adjectives battling each other. He was talking about two things: good versus evil. It has been an age-old battle since God created the Garden of Eden and the serpent slithered in to wreck everything."

"So you're on Tad's side," Jan declared. "Do you really believe the Reverend Orville Rawlings is controlled by a force from hell called evil?"

Joshua set the pot back on the coffeemaker and leaned against the kitchen counter. "Since I believe in God and heaven, I have to believe in Satan and hell. I don't necessarily believe that Rawlings made any deal with the devil for his soul, but I do believe in evil, whether it is a demon that serves Satan or Satan himself. I think there is an evil force. I'm not talking about *Star Wars*-type dark force stuff. I'm talking about a spirit that's deep inside you that motivates your behavior towards the greater good or your own agenda. Is your behavior motivated by good or evil? How else do you explain the likes of Bin Laden and Saddam Hussein? They are clearly motivated by evil."

Tad interrupted his cousin's speech. "Wait a minute! That doesn't make sense!"

"What are you talking about?" Jan argued. "He's agreeing with you."

Tad shook his head. "What Wilson told Josh about Rawlings doesn't make sense. That football game was over twenty years ago. Wally killed Cindy only nine years ago. Doc couldn't have had anything on Wally back then because he was still in high school and hadn't even married Cindy yet."

Jan smiled excitedly. "Then Doc Wilson must have gotten something on the reverend."

CHAPTER 27

▼

Ever since he had children, Joshua craved quiet.

Then, Valerie died.

In the days following his wife's death, Joshua thought the mournful silence in his home was going to drive him nuts.

Now, when Joshua returned to his house after meeting with Tad and Jan, the father thought his head was going to burst from the silent treatment his children inflicted upon him. When he announced in a good-natured tone, "I'm home!" the silence seemed to retort, "Drop dead!"

The dog didn't even greet him. Admiral remained stretched out on the sofa with his head on the cushion and one eye on his master, daring him to shoo him off. It was as if the dog purposely broke the stay-off-the-furniture rule in an act of rebellion for his master sending his family away.

"They'll get over it," Joshua told himself on the way into his study. He was grateful when the phone's ringing broke the silence.

"Bet you thought I forgot about you," Lieutenant Bruce Rogers greeted Joshua.

"No, I knew I'd hear from you soon." Joshua grabbed a notepad to write down the report from his military contact.

"Well, what you asked for wasn't easy to get. The Korean War was a long time ago. I had to work overtime to put it together."

"But you got it," Joshua stated with confidence.

"Have I ever failed you, Commander?"

After Joshua assured him he hadn't, the lieutenant went on with his report. "Captain Orville Alexander Rawlings—"

"He was a captain?" Joshua was surprised.

Bruce assured him the reverend was. "I got a copy of his file right here. What made it hard was that you told me he was in Korea. He wasn't."

Joshua chuckled. "It won't be the first time a veteran lied about his service to make it sound more impressive, especially for someone like Orville Rawlings."

"He did go overseas, but he never got further than Hong Kong. He served in a military hospital. Most of those he served with were other officers, and most died after the war of natural causes, a couple of car accidents—"

"Any who were reported missing after the war?"

"That is very interesting," Bruce's voice went up an octave. "If I hadn't gotten his file from the VA I would not have this information, because it's not part of our records. Captain Orville Alexander Rawlings was discharged from the U. S. Army on April 5, 1952. He left Hong Kong on April 6, 1952, to return stateside. Everything in here is in order. But a few days later, the police, and we have a copy of a report here in his file, questioned the base commander and others because Rawlings's family reported him missing. They claim he never arrived home. I have a whole bunch of letters here. The family claims the military is covering up his disappearance. The military's position was that he was discharged, checked out, and came back to the states on a military transport, and just decided not to go home. So, it's not our problem."

"Did the military ever investigate his disappearance?" Joshua's voice took on an official tone.

"I have a copy of a report from the Army. The Oregon state representative, that's where Rawlings's family is from, requested that the Army check into the disappearance. It was just the basic report. The Army investigator talked to everyone who was involved in the captain's discharge and found nothing out of the ordinary."

"Can you send me a copy of that report?"

"It's confidential, sir. It deals with Army personnel."

"Send it to the Navy recruiting office in East Liverpool to my attention."

Bruce hesitated. "I'll have to check with the chief on that, sir."

"Do that on Monday and give me a call."

"Yes, sir." Bruce was relieved that Joshua was going to leave it at that, but he was also concerned with what the commander would do if his boss's answer was no. "Anything else, sir?"

Joshua was about to answer no, but then thought of another question. "Can you tell me if the investigator questioned Charles Delaney?"

"Who is Charles Delaney?" was Bruce's response.

"He served with Orville Rawlings. He should be on your list."

Bruce rechecked his list, and then checked it again. "I don't have any Delaneys on my list."

"Are you in the military database now?" Joshua heard an exasperated sigh from the other end of the line as Bruce struggled to get into the database while talking on the phone.

"What's that name again?" Bruce's voice echoed after he switched to speaker-phone.

"Charles Delaney. He served in Korea. I can swear I was told that he and Rawlings met in Korea and served together." Joshua heard grunts and moans come from the other end of the line, which told him that Bruce was studying his findings. "He died like seven years or so ago of lung cancer," Joshua added in hopes that would help his former assistant, "so he should be listed as deceased."

"Found him," Bruce finally said. "Died in Pittsburgh? January 11, 1997?"

"That's him."

"This doesn't make sense."

"What?"

"You said he served with Captain Rawlings?"

"That's what I heard."

"Charles Lee Delaney, army sergeant. He was military police stationed in Seoul."

"So Delaney went to Korea?"

"That's where Seoul is," Bruce cracked. "But he wasn't in Rawlings's unit. Rawlings was an army chaplain at a hospital in Hong Kong. Delaney was an MP in Korea. We're talking about a whole other animal here, sir."

"Okay, I have another job for you."

"You must hate my guts, commander."

"This will be easier. I want to know who in Sergeant Delaney's unit was reported missing."

"During or after the war?" Bruce's voice was deadpan.

"Let's make it both. Maybe he was AWOL."

"You're not asking for much, are you, sir?" Bruce responded with sarcasm.

"I still outrank you, lieutenant. And find out who in Rawlings's family we can contact. I want to talk to them."

"Are you taking over the Army's case, sir? They don't like it when we do that."

"Then let's not tell them."

"Sir, may I advise that you run it through the admiral?"

"I'll call him on Monday. In the meantime, get that information for me and I'll buy you a drink on my next trip to Washington."

"I'd rather you invite me to your place for some peace and quiet in West-By-God-Virginia."

"May I remind you that I have five kids?"

"Yeah, right," Bruce remarked. "I'll buy you a drink."

*   *   *   *

"We have a witness who places the Hitchcocks at the Pittsburgh Airport, getting onto a plane for Chicago. The plane went down into a hillside right after takeoff and there were no survivors. There was nothing more to the investigation." Steubenville Police Officer Scott Collins's annoyance with the Hancock County sheriff's question about his case was clear.

Sheriff Curt Sawyer sized up the officer sitting across from him in the Steubenville Police Chief's office and concluded that Collins was a marine wannabe. While he had the build to be one of the best to serve his country, he did not have the character. His sandy blond hair was cut short to his head. He reeked of aftershave, which the sheriff could smell as soon as the police chief brought Collins into the conference room for their meeting. The uniformed officer also purposely wore his uniform tight to show off his bulging muscles.

As the sheriff questioned his investigation of the Hitchcock disappearance, Collins reacted like a dog defending his territory after catching another dog marking it. He sat forward in the chair across from his chief and puffed his chest out while he asserted that there was no crime to investigate. The family of three was tragically killed in the plane crash in Pennsylvania.

The police chief backed up his officer's report by adding, "I believe that we found during our investigation that no one had a motive for wanting to harm the Hitchcocks."

"And our witness had no reason to lie," Collins scoffed. "Why does Joshua Thornton want to know about a retired stripper and her bimbo daughter and kid anyway?"

When Sawyer shifted his attention from the police chief to the officer to answer his question, he was met with Scott Collins's daring glare. "Thornton believes that the Hitchcocks are connected to one of the victims in his murder investigation."

Officer Scott Collins laughed. "Well, if you want to find anyone with a motive to off them, then tell Thornton to look in his own backyard. His cousin, Tad

MacMillan, was the one trying to hunt them down. He looked pretty much to me like a jilted boyfriend, and we all know how deadly a broken heart can be."

*   *   *   *

Except for illness, the Thornton family never missed Sunday church services. Even though the children were leaving for the North Carolina Outer Banks, they were expected to go to church before departing.

The worship service went without incident. The Thorntons took up a whole pew in the front. Jan sat directly across the aisle from them. Tad played the keyboard and directed the choir. Pastor Steven Andrews's sermon was conversational in style. He spoke simply, like that of a friend telling a story.

The only thing not normal were the five long faces sitting to Joshua's left.

After the service, the kids stuck together on the church's green lawn while the pastor detained Joshua at the door. "I do hope all this mess over that poor girl's killing and Beth's involvement with her is settled soon," Pastor Andrews told his newest member while clasping his hand in both of his. "She was a good person."

"Yes, she was." In an instant, Joshua remembered the bright fun girl he had fallen in love with in his youth.

Stephen Andrews detected the mournful tone behind Joshua's strong demeanor. "I didn't really get to know Beth. From what I saw of her at the drug store and learned from Tad, I believe there was a lot of goodness in her. It is that goodness that we need to remember."

Carefree days, before adulthood responsibilities and addiction assaulted Beth, flashed through Joshua's mind. He cleared his throat. "I'll try to remember that."

The children migrated towards their father to hurry him along.

"Everything will be straightened out soon," Joshua stated with determination.

Jan came out the door to join them on the steps. "Oh, yes," she smiled. "We have a big break in the case. Josh found the key to everything."

"You found out what the key goes to?" Sarah shrieked. "No wonder he's sending us away!" she announced to her siblings, who looked no happier than she was.

"You're sending your children away?" Pastor Andrews looked quizzical. "Didn't their mother pass away only months ago?"

"You don't understand, pastor," Joshua tried to explain.

Donny interjected, "You found out what the key goes to after we spent days looking for it, and then you send us away and not let us in on anything."

Joshua fought to maintain a controlled, yet fatherly, attitude while his children aimed five pairs of daggers at him.

After shutting down the keyboard and meeting with the choir, Tad arrived to save his cousin. "Good morning. How are we this bright shining Sunday?"

"Your cousin is about to get lynched," Jan told him. "They found out about the key."

"Because someone has a big mouth," Joshua accused her.

Tad smoothly shifted gears. "How about if we all go to brunch?"

Joshua declined, "Thank you for the offer, but since the kids are going away—"

"We're not going away," Sarah snarled, "we're being sent away so you can have all the fun without us after we did all the work."

"Sent away?" Pastor Andrews was still confused.

"On account of us getting arrested for grave robbing the other night," Donny clarified.

"We weren't grave robbing," J.J. objected.

"Grave robbing?" Pastor Andrews gasped.

"They were looking for a dead body," Tad explained, "in Locust Hill Cemetery."

"Well, if you're going to look for a dead body, I guess a cemetery would be as good of a place to look as any." The pastor turned his attention to Joshua with an encouraging smile. "I can see that you do have your hands full, Joshua. Raising five very active children on your own can't be easy."

"Nah, he can handle it," Tad responded. "They're just high-spirited. Josh was the same way. I remember once, he was at this party. The parents of the kid were out of town, and the party got out of hand, and the neighbors called the police." Laughing, Tad pointed to a dismayed Joshua. "This guy jumped out of a second-story bedroom window to avoid getting arrested. Of course, they caught him."

"I remember that!" Jan burst out laughing.

The children turned to their father with wide grins.

Tracy snickered as she asked her father, "You jumped out of a second-story window?"

Joshua groaned and gathered the giggling children together. "Let's go to brunch."

The children made their way in the general direction of the van while Joshua hissed at Tad, "I noticed you neglected to tell them whose party it was that got out of hand."

✳   ✳   ✳   ✳

Sunday brunch had the tone of a wake.

Joshua took the children for a buffet at Elby's in East Liverpool before sending them off for a vacation away from murder.

After the waitress left with their orders for dessert, the father observed the sad faces surrounding him. "I haven't seen so many long faces since the cable went out right before Britney Spears's new video was to debut."

"You can cut out the humor, Dad," Murphy sneered, "we don't feel like laughing."

"Do you think I'm not going to miss having you kids around?"

"If you did, you wouldn't be sending us away," Sarah declared.

Joshua could always count on his older daughter to see his side. "Tracy, you understand, don't you?"

"We remember how it was with you and Mom, Dad," Tracy responded with sad eyes. "You thought we were too young to notice, but we knew what was going on."

Perplexed by what she was saying, Joshua gazed at her.

Tracy fingered her empty water glass while she continued. "Sure, you guys were happy. I mean, you were a lot happier than any of our friends' parents. But we also saw that when you were bound and determined to get someone who you knew was guilty, and you had to prove it, then anyone or anything else was just a distraction."

Tracy raised her eyes to her father's. "You didn't have to do all that traveling. You were a commander. You could order people to go for you, but you had to do it yourself."

"Mom would say that that was just the way you were." There was anger on Sarah's face.

Tracy added in a soft voice, "Mom would tell us that you loved us, but that you just could not think or do anything else until you got the answers to all your questions."

Murphy smiled at his brothers and sisters. "She also used to say we were all the same, like dogs that picked up a scent. That's why we had to find that body."

"Obsessive. That's the word," Joshua told his children. "If we are all the same way, and you understand why I have to do this, then why are you mad at me?"

"We don't know if you are sending us away to protect us, or to not be bothered," J.J. answered for the group.

"I'm sending you on vacation. Look," Joshua sat up in his chair, "every year your mother took you kids to the beach house for a few weeks, the whole summer if I was overseas. You haven't done that this year. You're simply going away for your vacation."

Tracy diagnosed his explanation. "You're rationalizing, Dad."

"Obsessive people do that," Joshua cracked.

"The difference was that Mom would go with us," Sarah said. "She didn't send us away."

"If your mother was here, she would be going with you," Joshua spoke in a low voice as the waitress delivered two sundaes for him and Donny.

"The point is that after all the work we've done to find that key, now that you know what it goes to, you are sending us away." Sarah glared at him. "Is this how it's going to be with you? You get all wrapped up in a case then, just as things get good, you send us away to get us out of your hair?"

"Don't you speak to me that way." Joshua's voice was low and threatening.

Her anger overriding her senses, Sarah refused to back down. "It's the truth."

Joshua looked at the five faces surrounding him. Donny's sundae was untouched. If he wasn't eating, Donny had to be as upset as his brothers and sisters.

Joshua pushed his sundae away and carefully folded up his napkin while he spoke to them. "Kids,—" He stopped and sighed, "I was never good at this." He placed the napkin next to his half-eaten dessert. "Your mother was good at this stuff, not me."

Joshua took his eyes off the napkin and looked at his charges—all five of them. "It is true that I am obsessive. I have gotten wrapped up in this case, which I didn't want to get mixed up in in the first place. Yes, I am also angry about you breaking into the cemetery in the middle of the night and breaking into the crypt and disturbing the dead. But truthfully, that is not my whole motivation for sending you away. I want you to be safe."

J.J. interrupted, "We can take care of ourselves."

"Can you? During the course of my career, I've known some fine men who could take care of themselves. They proved it time and again. They were trained to take care of themselves, and they are now dead."

"This isn't the Middle East, Dad," Sarah scoffed.

"How many bodies have we uncovered just during the last few weeks?" Joshua ticked off the bodies on his fingers. "The John Doe in the crypt. Lulu Jefferson. Her sister and the newspaper editor who tried to prove she was murdered. Eleanor Rawlings died taking a bath. Her father went crazy and threw himself off a bridge. Cynthia Rawlings was poisoned, or so we believe. Vicki Rawlings and Beth Davis. Eric Connally was blown to bits by a package mailed to Tad." He waved both hands as he continued the body count. "I've run out of fingers, so I can't count Morgan Lucas."

"Morgan Lucas?" Tracy asked.

"The news anchor who broke the story about Amber witnessing the murders. She breaks the story of her career, and now she's dead."

Joshua held up both of his hands to illustrate his point. "Eleven bodies. I'm all out of fingers. Eleven, so far. I'm not even counting the Hitchcocks, a whole family that seems to have disappeared off the face of the earth. These are eleven supposedly reasonable, sensible adults, who were just living their lives, and now they are all dead. Unless I can find evidence that can put their killer away, I can promise you, he or she will continue killing. I don't want any of you, the most important people in my whole world, in the line of fire. That is why I'm sending you away. Not to punish you, but to protect you."

"Dad," Tracy objected softly, "this has obviously been going on for decades. Are you going to make us stay in the Outer Banks forever?"

"Things are heating up. I know that key goes to Doc Wilson's cabin and he has all we need there. I can feel it. This will be wrapped up sooner than you think." Joshua forced a smile on his face. "When it is wrapped up, I'll drive out to the banks to meet you kids, and we'll have a good time for a couple of weeks before coming back for school."

After waiting a silent moment for his children to digest this information, Joshua summed up his case. "I can't take any chances with you kids. I promised your mother that I would take care of you, and that is what I intend to do."

CHAPTER 28

▼

"Left. No!" Tad corrected himself. "Right!"

"Make up your mind!" Jan wrestled the steering wheel of her little red Honda that was hurtling down the dirt road through the overgrown Pennsylvania woods.

In the back seat, Tad was yelling directions from those drawn on a yellow stickie by an elderly woman the doctor tended at the nursing home. She swore she was familiar with Dr. Russell Wilson's cabin.

Squeezed into the front passenger seat, Joshua searched for any sign of civilization.

After an hour and a half of maneuvering the maze of century-old dirt roads forged through woods not yet discovered by housing developers, the group wondered if they would ever find their way back, let alone find Dr. Wilson's cabin.

"Wait!" Joshua called out when they whizzed pass a boulder that stuck out into the road.

A swamp littered with dead trees was across the road from the rock. The road was so narrow that any miscalculation threatened the driver with either a dent or a bath in the swamp.

Joshua pointed at the boulder and the swamp across from it. "That looks familiar."

"Everything looks familiar!" Jan didn't slow down. "We're going in circles."

"Stop!" Joshua ordered.

Jan screeched to a halt.

The sudden stop propelled Tad into the back of Jan's seat.

Joshua jumped out, crossed the road, and raced over a small rise behind the boulder.

"Does he still get car sick?" Jan asked Tad.

"Nah!" Tad climbed out of the car, reached his arms high up above his head, and bent over to touch his toes.

They had just stretched when Joshua reappeared at the top of the rise and waved his arms triumphantly. "I found it!"

It was on the other side of the trees at the top of the rise. Dr. Russell Wilson's cabin was a wooden one-story structure in the center of a grassy clearing. The whole building leaned sideways like a house sloppily built of popsicle sticks. A bell tower that had fallen into itself was at one end of the structure. A brick chimney teetered away from the building on the other end. An overturned outhouse rested at the edge of the clearing.

Tad recognized it. "That's the one-room schoolhouse Grandmomma's mom used to go to." He eased himself down over the rise to the clearing.

Jan took pictures with the camera she brought to cover her exclusive story.

"And Doc Wilson went to school with Grandmomma's mother," Joshua reminded his cousin. He slid down the hill on his rump to inspect their discovery. "Grandmomma brought me out here when I was just a little kid. Doc bought it after it was abandoned. I remember Grandmomma and him talking about it."

"It's not a cabin," Jan told them while she snapped a picture from in front of the schoolhouse. The door rested ajar in the doorway. "And I don't see any lock that that key can go to."

Tad peered through a dirt-covered window. "Don't be so sure." The window was so dirty he couldn't see through it.

Joshua was forcing the door open. Tad joined him, and together they cleared the doorway. Joshua went in first.

"There's an old cot in here!" he called from inside. Tad and Jan went in.

It was one large room. The fireplace was made of brick. There were a series of windows along two walls and on either side of the door. The black chalkboard still hung on the opposing wall. The flag that once hung in the rusted remnants of the bracket on the corner of the blackboard was gone. The desks and chairs had disappeared ages ago.

Two of the three pictures that once hung on the walls were propped up against the decaying wall. One was of George Washington, and the other was of Abraham Lincoln.

The third picture, which contained the image of Jesus Christ, rested at the foot of the cot covered with a filthy thin mattress.

At the same time, everyone in the group saw the footlocker that the picture of Jesus Christ was leaning against.

Joshua actually gasped before diving for it, setting the picture aside, and turning the locker around to reveal the padlock sealing it shut. "Tad, give me the key!"

While his cousin studied the lock, Tad dropped to his knees next to him and fished the key out of his pocket. Joshua groaned when he discovered their next obstacle.

The lock was rusted.

"Maybe it will still work," Jan suggested hopefully.

Tad slipped the key into the hole. It fit but would not move. Joshua grabbed it out of Tad's hand and tried with all his might, but the rusted mechanism refused to budge.

Defeated, all three of them groaned and plopped down onto the rotted floor.

"It's simple. We'll take the trunk back home and break the lock." With a grunt, Joshua hoisted the trunk up onto one of his shoulders.

Tad kicked the cot. "I want to see what was in it now."

"Well, you can't always get what you want," Joshua said in his most paternal tone while he led the way out of the old schoolhouse. "But if you try sometimes, you'll find you get what you need."

"Mick Jagger sang it better." Tad followed his cousin.

"Mick Jagger sang what better?" Jan slipped the cover onto her camera lens.

"You need to get out more," Tad shot at her.

*   *   *   *

The first shot was fired when they appeared over the top of the rise.

The bullet kicked up dirt in front of Joshua, who dropped the trunk and hit the ground at the same time. The trunk rolled end over end down the hill and landed next to the boulder.

"He's hiding in the trees across the road up at the top of that hill," Joshua warned his cohorts.

Stunned, Tad and Jan searched the trees for the shooter without moving for cover until Joshua bellowed like the military officer he was. "Hit the dirt!"

Tad followed the order. Jan stood motionless.

The next shot snapped off a tree branch near her head.

"Jan!" Joshua yelled. "Get down! That's an order!"

When Tad tackled Jan, the two of them rolled together down the incline to the road. Tad covered both his head and hers while two more shots were fired. The doctor was instantly aware that the gunshots were being fired towards the shooter.

"Get in the car! I'll cover you!" Tad heard Joshua shout. Taking cover in the thick brush, Joshua waved his gun in the direction of the car.

"Get in the car!" Tad screamed at Jan.

Motionless, she gazed up at Tad with wide, frightened eyes.

He pulled Jan to her feet and dragged her to the car.

When a shot kicked up dirt between them and the car, Tad changed direction and yanked Jan to hide behind the boulder.

At the next round of shots from Joshua's hiding place, Tad once again darted for the car and shoved Jan into the back seat.

"What about Josh?"

Suddenly mobile, Jan fought Tad as if she could single-handedly save their leader.

"He's coming!"

"The trunk!"

"We'll get it." Tad pushed down on her head, thrust Jan into the back seat, and slammed the door on her.

The doctor heard another shot fired. Tad couldn't tell where it came from or where it hit until Joshua answered with two more shots from the rise above them. Tad jumped in the front seat and fumbled with the keys to start the car.

After the engine turned over, Tad lifted his head to look over the dashboard. He saw Joshua shoot towards their assailant before diving down the hill. Once he hit the ground, he went into a roll. He landed next to the trunk.

Unaccustomed to Jan's car, Tad punched the gas pedal to the floor. The car responded by leaping forward like a jackrabbit and landing with a jolt between the shooter and Joshua.

Three shots were fired at them while Jan opened the back door and helped Joshua dump the trunk into the back seat. He leaped in behind it.

"Move! Move! Move!" Joshua roared like General Patton.

Tad hit the gas without waiting for them to close the back door.

They heard a series of shots over the pitter-patter of the small engine while the car fishtailed down the dirt road.

*   *   *   *

The phone was ringing when Joshua carried the old trunk into his study. Tad and Jan hurried in ahead of him to find something to use to break into it.

"There's the phone," Jan stated the obvious.

Joshua's hands were still full with the trunk.

"Where are your bolt cutters?" While ignoring the ringing phone inches from his hands, Tad searched the desk.

Admiral came into the study from where he had been sneaking a nap on Sarah's bed. As he watched them scurry about to open the trunk and answer the phone, the dog sat and uttered a long, low grunt.

Meanwhile, the phone kept ringing.

Joshua plopped the trunk down into the middle of the floor. "Answer that, will you?" he ordered while lunging for the phone. He reached it just before the answering machine picked up. "Hello," he gasped out.

"Commander Thornton!" the admiral barked at him.

After years of conditioning, Joshua stood at attention.

Admiral Andrew Zimmerman, a Navy Seal from the Vietnam War, continued, "What have you been doing? Inactive duty bores you, so you decided to go dig up dead bodies in graveyards?"

"Where are your bolt cutters?" Tad repeated his inquiry.

Jan was yanking on the lock in a vain effort to break it off with her bare hands.

"I'm only trying to identify a body, sir." Realizing what the admiral had said, Joshua asked, "How did you know a body was found in a cemetery here in Chester?"

"Where is your toolbox?" Tad asked Joshua, who tried to ignore him.

Joshua put his hand over the phone's mouthpiece and whispered, "Check the garage."

Meanwhile, Admiral Zimmerman barked, "What is it with you, Thornton? Wherever you go, bodies just keep dropping out of nowhere. Now, they're popping out of crypts."

"Who is that?" Tad wanted to know.

"Shut up," Joshua snapped at his cousin while trying to piece together what the admiral was reporting.

"What did you say, commander?" the admiral shouted.

"I was talking to my cousin, sir. I apologize if you think I directed that at you. Excuse me." Covering the mouthpiece, Joshua hissed at Tad, "Go check the garage and take Jan with you."

Shooting Joshua a stern glare, Tad and Jan did as they were ordered and slipped out of the study.

Returning his attention to his commanding officer on the other end of the line, Joshua grabbed his notepad and pen and sat at his desk. "I'm sorry, sir, but how did you know about the crypt?"

"We just got a report from the VA that the body of a former inmate at Leavenworth was found in a crypt that didn't belong to him in Chester, West Virginia. Of course, I knew instantly that you were connected to the case somehow."

"They identified him by his fingerprints," Joshua muttered more to himself than the admiral.

"That's right. He was Army, but I was given his file and asked to give you any assistance you need." The admiral asked firmly, "What are you up to, Thornton?"

"Losing my mind, sir," Joshua smiled. "Who was this inmate?"

Joshua was relieved to hear a smile come into Admiral Zimmerman's voice. "Your John Doe was Private Kevin Rice. He was convicted of stealing government property to sell on the black market while stationed in Seoul, Korea. He was caught red-handed delivering the goods to a fence. It was also believed that he fragged his platoon sergeant, but the prosecutor couldn't get enough evidence to charge him with murder."

"Did you say he killed his sergeant?"

"Yes," the admiral sighed. "Rice was questioned about the series of thefts, but they let him go because the investigators felt he wasn't smart enough to run the operation as smoothly as it was. The investigators hoped Rice would roll over on his boss. That was Master Sergeant Caleb Penn. He ran the supply depot. Rice confronted him, and they got into a big fight. Penn beat the shit out of him. Before the investigators got enough on Penn to arrest him, he was blown up."

"How did it happen?"

"Ignition bomb. He got into his jeep to drive across the base and boom." The admiral went on. "Rice was convicted of stealing, but they couldn't connect him to the bomb. They gave him seven years in Leavenworth for theft of government property and a dishonorable discharge."

"What was Rice's defense?"

"He said he was only following his sergeant's orders and made no profit from the thefts. He knew something fishy was going on, but he felt he was in no position to make waves. The prosecution found evidence that he did take money for his part. Therefore, he had to know that whatever he was doing was illegal." Zimmerman added, "But the prosecution did believe Penn was the mastermind behind the operation."

"But you can't lock up a dead man," Joshua pointed out. "If his sergeant was alive, Rice could have rolled over on him and gotten a lighter sentence. Was he smart enough to realize that?"

"From the tone of the statements in this file, I don't think so." The admiral continued reporting from the case file, "Sergeant Penn seemed to be a smart guy. When he got himself blown up, the Korean police wanted him for questioning about the death of a Korean civilian."

"What civilian?"

"The fence. He was shot in the head as soon as he was released by the military police."

"And the prosecution didn't try to pin it on Rice?"

"He had an alibi. He was still being held in the stockade."

"What time period was this?"

"Beginning of 1952. Rice was picked up on suspicion of killing his sergeant just one week after he was caught with the truckload of goods." Joshua could hear the papers being shuffled on the Admiral's desk. "February 1952."

"And the Korean?"

"What about him?"

"Did the Korean police ever find out who killed him?"

"Since Rice had an alibi, they decided it had to be one of his other suppliers. This guy dealt in everything."

"Maybe Penn did it. You said they wanted to question him about it."

Joshua listened to the admiral hum to himself on the other end of the line while Zimmerman read the reports in the file. "Penn had an alibi. He was in a meeting with another sergeant."

Joshua tapped the end of his pencil on the notepad while he thought. "First, the fence is shot, and then the suspected mastermind is blown to bits."

"The prosecutor's case was that Rice was not as much of an innocent stooge as he played for the investigator. The extra money in his bank account proved that. He got caught with his hand in the cookie jar, and the guy who put him up to it was putting all the blame on him, so he got mad and decided to blow him up."

"Why and how did Rice end up in Chester, West Virginia?"

"I have no idea. He was released from Leavenworth in 1959. That's the last the military knew of him." The admiral abruptly asked, "Since when have you gone to work for the DEA, Thornton? I thought you requested inactive duty so that you could run for president of the PTA."

"I'm not working for the DEA, sir. The state attorney general appointed me special prosecutor in a double homicide."

Realizing the significance of the admiral's inquiry, Joshua fired off a question that flashed in his mind, "How did the feds know about this John Doe?"

"Your state medical examiner ran his fingerprints through the federal database to ID him. The Penn case was flagged because the feds have a suspect but haven't been able to nail him with anything. Since Rice was in Leavenworth, his records belong to the military. The Army sent his file to me, since, officially, I'm still your commanding officer, even though you are on inactive status. As your commanding officer, I need to know what is going on."

Joshua rubbed his forehead as he recounted for the admiral the adventures of his move back home, and Lulu's news that Rice and Rawlings had served together in Korea.

"Well," Admiral Zimmerman told Joshua, "from what our records indicate, Rawlings had no reason to know any of them. He was a chaplain serving in a military hospital in Hong Kong. Rice and his friends were all in Seoul."

"Speaking of Rice's friends, I wonder if he knew Charles Delaney?" Joshua mumbled. "He served in Seoul. Maybe Rice came to Chester to see him."

Joshua recalled that it was Sheriff Delaney who warned his accomplice to hide Rice's body after his parents found it in the barn. But how could they prove the call was to Rawlings if the reverend didn't serve with Rice in Korea after all. What possible threat could Rice be to a chaplain who served in Hong Kong? Could Delaney have made the phone call to another war buddy who may have been mixed up with Rice and his illegal dealings? There was no telling what else Rice could have gotten himself into after his release from Leavenworth in 1959.

But then, if Reverend Rawlings wasn't involved, why did Rice have that article about him in his pocket?

"Thornton, are you still there?" Admiral Zimmerman's voice snapped.

Joshua started out of his thoughts. Apologizing, he asked the admiral to repeat what he was saying.

"I was telling you that Rogers told me to tell you that there was one enlisted man, a Corporal Milton Black was AWOL from Sergeant Delaney's command."

Forgetting his request for the lieutenant to find out who in Sheriff Delaney's unit had been reported missing in his quest to identify the missing body, Joshua asked why Rogers wished for the Admiral to report that information to him.

"Because you told him to," the admiral reminded him.

Politely, Joshua cleared his throat and asked for the rest of Rogers's report. As long as his assistant had done the work, the least Joshua thought he could do was to listen to the report, even though he now didn't consider the information relevant to the case. "When was this corporal reported AWOL?"

"February 5, 1952."

Joshua squinted at the date he had scribbled on his note pad that Rice's commanding officer was killed: February 1952.

Admiral Zimmerman went on, "According to the report that Rogers got from his file, Black was a disciplinary problem from the get go. Didn't fit in. His CO finally gave him a three-day pass. He went to Hong Kong and never came back. I don't think he has anything to do with any of this. He had no connection with Rice or supply. He was military police."

Joshua nodded as he wrote down the dates and made a timeline on the notepad. "Under Delaney?"

"Delaney was his CO. He was the one who signed off on the three-day pass. Got a reprimand for that. Command wanted to know why he gave a three-day pass to a man with disciplinary problems. He said he thought a break would do him some good. Anything else, commander?"

"Yes, sir," Joshua answered. "Were any American John Does ever found in Hong Kong during that time period?"

"Now, why do you want to know that, Thornton?"

"I'm looking for all the pieces of a puzzle, sir. You did say that Black went to Hong Kong. What became of him? Did they check to see if maybe he didn't come back because he was dead?"

"He most likely came back to the states and went into hiding."

"In Chester, West Virginia," Joshua chuckled. "Can you have Rogers check on American John Does found in Hong Kong about that time period for me, sir?"

Joshua heard an exasperated sigh from the other end of the line. "Okay. Can I do anything else for you, commander?" the admiral asked in a sarcastic tone. "Would you like me to send Rogers to rotate the tires on that Corvette of yours?"

Joshua smiled as he heard Lieutenant Rogers laugh in the background until he abruptly stopped. Joshua could imagine the commanding glare the admiral fired off at him to halt the laughter. "Could I please have copies of all those files?" he asked politely.

Despite the admiral's order to cooperate with his subordinate, Joshua was still surprised when Admiral Zimmerman responded that he would have the files sent overnight via courier to the recruiting office in East Liverpool.

*   *   *   *

Joshua's black Corvette was parked inside the garage tucked away into the corner of the property. Built of stone that matched the house back when owning a car was a luxury, before having two cars was a necessity, the garage was only wide enough to house one car, in this case, Joshua's prized toy.

An old wooden workbench was stretched across the length of the garage. Tad recalled many Sundays, as a child, when he and Joshua's grandfather, Jacob Thornton, worked at the same bench on one project after another. Tools would be scattered all over the bench, but Jake Thornton knew where each one was at all times. He would just reach out and grab it.

As a teenager, Tad built a motorized go-cart in this same garage. His little cousin, Joshua, watched him with the same adoration Tad had for Jake. They rode the go-cart up and down Chester's cobblestone streets for a whole summer, before the front axle broke and the cart was scrapped.

Now, the tools shone. They were lined up on a rack, according to size and use. The bench was clear, and the garage showed no sign of any project in process.

"Do you see them?" Jan reminded Tad of her presence.

"No," he muttered.

The cell phone in the doctor's pocket rang. While pointing out the toolbox on the workbench, Tad answered his phone.

Jan rummaged through the collection of tools for the bolt cutters while the medical examiner spoke into the phone.

"This is Dr. MacMillan," Tad said into the phone. He nodded when Jan held up the bolt cutters and wordlessly asked if they would do the job. "Yes, I did want that information as soon as you got it." He patted his pockets for a pencil. "Wait a minute."

Tad climbed into the Corvette to find a pen in the glove compartment. He then got out of the car only to discover he didn't have a slip of paper. The doctor wrote the information on the palm of his hand. Thanking the caller, he hung up.

"And you make fun of Josh for always being prepared." Jan remarked as Tad took the bolt cutters and led the way back into the house.

*   *   *   *

Joshua was examining the lock and the key when Tad and Jan returned.

"Are we permitted to enter now?" Jan asked sarcastically from the doorway.

"I am still in the reserves." Joshua held his hand out for the bolt cutters. "I had to maintain a military attitude, or get my ass kicked the next time I go to Washington."

"Well, while you were talking to your admiral, I was talking to the state lab about our John Doe," Tad told them.

"He's Kevin Rice," Joshua beat Tad to the punch. "Got out of Leavenworth a few years before Mom and Dad found him in Bosley's barn. That was what the admiral called to tell me." Joshua went on to recount the information he received from his commanding officer, which Jan wrote down in her reporter's notebook.

"Did he also tell you the murder weapon is a forty-five caliber Colt?"

"Forty-five caliber Colt?" Joshua stopped working on the padlock. The military was often issued Colts as weapons. "Are they sure?"

"How would they know that?" Jan asked them.

"Every gun causes a particular type of marking on the slug when it leaves the barrel," Tad started to tell her.

"I know that," Jan interrupted. "What I'm asking is how do they know without the gun that it was a Colt, and not a Smith and Wesson or a Magnum?"

Tad responded while Joshua stared in deep thought. "Computers. Certain types of guns leave certain types of markings that are characteristic of only that type of gun. Now, when they find the murder weapon, there will be other markings that are characteristic of only that individual gun."

"Forty-five caliber Colt, huh?" Joshua muttered and resumed working on the lock.

"Yeah," Tad responded, "and here is something else for you to chew on. The toxicology report came back on the drug used to incapacitate Vicki. It was succinylcholine. A big dose of it, too. That alone would have killed her."

"A controlled substance?" Joshua wondered.

"Of course. It's a powerful muscle relaxant that causes paralysis in breathing. It's usually used by doctors when a breathing tube is inserted."

Jan asked Tad, "Didn't you say she was shot up with it?"

Tad shrugged and sat back as he told Jan about Vicki's murder. "Vicki was looking for a good time with her killer. They were having foreplay. She thought her killer was shooting her up with something to enhance their sex when in fact, the succinylcholine cut off her breathing."

Mesmerized, Jan watched with wide eyes while Tad summarized Vicki Rawlings's death.

"By that time, Vicki had to know what was going down, but there was nothing she could do about it. She had to fight just to catch her breath and the drug prevented her from doing that. All she could do was lie there while her killer held that steel spike over her head and shoved it into her heart."

Jan gulped and shuddered.

Seeing that the would-be reporter had no other questions, Tad returned his attention to the trunk and broke through the lock.

They smiled triumphantly at each other.

"Now, watch this be filled with old sheets," Joshua joked. He rubbed the lid like a magician about to perform an illusion.

"Don't even joke about that," Tad warned. "As long as I've been waiting for this, God has to be kind."

"You do the honors then." Joshua sat back to give Tad access to the lid.

Tad said a small prayer of hope before opening the lid to reveal a chest filled to the rim with thick brown envelopes. Each one was sealed and labeled. A yellowed white envelope lay across the top of them with Dr. Wilson's familiar, arthritis-plagued, jagged handwriting across the front. It was addressed "To Whom This May Concern".

Tad opened the envelope and read it. A frown, followed by a broad smile, crossed his face while he read it.

"What is it?" Jan demanded to know.

Joshua took out the thick envelopes and read each label.

"It's everything," Tad breathed. "This letter is from Doc Wilson. He had it notarized in Pittsburgh. He says these are the real autopsies with the true findings on—"

"Here's Lulu Jefferson's autopsy." Joshua held up the envelope. "And Eleanor Rawlings and Sam Fletcher." He continued to take envelope after envelope out of the trunk.

Joshua's pace slowed as he read the label on one of the envelopes. "Here's the patient file for Victoria Rawlings."

"Vicki's patient file?" Tad asked.

Joshua read the label on the next envelope. "And here's Wally's patient file." He flipped through the next few envelopes. "The patient files for the whole Rawlings family are in here."

Tad, who was still reading the letter, interjected excitedly, "He says he tried to do the right thing, but Chuck Delaney threatened him and his family if he said any of these deaths were anything but an accident or natural causes. The autopsies he had done previously only said what he was told to report. These are the real reports with the real findings. Each one is witnessed and notarized by an official from Pittsburgh. He could not use a local notary because she was a member of the Reverend Orville Rawlings's church."

"That should nail him!" Jan exclaimed.

"Here's the autopsy report you were looking for." Joshua handed Tad the thick envelope.

With a grateful grin, Tad took the envelope. When he opened it, what looked liked a black marble fell out with a clap and rolled across the hardwood floor. Jan slapped at it with her palm against the floor until it came to rest against Admiral's head.

With an annoyed groan, the dog lifted his head to look at what interrupted his nap.

"What is it?" Joshua asked.

Jan held it up. "It's a bullet."

"It came from here." Tad showed them the small round hole in the front of the envelope.

Joshua took the slug from Jan. While he examined it, Jan knelt to check out the trunk.

"It's a forty-five." Joshua held the slug up to the light.

"And here is where it went in." Jan fingered a hole on the outside of the trunk.

"So he was able to hit the broadside of a trunk," Joshua smirked as he went to his desk.

"And you weren't able to hit him, I saw," Jan cracked. "I had heard you were supposed to be a good shot."

"He is." Tad was removing the contents of the envelope. "I guess old age caught up with him." He read a report attached to the top of the report.

"I wasn't trying to kill him." Joshua removed a small envelope from a desk drawer and slipped the slug into it. "If he was a half-decent shot, you two would have been dead the way you were standing up on top of that hill. Either he wasn't trying to kill us, or he didn't know how to shoot." He labeled and sealed the envelope.

"Doc mentions my coming to see him the day after Cindy's death and reports what I told him. He even has the date and the time. He says he told Sheriff Delaney who said that my testimony would be worthless since I was a drunk."

"Why try to blow you up ten years later?" Jan wondered.

Tad continued reading the report that was several pages long. "He was treating Cindy for gastrointestinal illness, which he concluded was brought on by nerves. The patient was high strung."

"Cindy was not high strung!" Jan objected.

"No, she wasn't," Tad agreed before he resumed reading. "Doc noticed on more than one occasion that Cindy did not seem to want to be alone with Reverend Rawlings. He recounts an incident here where the reverend came into the room while Doc Wilson was taking Cindy's pulse and her heart rate increased significantly. Then, she had a panic attack."

Tad turned to the next page. "Doc diagnosed her condition as nerves. After her death, when I came to see him, he realized all the symptoms were also indicative of poison. Based on my statement to him, he did a toxicology test to look for arsenic poisoning and found it."

"So, it was your going to him that made him find the truth." Joshua smiled at Tad, who lowered his eyes sadly.

"But why didn't he do anything?" Jan wondered. "He reports that being alone with Rawlings made her have a panic attack."

Tad told her, "He only had proof she was poisoned, but not by whom. She told me Wally was poisoning her. She had her panic attack when the reverend came into the room. If Wally was the one killing her, why get upset about being alone with the reverend?"

Jan shuffled through the rest of the reports. "But why would he not suspect that she was being poisoned if Rawlings killed all these other people?"

Joshua observed the stack of thick envelopes. "Doc Wilson found all these people were murdered and used their deaths to get Rawlings to stay in line. In most cases, he probably couldn't prove who the killer was, but he could cause a scandal too big for Reverend Rawlings to risk."

The evening sun shone through the window onto the stack of brown envelopes fanned out before them.

Joshua checked his watch and stood up. "Well, as much as I'd love to continue reading these and piecing together our dear reverend's sins, I have a meeting to go to."

"With who?" Jan accepted Joshua's hand to pull her to her feet.

Tad was filing the envelopes back into the chest.

"None of your business," Joshua responded to Jan's query.

"You have a date." A note of jealousy had crept into her tone, which caused both Joshua and Tad to do a double take. "That's why you sent your kids to the beach."

Tad closed the lid to the trunk. "I'll leave you two love birds to fight this out. Call me if anyone starts bleeding." He picked up the trunk and headed for the door.

"Wait a minute," Joshua called to his cousin. "She's going with you."

Tad ignored Joshua's command and kept on going.

"Who is she? Tess Bauer?"

Joshua turned to Jan. "Can't a man spend an evening alone without being accused of all sorts of illicit activities?"

"You said you had a meeting. Now, it's an evening alone. Which is it?"

Joshua gave her the look. While it would have made his children make for a hasty retreat, Jan shot it right back to him. "I think you should leave," he said in a low tone.

"So do I." Jan grabbed her purse and camera, and stalked from the room.

A second later, Joshua heard the door slam behind her.

✳   ✳   ✳   ✳

Tad was washing his hands at the kitchen sink when Joshua knocked on his apartment door. The sound system was playing classic rock music from in the living room.

"How are you doing?" Joshua came in without waiting for him to answer and closed the door behind him.

"I've been better." Tad turned off the water and reached for a dishtowel. "I see you escaped Jan unscathed."

"Barely." Joshua grabbed a chair from the kitchen table and straddled the back to sit in it. "What has gotten into her?"

Laughing, Tad leaned against the kitchen counter and dried his hands on the dishtowel. "You really aren't very smart when it comes to women."

Even though he agreed with Tad, Joshua shook his head in confusion by Jan's behavior. "Valerie was easy. There were never any games with her. She always laid it right out in the open. Other women are so—"

Jan burst in through the kitchen door. Startled, Tad jumped to his feet. Joshua, even with his training in always being prepared, stood up just in time for her to blast him. "You said you had a date!"

"You followed me!"

Tad stepped between the two of them.

Joshua backed up to the living room doorway while Jan attempted to shove Tad out of her way so that she could advance on her target.

"Oh, you are so cute!" she seethed.

"Jan, you've got to leave!" Tad gently pushed her towards the door. He turned to Joshua for help. "She has to go. Now!"

Jan was too angry to hear Tad's warning. "You promised me an exclusive!"

"Jan, we'll talk about this later!" Joshua assisted Tad in moving her to the door.

Jan wrestled out of both their grasps and rushed across the room in a rage. "It is not fair! Both of you have what you wanted! Tad, you're one of the most respected doctors in the valley and you've slept with every bimbo in the tri-state area. Josh, you've traveled all over the world investigating famous murder cases, while I'm stuck here writing little articles for little papers and directing people to the enema aisle! All I wanted was a little help to achieve my little dream, and how do you help me? You leave me out in the cold!"

Joshua's calm tone contrasted her fury. "Jan, we will talk about this later."

"No, we'll talk about it now!"

"I suggest you talk about it later."

Tad closed his eyes and shook his head.

Jan was turning around to find the source for the deep voice that uttered the suggestion when Joshua yanked her from the living room doorway by the arm and shoved her behind him in order to shield her from the danger awaiting them.

"I guess I'm going to have to adjust my plans," Sheriff Curtis Sawyer announced as he removed his gun from its holster.

CHAPTER 29

▼

"Dad is going to kill us."

"You've already told us that, Donny." Sarah laid her head back on the head-rest and tried to go back to sleep.

"Yeah, well, no one will listen to me, and I'm too young to die."

"We've been listening to you for the last two days." Murphy told him from the driver's seat of the van. "If you wanted to stay with Aunt Carol, then why didn't you?"

"I'm just telling you that Dad's going to kill us."

It was a mutiny led by J.J. and Murphy, and vetoed by Tracy, who knew how unwise it was to not follow their father's orders.

During the course of the road trip to North Carolina, J.J. and Murphy became more determined to return home. When they told their siblings their plan, Sarah was more than willing to go with them. Donny wanted to go, but announced they would all die. Tracy knew the extent of their father's wrath, but her brothers and sister needed her reasonable guidance on their insane mission.

So, the morning after their arrival, Murphy told their aunt that they were going to spend the day on the beach. Then, they all simply piled into the van and drove off. Their aunt would not realize they were not coming back until it was too late to stop them.

It was dark when Murphy took the Chester exit off Route 30 into town. All of their butts were sore from riding in the van for two days-one day to the Outer Banks and one day back. They had to gear themselves up to confront their father. Each of them silently rehearsed his or her defense.

Multi-colored lights of emergency vehicles lit up the sky above the small town. As they turned onto Carolina Avenue to make the turn onto Sixth Street to take them up to Rock Spring Boulevard, they found a police barricade blocking their access onto Sixth. The center of the activity was up the street between Indiana Avenue and Church Alley.

"What's going on?" Tracy asked her older brothers.

They eyed a collection of police vehicles, ambulances, and various news crews jostling for views of one of the houses up the street.

"I don't know." Murphy pulled up to the curb.

J.J. climbed out of the passenger side of the van and wandered over to the barricade for a better look. His brothers and sisters got out behind him to stretch their legs.

Tess Bauer, dressed to impress, and her crew were set up on the corner of Church Alley. Unaware of the group of children listening to every word, just out of camera range, Tess gave her report to her television audience:

"The police have yet to release the details of the shooting on this quiet suburban street. However, witnesses have told Channel 6 News that the shooting took place in an apartment above a doctor's office and three people are believed to be dead. All of the victims are local residents; two men, one a doctor, the other a lawyer, and a woman."

"No!"

The camera operator quickly focused in on the wail.

"Dad! No! It can't be—"

J.J. broke through the police lines, even while uniformed officers made vain efforts to stop him.

With strength in numbers, the rest of Joshua Thornton's offspring, not even aware of their wailing, followed their eldest sibling up the street towards Tad's home from which they saw a parade of stretchers with body bags on them coming down the steps of his second floor apartment.

The news camera caught the action when Sheriff Curtis Sawyer intercepted Murphy before he could rip open one of the bags. The rest of the deputies and state police officers tackled the hysterical children while the journalists reported the scene reminiscent of a 1960's riot.

The police forced the five children into a state police van and slammed the doors shut behind them.

The Thornton children screamed and pounded on the doors while Sheriff Curtis Sawyer climbed into the driver's seat and sped out of the alley.

"What do you think you're doing?" the sheriff demanded to know as he pulled the van around the barricades into the direct line of fire of the news cameras.

"You killed Dad!" Tracy screamed at him from the front passenger seat across from him. Her siblings sobbed in the back.

"Where did you get a crazy idea like that?"

In their hysteria, the children didn't notice that the sheriff had turned onto Route 30 and headed towards the Pennsylvania border.

"Everyone knows you work for Rawlings!" J.J. told him. "You don't make a move without his say so!"

"Why'd you have to kill him?" Sarah cried.

"Isn't it obvious?" Murphy answered her. "Because Dad was too smart. Rawlings knew that it was just a matter of time before Dad put them all away for good!"

"How much did Rawlings pay you to kill Dad?" J.J. asked Sawyer.

"I did not kill your father." The sheriff crossed the state line into Pennsylvania.

"Give us a break!" Sarah scoffed.

"We've only been here a matter of weeks and we know that Reverend Rawlings runs the drugs in this valley. It's common knowledge," Murphy yelled. "If you aren't in his pocket, why don't you arrest him?"

"Because we can't put anyone away for what everyone knows without any real evidence to back it up," Sheriff Sawyer argued. "If we could, Al Capone would have gotten the chair for ordering the St. Valentine's Day Massacre instead of locked up a few years for tax evasion. Everyone knows a lot of things about Reverend Rawlings, but no one has squat that can put him away. Did you ever think that I was trying to get that?"

"By killing our dad?" Tracy blubbered.

"I did not kill him."

Suddenly, J.J. noticed they were not heading down the river to the sheriff's department. The van was racing down a gravel road in the country. "Wait a minute! Where are you taking us?"

"Some place where you can stay out of trouble."

All five children had the same thought at the same time. The sheriff was doing what he had to do. They knew too much. It was simple. Do away with them and he would not have to look over his shoulder to make sure they didn't extract their revenge on him.

Fearfully, they watched Sheriff Curtis Sawyer turn the van onto a dirt lane that led up to a darkened white farmhouse that rested on a small hill behind a cow pasture.

Wordlessly, they came up with a plan.

They waited until he turned the police van into a driveway that ended at an apple tree before Tracy lunged at the sheriff. She grabbed the steering wheel with both hands, stomped on his foot that was on the gas pedal, and kept it there.

The van hurtled into the tree.

The impact threw everyone forward.

"You damn kids!"

Before the trained and experienced lawman could gather his senses, Tracy's long fingers were like ten daggers into his eyes. After blinding him, she gave him a left hook that stunned him long enough for her to grab the keys out of the ignition, and follow her siblings in their escape.

Screaming for help from whoever could hear them, the five children ran in five different directions across the farm.

Each one of Joshua Thornton's offspring paused only long enough to see if the sheriff was chasing them.

Instead of pursuing them, their abductor stayed in the van and bellowed. "Thornton! You better get out here! Now!"

In the dark, from their hiding places, the escapees saw the silhouette of three people rush from the house to the van. They recognized the state police uniforms. While two of the three figures helped Sheriff Sawyer from the van, the third came around and called out to them.

"All right, kids! Front and center! Now!"

The Thornton children's hysteria was replaced with elation, only to just as quickly be replaced with fear, when they recognized their father's familiar commanding tone.

$$*\qquad*\qquad*\qquad*$$

"You know, one of my biggest concerns when I became a parent was that one of my children would grow up to become a delinquent."

Dressed in the dark green uniform of the West Virginia State police, Joshua paced the kitchen in the deserted farmhouse. His children were lined up across the center of the floor in wobbly, kitchen table chairs.

"But never, in my wildest imagination, did I ever dream that it would happen to all of them." Joshua paused to glare at each of them, one at a time. "You have in one week gone from trespassing into a cemetery to assaulting a police officer."

Guiltily, they looked over to the kitchen table where Tad and Jan were administering first aid to the scratches on Sheriff Sawyer's face. His right eye was already swelling from Tracy's punch.

Sarah defended herself as best she could. "Tracy was the one who punched him."

Tad and Jan smirked at each other. "Curt, you didn't tell us it was a girl who beat you up," Tad snickered.

"If you tell anyone that, I'll really kill you," Sheriff Sawyer growled. He suppressed a cry when Tad touched one of the scratches with antiseptic.

"Sorry, I left my medical bag at home. I have to use this old first aid kit I found in the cabinet, and it doesn't have everything."

"What are you kids doing here?" Joshua turned back to his defiant offspring.

"Sheriff Sawyer brought us," Donny answered with a grin in an attempt at humor.

Joshua didn't fall for it. "You are supposed to be at the beach."

"Would you believe we took a wrong turn?" Sarah also failed to make her father smile.

"We didn't want to go to the beach," J.J. told their father. "We wanted to be with you."

"We already discussed that," Joshua countered.

"And you decided that we were going to go on vacation, and you would join us later." J.J. said.

"It was my decision to make. I'm the father."

"But after Mom died, you also decided that you were going to leave the Navy because you wanted us all to be together," J.J. reminded him. "Well, how can we all be together if you send us away?"

Joshua stated firmly, "That was totally different. My decision to leave the Navy was because I am the only parent you have left to raise you."

"And you still are," Murphy pointed out.

"I know this is none of my business," Tad interjected, "but your father sent you away for your own safety, and the completion of this operation we got ourselves into."

"Which is what?" J.J. asked. "Faking your death?" He observed the police uniform.

"Faking a hit." Joshua pointed to Curtis Sawyer, who now held an ice pack made of cubes wrapped in a torn, yellowed dishtowel to his swollen eye. "Believe it or not, our sheriff is one of the good guys. He's been working with the feds since before he was elected."

"You kids were right," the sheriff told them. "It is common knowledge that Rawlings controls all the drugs in the valley. His empire is small potatoes compared to the big cities, and that's why the big dealers don't try to muscle in on his turf, but it is still lucrative. The reverend has such a 'holier than thou' reputation that he is above reproach by those in high places. If you tell anyone that the Reverend Rawlings is a major drug dealer, the response is, 'Reverend Rawlings would never do that.' His granddaughter was the front man."

"Who was it before Vicki?" Jan asked. This was her first chance to interview the sheriff. "I mean she is—was—only seventeen years old. If the reverend was a major drug dealer for generations, then who did it before her?"

"His daughter Bridgette. And before her, it was Sheriff Delaney, who had punks working for him. After Sheriff Delaney died, the feds saw their opportunity to get a man on the inside. Since Mom is their maid, my bosses thought I already had a foot in the door. So, I came home from the service," the sheriff held up his fingers in the form of quotation marks, "and worked my way into the reverend's confidence."

"Wait a minute," J.J. interrupted. His face showed his confusion. "If Rawlings is a small-time operator in drugs compared to the big city dealers, then why do the feds even care? Shouldn't they be going after the big drug dealers?"

Sawyer was impressed by J.J.'s perceptive intellect. "Good question. Yes, Rawlings is small potatoes compared to the dealers we haven't been able to touch, but his suppliers are big potatoes."

Jan was not so impressed. "So the feds are looking to nail him so that they can offer him immunity from prosecution in exchange for rolling over on his suppliers. What about all the people he's had killed throughout the years?"

"I'm not the one who will offer him any deals," the sheriff said in his defense. "My job is to bust him the best way I know how."

Joshua chose this moment to confirm a suspicion. "It was your bosses who got the admiral to get the military records released to me on Private Rice."

Curtis Sawyer grinned. "I'm no JAG lawyer. After I read Lulu's letter and those fingerprints on that John Doe showed that he had been in Leavenworth, I knew that Rawlings and Rice had a military connection. Rice was convicted for stealing government property to sell on the black market. Maybe Rawlings was one of Penn's Hong Kong connections and, after Rice read about the great Reverend Rawlings and his church in that magazine, he came to Chester to blackmail him. Imagine what would have happened to the reverend's church if Rice leaked to his congregation that their leader was nothing more than a common thief stealing from our own government."

"That's a thought," Joshua agreed. "But we can't prove that Rawlings had anything to do with Penn, Rice, or the black market. According to the military records, Rawlings had no way of knowing any of them."

"Look," the sheriff asserted, "Rice and Rawlings knew each other somehow. Rice tore that article out of that magazine and came to Chester for a reason. Now, Thornton, my people told me that if anyone can put this together, you can. After all the trouble we went through to get those military records released to you, you can't go stupid on us now."

"You've been working on this a long time," Tad said to Curt.

"A very long time," Curtis Sawyer suppressed a groan while the doctor worked on his wounds. "And this is the first time, in my whole career, I've ever gotten injured in the line of duty."

"So the reverend did hire you to kill Dad?" Tracy confirmed their earlier suspicion.

"He didn't actually hire me. I believe he ordered it, but it was Wally Rawlings who paid me half of five thousand dollars to kill both your father and Dr. MacMillan. I get the rest tomorrow. The only problem is the son didn't actually say it was the reverend's orders and his father was never present for any of the meetings. So far, I only have enough to get Wally."

Joshua was more confident. "That may be enough to get him to roll over on his father. Loyalty is not one of Wally's strong suits."

"When did you set this all up?" Murphy wanted to know.

Tad explained, "The sheriff contacted your dad as soon as he was contracted to do the job. Josh told me what was going down."

"This was already set up when he caught you kids at the cemetery," Joshua informed them. "That gave me the perfect excuse to send you away and out of danger."

"But why send us away?" Sarah wondered.

"What have you kids been through in the last hour?" Joshua responded with a question.

"An emotional roller coaster." Tracy already knew the answer to Sarah's query.

Sheriff Sawyer told them, "Even if you were in on it, we couldn't be sure with all of you that you wouldn't confide in a friend, who would tell his or her friend, who would tell someone, who would tell the Rawlings. His church has hundreds of members, who are everywhere, who think he's the holiest thing since the pope."

"If one of them warned Rawlings, then Sheriff Sawyer would be killed and someone else would be hired to finish the job he was hired to do." Joshua concluded, "I've seen it happen. I knew a guy in Naval Intelligence who was undercover. A friend of his wife saw him in a shopping mall with his target, a terrorist suspect. She didn't know he was undercover and started asking about his wife and the kids and an upcoming barbecue. They both got bullets in the brain. I don't mean to be blunt, but that is the mentality we are dealing with here. In an operation as delicate as this, the less who know the better."

"I didn't even know about it until Sheriff Sawyer walked in with a gun pointed at us," Jan told them. "I about peed my pants."

Joshua gestured towards Jan while he told his children, "There's someone else who wouldn't do what she was told. So, we had to improvise. Tad and I got to walk out in nice clean police uniforms so the media wouldn't notice us, while Jan got to experience being carried out in a body bag with air holes punched in it."

"All the more material for my book." The budding journalist grinned.

"I thought it was an article for the paper," Tad said.

"Hey, I've been killed in a professional hit. Do you think I'm just going to confine myself to *The Evening Review*? I scooped Tess Bauer. I wish you guys could have stopped off to let me get my laptop."

Joshua turned apologetic towards his children, who were still lined up in their chairs. "I meant for you to find out about this after it was all over. Carol was going to tell you tomorrow morning."

Ashamed, the kids hung their heads. J.J. offered an apology for himself and his siblings. "Dad, I don't know what to say. We really blew it this time, huh?"

Sheriff Sawyer let them off the hook. "Maybe you didn't. Maybe you sealed it. The news people got everything on tape, and you can be sure it will be all over the news. You kids really believed your father was dead, so your reaction was genuine."

The sheriff told Joshua, "If Rawlings got suspicious about you sending your kids off just before the hit went down, their reactions in front of Tess's cameras would certainly do away with it. That meant you didn't suspect anything and letting them find out that way—" Sawyer shook his head with a naughty snicker. "What kind of father would do that to his kids?"

"So we didn't blow it?" Sarah grinned hopefully.

"You're still grounded for life," Joshua pronounced deadpan.

"So what do we do now?" Murphy stood up. "Start making funeral arrangements?"

"We're not going so far as to have a funeral."

"Oh, come on, Dad," Murphy slipped an arm around Joshua's shoulders. "It will be fun. We'll have a wake. All your friends will be there, and then you'll find out what people really think of you."

"Then, we'll get to find out what he left us in his will," Donny chimed in.

Joshua slipped Murphy's arm from his shoulders. "This will be over as soon as Sheriff Sawyer arrests Wally and, hopefully, Reverend Rawlings, when he pays him off. For now, you are going to go home, call Aunt Carol and tell her what you did, and say nothing to anyone."

Jan had other questions for Sheriff Sawyer. "I can understand why Wally wanted Josh killed, but why Tad?"

The potential hit man shook his head. "Only that he hated him." He squinted at Tad. "One interesting thing, MacMillan, Wally said you were Vicki's father." As he made his announcement, Sawyer glanced at Joshua out of the corner of his eye.

Recalling earlier conversations with his cousin on the subject, Joshua gazed at Tad, who responded firmly. "I am not Vicki's father. Cindy and I never had intercourse. In a week, you'll get the results from my DNA test to prove that there is no biological connection between me and Vicki."

"Well, we'll find that out." Sheriff Sawyer drawled, "But if you aren't Vicki's father, and Wally is telling the truth, then we've got an interesting twist in this case because Wally swore to me that he never consummated his marriage to Vicki's mother."

"Hot damn!" Jan gasped and scribbled furiously on her stationary pad. "This is more than a book! This is a movie! I wonder if they'll get Drew Barrymore to play me."

"How much do you want to bet Reverend Rawlings will claim it was Immaculate Conception?" Murphy smirked.

Sheriff Sawyer cracked, "With Vicki Rawlings, the devil himself would have had to have been the father."

Joshua was in deep thought as he murmured, "Maybe he was."

CHAPTER 30

▼

"I was not Vicki's father," Tad reasserted after the sheriff took the children home.

They were reading Dr. Wilson's files by the dim light from the overhead lamp above the kitchen table. Tad had put the trunk into the patrol car before being 'murdered'.

"Keep saying it. Maybe we'll start to believe it," Jan scoffed. "I remember how you two used to hang out together. It was like the princess and the frog."

"More like Princess Di and Mick Jagger," Joshua chuckled. "Don't worry. Your DNA tests will prove everything. The only problem is that it will be at least a week before we get them and we need them now."

Jan snickered.

"Like I care if you don't believe me," Tad responded to Jan's laughter.

"What woman in the tri-state area have you not slept with?" Jan asked with scorn.

"You," Tad answered without humor.

"Why would he lie?" Joshua casually asked Jan. He was sitting back in his chair with his arms folded across his chest.

Tad smirked at Joshua's defense in the form of the single question.

Jan struggled to come up with an answer to Joshua's abrupt query. "Why should we believe him?" she finally responded.

"Because Tad has no reason to lie about it," Joshua pointed out. "Think about it. You just said that Tad MacMillan has the reputation of having slept with every woman in the tri-state area. He's had a reputation of being a stud since the day he lost his virginity, and he's never done anything to dispute it."

Jan agreed, "He likes people thinking he's a rogue."

"Better than being frigid," Tad chuckled at his biting insult to the proper journalist.

Joshua interrupted Jan as she was about to lunge towards Tad in her defense. "My point is that it would only improve his reputation as a stud if he bedded the virginal Cindy Welch. Just think. Here we have a stud so virile that not only does he seduce the valley's virgin queen, but he sires her baby after she is newly wed to the son of the valley's most prominent citizen." Joshua laughed quietly, "Talk about a notch in your belt."

Jan countered, "Tad admits that he loved Cindy. Maybe he cared enough about her to not want to ruin her reputation." As the thought struck her, she added, "Or maybe he cared enough about his hide to not want Wally to kill him for sleeping with his wife!"

"Wally assumed Tad slept with her anyway, and he's lived this long," Joshua replied.

"Until he hired Curt to kill us," Tad pointed out.

Joshua surmised, "Most likely the reverend ordered Wally to have me killed to stop the investigation, and Wally had become so consumed with hatred for you that he decided to throw you in on the contract as a favor for himself."

Returning to the subject of Tad's claim of innocence, Joshua shook his head at Jan. "No, for Tad to lie about being Vicki's father does not make sense. He had the reputation before he even met Cindy. It only improved his reputation for people to think that the virtuous Cindy Welch gave in to his animal magnetism and fell in love with him.

"Ah!" Joshua sighed mockingly, "Tad MacMillan must be some man for a woman of Cindy Welch's purity to give in to him."

"Give me a break," Jan scoffed.

Joshua continued, "What I want to know is why Wally would lie about being Vicki's birth father?"

"Because he hated her," Jan answered.

"Then why not just disown her? It isn't like he didn't have the heart to do that."

Tad suggested, "Maybe his father forbade it."

"And Rawlings didn't forbid Wally from publicizing it to me and the sheriff that he did not have a loving relationship with his wife and she bore another man's child?" Joshua asked rhetorically. "I doubt it. Why make up a lie about sleeping with Cindy and claim that Tad is Vicki's father? Could it be because it's true that he never consummated his marriage? Therefore, someone else has to be Vicki's father."

Jan giggled at the simple solution to find out the answer to their questions. "Why not just get a DNA test from Wally? That will prove if he is, or isn't, Vicki's father. Besides, what does it matter if he isn't?"

Joshua confessed, "Because DNA evidence left on the scene proved to come from Vicki's half sister. If Wally is not her father, then we are not looking for one of his offspring by another relationship." He added with a snarl, "And to answer your question about why we don't get DNA evidence from Wally, Mannings said no and since there is no probable cause to connect Wally to the murder scene since he has an alibi, we can't get a warrant to get it from him."

"Who else could be Vicki's father except Tad?" Jan asked.

Tad mused thoughtfully, "If Wally isn't Vicki's father, then that would eliminate Alexis Hitchcock as a suspect."

"Who is Alexis Hitchcock?" Jan snapped.

"Wally's illegitimate daughter," Tad answered. "She and her mother have been missing for the last four years. I thought Wally killed them. But when that DNA turned up at the murder scene, I started to think differently. I was beginning to think Alexis was posing as Amber."

Jan's eye widened at learning this latest information.

Joshua sorted the brown envelopes into two separate files. "Doc Wilson has the patient files for the whole Rawlings family here. There has to be a reason he wanted us to read them." He shuffled through the folders. "Here's Vicki's."

Tad observed, "She was just a kid when Doc died."

"Was it before or after Wilson died that Vicki started harassing you?" Joshua asked.

"After." Tad added in a low voice, "Soon after."

Joshua nodded with a small smile and made a "Hmm" noise before he returned to the stack of files. "We also have Bridgette's file, and Hal Poole's."

"Hal was living in the same house as Cindy," Jan reminded them. "Maybe the two of them formed some sort of alliance that led to other things."

"Let me see Wally's file." Tad reached for Vicki's folder and opened it up.

Joshua laid Wally's folder open on the table next to Vicki's folder in front of Tad. The doctor checked only one fact before ordering, "Now, give me Cindy's file."

"What are you looking at?" Jan peered at the papers on the other side of the table in an attempt to read them upside down.

"I'm going to use the old-fashioned way to find out if Wally is telling the truth about not being Vicki's father."

"Vicki's blood type was A positive. She was RH positive," Joshua observed. As a father, he suspected he knew what information Tad was studying in the patient files.

"Cindy was O, RH negative." Tad moved his finger over to Wally's folder. "Wally was A RH negative." He looked up at both of them and said what Joshua already knew. "Wally couldn't be Vicki's father, not if she was RH positive. One of her parents would have to have been RH positive. Since Cindy was negative, then it had to come from the father."

"Wally must have been telling the truth about never consummating the marriage," Joshua concluded. "You said Cindy confessed her love for you on their honeymoon."

"Whoa!" Jan breathed, "What a damper to hand your husband on your honeymoon."

Joshua agreed. "For a man of Wally's ego, that had to be like driving a stake through his balls." He told Tad, "If Wally was telling Sawyer the truth about never sleeping with Cindy, and she confessed to loving you, then it would be natural for him to assume you were the baby's father when she got pregnant."

The doctor laid his hand on Vicki Rawlings's patient file. "Doc Wilson had to have known the second he saw the results of Vicki's blood tests that Wally wasn't the father. Like Wally, he probably just assumed that I was." He answered their unasked question. "I'm A positive and Wilson knew it. Theoretically, I could have been Vicki's father, but I'm not."

"Then that leaves only one other option. Cindy was with someone else," Joshua observed, "someone who has RH positive blood factor, who also fathered another child that was on the scene when Beth was killed." He asked his two companions, "Am I correct in assuming that you both, having known Cindy, are in agreement that she didn't have another child that no one knows about? That she's not the common parent between Vicki and the suspect we're looking for?"

"Impossible," Jan answered. "Cindy led a very public life. She was the princess of Rawlings's church. She was their lead vocalist and the leader of the women's group. If she had another pregnancy, other than when she was pregnant with Vicki, everyone would have known about it."

Joshua muttered, "That's what I thought."

"What about Hal Poole? Who would blame him if he had a mistress or two?" Jan suggested again. "Bridgette treats him like crap. Cindy was so sweet. They probably got together to give each other strength. Vicki could have been Hal's and who is to say that Hal didn't have another bastard child from someone else."

"Hal Poole? I don't think so," Tad said with certainty.

"He may be a wuss in public, but you never know what a man is like behind closed doors," Jan argued. "If Hal and Cindy were having a love affair and Bridgette found out about it, then Hal would stand to lose a whole lot. Bridgette is the one with the money. That would give Hal motive to kill Cindy."

When he considered the scenario, Tad shook his head with a knowing smile. "From what I heard, Wally and Cindy weren't the only Rawlings couple that never consummated their marriage."

Joshua gasped, "You have to be kidding!"

Tad's chuckle turned to laughter.

"He is kidding." Jan was not amused by what she considered to be Tad's sick sense of humor.

Tad shook his head. "No, I heard from a former church member and friend of Hal Poole's that Bridgette convinced her groom that sex, other than to make babies, was a sin. Now, they have no children. You tell me."

Joshua scoffed, "Why would she marry him if—?"

"Because her daddy ordered it," Tad answered. "The Poole family is a big supporter of the Rawlings's church, both financially and politically. By political I mean that since early in Reverend Rawlings's ministry Hal's parents have brought a lot of people into the church and a lot of Rawlings's followers follow the Pooles. If the Poole family left, it is safe to say that a large portion of the congregation would go with them, along with a dependable source of income."

Joshua recalled that Hal Poole expressed his love and obsession with Bridgette back in high school. While it was clear her feelings for him were not the same, she did not discourage his affection either.

Tad went on to explain the marriage. "It is a classic power marriage. If Bridgette turned down Hal's proposal, do you think his family would have continued attending their church?"

"So Bridgette married a man she didn't love, and then manipulated his little pea brain to keep him from touching her?" Jan scoffed. "I think the two of them deserve each other!"

Tad's shoulders shook as he chuckled. "Now you know why I find it so laughable for you to suggest that Cindy would have an affair with him."

"Cindy was married to a monster. I imagine that would make any woman vulnerable to have an affair with anyone who offered her an ounce of compassion," Joshua offered as an explanation for Cindy Rawlings's possible adultery.

Joshua's ringing cell phone interrupted the debate. His watch said that it was near midnight. Sheriff Sawyer was calling to report that the children were home safe, and he had already spoken to Wallace Rawlings, who assured the sheriff that he could pick up his money in the prosecuting attorney's office at ten o'clock in the morning.

Joshua found it ironic that a hit man was picking up his pay off for two murders in the prosecutor's office. He hung up the phone and looked at his two partners in crime.

"Ten o'clock tomorrow it will all be over," Jan sighed.

"No," Joshua sat back thoughtfully and studied the tips of his fingers in the dim light. "I expect at ten o'clock tomorrow, it will be just beginning."

*   *   *   *

Every one of the Thornton children was exhausted. They had been on the road all day; and then the emotional upheaval of learning of their father's death; then his being alive; and then his wrath; they were physically and emotionally wrung out by the time Sheriff Sawyer dropped them off at the back door of the Thornton home.

After Tracy won the race for the one bathroom to take a bath, her brothers and sister, grumbling about how long it was taking to bring their house up to the twenty-first century, went to their rooms.

J.J. took the cordless phone from his father's room upstairs to call their aunt to apologize for their deception and any worry they had caused her. She was not surprised. She knew her sister's children well.

The twins opted to try again in the morning, before going to Reverend Andrews's home to retrieve Admiral from where their father had dropped off the pet before he was "killed". They went up to the attic to go to sleep. Donny didn't care if he ever got a bath. He went to bed. Sleep also being her main priority at that moment, Sarah went to her room to go to bed.

Dressed in her bathrobe, Tracy turned on the overhead lamp before turning on the water in the claw-footed tub. In the mirror, she was studying a small pimple appearing on her chin when she saw the bathroom door closing behind her and a figure dressed all in black step out from behind the door. Tracy forced out a scream just as the door slammed shut and the lights went out.

J.J. and Murphy had both put on their sweat pants they wore for their pajamas when they heard Tracy's shrill scream. "Intruder!"

"What was that?" J.J. paused long enough to ask.

Murphy was already racing down the stairs.

J.J. was compelled into action when he heard a body slammed up against a wall. Forgetting about using the phone he had just set on his nightstand to call the police, he bound down the stairs.

On the second floor, Sarah was pounding on the bathroom door when Murphy bound out of the stairwell. Cat screams came from inside the bathroom.

"Help!" Tracy shrieked.

As if she was the obstacle to getting inside the bathroom to help Tracy, Murphy yelled at Sarah to open the door.

Too frightened to move, Donny watched from his bedroom doorway at the end of the hall.

"The door is locked!" Sarah wrenched the glass doorknob.

"Stand back!" Murphy ordered her as J.J. raced down the hall.

Even though he was known for his athletic prowess, Murphy was surprised when the force of his kick, combined with the deterioration of the century-old glue sealing the panels together, knocked out the top portion of the door. Tracy dove toward the light entering the room through the hole her brother created.

Nearly hysterical, Tracy sobbed while Sarah and J.J. pulled her out through the hole in the door, before Murphy shoved it open and rushed inside. Her hands and arms were slippery from the blood rushing from her wounds.

The sight of his bloodied sister startled Donny into action. He raced down the stairs to the phone to call their father for help.

The assailant shoved Murphy into the water-filled bathtub before making an escape. Even with three witnesses in the hall, no one was prepared to stop the figure dressed from head to toe in black that raced past them and down the stairs.

While the blood that covered Tracy motivated Donny to call their father, it triggered Sarah to go on the offensive. She didn't stop to consider what she would do if she succeeded, but Sarah did know that she was going to catch her sister's assailant.

Despite her siblings' calls to stop, Sarah hurled herself down the stairs and tackled the intruder on the steps. When Tracy's attacker turned to take a swing with the blood-covered knife at the girl, Sarah dove and caught the intruder by the waist, which sent both of them down the staircase in a tangled mass of rolling bodies.

"Sarah! No!" J.J. screamed. All he could do was watch them tumble down the long curved staircase.

From the bottom of the stairs, Donny watched Sarah and the black clad figure rolling together down the stairs towards him. "Sarah!" he squawked through a throat tight with fear.

With the plop of her head hitting the hardwood floor, Sarah landed in a heap at the foot of the stairs.

Sarah's body cushioned the intruder's fall. The assailant halted only long enough to get up, before racing out the front door into the night.

*   *   *   *

"What am I doing?" Joshua cursed while he paced the morgue.

"I believe it's called pacing," Jan answered.

Tad, wearing a surgical mask to hide his identity, was upstairs talking to the emergency room doctor, a trusted colleague, to find out the condition of two of Joshua's children. His sons sat in a state of shock in the waiting room.

"No! I should not be here! I should be upstairs with my kids! I should have been home tonight and not out playing cops and robbers! Damn it!" Joshua shouted loud enough to wake the dead bodies in the room. "I quit!"

He threw open the doors to head for the elevator to take him up to his children.

Jan threw herself at Joshua and grabbed his arm to pull her friend back into the safety of the morgue. "If you go upstairs then everyone will know that you aren't dead, and we won't have Wally, and he'll stay the prosecutor, and the reverend's business will go on as usual!"

"They came after my kids! Tad said they killed a whole family. Why would they draw the line at my kids? What was I thinking?" Joshua shook Jan off his arm like she nothing more than an annoying gnat and punched the button to call the elevator. His voice shook as he asked her, "Do you know what I've been doing?"

Confused by the question, Jan shook her head to convey that she didn't know about what he was asking her.

Joshua slumped against the white concrete block wall and sighed heavily before he answered. "I've been hiding."

Jan scoffed. "I know. I was at that farmhouse, too."

Slowly, Joshua shook his head. "No, not that. I've been hiding from fatherhood." He explained, "I don't want to be a single father. I don't like it. I never know if I'm doing the right thing or not. So I let myself get all wrapped up in this case and sent my kids to my sister-in-law's because I didn't want to deal with feeling clueless. Murder is more fun than single parenthood."

"More fun or more comfortable?"

"What do you mean?"

Jan grinned softly. "Josh, God gave you a gift. The gift of being able to put together puzzles and uncover the truth where no other man can. You've spent your life using that gift to help people. You're good at it and you know it." She added, "And Valerie was good at raising kids. Look at your kids. You can see it. She stayed home and took care of them while you went off chasing bad guys and getting shot at because that was what she was good at."

Stunned, Joshua slowly nodded his head. He blinked his eyes to hold back tears of guilt and fear.

Jan shrugged with a grin. "You're probably right about getting all involved in this case to escape from your parental responsibilities, but—Damn! You're not the only one here." She giggled. "I'd choose playing dead and being carried out of Tad's apartment in a body bag to stocking the laxative aisle at my store any day."

A grin crept to Joshua's lips. "I think raising my kids is more important than unpacking laxatives. The price parents pay for neglect is much higher."

"What are you going to do about it?" Jan asked.

"Quit."

"You can't quit!" Jan responded firmly.

"Watch me." Joshua turned around and punched the call button once more.

Jan grabbed Joshua's arm with both her hands. Determined not to let him go, she forcibly yanked him a couple of feet back from the elevator. "What about your responsibilities to this valley? You said that Doc Wilson told you that the reverend was evil. They went after your kids. That proves that they're evil, and they need to be stopped, and if you don't do it, then no one will. Didn't you say in your valedictorian speech something about man's responsibilities to his fellow man?"

The elevator doors opened to allow Joshua's escape to his family.

Jan's words made him hesitate.

Seeing that Joshua was listening, Jan resumed. "This is our chance to take them down. If we don't take it, then there may not be a next time. We're only a couple of yards from the goal."

The doors shut again. Joshua let Jan lead him by the arm back to the morgue.

"Sarah and Tracy could be dead," Joshua muttered.

"Then give the Rawlings hell! The way only you can." Jan held open the door to the morgue.

Joshua hesitated when he heard the elevator doors open again.

Dressed in a surgical gown, Tad stepped off the elevator. He carried a gown and mask over his arm.

Murphy, J.J., and Donny stepped off the elevator behind him. When he saw his father, Donny ran to him and threw his arms around his waist.

Reading his son's sobs as indications of the worst news, Joshua hugged his youngest son tightly.

While the Thornton men went into a group hug, Tad relayed his report. "Everyone is going to be okay. Tracy is being patched up right now. Whoever it was went after her with a knife, but she defended herself well. All she got were defense wounds on her arms."

"Her face?" Joshua choked.

Tad shook his head as he ushered them back into the morgue. "No cuts on her face. I've already called the best plastic surgeon in the area. He will be out tomorrow morning, and he'll be able to fix her up so there will be no scars. I looked at them myself. They'll heal up fine."

"Sarah?"

"A concussion and a couple of broken ribs. She's going to be fine. Tracy will be released in the morning, and Sarah can go home in a couple of days."

They heard the elevator doors open down the hall.

Tad gave Joshua the gown and mask. "We'll go back upstairs and you can see them," the doctor was saying when Sheriff Sawyer came in.

"Well, our plan hasn't gone completely haywire," Sheriff Sawyer announced. "Tess Bauer is already upstairs reporting about the tragedy of the Thornton family. It's a real tearjerker."

"How did she find out about it so fast?" Jan asked with a note of jealousy.

"She's got sources everywhere," Sawyer snarled.

"Did you find out who did it?" Joshua queried the sheriff while Tad tied the back of his gown.

"I called Wally Rawlings again. I made like I was pissed that he hired someone else to do what I could do with fewer complications. He claims he had nothing to do with it. His orders were just to kill you and Tad and no one else. Then, he chewed me out for offing Jan and said he wasn't giving me any bonus for taking her out."

"Do you believe him?" Jan wanted to know.

"I believe that he didn't hire someone to do it. He was worried about the direction suspicions might fly."

"It wasn't a pro," J.J. stated with certainty. "I mean, Dad, wouldn't a pro have been neater about it?"

"Tracy swears it was a girl," Donny told them.

"There are female assassins," Jan said.

"No, it was a cat fight in there," Murphy disagreed. "There were screams from two girls. She was pulling Tracy's hair and trying to cut her up. When I went in there, and she shoved me, I grabbed her and felt her boobs—" Conscious of Jan's presence, he corrected himself, "I mean, breasts."

Tad told them, "Whoever it was, Tracy says she got in a few good punches. She swears her attacker now has a couple of broken ribs."

"I wouldn't be surprised," Sheriff Sawyer rubbed his injured eye.

Tad tried not to snicker at the sheriff's wound. "We'll keep an eye out here in the hospital for any female patients with broken or bruised ribs."

Joshua warned them, "Let's not make any assumptions that this is connected to the Rawlings." He asked his sons, "Was Tracy having any disagreement with any girls in town?"

"We just moved here," Murphy reminded him.

"How about Ken? Does he have any old girlfriends who might be jealous?"

Tad shook his head. "I know Ken. He's a nice kid. He was not seeing anyone who would go nuts like that."

Jan suddenly gasped, "You don't think one of Vicki's weird friends did it to make you stop trying to put Rawlings out of the drug business."

Joshua squinted at Jan as the thought sickened him. "Like Amber."

Sheriff Sawyer shook his head. "Amber is long gone. The word on the street is that Reverend Rawlings has an open contract on her. If she's still around, she's more stupid than we thought." He added, "And speaking of contract killings—"

Joshua breathed, "There's another contract on me?"

Sawyer grinned, "That one was already filled. Everyone still thinks you're dead. I'm talking about the Hitchcocks. I called the FAA to check that passenger manifest for that DC-10 that the Hitchcocks were supposed to be on. Their answer was waiting for me on my desk when I got to the office tonight. There were no Hitchcocks. As for the girl—" the sheriff asked Tad, "You said that Alexis was around twelve years old then?"

After Tad nodded his head to answer his question, Sawyer went on, "There were no children on that flight, period. So, we know for certain that, at least, Alexis Hitchcock was not on that plane." He chuckled, "So much for Officer Scott Collins swearing that that witness put them on that plane." His chuckle turned into a sarcastic laugh. "Funny thing about that witness. Hannah Pickering is her name."

"What about her?" Joshua wondered.

"She was a member of Rawlings's church, and Bridgette's secretary."

"They're dead," Tad announced sadly.

Jan grinned. "Alexis is Wally's daughter. That makes her Vicki's half sister."

"No," Joshua reminded her. "We just found the evidence that proves that Vicki was not Wally's daughter. That eliminates Alexis as a suspect." He muttered, "I want to know why Collins didn't check out that woman's statement. A simple check of the manifest would have proven she was lying."

The sheriff was grumbling, "I want to check that out myself. I hate crooked cops."

Joshua wasn't paying any attention. He was muttering thoughtfully. The wheels in his mind churned. "Alexis Hitchcock and her family disappear. Tracy was attacked with a knife. Morgan Lucas interviews Amber and she is stabbed to death. Vicki was impaled." He turns to his sons. "How was it that Tracy ended up in that bathroom and not one of you?"

Not sure where Joshua was going, all three boys shrugged and exchanged questioning looks. It occurred to J.J. what Joshua wanted to know. He answered slowly, "She got there first."

Joshua sighed heavily and hung his head before he asked his cousin, "Tad, do you know the medical examiner in Pittsburgh?"

Tad laughed. "Know her? She's a woman in the tri-state area."

"Hound," Jan cracked.

"I want you to get me everything you can on Morgan Lucas's murder." Joshua turned to Sheriff Sawyer. "And I need you to call the news station. I need all the taped, the unedited ones, of Amber's interviews."

Tad asked, "Are you still thinking that Amber is Alexis Hitchcock out for revenge?"

Jan argued, "Didn't you just say that Alexis was eliminated as a suspect because the killer was Vicki's sister and we just proved that Wally wasn't Vicki's birth father? So why is Alexis still on our list of suspects?"

"In either case, Tracy never met Amber or Alexis," Murphy objected. "So why would whoever it was want to hurt her?"

"To get to me, that's why," Joshua answered somberly.

*   *   *   *

"Okay, here's how it is going to go down," Sheriff Sawyer told the state police, his trusted deputies, federal agents, and his "victims".

The morning after the "hit", everyone met at the sheriff's satellite office in Newell. They could not risk warning the county's prosecuting attorney of his arrest by gathering at the courthouse across the parking lot from his own office.

Sheriff Sawyer's office in Newell consisted of a single room with a phone, desk, and chair. The officers and agents, dressed in bulletproof vests, were crowded into the bare office. To blend in, the sheriff's three victims wore state police uniforms.

Jan held her recorder out to catch every word.

"I'll go in like usual." The sheriff gestured towards his arresting officers. "You wait in the stairwells and around the building until I give the signal. The signal will be when I say, 'Nice doing business with you, Mr. Prosecutor.'"

"What if Reverend Rawlings is there?" one of the deputies asked, "Do we arrest him, too?"

"If he's there," Curtis Sawyer said, "I going to make damn sure I get a statement from him confirming that the hits were on his orders. So far, we don't have anything from Wallace Rawlings to connect the reverend to the contract."

"But wouldn't his being present for the payoff be enough?" Jan inquired.

"No," Joshua responded. "He could make a case for reasonable doubt by saying that he thought Wally was paying back a loan, or buying a car, or any legal transaction."

The sheriff asked for any more questions. With assertions that everything was clear, they dispersed and headed down the river to the prosecuting attorney's corner office in the basement of the school to make the big bust.

Joshua, Tad, and Jan made the trip with two federal agents in the back of the surveillance van that picked up Sheriff Curtis Sawyer's wiretap. The van parked in the lot next to the door leading down to Wallace Rawlings's office.

In the deserted school building, Curtis Sawyer tested the wiretap by softly singing *To All the Girls I've Loved Before*, which caused his audience in the van to snicker, while he descended the stairs to the corner office.

"He'd better not give up his day job," Tad joked.

Joshua could see the excitement in Jan's eyes at being in on the biggest thing in her life. When their eyes met, he shot his oldest childhood friend a smile. He was unaware of how her heart leapt at the sight of his smile, meant for her and only her.

"I'm going in." They heard Sheriff Sawyer step into the reception area.

Wallace Rawlings's bleached blond secretary looked up with a toothy grin when Curtis Sawyer stepped up to her desk in his freshly pressed navy blue sheriff's uniform. He wanted to appear as intimidating as possible. "May I help you, sheriff?"

"I have a ten o'clock appointment to meet with Mr. Rawlings."

"I'm sorry, but Mr. Rawlings isn't in yet."

Everyone in the back of the van groaned.

Sheriff Sawyer frowned. "You must be mistaken. His car is outside in his parking space."

Now, it was the secretary's turn to frown. She shook her head. "I haven't seen Mr. Rawlings all morning. He must be at the courthouse."

Sheriff Sawyer was starting to feel sick. Was he the one set up? Had the Thornton children blown it after all?

"I've been here since eight-thirty, and I haven't seen him," the secretary was saying.

"Maybe he's in his office and just hasn't come out yet." Sheriff Sawyer's annoyance was evident in his tone.

The secretary insisted that was not possible. Wallace Rawlings always locked his office when he was out, and when he was there it was unlocked, and the office door was now locked. Therefore, he must be out.

The secretary was afraid to knock on her boss's door when the sheriff suggested she do so. Wallace Rawlings's temper was infamous.

For this reason, the MP-slash-sheriff-slash-federal agent took charge and knocked on the door.

There was no answer.

In the van, Joshua groaned. "This is getting very irritating."

"You're irritated?" one of the agents jeered. "I can hear Sawyer's blood pressure rising."

Seeing no appointments listed on his calendar, the secretary called around to the various offices in the courthouse across the parking lot to locate her boss. She instructed Sheriff Sawyer, whose appointment was not listed since it was made late the night before, to sit and wait.

"I've got a very bad feeling about this." Joshua stepped out of the back of the van, walked the dozen or so feet to the corner of the school building, and crouched down to peer into the basement window that belonged to the office of Hancock County's prosecuting attorney.

"Damn!" Joshua stepped to the next window and peered inside.

The secretary was dialing another number on the phone in an attempt to locate her boss and get rid of the lawman standing over her like a vulture waiting for her to expire.

Joshua tapped on the window.

The secretary, the phone still at her ear, whirled around. "Who is that?" she barked when she saw Joshua, dressed in his state police uniform, looking in at them.

"Do you have a key for that door?" Joshua pointed in the direction of Wallace Rawlings's office.

"Yes," the secretary looked from Joshua to the sheriff, "but I can't let you have it."

"Then you unlock the door," the sheriff requested.

"I can't. If I did, Mr. Rawlings would—"

"You don't have to worry about Mr. Rawlings," Joshua assured her. "I can promise you that."

Sawyer's request turned into an order. "Unlock that door."

Worried by the tone of the sheriff's command, the secretary took the key out of her desk drawer and scurried through the reception area to the office door. With her own sigh of disgust at the bothersome sheriff, she turned the key in the lock and stood back to let Curtis Sawyer enter. When she stepped in behind him, she screamed.

Joshua Thornton and the rest of the sheriff's team were already rushing in when the sheriff gave his signal into his wire mike. "It was nice doing business with you, Mr. Prosecutor. Bring two body bags with you."

Wallace Rawlings sat behind his desk in a position of no dignity with his arms stretched out on either side. His head hung back. He gazed up to the heavens with a third eye in the center of his forehead. Blood, reminiscent of a red halo, was splattered on the wall behind him. The balance of Sheriff Sawyer's blood-stained payoff sat in the center of the desk.

Sprawled to one side in his chair from the force of the gunshot to his right temple, Hal Poole sat across from his brother-in-law's desk. A forty-five caliber Colt lay on the floor next to his chair.

"Now who's going to put the spin on this for the reverend?" Sheriff Sawyer wondered out loud.

CHAPTER 31

▼

Joshua studied the pistol in its clear evidence baggie. He was thinking so deeply that he was unaware of the fury of activity around him. The federal agents, state police, and sheriff's deputies were already busily working the scene.

As soon as she caught a glimpse of the bloody corpses, Jan retreated back to the van to document it in her notebook before erasing the horrid site from her memory, an act that Joshua knew would be impossible to accomplish.

After the victims were thoroughly photographed and Tad finished his on-scene examination, the medical examiner permitted the attendants to begin their job of bagging the bodies for transport to the morgue.

"Nice looking weapon, huh?" Sheriff Sawyer observed the gun in Joshua's hand. "Well taken care of."

"And very old." Joshua turned the gun over. "It still has the registration numbers on it."

"We're running a check on it. Most likely belongs to Wally. He had a gun collection. None were registered. His sister says she believes the gun that killed Beth Davis belonged to him."

"Wally has—" Joshua corrected himself, "had—a gun collection, huh?"

"It wasn't common knowledge. My mother says he has more than a couple dozen."

Joshua gingerly laid the precious piece of evidence on the corner of the desk. "I wonder where he got this one."

"Unless it was registered by the previous owner, I doubt if we'll find that out now. Why do you want to know?"

"Oh, it's just another piece of the puzzle."

Curtis Sawyer spat out his frustration, "Yeah, well, right now we have hundreds of puzzle pieces scattered all over the place. Meanwhile, Reverend Rawlings is sitting up in his mansion and laughing at all of us."

Joshua was surprisingly cool. "We'll get the last laugh, all in good time."

Across the room, Tad zipped up Hal Poole's body bag. The morgue attendants wheeled his body out into the reception area and past the late county prosecutor's distraught secretary.

"It was a murder-suicide. Happened around one o'clock this morning," Tad announced to the sheriff and special prosecutor.

"I called Wallace at his cell phone number shortly before one this morning to find out if he had anything to do with that attack on the kids," the sheriff told them. "I don't know where he was when he took my call."

"Well, that was around when he died," Tad stated. "Hal Poole shot himself. There's no denying it. There are no signs of a struggle. The gun dropped in the right spot." The doctor shrugged. "Those are my preliminary findings. Maybe forensics can find something else."

"Hal could have gotten the carbon you found on his hands when he was shooting at us yesterday," Joshua surmised.

"He was shooting at you? I was hired to kill you. Why would he be shooting at you?" The sheriff sounded offended.

Joshua said in a teasing tone, "Oh, I'm sure he didn't mean to cheat you out of your business arrangement with Wally. He was on a mission to protect his spiritual leader from his enemies."

*   *   *   *

Reverend Orville Rawlings covered his face with his hands and wept upon learning the news of his son's murder and his son-in-law's suicide.

There was no denying that was what it was. Hal confessed his sins in an e-mail sent to the reverend. The note said simply that Wallace Rawlings was possessed by the same demons that possessed Vicki and he had to be killed in order to exorcise them.

Upon their arrival at the Rawlings mansion, a shapely young maid escorted the sheriff and special prosecutor into the formal living room to break the news to the reverend and his daughter of the discovery of the bodies.

"Reverend Rawlings and Mrs. Poole should be in the living room," the new maid was telling them as she escorted them inside. "Their hair stylist just left."

Dabbing her eyes with a lace handkerchief, Bridgette handed Curtis Sawyer a printed copy of the e-mail. He quickly read it before handing it off to Joshua. It read:

Dearest Father,

Forgive me, Father, for I am about to sin. Brother Wallace has been possessed by the same demons that took his daughter, and they must be exorcised. First, he led his daughter down the path of drugs, alcohol, and promiscuity. In her travels down the path of evil, Satan seduced her into conspiring with him in his battle against God and goodness by defeating our family. I had no choice but to thwart Satan in his scheme by killing his concubines.

The killing has to stop. I have no choice but to stop him. It was too late to call Brother Wallace back to God. The only way to exorcise our family of these demons is to kill him, and then myself, to spare the family the shame of our sins.

May God have mercy on our souls.

"God forgive him," Reverend Rawlings gasped through heavy sobs. He laid his head on his daughter's shoulder.

Joshua gave the note to Sheriff Sawyer, who slipped it into an evidence bag.

"When did you get this e-mail?" Joshua asked the reverend.

"This morning," Reverend Rawlings answered with a warning look. "I downloaded my e-mail on my computer after breakfast as I always do. I found it then."

"What time was that?"

"Ten o'clock. I called Hal's office at the church and got no answer."

"Why didn't you call your son's office? He was the one Hal was going to kill," Joshua shot back.

"Why do you ask?" The reverend looked to Sheriff Sawyer. "Why is he here? His job is to find my granddaughter's killer—a job at which he has failed miserably. He'd still be chasing his own tail if Hal hadn't confessed."

Sheriff Sawyer answered with a repeat of the question. "Why didn't you call your son's office?"

"Who is to say I didn't?"

"I was there at ten o'clock, and no call came from you."

"The line was busy." His eyes now dry, Reverend Rawlings stood up. "If you will excuse me, I must plan a memorial service for my son and son-in-law, and prepare a statement for the media in time for this evening's news cast. Our maid will show you out."

On cue, the young maid appeared in the doorway and gestured in the direction of the front door. Their visitors dismissed, Reverend Rawlings and his daughter exited out the other door.

Joshua and Sheriff Sawyer rose to their feet. The prosecutor squinted at Bridgette, who, feeling his gaze on her, shot him a cocky smile before closing the door behind her.

"What are you looking at?" the sheriff wondered as he saw Joshua staring at the door that Bridgette had just shut between her, her father, and their visitors.

"I was just noting what a lovely shade of red Bridgette's hair is," Joshua said.

To reinforce the reverend's command for them to leave, the new young maid cleared her throat.

"It's not natural." The sheriff gestured for Joshua to follow him to the foyer.

"Neither was that hair found caught in the chamber of Beth's murder weapon," Joshua whispered.

"Bridgette was Vicki's aunt, not her sister."

"Not even that, since Wally wasn't Vicki's father." Joshua stopped at the front door the maid held open for them.

"My mother was fired this morning," Sheriff Sawyer announced when his mother's replacement slammed the front door on them.

"What time this morning?"

"Bridgette called her at home before she left for work to tell her that her services would no longer be needed."

"So that was like—?"

"Six o'clock this morning."

"Sounds like there was a leak somewhere," Joshua murmured.

They continued their conversation on their way to the sheriff's squad car.

Curtis speculated, "Tess Bauer and her minions were at Tad's place just minutes after 911 got the call. If one of those news hounds caught you and Tad in the police uniforms leaving his apartment last night, and word got to one of Rawlings's informants, that can explain the attack on your family and Wally's sudden death. Needless to say, the reverend is capable of anything, even killing his own son, to cover his butt."

"Tad says the physical evidence suggests Hal Poole shot Wally and then himself. He confessed to killing Vicki and Beth," Joshua sighed regretfully.

"Then, it looks like we don't have anything on the Rawlings. We can't even prove Orville Rawlings was behind hiring me to kill you and Tad."

"I wonder what time that e-mail was sent." Joshua turned to the sheriff. "Why would Hal kill Vicki and Beth?"

"He was a fanatic. Everyone knew that. He kissed the ground the reverend walked on."

Joshua wasn't listening. Something else had his attention. Across the driveway, just around the corner of the house, the rear bumper of a black MG convertible peeked out from behind a hedge.

There was one more piece of the puzzle.

"Amber said she saw the Reverend Rawlings kill Vicki and Beth." Joshua stepped around the law officer to take a closer look at the sports car with a bumper sticker announcing "Jesus Lives!" He could just make out the license plate: "RWLNGS4".

"She was lying," Sheriff Sawyer shrugged. "Won't be the first time someone lied about witnessing a murder to get their mug on television."

"What about Wally's trench coat with the red hair from the same suspect who left her hair in the gun? What was that doing in the closet? It's summer. It's hot. Why wear a coat?"

The sheriff chuckled at the question that had an obvious answer. "He wore it to frame Wally."

"Hal was almost bald and he certainly never colored his hair." Joshua was on a roll. "In your experience, sheriff, do fanatics usually go to the trouble of framing other people for their deeds in the name of God?" He quickly answered his own question. "It's been my experience that fanatics trip over each other to take the credit."

"Are you saying you think Hal Poole didn't kill Wally and then shoot himself?"

Slowly, Joshua thoughtfully shook his head. "No, he did it," he muttered. "I just think he had some help."

*   *   *   *

Joshua forgot all about the murders and his daughters in the hospital when he saw the sealed moving box resting on top of his desk in his study. Hurriedly, he ripped it open and dug through the plastic bubble wrap to find the picture in the cut glass frame he had always kept on the corner of his desk.

He gazed at the image in his hands. Valerie was so young, so filled with love. Her long auburn hair was swept up. It almost seemed entwined with the pearl crown from which her veil flowed. Her cheeks were flushed with excitement as she smiled softly at the photographer's camera.

Blinking back tears he felt welling up in his eyes, Joshua traced the outline of her image with his fingertips.

"Hey, Dad, I think everything is here!"

At the sound of Murphy's call from the hallway, Joshua quickly wiped away his tears with the back of his hand and placed the picture on his desk. He turned his attention to the remaining contents of the box.

Murphy came in and held the inventory clipboard up for his father to see. "Everything is checked off. It seems to be in good shape, too, considering that it has probably been tossed around half the summer."

"Good." Joshua removed from the box a stack of framed photographs that had been stored in a cabinet in their previous home and proceeded to sort through them.

Murphy chuckled as he saw the subject of one of the pictures. "Hey, Dad, what's this?" He picked up the picture. Upon noticing the one beneath it, Murphy laid the two pictures next to each other on top of the desk. One picture depicted a black cat with a white background. The other was a mirror image of a white cat with a black background. "Looks kind of tacky for Mom's taste."

Joshua smiled with fondness at the memory. He took the pictures and wiped the glass frames with his forearm. "Those are a couple of puzzles your mother got me the first Christmas we were married. It was two puzzles in the same box. It took me two months to do them. I was so proud of myself, your mother had them glued together and framed."

"Two puzzles at once. Wow!" Hearing that, Murphy admired them. "That must have been hard."

Joshua shook his head while he laughed. "It took a real adjustment of my thinking to figure them out." He called thoughtfully, "It wasn't just one puzzle I had to figure out. It was two that were connected only by virtue of being in the same box. Once, I figured that out, it all made sense."

He stared at the two puzzles he held in his hands and saw Vicki's and Beth's dead bodies.

Two murders. Two times of death. Two murder weapons. One crime scene.

Two puzzles in the same box.

Joshua handed the frames back to Murphy, and headed for the door.

"Where are you going?"

"To catch a couple of killers."

*   *   *   *

The Thornton girls were on Sarah's bed watching music videos of the latest boy group on the television and giggling at a private joke between them. As soon as they saw their father bearing gifts of flowers and candy, the girls exchanged naughty grins and made failed attempts to stop giggling.

If it weren't for her hospital gown, Joshua would never have known that Sarah was even injured. Bandages all the way up her arms to her elbows evidenced Tracy's wounds.

Tracy hugged Joshua, who held her tightly for a long moment. "Ready to go home?" he breathed into her hair. He brushed her long hair with his fingers when she pulled away.

"Sure," Tracy turned to her sister. "Hear that, Sarah? I'm going home."

"Good." Sarah continued to giggle at their private joke until she cried out in pain. Her eyes filled with tears.

Joshua rushed to her. "Are you okay, honey?"

Sarah grimaced and choked down her tears. Determination crossed her face. "I'm fine."

"The doctor told her not to laugh because of her broken ribs," Tracy told their father.

"Yeah," Sarah hugged her ribs. "So don't tell any jokes. Okay? Because it hurts like hell-heck! It hurts like heck!"

Joshua swallowed. "Okay. No jokes. From here on out, we'll be serious." He and Tracy put on mockingly serious expressions that made Sarah laugh again before crying out.

After consenting to let Tracy go thank the nurses and say good-bye, Joshua set Sarah's flowers on the bed tray next to the remnants of her devoured lunch.

Alone for the first time, Joshua gave his daughter his look that failed to come off. "That was a dumb thing you did last night." The father tried to sound harsh.

"What?" Sarah asked innocently. She noticed the small smile behind his stern expression.

"Chasing after that attacker. She or he had a knife and, judging from the looks of Tracy, was not afraid to use it. You could have been killed."

"Dad," Sarah said with a small smile, "I did nothing you wouldn't have done."

"I've been trained how to defend myself."

"I know how to take care of myself."

"Maybe against your brothers during a friendly wrestling match where there are rules of engagement. But when it comes to homicidal maniacs, there are no rules, and unless you are trained to defend yourself in that type of situation—" Joshua gestured to indicate their surroundings, "This could have been a lot worse."

Unsure if she should apologize or defend herself for protecting her family, Sarah shook her head and shrugged at the same time.

"I'm sorry." Joshua sat at the foot of the bed and laid his hand on her foot buried under the covers. "I should have been home last night."

"But you had to hide out so that you could get Mr. Rawlings."

Joshua plucked at a piece of lint embedded on the blanket covering the bed. "I think that was a mistake."

Sarah cocked her head. "What was a mistake?"

Guilt made the words difficult to force from out of his throat. Joshua felt as if he was confessing his sin to his late wife instead of his young daughter. Never before had he confessed an error to one of his children.

"Before…before your mother…she was always around to take care of you kids. And that let me be free to do this type of thing. That was why I left the Navy." Joshua swallowed. "But I forgot about that and—"

"Are you saying you were wrong?" Sarah blurted out.

Joshua hesitated. Sarah was gazing at him with wide eyes. Should he admit that he wasn't the all-knowing, always right, dominant figurehead whose image he had skillfully created since the twins' births?

He chose his words carefully before responding, "I've made mistakes on occasion, but I'm never wrong."

A small smile crept to Sarah's lips. "Sure, Dad."

$$* \quad * \quad * \quad *$$

Dressed in his mask, gloves, and leather apron, Tad was hosing down the autopsy table with scalding hot water when Joshua came into the morgue. The prosecutor had two thick brown envelopes tucked under his arm.

"Is Tracy all checked out?" Tad yelled over the noise of the spraying hose.

"Yep. I'm taking her home with me." Joshua added with concern, "Sarah is hurting."

"She'll be better tomorrow." Tad turned off the hose and put it away before patting his cousin on the shoulder. "You're a lucky man." The medical examiner took off his mask and gloves.

Joshua responded with sincere gratitude, "Yes, I am."

Tad nodded at the envelopes. "What have you got there?"

"The transcript from Eric Connally's trial for vandalizing the post office and files sent from the JAG office." Joshua indicated the table where Tad had just examined the remains of Wallace Rawlings and Hal Poole. "What can you tell me?"

Tad took off the heavy leather apron and hung it up on a hook by the table. "Same as I said in New Cumberland. Wally was shot from at least three feet away. Died around one o'clock. Hal died about the same time. Contact wound to the temple. No signs of a struggle. He had fired a gun."

"No other evidence on or in them? Drugs?"

"You'll need to wait for the toxicology reports for that information. I sent a sample of both of their DNA to Weirton for comparison to what we've already got for Vicki's and Beth's murders." Tad sat down at his desk to complete his reports from the exams he had just performed. "Oh, I talked to the medical examiner in Pittsburgh about Morgan Lucas like you asked me to."

"And?" Joshua sat on the corner of Tad's desk.

"I have a date with her for this Friday, but she did give me a preview. The police are figuring it to be a crime of passion. She was stabbed like seventeen times. Plus, what they didn't release to the media is that her pretty face was sliced up."

"Jeez."

"That's what I said. She was dead before she got the cosmetic surgery and there was no sign of forced entry into her place."

The prosecutor digested that news while continuously nodding his head. To Tad, his cousin looked like one of those dogs with the bobbing heads that used to sit in the back window of a car.

After a long moment of watching Joshua nodding his head while staring into space, Tad concluded that their conversation had taken a break and began filling in the blanks on the medical examiner forms for his latest autopsies.

Abruptly, Joshua tore open one of the envelopes and removed the report from Washington. He scanned the information he held in his hands while asking nonchalantly, "What can you tell me about Tess Bauer?" He learned early in his career how to divide his attention between two activities.

Tad filled in a couple of blanks on a form before he replied, "What do you want to know? I know her family. They were real holler people, what they used to call hillbillies."

"What else?" Joshua put the report back into its envelope.

Tad stopped writing and looked up at Joshua questioningly. "What are you looking for?"

"Anything? Just tell me what you know about them."

"Tess is more sophisticated than the rest of her folks." Tad stopped and shrugged. "Guess she's trying to forget her roots. You can see that in how she dresses."

"Keep going. What else?"

Clueless about what Joshua was seeking, Tad took a deep breath and slowly let it out while he thought of what to say. "Her mother used to sleep around."

"What do you mean?"

Tad laughed. "What do you think I mean?"

"I thought you said they had six kids."

"And word is that they weren't all from the same man." Tad grinned. "Ingrid Bauer had a body that wouldn't quit. She had a face like a horse, but her body made up for it. Russ Bauer took that for granted. He had this routine. When he got paid, he'd go to the bar and drink like half of it away before going home. He never took Ingrid out. She was literally stuck up in that hollow with all those kids. So, when she got lonely, she'd get a ride into town and end up getting picked up by some guy and have a fling. Don't ask me if she planned it that way. Maybe she did it to get even with Russ, or maybe it was just to get out. But afterwards, she'd run back to the hollow and go on with her life."

"Did her husband know about this?"

Tad shrugged. "If he did, he never let on to anyone outside the family. Everyone else in the valley knew."

"What type of men did she have flings with?"

Tad snickered, "Anyone who had a pack of cigarettes and a pulse."

"Rawlings?"

"Which one?"

"Name one."

"Wally, maybe. I can't see him passing up an opportunity. However, he liked his women real young and she was older than him. Not only that, but she wasn't exactly high class. Tess has class. I guess she got it from the milkman."

Joshua joked, "Wasn't your father a milkman?"

"My dad was a dairy farmer. Besides, he knew well enough to stay away from Ingrid." Tad mused thoughtfully as he considered Joshua's previous question. "As for the reverend, I can't see him chancing his reputation for a quickie with a hillbilly."

Joshua found himself agreeing with Tad's assessment. "What else can you tell me about Tess?"

"I was surprised with her reaction to her sister's death. They were never particularly close." Tad paused for a long thoughtful beat. "Maybe Tess regretted how she treated Diana before she died and that was why she decided to be so gung-ho about seeking vengeance against the Rawlings for her sister's death."

"How did she treat her?"

"Diana was pretty, not that Tess is hard on the eyes; but when Di entered the room…" Tad chuckled with a naughty tone. "She took after her mother. She was very sexy and she knew how to play the guys. She'd use them, and then toss them aside."

"Did you sleep with her?"

"I don't do jail bait," Tad responded firmly. "Diana was only sixteen when she died."

Despite Tad's reputation, Joshua believed him that he did not sleep with under-aged girls. His cousin was never stupid. "Go on," Joshua urged Tad to continue.

"I guess it was only natural for Tess to be jealous of Di. I heard about a fight those two got into once."

"Fight?"

"Cat fight."

"Cat fight?" Joshua repeated the same term that his sons had used the night before to describe Tracy's encounter with the intruder.

Tad made a motion with both his hands in the pretense of cat claws and made a screeching noise. "You know. It was a cat fight. Diana had slept with Tess's boyfriend." He took time to recall the long forgotten details before continuing. "I think that was the only man Tess was ever serious about." He shrugged and doodled on his notepad. "I don't know Tess that well. She may have had other men, but this guy dumped her for the little sister, and Tess about scratched her eyes out at this party out in Hookstown. Diana dumped the guy, I think. He took off. Then, Diana got high and slashed her wrists, and Tess gave up her chance to go to the networks to avenge her death. Go figure."

Startled, Joshua stared at Tad. His shock was so evident, that Tad stopped doodling and looked up at him. "What's wrong?"

"Wait a minute," Joshua shook his head. "I thought Diana Bauer died of a drug overdose."

It was Tad's turn to shake his head. "No, she slashed her wrists. She was pumped up on drugs at the time and bled to death. I can call the medical examiner in Hookstown to confirm it if you want me to." Tad smiled. "Do you mean to tell me that Commander Thornton made an assumption?"

Joshua groaned, "I guess I did."

"Well, I guess that proves it," the medical examiner continued laughing, "The mind is the first thing to go."

Humiliated by his error, Joshua pressed on. "What were the circumstances?"

"I'm not that familiar with the case. It happened across the state line in Pennsylvania, which is out of my jurisdiction."

"So you didn't do the autopsy."

Tad shook his head. "All I know is what I heard through the grapevine. The medical examiner there is an old drinking buddy of mine."

"It was a suicide?"

Tad shrugged. "That's what I heard."

"Why was I led to believe it was a drug overdose?"

"I never said it was a drug overdose. She was on drugs at the time, but I don't think it was an overdose. She bled to death."

"You never said it wasn't an overdose," Joshua raised his voice. "You and everyone told me that Tess Bauer has been after the Rawlings because her sister died of drugs. What am I suppose to think?"

"Which goes to prove that when you assume you make an ass out of you and me," Tad said in a calm voice with a wide grin.

"How did Diana Bauer die?"

"She was found in her bath tub, in her room, in a cheap boarding house in Hookstown with her wrists slashed by a broken wine bottle." Before Joshua could ask his next question, Tad answered, "I did hear there were no hesitation marks in the cuts, but she was so full of booze and sleeping pills that that could explain why there wasn't any hesitation."

"Lack of hesitation usually points to murder." Joshua asked, "Any suspects?"

"None that could be found. The boyfriend was gone."

"Gone where?"

Tad sighed from exhaustion of the continuous questioning. "I don't know."

"Who was he? Was he into drugs?"

"He was an insurance salesman who liked sixteen-year-old girls. Everyone just assumed that after all the scandal Tess created over catching him with her under-aged sister that he skipped town."

Now, it was Joshua's turn to smile. "Everyone just assumed, huh?"

Tad snickered. "We are talking statutory rape and Diana did have three big brothers. I would have left town under the darkness of night, too, if I were him."

"So he just disappeared? Before or after Diana was found in the bathtub?"

Tad shrugged for his answer. Seeing the familiar look in Joshua's eyes, he sighed. "You want me to find out." It was a statement.

Joshua's grin broadened.

"I'll call Hookstown."

"Thank you, Dr. MacMillan," Joshua mocked with sickening sweetness.

"Yeah. Right." Tad made a note on a yellow notepad to call his old drinking buddy. "Anything else you want from me?"

"No, that's okay. Can I use your phone?" Without waiting for Tad's consent, Joshua proceeded to dial the phone number.

Joshua didn't identify himself when Curtis Sawyer picked up the other end of the line. "Curt, did you run those fingerprints on Rawlings's glove through the federal database?"

On the other end of the line, Sheriff Sawyer, confused by the question, stopped and looked at the phone receiver he held in his hand. "No. Why?"

Joshua smiled in anticipation. "If it comes up the way I think it will, then I think we will find Amber."

"Speaking of Amber," Sawyer said, "I got those tapes from the news station you asked me for. They were real easy to get. The station manager says we'll have more than his cooperation, if it helps finding out who killed his anchor."

"Great. I'm on my way to pick them up." Joshua hung up. Excited, he paced as he rubbed his hands together.

"Do you have something?" Tad grinned.

"An idea. All the pieces of the puzzle have finally come together, and it is all so clear now. Where's Doc's trunk?"

"I took it back home. Why?"

"I have a lot of reading to do," Joshua pointed at Tad, "and so do you."

"We both already read everything that's in there."

"I need for you to find out who Vicki's father was. I think Doc Wilson knew. That's why he put Vicki's patient file in that trunk."

Tad shook his head. "Doc thought he knew. He was wrong."

"You knew Doc better than I did. Was he a man who listened to rumors, or was he a man with his own mind?"

Tad hesitated. "He thought I was a drunk."

"You were a drunk. Now, you're sober. You sobered up before he died and won his respect." When Tad scoffed, Joshua added, "Doc Wilson never would have run that tox test on Cindy if he didn't respect your opinion."

As the realization of Joshua's statement hit home, Tad slowly sat up in his seat.

Joshua continued pleading his case. "I think you were right. Doc knew when Vicki was born that Wally wasn't her father, and he had a pretty good idea who the father was, not based on rumors about you and Cindy, but on medical facts. He put everything he knew in those files and hid them so he could hold them over the Rawlings's heads. Now, you have them, and I'm counting on you to put it together for me."

✳ ✳ ✳ ✳

"Where's Admiral?"

Tracy was the first one to notice the dog's absence at dinnertime.

Joshua only noticed the pleasurable experience of eating his pizza without dog drool pooling on his thigh.

Before her death, Valerie, despite her insistence that their anticipated well-behaved family pet would never beg from the table, would sneak food to Admiral from her chair at the head of the table. After her death, Admiral switched to the other end of the table to beg at Joshua's chair.

In order to relieve Tracy, fresh from the hospital, of cooking dinner, Joshua had ordered two extra large pizzas, one with extra cheese, the other with everything, including anchovies. Joshua, his sons, and Tracy were gathered around the kitchen table for a feeding frenzy, when the girl noted that she had not seen Admiral since she arrived home.

"He's probably sneaking a nap on my bed." Joshua suppressed a yawn. It was only after he sat down to eat and enjoy a cold beer that he realized that he had not slept in thirty-six hours. Exhaustion set in. He fought to stay awake long enough to finish his slice of pizza.

Joshua wondered if he had dozed off when he was startled by the touch of Tracy's hand on his. "I guess this has been a long day for you, huh?" She smiled sweetly.

Joshua frowned as his eyes lay on the bandages on both of her forearms. "I guess I'm not very good company tonight." Excusing himself, he left his half-eaten slice of pizza and went upstairs to his room.

Up in his bedroom, Joshua plopped onto the bed he had shared with his late wife, and buried his face into the sweet smelling comforter that still held a hint of Valerie's scent.

A cool evening breeze drifted in through the open French doors leading out onto the verandah and brushed across Joshua's back. He was relieved to feel the coolness. At noon, the room was so stifling hot that he had opened the doors to air it out.

Admiral's low growl interrupted Joshua's descent into sleep.

Joshua turned his face from the pink floral comforter that Valerie selected for their bedroom in San Francisco, and spied the missing dog.

Admiral was sitting at attention with his gaze trained on the closet door.

"There you are," Joshua sighed. "You missed dinner." He pulled a pillow down from the head of the bed and hugged it to his face.

Admiral growled again. This growl ended in a pleading whine.

Joshua opened one eye and looked at where the dog was still on point. Admiral was looking over his shoulder back to his master. After his eyes met his master's, the dog turned back to the closet door.

"Admiral, what's wrong with you?" Joshua smelled the sickeningly sweet scent of cheap aftershave.

It wasn't his brand.

No, he thought. Not two nights in a row.

Quietly, Joshua slipped off the bed and searched for a weapon he could use in his defense. He found his baseball bat resting in the corner.

Seeing that his master had finally caught his message, Admiral stood up and growled at the door as if to say, "Now you're going to get it."

Armed with the bat, Joshua braced himself against the wall next to the closet and ordered, "You! In the closet! I know you're in there! Throw out your weapon and come out! Hands first!"

Silence answered his order.

"I know you're in there! I'm calling the sheriff!"

After a long pause, in which everyone in the room, including the dog, held his breath, the glass doorknob to the closet door turned. A hand stretched out.

"I want to see both hands!" Joshua held the bat off his shoulder. He was ready to swing.

As the door burst open, the intruder fired one hasty shot that went wild.

Before the shooter could stop to determine what he'd hit, the closet door swung shut again and hit him in the face. The wood in his face stunned him senseless long enough for Joshua to use the bat to knock the gun out of his hand to the floor, yank the door open again, grab him by the shirt, whirl him around and shove him down onto the bed with his intended victim on his chest.

"What was that?" Tracy looked up from the front porch.

Ken came to visit with gifts of flowers and candy. Tracy's brothers took her hint to leave them alone and went for a walk.

"It sounded like a gunshot," Ken observed.

"It sounded like it came from Dad's room." Tracy ran into the house and up the stairs.

"Who are you?" Joshua spat into his assailant's face. "Why did you attack my daughters?"

If it weren't for the aftershave, Joshua would have expected to find Amber in his closet in an attempt to carry out her threat against him. Instead, it was a muscular young man, who, in spotless jeans that looked almost pressed, did not fit the profile of a common breaking and entering type.

"Your worst nightmare!" Scott Collins responded in the tradition of his he-man movie idols. He punctuated his statement by head butting Joshua between the eyes and tackling him to the floor.

Scott Collins's delight at pinning Joshua down was temporary. He was so focused on carrying out his assignment to eliminate the special prosecutor that he forgot about the dog that had him trapped in the closet for almost six hours.

It was like one hundred and fifty-five pounds of fur and teeth had descended from the heavens onto the assassin.

Covering his preciously pretty face with one arm, Scott rolled off Joshua.

The growling slobbering mass had him by the other arm.

Joshua scurried on the floor in search of the gun he had knocked out of Scott's hand.

Scott reached for the ball bat and swung it at the dog's head.

Yelping, the pet retreated into the closet.

"Dad, are you all right?" Tracy called from behind the closed bedroom door.

Spying the ball bat that Scott now welded, Joshua screamed at his daughter. "Get out of here! Call Sawyer!"

In his line of work, Joshua taught his family early on what to do in situations in which intruders came into the home. Despite Tracy's natural instinct to go into the room and try to help, her father had drilled into her head that to do so would only make her a possible hostage to be used against him.

"Shouldn't we go inside to help?" Ken asked when he saw her turn away from the door and run down the stairs to the foyer.

"We need to go to your house and use your phone!"

Inside the bedroom, the two men were at a standoff.

Scott Collins grinned with pride as he saw Joshua, unarmed, eying the ball bat.

"Who hired you?" Joshua asked as he circled Collins.

"Take a guess."

"Rawlings. Bridgette Rawlings." Joshua positioned himself before the French doors leading out onto the verandah.

"Smart man. Too bad all your brains are going to be splattered across these four walls."

Joshua gestured for Scott to come at him. "Take your best shot."

It was a dare the prosecutor knew the intruder couldn't pass up. Joshua could see in the way he dressed to show off his finely-toned muscles and smelled of cheap aftershave, that his attacker was a man of superior ego.

As Scott rushed forward with his weapon poised to bash in his head, Joshua ducked, grabbed the assailant around the waist, lifted him, and threw him up and over his shoulders.

Joshua sent his assailant flying head over heels, not unlike how he himself had flown during that great Oak Glen-Weirton game. Only Scott Collins didn't land on his head, he flew over the verandah railing down into the late Rachel Thornton's prized rose garden.

CHAPTER 32

▼

Tad reached out to Joshua's motionless body to lay his hand on his shoulder. His touch made the sleeping man yelp and sit up in the hospital bed.

"Quiet!" the doctor hissed. He pointed towards Sarah, who was still asleep in her bed in the semi-private hospital room.

Reminded of where he had gone to sleep while waiting for the emergency room doctor to permit him and Sheriff Sawyer to question Scott Collins, Joshua sucked in his breath to quiet his nerves.

Tad whispered, "This case is getting to you, isn't it?"

"Exhaustion is getting to me." Joshua gestured for the doctor to follow him out of the room to prevent waking up Sarah.

It wasn't until they were in the dimly-lit hospital corridor that Joshua noticed that Tad was wearing his leather motorcycle jacket. He was checking on Sarah before going home when he found Joshua asleep in the vacant bed next to hers.

They strolled down the hall toward the stairs to take them to the waiting room. "Do you want to know something, Tad? This is the first case that I have ever had that struck home."

"I thought you brought every case home with you. Wasn't that one of Valerie's complaints?"

"Mentally, I brought them home. They weren't personal," Joshua corrected himself, "not most of them. I brought them home in my mind, the way a crossword puzzle nags at you in the back of your mind all day until you can find that word that completes the whole puzzle. It stays with you, but it doesn't attack your family. This one attacked my daughters, and now me."

Tad stopped with the palm of his hand on the stairwell door. "Sawyer said that this guy told you that Bridgette Rawlings hired him."

Joshua nodded his head.

"Are you sure he's the same guy who attacked Tracy last night? Why would Bridgette hire Collins to kill you when Wally already hired Sawyer to do it?"

Joshua hesitated as he considered Tad's question. "Tracy swears that she broke her attacker's ribs. This guy's ribs didn't get broken until I tossed him off the verandah. If she had broken them, he wouldn't have been able to move the way he did."

The two men stepped into the stairwell and climbed down the stairs.

Joshua asked Tad, "Do you remember Collins back when you reported the Hitchcock family's disappearance?"

"It never occurred to me that he was in on it. I thought he was just an incompetent."

"Maybe that's what he wanted you to think."

Officer Scott Collins was lucky to be alive. His back was broken. The fall also broke one each of his arms and legs, and six ribs. The thorns from the overgrown rose bushes that broke his fall left their mark all over his well-formed body.

It was morning before Joshua Thornton and the sheriff were permitted to question him about his involvement with Bridgette Rawlings and the job for which she hired him.

As the prosecutor expected, while Scott Collins's body was wrecked, his mind was still operational. From his hospital bed, he insisted on lawyering up before speaking to the Hancock County sheriff and the special prosecutor.

"All you have on my client is simple trespassing," Frederick Dawson challenged Joshua and the sheriff after they informed them of what they had against his client. The lawyer was perfectly-dressed in the most expensive suit he could afford on the modest income generated in the valley that was not known for a high crime rate.

Joshua responded to the challenge with a chuckle. "What law school did you go to?"

"I may not be any local hero," Dawson snorted, "but I do know my way around a courtroom."

"Do you know what evidence is? That is the stuff that is going to send your client to a federal pen. I saw him pull a trigger on a gun and take a shot a me. I also saw him swing a bat at my dog and try to, and I quote, 'splatter my brains on all four walls of my room'. We also have two more witnesses who place him at the scene. Do you want me to add to that the gunshot residue we found on his hands; and the gun with his fingerprints on it that we found on my bedroom floor? That is more than simple trespassing, Mr. Dawson."

"He tried to murder a state prosecutor," Sawyer told the lawyer. "That makes this a federal case of conspiracy to commit murder."

Dawson countered, "None of your evidence is going to see a courtroom. I'll get it suppressed."

"I have his statement that he was there to kill me on Bridgette Rawlings's orders," Joshua told Collin's lawyer.

"That's your word against his," Dawson argued. "You have no other witnesses who heard him make that statement."

"Your client tried to kill me. He also tried to kill my daughters—"

"I did not!" Collins exclaimed.

"Prove it," Joshua challenged, "Where were you the night before last?"

Collins sputtered like a lawnmower that was unable to start.

"You assaulted my daughters the night before last, and then last night you tried to kill me. That's three counts of attempted murder, plus three counts of murder when you count the Hitchcocks."

"I didn't kill them!"

Joshua laughed. "Of course you did!"

"No, I didn't!" Collins looked to his lawyer for help.

"Nice try," Dawson laughed cockily. "You have nothing to connect my client to the Hitchcocks."

Joshua shook his head. "A jury is going to want to know why he closed the case without checking the passenger manifest when Hannah Pickering claimed she dropped them off at the airport to take that flight to Chicago. A simple check showed they weren't there. Was your client lazy, or did he get Bridgette Rawlings's secretary to make that statement to cover his tracks?"

"I didn't even know Hannah Pickering!"

When Frederick Dawson hushed him, Collins turned on him. "Do something."

Joshua could see the wheels spinning in Dawson's mind as he tried to think of his next legal move. The public defender had told the small town lawyer that this was a simple case of attempted murder. He thought two men had simply gotten into a fight and one threw the other off a balcony into a rose bush. He didn't expect his client to be accused of three murders.

While Dawson scrambled for his next line of defense, Joshua plunged onward. "Why did Hannah Pickering lie about the Hitchcocks being on that flight if you didn't make them disappear beforehand? Was it because that plane crash the day after you killed them was just too convenient a way of ending the investigation that Tad MacMillan started by reporting them missing? Once you got yourself assigned to the case, it would have looked bad for you to let it go cold. This way, you closed the case without anyone suspecting that you were the one responsible for their disappearance."

Sawyer interjected, "Your chief is very curious about you now, Collins. He said that their efforts to squelch the drug traffic in Steubenville have been ineffective. Every time they think they have a handle on it, it slips through their fingers. Since we told him about your statement to Josh about working for Bridgette Rawlings, they're now wondering how you got the money to buy that fancy sports car you drive on a city cop's salary."

Collins spat out, "It was an inheritance."

"Who died? How did they die and how many?" Joshua shot back.

"This interrogation is over!" Dawson stood up to usher the prosecutor and sheriff out of the room.

"For us, but not your client," Joshua countered. "The feds want to know why your client was so stupid about not checking the flight manifest. They are also going to be asking him a lot of questions about his lax nature about the drug traffic in Steubenville." He told Collins, "Both of your careers are over. You'll be lucky if you don't end up with a needle in your arm."

Collins shouted, "I didn't kill the Hitchcocks! I didn't kill anyone. I didn't have to!"

"Come on!" Sawyer scoffed.

"They were already gone!" Collins gritted his teeth and hugged his aching ribs. "You're right. I was hired to kill the Hitchcocks. Bridgette Rawlings paid me to make them disappear. She didn't care how. She said that as long as they were around, then Wally would never get elected prosecutor." He said firmly, "But they were already gone when I got there. I couldn't find them! Then, when that Pickering broad said she had put them on the plane, I figured okay. I told Bridgette that I did the job, she paid me the twenty-five thou and I kept my mouth shut."

Joshua squinted. "Bridgette Rawlings never asked for proof that you killed them?"

"She figured I got the Pickering lady to lie for me just like you did."

*   *   *   *

"Do you believe that?" Curt waited until he and Joshua were in the elevator going down to the ground floor lobby before he asked the prosecutor to concur with his impression that Scott Collins had come up with an unbelievably desperate lie to cover his crime of killing the Hitchcock family.

"Maybe." Joshua thought he had put together most of the pieces of the puzzle, but Scott Collins's assertion that he did not kill the Hitchcocks did not fit.

Joshua sighed. "I think we should ask Hannah Pickering who she was lying for."

*   *   *   *

Hannah Pickering did not look or live as Joshua Thornton and Sheriff Sawyer had imagined. Knowing that she both attended and worked for Reverend Rawlings's Valley of the Living God Church, they were under the impression that Hannah Pickering's lifestyle would match that of the Rawlings. For this reason, they were surprised to find the unmarried, middle-aged woman living in a mobile home out in the country on the edge of New Manchester.

When Joshua and Curt pulled up in the sheriff's cruiser, Hannah was working with her bare hands in the soil of her vegetable garden in the front yard of her one-acre lot. The skirt of her loose fitting cotton dress was pulled forward between her bare legs and tucked into the worn canvas belt she wore around her waist. The belt was also used to hold her gardening gloves and tools. Her waist length hair, gray before its time, was twisted and clipped on the top of her head.

"Ms. Pickering?" the sheriff confirmed they were at the right address as they stepped along the stone sidewalk to the garden.

Hannah Pickering stopped gardening to shade her gray eyes while she studied the sheriff in his uniform and the man with a blue sports coat over tan slacks who appeared to be threatening to step on her garden.

She hesitated before confessing that she was the woman they were seeking. "Who are you?" she asked Joshua. Sheriff Sawyer's uniform told her who he was.

"I'm Joshua Thornton—"

Hannah finished the introduction, "The man investigating Vicki Rawlings's murder."

"Yes."

"I quit working for the Rawlings four years ago."

"Why is that?" Joshua asked.

Hannah shrugged. "Why does anybody quit a job? I got a better one. I'm a single woman living on my own. I have to take care of myself. I got offered a job with an insurance company with better benefits, so I took it."

Joshua took note of the gold crucifix she wore around her neck. "You also went back to the Catholic Church."

"Is that a crime?"

"Has a crime been committed?"

"Vicki was murdered after I quit working for the Rawlings and went back to the church."

"Do you know what the root of the word 'secretary' is?"

Joshua's unexpected question startled the sheriff. This was not how he usually began an interrogation.

Hannah answered by looking down at the tomato plants surrounding her bare feet.

"Secret," Joshua answered his query. "The secretary is the keeper of the secrets. You were Bridgette Rawlings's secretary. I suspect you heard something you weren't meant to hear. You overheard Bridgette hiring a Steubenville cop to kill the Hitchcocks, a family who attended the church. You had to have seen them since you were the church secretary and they were members."

Hannah admitted, "I knew them."

"You couldn't just sit back and let them be killed." Joshua stared at the crucifix.

Curt Sawyer gasped as he saw where Joshua Thornton was heading. "You hid them from Collins," the sheriff finished the prosecutor's theory.

Hannah smiled proudly. "Bridgette Rawlings gave me a very generous bonus for my helping that cop when I told the police that I put them on that flight to Chicago and they closed the missing person's case."

"But they weren't on the flight to Chicago," Sawyer pointed out more to Joshua as a kink in his theory.

"That crash not only helped Collins in ending the missing person's investigation. It helped Hannah by making the Rawlings think that the Hitchcocks were dead. In reality, they were—?" Joshua and Sawyer waited for Hannah to finish his statement.

"On a bus to Canada. I drove them out the Pennsylvania turnpike to Breezewood and put them on a bus. It took me hours to convince the old lady I was telling the truth about the Rawlings hiring someone to kill them. Monica Hitchcock believed me practically before the words came out of my mouth. She said a cop called before I got there and said he had to come over to ask them some questions about one of Trixie's former customers who had died and left them a bunch of money. She said she had a bad feeling about it and called Tad MacMillan." She added, "That was another reason they wanted to get rid of them. Hal had told Bridgette that Monica had gotten real close to MacMillan. They were afraid she'd tell him something they didn't want him to know."

Joshua pounced on her revelation. "What? What were they afraid she was going to tell him?"

Hannah shook her head. "I have no idea. I just know that that family has a lot of dirty little secrets, so many that I was afraid to find out any of them. What I did find out about them was enough to drive me back to the church."

"Where are the Hitchcocks now?" Joshua asked.

Hannah hesitated.

"Wally Rawlings is dead," Joshua reminded her. "They can't hurt him politically anymore."

"Trixie Hitchcock died a couple of years ago. Monica married a professor. She and Alexis moved with him to Europe. Monica runs an inn in the English countryside."

"And Alexis?"

Hannah smiled demurely. "She's going to school, playing soccer, and chasing boys like every other teenage girl. Why?"

"In the English countryside?" the sheriff confirmed. "In Europe?"

Hannah laughed quietly. "You're not thinking Alexis killed Vicki, are you?"

"Not anymore," Joshua responded.

∗   ∗   ∗   ∗

In the family room on the ground floor of the stone house, Sarah curled up on the Thorntons's comfortable old sofa to work on the Whitman's box of candy Ken had brought for Tracy.

A cool breeze blew in through the open French doors that led to the patio, which spilled out into the back yard.

Joshua had hoped to study alone the recordings sent over from the news station; but, upon learning his plans, each of his children found a reason to be in the family room. Tracy was organizing the family's VHS tapes to determine what ones they didn't watch anymore to box up and what ones to keep out. Murphy offered to operate the DVD player because the technology still confused his father. J.J. was practicing his flute. Donny and Sarah made no pretense about their curiosity.

"What are you looking for?" Sarah pressed her finger into the bottom of a piece of candy. Finding that it was a caramel, she returned it to the box before resuming her search for the pieces she liked.

"Proof of who attacked you and Tracy." Joshua handed the DVDs with the recordings burned onto them to Murphy.

"I thought it was that cop." Sarah popped a coconut cream into her mouth.

"He's too big and the wrong sex," Murphy disagreed. "A woman attacked Tracy. Right, Dad?"

Joshua frowned. "Collins has an alibi. Turns out he was meeting with a drug dealer to warn him about a bust the police were planning. The feds have had an informant in the Steubenville police department following him."

Murphy turned on the player and inserted the first DVD. "According to the label on this disk, this is Tess's series of interviews with Amber on the drug market. They're uncut."

Amber grinned with watery eyes at the camera. Her dark eye makeup and lipstick accentuated her pale skin. A tear in her black top revealed the black widow spider tattoo on her left shoulder. Bracelets and necklaces littered her arms and neck. She had rings on every finger and thumb, which were adorned with long claw-like fingernails that were painted magenta.

Joshua studied the interview in which Amber told in slurred speech about her drug habits and dealings with Vicki Rawlings.

None of it was anything new from what the Thorntons had heard in other reports or realistic television shows about drug users. Amber never knew her father, her mother's boyfriend raped her, and she ran away from home.

With all that information in mind, Joshua wondered how Amber ended up in Chester. Runaways generally, as a rule, go to big cities to get lost in the immense population of other runaways.

"Next." Murphy selected the following interview from the menu on the disk.

It was more of the same. Amber seemed less out of it, and even less in the next interview, which was the one Joshua saw the first day they had arrived in town.

"Anyone home?" Tad's voice called from the foyer on the floor above them. They heard the front door slam shut.

"Down here!" Joshua yelled up the stairs while keeping his eyes on the television screen.

Dog bounded down the stairs and leapt onto the sofa between Joshua and Sarah. While his daughter petted the bouncing dog, Joshua shoved him off the furniture. Spying Admiral under the coffee table, Dog chased what he considered a new playmate out into the yard.

With a large brown envelope flapping in his hand, Tad galloped down the stairs. From over the back of the sofa, he slapped Joshua's chest with the envelope before holding it against his cousin's left breast. "For you."

Joshua caught the envelope when Tad released his hold and it slid towards his lap. "Are these the results of your DNA test?"

"Nope." Tad crossed to the open French doors. "Let's go for a walk." He gestured for his cousin to follow him.

The children watched with puzzlement as their father and Tad stepped out into the freshly mowed back yard.

"What is this?" Joshua asked once they were out of earshot of his offspring. He opened the envelope and removed the long sheet of white paper with a row of dashes in a pattern unique to the subject's genetic blueprint.

Tad paused to study the blooms on a lilac bush. He recalled when it was only a few feet tall. Now, it almost reached the third story of the house. "They're Maggie's DNA test results. I thought you might like to see it."

"We've determined that there is no way Vicki Rawlings could be Wally's biological daughter. That cleared Maggie."

Tad plucked a purple lilac from the bush. "I know. That's what makes this so very interesting."

His cousin's tone of voice when he said the word "interesting" prompted Joshua to momentarily forget about Amber's interviews with Tess Bauer playing inside the house on the other side of the yard.

Inside the envelope, another sheet of paper accompanied Maggie's test results. The name written in the upper right hand corner told him that it was Vicki Rawlings's DNA results. Joshua studied the two results.

Tad stated the findings of the two tests, "According to their DNA, Maggie and Vicki are related."

Startled, Joshua squinted at Tad. "Wait a minute. You proved with elementary biology that there is no way Wally can be Vicki's father. If Maggie is his daughter, then she and Vicki can't be related."

Tad pointed to the markers on the two DNA results that matched. "Yet, Vicki and Maggie have enough markers in common to prove that they are blood relations."

"Siblings?" Joshua asked.

Tad shook his head. "Not enough common markers to be siblings."

"Then they are cousins?" Joshua concluded with a questioning tone.

"Once you get out of the immediate family, then it gets foggy as far as proving how people are related." Tad shrugged. "It is a known fact who their mothers are. Cindy and Beth weren't related. The girls have to be related by their fathers. Wally didn't have a brother, so they can't be cousins."

"Wally didn't have a brother that we know of," Joshua pointed out.

Tad agreed. "The nut never falls very far from the tree. Reverend Rawlings moonlights as a drug lord. Why stop there? Why shouldn't he have a woman stashed away somewhere; a woman who gave birth to his son, who grew up to become Cindy's lover and father Vicki?"

Joshua wondered out loud. "Could Beth have been mistaken about who Maggie's father was?" He reminded Tad, "You did say that she was on her way to becoming an alcoholic when she was pregnant with Maggie. Maybe she had a blackout when she conceived Maggie. If that's the case, there's no telling how Vicki and Maggie are related."

Tad answered firmly, "Beth swore that Wally was the only one who could be Maggie's father. Besides, there aren't enough markers for them to be siblings, even half siblings."

"Well, this certainly gives me something to think about." Joshua slipped the test results back into the envelope. Deep in thought, he led Tad back up the yard and into the family room where his children were still watching Amber's interviews.

"Hey!" Donny exclaimed as he rummage through the box of candy in search of an unmolested piece. "Who poked holes in all the candy?"

Joshua and Tad walked in as Murphy was switching DVDs. He announced that this disk contained Amber's special announcement about witnessing the murders.

As he watched his son cue up the report, Joshua asked Tad, "Have the DNA tests come back on Wally yet?"

Tad responded that they hadn't.

Morgan's face splashed across the television screen. The image reminded Joshua of how pretty Morgan Lucas was compared to the subject of her interview.

"I guess I need to have someone from the attorney general's office call that lab," Joshua told Tad. "I need those results."

The lawyer refocused his attention on Amber. That was when he saw Amber's mistake. It jumped out at him from the television screen the way a typo leaps out from a whole page of text when it is read with a fresh pair of eyes.

"Stop the disk!" he ordered Murphy, who hit the stop button on the remote. "Put in the other disk."

"What track?" Murphy asked.

Everyone in the room strained to see what Joshua had noticed.

"It doesn't matter," Joshua told him. "Just cue up any one of the interviews with Tess."

Murphy popped in the previous DVD and hit the play button.

Amber's image filled the television screen.

"Now go back to the interview with Morgan." Joshua ordered his son.

Murphy did as he directed.

When Amber re-appeared, Joshua smiled up at Tad. "Do you see it?"

Tad's grin told Joshua that he did.

"What?" all the children wanted to know.

"Keep your eye on the spider." Joshua told them.

CHAPTER 33

▼

Center stage, Reverend Orville Rawlings openly sobbed while leading his worship team and followers through song after song and prayer after prayer for the lost souls of his son and son-in-law at the memorial service.

Meanwhile, the projection screen behind him illustrated Wallace Rawlings's and Hal Poole's lives through a montage of videos and slide shows to a variety of contemporary songs fitting the theme of the memorial performance.

Off to one side of the stage, Bridgette Rawlings Poole sat in the image of a woman in mourning. She was dressed all in black, complete with a broad rimmed hat with a veil that hung down to her bodice.

If the Rawlings family charged admittance, it would have been a sold-out performance. In lieu of tickets, the church did request donations towards a memorial fund for the deceased. No one specified how the money would be used. Judging by the pile of cash and checks in the collection plates, most of the church members either did not care about, or notice, that lack of detail.

The Thornton children sat between Joshua and Jan at the back of the worship center. Their father had agreed to let them come to the service, but ordered that they wait outside for the show after the performance.

Looking like a Native American tribal chief with his arms crossed across his broad chest, Sheriff Curtis Sawyer stood at attention by the exit at the back of the room. Since his chance at getting Orville Rawlings was blown by Wallace's murder, not to mention his mother was fired from her job after more than twenty years of service to the Rawlings, the gloves were officially off.

On the other side of the audience, Tess Bauer and her camera crew were taking in the show. The journalist shifted in her seat in the front row. She was anxious for the real show after the memorial performance. Joshua Thornton had proven to be a good source. As a reward for sending Amber to see him, he was giving her an exclusive of Reverend Orville Rawlings's arrest and promised her an exclusive interview after the arrest.

Seated front and center in the audience, Clarence Mannings's unemotional reaction to the service indicated that he was there only for professional reasons. Under his bushy eyebrows, he appeared to be asleep.

"Oh, Lord," Orville looked up to the ceiling. His face was contorted with emotion. "Why have You forsaken me? You don't have to answer that! I know why! And that is why You have taken my son from me! That is why You have punished my daughter by taking her husband from her! We have sinned, oh, Lord! We are weak, and we have failed, and we throw ourselves on Your mercy!"

In a display of repentance, Orville knelt to the floor of the stage and clasped his hands while sobbing loudly. "We ask that Your will, not ours, be done!"

Quietly, Tad came in at the back of the sanctuary. He practically held up an elderly man dressed in a dark tweed suit with a fedora hat perched on his gray head. At a snail's pace, the two men made their way to the first seat available, which was across the aisle from Joshua Thornton and his family. The old man, stooped over into a C-shape, sighed wearily after the doctor eased him into his seat.

Once the doctor was certain his companion was comfortable, Tad ducked across the aisle and knelt next to Joshua's seat. As he slipped a large white envelope into the prosecutor's hand, Tad declared with a grin, "It's all there."

At the end of the service, the Thornton children, hoping their father would change his mind about them waiting outside (either that, or be too busy to notice their presence), hesitated while Joshua, Curtis Sawyer, Tad, and Jan huddled together to confer about their next move. The children's hopes were dashed when their father gave them a wordless order to leave with a single shot of his look. He watched motionlessly while they rushed outside.

Joshua Thornton led Tad and the sheriff down to the stage. Jan Martin hurried along close at their heels. Tess's camera operator continued filming from the back of the church while she took a seat a few rows back from the stage.

Clarence Mannings didn't bother getting up at the end of the service. As if the show had just taken an intermission and the next act was now beginning, he remained in his front row seat and brushed his mustache while he watched Joshua and his team advance on his client.

When Tad's elderly companion remained silently watching the show from his seat in the back of the auditorium, most assumed he was one of the doctor's patients who was too frail to leave without assistance.

Grinning cockily, Reverend Rawlings spread his arms and greeted his adversaries. "Ah! Welcome! Welcome to the Valley of the Living God Church!"

"We haven't come to join your congregation, Reverend Rawlings," Sawyer announced.

"You haven't come to pay homage to God, but to bury Him."

"God has nothing to do with this," Tess announced in challenging tone. "Your activities have been an insult to all religious leaders."

"I'd watch what I say, Ms. Bauer. You and your station are already being sued. I have witnesses. My lawyer for one." Rawlings pointed down to Clarence Mannings, who smirked at Tess from his seat in the front row.

Joshua stepped forward. "Reverend Rawlings, sir, what has happened to your tears?"

Reminded of his time of mourning, the reverend contorted his face and wiped an imaginary tear from his eye.

Joshua chuckled up at him. "That's okay. We understand."

Crisscrossing before the front row of the auditorium, the prosecutor presented his argument. "I like puzzles, though I don't have time to put them together, because it's hard to have time to work on something like that when you have five kids who are always into something. My wife gave me this jigsaw puzzle as a present our first Christmas together. It was very interesting, because it wasn't just one puzzle. It was two puzzles in the same box. Since I was good at puzzles, I thought it was a cinch to put together, but I was wrong. I had to readjust my thinking. When I looked at a piece, I had to ask myself not just where did it go, but first, I had to ask myself which puzzle did it belong to."

Joshua stopped and smiled up at Orville Rawlings and his daughter, who remained in their center stage positions. "That was my problem with this case. I kept looking at everything as one puzzle, when it was actually many puzzles with all the pieces in the same box. Once, I looked at it that way, the pieces fit together much more easily."

Clarence Mannings cleared his throat, sat back in his seat, and crossed one leg over the other. "Commander Thornton, this is all very interesting, but my client and I don't have time for your rambling."

"Oh, I suggest you make the time, sir, because your client built the box into which all the pieces to all these puzzles belong. By the time I'm through, this box is going to be his coffin."

Reverend Rawlings pointed to Joshua as he told his lawyer. "You heard him say that, Mannings. Be prepared to file a lawsuit first thing in the morning! Not only is he slandering me less than two days after my son has been killed, but he's threatening me, too."

"Let's talk about that, Reverend Rawlings." Joshua sat on the arm of one of the chairs. "You said you did not realize that your son was in danger until ten o'clock the morning after his death."

"That's right, when I received the e-mail from Hal confessing his sins."

"You dye your hair, don't you?"

"What?" Orville Rawlings was outraged by the unexpected intrusion into his private grooming habits.

"Is this really necessary?" Bridgette stood up from her seat on the stage and crossed to take her father's arm.

"You color your hair, too, don't you, Mrs. Poole?"

"That is none of your business!" Bridgette shrieked.

"But it is pertinent."

Curtis Sawyer crossed his arms over his broad chest. "You see, Reverend Rawlings, my mother told me that for years you have had a standing appointment in your home every fourth Friday morning to have your hair colored. The same hair stylist colors Mrs. Poole's hair. Her shade is Irish Setter red. When I told Mom that you had an appointment with your hair stylist the morning Wally and Hal were found, she found that interesting, because it was Tuesday, not Friday. We called the stylist. She said that Mrs. Poole called her at almost seven o'clock the night before, Monday night, to request that she come three days early. She said that you would be too busy for her to come Friday."

Joshua detected the look of disdain Reverend Rawlings shot towards his daughter as he extracted her hand from the crook of his arm. "Maybe you knew that you would be the focus of a lot of media attention," he indicated the camera, "and you didn't want to be caught with your roots showing."

Mannings shook his head at Joshua. "That is totally circumstantial."

"Let's talk about Wally and another one of the puzzles." Joshua held out his hand to Sheriff Sawyer, who handed him a thick paper book. "Wally defended Eric Connally, pro bono, by the way, in federal court when he was charged with vandalism of federal property, and breaking and entering. He won the case."

"Wally is dead," Bridgette sighed with boredom.

"I'm aware of that. Interesting thing about the evidence that came out in that trial. The post office break-in in Chester was the same night that New Cumberland's courthouse was broken into. Those two crimes were never connected. One was a federal building. The other was a county building. One was in Chester. The other was in New Cumberland. But when you look at both break-ins, then you see there are similarities. Whoever broke in knew how to bypass security systems. That was how Wally got Eric off. He proved Connally knew nothing about security. In presenting his defense, Wally proved that he knew all those things. As a defense attorney, he was familiar with the courthouse, and the post office's system was not complicated at all."

"Wallace didn't know anything about security systems," the reverend argued.

"But you do, sir."

"I do not!" Rawlings retorted.

"We'll come back to that." The prosecutor strolled over to the stage. "Now, let's talk some more about that post office break-in. Why would Wally break into a post office?"

"He had no reason to break into the post office." Sighing at the inconvenience of the whole proceedings, the reverend crossed the stage to sit in the chair Bridgette had formerly sat in.

"I don't think he broke into the post office." Joshua waited for a response from the reverend, who gave none.

"Who broke in?" Sheriff Sawyer called out.

"Wally's father and sister."

Bridgette's response was loud and exaggerated laughter. "Are you drunk?"

"Keep it up, Thornton. You're only upping the ante in a slander suit," Mannings warned him.

"You know all about security systems," Joshua told the reverend.

"I do not."

"You didn't learn them in the Korean War?"

"I was a chaplain in the Korean War."

"Oh, yeah, that's right. That's where you met Charles Delaney, your good friend."

"Yes."

"It's all in your military records." As he spoke, Joshua took a thick binder from Tad.

For the first time, Reverend Orville Rawlings betrayed a hint of fear in his eyes as he observed the binder that Joshua placed on the seat in the front row.

Joshua played him out. "I believe you and your daughter broke into the post office to intercept a letter that was supposed to be mailed to the then prosecuting attorney of Hancock County, a letter you were told would be mailed out upon the death of Dr. Russell Wilson. When you didn't find the letter in the post office, you assumed you missed it, and broke into the courthouse to look for it there." Joshua chuckled, "I'll admit that is speculation."

"Your speculation is worth shit," Bridgette responded. "Computer equipment was stolen from the courthouse. Why would my father steal computer equipment when we can buy the best on the planet?"

"To cover up that you were looking to steal the letter I have right here." Joshua took a letter out of his inside breast pocket. "It tells us everything. We found it with the real autopsy reports in which Doc Wilson stated the true causes of deaths for the victims of the Rawlings."

"And why, pray tell," Clarence Mannings sighed, "did he not report the true findings when he did the autopsies?"

"Doc Wilson and his family were threatened into reporting what Reverend Rawlings and Sheriff Delaney, the reverend's good friend and employee, told the medical examiner to report. He did as he was told, but he documented everything. Records do confirm that the dates of the break-ins occurred the night after Dr. Russell Wilson died."

"I resent that!" Bridgette yelled.

Joshua handed the copy of the letter to Clarence Mannings as he told Bridgette, "Resent it all you like. Every autopsy is now in the hands of the attorney general, along with the original of this notarized letter."

"And the jury is going to believe a blackmailer?" Clarence Mannings smirked.

"Check his bank accounts. Dr. Russell Wilson never took one penny in blackmail. His extortion was to keep the Rawlings out of positions of power. That's why Wally Rawlings didn't run for prosecuting attorney until after Doc Wilson died. When the letter was never sent or received, then he thought he was safe. Now, there was only one small hurdle standing in the way of his political career."

"What?" Reverend Rawlings's glare dared Joshua to continue.

"The Hitchcocks."

Joshua watched as Reverend Rawlings's eyes narrowed to slits. He directed the fire in his eyes at Bridgette, whose attempt at innocence did not come off as she squeaked, "Who?"

Joshua suppressed a grin to see them rattled by the mention of the Hitchcock name. "Wally's mistress and her family, including the child they had together while he was married to Cindy. Don't pretend you didn't know them. They were members of this church."

"Oh, I remember them now," Bridgette said. "It was such a tragedy. They were all killed in plane crash a few years ago."

"No, they weren't," Joshua shot back. "Your former secretary lied. She didn't put them on any plane." He shocked Bridgette further. "And they're not dead either. The mother died of natural causes, but Wally's former mistress and their daughter are alive. Your secretary hid them from the cop you hired to kill them and faked their deaths on that flight."

Bridgette giggled. "You must be smoking crack."

"We have her and Scott Collins's sworn statements. You hired Scott Collins to kill three people to clear the way for Wally to run for prosecuting attorney."

Mannings interjected, "Even if it's true, no one was killed. In which case, all you have is a conspiracy, which happened four years ago."

"And the attempt on my life was a few days ago," Joshua retorted. "It was the same drill. Bridgette hired Scott Collins to kill me after she found out that Sawyer hadn't."

"He says," Bridgette announced with a cocky tone.

Joshua repeated. "He says."

Mannings pointed out. "The statement of a crooked cop doesn't hold much weight in front of a jury."

"No, it doesn't." Joshua gestured towards the letter Mannings still held in his hand. "The Hitchcocks were only a small hurdle standing in the way of Wally's political career. They aren't even mentioned in Wilson's letter. But Wilson didn't need the Hitchcocks. He had enough without them to ruin the Rawlings. Over the years, he collected a mountain of evidence while he was medical examiner. It began with Sam Fletcher's murder and ended with the death of Wally's wife."

Before the defense attorney or church pastor could stop her, Bridgette retorted, "Wilson had no proof of who poisoned Cindy."

"It's interesting that you used the word 'poisoned'." Joshua's lips curled.

"Shut up, Bridgette," her father warned.

"I never said Cindy Rawlings was poisoned," Joshua pointed out. "I only said she was murdered."

"Well, I was there," Bridgette scoffed. "She wasn't shot. She wasn't knifed. How else could she have been killed?"

"She could have been smothered," Tad suggested.

"She was throwing up. She was vomiting blood and having convulsions."

"Shut up, you stupid girl!" the reverend hissed.

"According to your statement at the time, Mrs. Poole," Joshua said calmly, "you weren't home when Cindy died."

"Why would any one in the Rawlings family want to kill Wallace's wife?" Clarence Mannings smiled with a cocky grin at his adversary.

"To cover up the sins of the father." Joshua strolled over to where Tad was sitting in the audience. "It all started on Cindy's and Wally's wedding night, when the bride made the fatal mistake of confessing to her new husband that she was in love with another man, Dr. Tad MacMillan."

"Wallace Rawlings killed his wife because she was in love with another man." Clarence Manning scoffed. "You're wasting our time prosecuting a dead man?"

"No, Wally got his kicks out of making people miserable. If he killed Cindy, then he'd miss out on the fun of torturing her. He refused to divorce her. For Cindy, divorcing her husband would be a sin. She vowed for better or worse, and it was the worst. Wally exacted his vengeance by making his wife cut off all relations with Tad MacMillan and her friends. He punished her emotionally by refusing to have marital relations with her, while at the same time embarking on an affair with another woman who bore his child. I have no proof, but I don't doubt, knowing Wally the way I did, that he flaunted his affair to Cindy, purely to humiliate her. So, you can imagine Wally's fury when Cindy got pregnant by what had to be another man."

Each member of the audience, making the same assumption, looked at Tad.

"I was not the father!" the doctor claimed.

The prosecutor reminded them, "Remember, I said that Wally ordered Cindy to stay away from Tad." He continued, "Cindy vowed to obey her husband. She did stay away from the man she loved. Yet, Wally couldn't, and didn't, believe her when she told him that Tad was not their daughter's father."

Joshua asked with an exaggerated shrug, "Who else could have been the father?" He went on, "Wally even told Vicki, in a moment of extreme cruelty, that Tad MacMillan was her father, because he knew he wasn't. Therefore, it had to be Tad."

"Wally was Cindy's husband," the reverend stated. "If Dr. MacMillan wasn't Victoria's father, then Wally—"

"Wally told me he never consummated his marriage to Cindy," Sheriff Sawyer said.

"He said the same thing to me," Joshua told them.

"Hearsay," Mannings snickered.

"Blood is not hearsay," Joshua said, "and blood does not lie."

"It was Vicki's blood tests, done as part of the usual natal examination at the hospital when she was born, that told Doc Wilson that Wally was not her father." Tad stated, matter-of-factly, "There is no way possible for a man and a woman who both have RH negative factor to produce a child with an RH positive blood type. One or both of the parents have to be RH positive."

"So obviously, sweet little Cindy was sleeping around," Bridgette giggled.

"A jury would call it rape. Multiple rape." Joshua handed Mannings a copy of Wilson's file on Cindy Rawlings. "Doc Wilson recalls in his statement an incident he witnessed in which Cindy Rawlings had a panic attack when her father-in-law came into her bedroom without knocking."

"That doesn't prove anything," Mannings insisted.

"It proves a factor of their relationship, which is that it was not a relationship of invited intimacy."

Mannings laughed. "Are you suggesting that my client was his granddaughter's father?"

"Yes, and we have the DNA tests to prove it," Joshua announced before handing off the envelope Tad had handed him earlier to the doctor.

Tad took center stage. "It was one of those things where when you saw it spelled out you wondered why you didn't see it before."

Reverend Rawlings challenged with a cocky chuckle, "Even if I was Vicki's father, there is no way you can prove it. My lawyer blocked your prosecutor from taking any of my DNA due to just cause. You still don't have just cause to get it."

"We didn't need your DNA to prove it," Tad smirked. "Have you forgotten already? Your son Wally was murdered. That made his body evidence. It was with his DNA that we found the evidence to prove that you fathered Vicki."

"And who was it that put this proof together?" Mannings's sly grin under his walrus mustache indicated that he was already putting together his client's defense.

"The West Virginia state lab in Weirton."

"I don't suppose you mentioned to the forensics people who put together these results that you were intimately involved with Vicki Rawlings's mother."

Tad answered without shame. "No, I did not."

Mannings circled Tad like a predator sizing up his prey. "So, I presume that you have determined that my client, not having his DNA, is Vicki Rawlings's father, without the use of your own DNA to eliminate you as the father."

Tad yanked a sheet of paper from the envelope and presented it to Mannings. "Your presumption is incorrect. I voluntarily gave my DNA to a state medical examiner at the Weirton lab. They even recorded it on video to prove that is was my DNA, and no one else's." He gestured for Mannings to read the results. "There is no way possible that I can be Vicki's father." Tad added, "Wally's DNA proves the same thing. There is no way that he could have been her father, however, there are enough common markers between Wally and Vicki to make them half siblings, just like DNA evidence found at the murder scene."

Bridgette interjected, "That proves that Wally killed Vicki!"

Joshua pointed out, "Since Wally was Vicki's half brother, that makes you her half sister, Bridgette."

Bridgette reacted with an insulted snort.

"Orville Rawlings was Vicki's grandfather," Mannings argued. "Of course, any tests will prove that he is related to her, which is already an established fact."

The reverend announced sharply, "I will not dignify this perverted accusation by submitting any of my blood to any tests!"

"As I stated before, Reverend Rawlings, we don't need any of your blood to prove your relationship to Vicki," Tad explained calmly. "The DNA tests prove that Wally and Vicki were indeed related. The RH factor proves that they can't be father-daughter. The markers prove that they shared at least one parent. It is a proven fact that they don't have the same mother; therefore, they must share the same father. Since you are Wally's father, then you have to be Vicki's father."

"And," Joshua concluded, "in order to be Vicki's father, you had to have intercourse with her mother, your son's wife."

"None of this proves anything," Clarence Mannings gestured for Reverend Rawlings not to say anything. "By the time we are through, Commander Thornton, I'll have this whole valley convinced Cindy Welch Rawlings was a bed-hopping nymphomaniac with a Daddy complex, who seduced her poor father-in-law in a weak moment."

"I'm sure you will," Joshua responded softly.

Disappointed, the witnesses thought Joshua had given up when he strolled up the aisle with Clarence Manning's smirk of superiority directed at his back.

Wordlessly, Tad took his envelope of evidence and returned to the audience.

Reverend Rawlings stood up and smoothed his clothes. "Well, if you will excuse me—"

Joshua whirled around and roared at the reverend. "I'm not through with you! Sit down!"

To everyone's surprise, including his, Reverend Orville Rawlings dropped back down into the chair.

"No, we cannot prove you used that poor girl's faith in your church, and her trust in you, to force her into submitting to your perverted punishments in the name of God, but Dr. Russell Wilson claimed it was murder, and I believe you killed her."

"Even if they were sleeping together, why, after years of her being married to his son would the reverend kill her? You would have better luck proving his son did it." Clarence Mannings plopped down into his seat with an air of bored annoyance.

"Your client killed her because the worst thing imaginable happened." Joshua turned to his cousin. "Dr. Tad MacMillan became a respectable citizen."

Joshua resumed his pacing, this time up and down the aisle. "You see, as long as Dr. MacMillan was a drunken rebel, Cindy wouldn't want to be with him. She could love him from afar and long for what could have been. Then, Tad Mac-Millan did the unimaginable. He sobered up. That made him more appealing to Cindy. People started listening to him. The reverend knew that if Cindy spoke to Tad, which would surely happen with them living in the same town, the two of them might get together. If that happened, then a catastrophe would occur."

Seeing where the prosecutor was going, Curtis Sawyer uttered an involuntary gasp. "She would confide to Tad that the reverend was raping her."

"If Cindy told Tad that while he was drinking, no one would listen to him. Now that he was sober, if she told him, he could do something. If the truth came out, the reverend would lose everything. That's why Reverend Rawlings slowly started killing her.

"Then, when the reverend learned that she had indeed spoken to Tad—I suspect he had his personal spy, Hal Poole, following her—he killed her with one final dose of arsenic. At first, Doc Wilson dismissed Cindy's health problems as an ulcer brought on by a nervous condition. When she died, he thought her ulcer had hemorrhaged, until Tad informed him that Cindy said she thought she was being poisoned. Doc Wilson did a toxicology test and found the arsenic. Now, since he couldn't prove who did it because Cindy told Tad it was Wally, he could only hang it over the family's head as a major scandal if they didn't behave themselves."

"Like you said," the reverend retorted, "you can't prove I did it."

"Just like Doc Wilson couldn't prove you killed your wife, huh?"

"Oh, please," Clarence Mannings groaned as he stood up. "Do you plan on accusing my client of every death in his family tree?"

"Just about," Joshua smirked back at him. "Oh, it is a very interesting family tree. You shake it and skeletons drop like rotten apples. You see, while everyone else bought that your client was a saint, Doc Wilson was too sharp to fall for his act. No one could pull the wool over his eyes. He believed Tad when he told him that Cindy was murdered because he already knew the type of man your client was.

"Doc Wilson knew something evil was going on in the Rawlings family when Eleanor Rawlings drowned in her bathtub. Back then, Doc says it in his report, he was bothered by two bruises on each ankle."

"My dear wife was not a well woman!" the reverend objected.

Joshua didn't slow down. "Your wife died four years before Cindy. Vicki was five years old when your wife died, which means that you had been raping Cindy for at least six years at the time of your wife's death. Need I point out that Vicki told more than one witness that you killed her grandmother? She must have seen something, and I have no doubt that was a factor in her rebellion.

"Doc Wilson heard the rumors and was bothered by those bruises on your wife's ankles. While you had managed to get everyone in the valley to believe that a man of God could never do such an awful thing, you couldn't convince Doc. Not only did he have suspicions about your wife's death, but also he had the evidence that Vicki was not Wally's daughter.

"That was enough to keep you in line. You were very aware that Dr. Russell Wilson was probably the one man in this valley people respected more than you. If he said you were a murderer and rapist, people would believe him. That is why you ordered Wally to withdraw from the race for county prosecutor. Wally's withdrawal from the race satisfied Doc Wilson enough to keep him quiet until Cindy was murdered. Then, he took another look at his report on Eleanor's death and figured it out."

Tad and Sheriff Sawyer wheeled a claw-footed tub filled with water out onto the stage. Joshua climbed up onto the stage to join Jan, who came out wearing a bathrobe. As he presented his demonstration, Jan removed her bathrobe to reveal a bathing suit and a pair of nose plugs that she put on before climbing into the tub.

"It was so painfully simple. Eleanor Rawlings was found in this same old claw-footed tub in the master suite of the Rawlings mansion. It was hard, but we found it at the antique shop you sold it to. Eleanor Rawlings was taking her bath when her dear husband came in to speak to her. He was standing there talking away, lingering next to her feet, which were resting up on the edge, when he simply—"

Joshua grabbed Jan's feet and yanked them up. Jan lost her balance and fell under the water. With nothing to grab to pull herself up, she flailed helplessly under the water. Everyone in the chapel, thinking they had witnessed another murder, screamed in unison and jumped to their feet.

Just as quickly as he yanked Jan under, Joshua let go of her ankles, grabbed his victim from under her armpits, and pulled her, gasping and sputtering, up out of the water.

Horrified by the vision of Reverend Rawlings effortlessly drowning his frail wife, the audience watched in silence while Joshua helped his victim, her legs trembling, out of the tub and into her robe. Tad helped her off the stage to redress backstage.

To further imprint the image in their minds, Joshua waited for his victim to be out of sight before breaking the silence.

"Now, there we have a young athletic woman, who was prepared for what I did. If I had held onto her feet, I could have drowned her, and there was nothing she could have done to stop me. Eleanor Rawlings was an elderly woman in ill health. She was weak. Killing her was as simple as drowning a kitten."

"Motive?" Clarence Mannings sputtered out his demand to know the answer to his question.

"Everything was in her name." Sheriff Sawyer indicated the massive building. "All of this. Everything. The land. The mansion. Eleanor's father left everything to her."

"Sam Fletcher," Tad joined in as he stepped back into the auditorium from backstage, "didn't trust his son-in-law. He didn't leave Rawlings a dime. He left it all to Eleanor, and she was passive enough to let her husband do with it as he wanted. If she found out that her husband was raping their son's wife, that may have been enough to make her leave him, take everything with her, and ruin Rawlings's reputation by revealing the snake he really was."

The reverend laughed. "I suppose now you are going to say I drove my father-in-law nuts and made him jump off the Chester Bridge."

"LSD." Tad strolled up to the steps leading up onto the stage. "When I read the revised autopsy report on Sam Fletcher's death, I remembered a conversation I had with Doc Wilson. You see, Sam Fletcher died back in the late fifties. His death was ruled a suicide brought on by mental illness. But I remember very clearly how my father could not understand how someone so together could just suddenly go nuts. No one understood, especially Sam's good friend, Doc Wilson."

Tad leaned on the stage and looked up at the reverend. "About a month after Cindy died, Doc calls me. Now, as my cousin mentioned, I was sober then, and I had built a new reputation. Doc Wilson never trusted me for anything, no matter how much I tried to help him. It was the only time, the one and only time, he called and asked me, of all things, about LSD. He knew I had experimented with it when I was a teenager, when everyone else was doing it. I told him about the hallucinations, the delusions; how some people had good trips and some had bad, and about a guy I knew who OD'd on it.

"Then, he asked me how it would affect someone who was given doses of it without their knowing, and, if no one knew he was on it, how would he be perceived. I told him the doctors would think the patient had become schizophrenic and paranoid. Doc Wilson asked me if this patient would jump off a bridge. I said, 'Yes, either to kill himself to end the trip, or because he thought he could fly.'"

Tad squinted up at Reverend Rawlings. "Doc Wilson put that conversation in Sam Fletcher's file. He says that he was always bothered by how Sam Fletcher died and, after speaking to me, he recommended that his body be exhumed so that tests can be run to see if LSD can be detected in his remains." Laughingly, he added, "Which they can."

"Of course," Joshua pointed out, "Doc Wilson could never get Fletcher's body exhumed because you and Sheriff Delaney had the power to keep that from happening. Now that Delaney and your son, the prosecutor, are both dead, we should be able to get a look at Sam Fletcher's body. Like Tad, I'm confident LSD will be found in his remains."

"How would I get LSD?" the reverend laughed.

"I'm glad you asked that question. Back in the 1950's the CIA was experimenting with LSD to extort information from prisoners. They had it in Korea."

Joshua responded to Mannings's question before the lawyer could utter the words. "As for motive, after Sam Fletcher died, Eleanor had control of her father's land and money, and the reverend had control of Eleanor. Therefore, he had control of everything."

"But you have no proof," Reverend Rawlings glared at them. "I believe this is all called speculation. Sam Fletcher went crazy. He was crazy when I met him, and he was crazy when he threw himself off that bridge, and you can't prove otherwise."

"That's right," Joshua said. "Those puzzles we can't get you on. We can't prove to a jury that you killed any of them. Just like we can't prove you had Chuck Delaney give Lulu Jefferson that overdose of heroin."

"Who the hell is Lulu Jefferson?" Clarence Mannings yelled.

"She was the young woman who wrote this letter to my mother." Joshua pulled a copy of the letter out of his binder and handed it to the lawyer. "She recounts a night in which she, her date, and my parents found a dead body in an abandoned barn. They went to get Sheriff Delaney, and he made a phone call to a 'deputy'." Joshua used his fingers to indicate quotation marks. "When they came back, the body was gone. That body is now in the morgue in Weirton. It was identified as Kevin Rice, who Lulu Jefferson saw in a picture in your client's office years later. She made the fatal mistake of asking the reverend who he was. Suddenly, your client remembered she had seen the body in the barn and, being a man who took no chances, ordered Sheriff Delaney to eliminate her. Sheriff Delaney, being an officer in your client's drug business, easily got his hands on the heroin to do the job. However, before Delaney could do the job, Lulu wrote a letter telling everything to my mother. Unfortunately, my parents never received the letter."

"Lulu Jefferson was mistaken. I don't even remember her asking me about any picture. I barely remember her!"

"How long do we have to put up with this?" Bridgette snatched off her hat and veil in an air of disgust. "This is boring."

"Oh, I assure you, Mrs. Poole," the prosecutor told her, "before I'm through, you are going to get more excitement than you can handle."

Joshua picked up his binder and climbed up onto the stage. "Reverend Rawlings, let's go back to your service record. You stated on more than one occasion that you met Charles Delaney in Korea." He opened the binder and referred to a report. "You even stated that here in this very room earlier this evening."

The reverend sighed. "Yes, I did."

"Where in Korea?"

"Seoul."

"Did you see any action?"

"As much action as an army chaplain can see."

"But Charles Delaney was a master sergeant in the military police stationed in Seoul."

"We were stationed at the same base."

"Not according to the records I have here from Washington. According to the VA, Orville Alexander Rawlings never set foot in Seoul. He spent his whole time overseas in Hong Kong." Joshua handed the reverend a copy of the report.

"He could have gone there on leave," Bridgette responded.

"Your father just said he was stationed there." Joshua emphasized the word "stationed".

"So he added color to his service record," Mannings scoffed. "Many public figures do that."

"He lied!"

"Lying is no big deal. Presidents get away with it!"

"What was your rank?" Joshua shot at the reverend.

Reverend Rawlings snarled. "I was a captain."

"You were an officer. A chaplain. Charles Delaney was a sergeant in the military police. How did you become friends with an enlisted man in Seoul while you were an officer serving at a military hospital in Hong Kong?"

For the first time in his life, the reverend was speechless.

Mannings ordered him as he came up onto the stage. "Don't answer that. He has no proof of anything. If he did, we'd be down at the police station, not here."

"I have proof." Joshua held up his hand to stop Mannings, who froze in his footsteps.

Joshua stood over the reverend. "I have proof that ties everything together. You were in Korea in 1952. That was where you met Master Sergeant Charles Delaney. The two of you were partners in crime. Private Kevin Rice was one of your minions. You weren't a chaplain. You were a master sergeant in charge of the supply depot—"

"Oh, please!" Bridgette laughed. "My father was no enlisted man!"

"Orville Rawlings was a chaplain!"

Joshua walked towards her. Once he was face to face with Bridgette Rawlings, the prosecutor whirled around and pointed at her father. "This man is not Orville Rawlings! He is Master Sergeant Caleb Penn!"

There was a stunned silence.

The reverend smirked up at Joshua.

Bridgette laughed, at first out of humor. Then, her laughter took on a hysterical tone. "You must be on the same drugs your cousin takes." She crossed the stage as if to leave.

"Are you going to tell them, sergeant?" Joshua asked the man known as a respected pastor.

The suspect responded in a low tone, "You can't prove anything."

"Who is Sergeant Penn?" Smiling with amusement, Mannings crossed his arms.

"The man for whom Private Kevin Rice spent seven years in Leavenworth. Oh, it was beautiful plan!" Joshua smiled at the reverend. "I have to give you credit."

Joshua crossed the stage as he explained the scheme. "You have to pay close attention to the details here. Sergeant Caleb Penn was in charge of the supply depot in Seoul. Rice was a private, who was simply following Penn's orders when he was caught delivering stolen goods to a fence."

Joshua climbed down off the stage. "When the operation started falling apart after Rice was arrested, Penn shot the fence to death to make sure he didn't turn him in, and then he staged his own death."

So his audience could hear him, Joshua raised his voice as he casually backed up the aisle towards the back of the auditorium. "Either Penn or the master sergeant of the military police, Charles Delaney, abducted a Corporal Milton Black. Delaney, Black's commanding officer, approved his three-day pass to go to Hong Kong. That tells me that Delaney was involved in this up to his crew cut. Black never went to Hong Kong. He was killed, and then blown up in a jeep. The body's identification was based solely on Penn's dog tags, which they had switched, and Delaney's statement that he saw Penn getting into the jeep right before the explosion."

Joshua was now at the back of the auditorium. "By then, Penn was in Hong Kong, looking for his next murder victim, to steal his identity to get himself back to the states."

"Why not come back to the states as Black?" Jan called from the front row.

"Because Black still had another year to serve overseas. When he didn't come back, Delaney reported him AWOL, and then as a deserter. That was his duty as his superior officer. They knew that Black would be wanted when he didn't return. It wouldn't be smart to keep the identity of a wanted man."

Joshua stood behind the elderly man to continue presenting his case. "It was part of their plan. After getting to Hong Kong with Black's ID and three-day pass, Penn had to find someone who was on his way home. He was in Hong Kong a month before he found the perfect victim, an army chaplain by the name of Orville Alexander Rawlings, who had his papers and was ready to leave. I imagine Penn found him in a bar the day before he was to ship out. He shot him in the head like he did the Korean fence, took his papers and dog tags, boarded the plane, and then came home and checked out. From sergeant to captain in less than a month. Not bad."

"But wouldn't someone notice he wasn't Rawlings?" Tess wondered.

"It wasn't that big a chance," Joshua explained. "The military is one giant bureaucracy, especially in war time. Things happen so fast." He snapped his fingers on both hands to illustrate his point. "Most likely no one even looked at his face. Plus, the odds of finding someone who actually knew Rawlings stateside, when he served in Hong Kong, weren't that bad."

Mannings was no longer objecting or laughing.

Joshua continued. "Orville Rawlings did have a family. When they reported him missing after he didn't come back home to Seattle, Washington, the military just checked their paperwork, saw that Rawlings had checked out, and it went no further. It never occurred to anyone that he didn't come back from Hong Kong."

"You can't prove any of this!" Bridgette shouted to the back of the auditorium.

For his response, Joshua helped the elderly man to his feet.

Amid silent curiosity, the two of them crept up to the front of the auditorium.

The elderly man put on thick eyeglasses to peer up at Reverend Orville Rawlings. His lips trembled as he shook his head. He turned to Joshua and said with a weak raspy voice that shattered the silence, "No, that's not him."

Mannings's cockiness gave way to concern over a surprise witness. "Who is this?"

Joshua spoke up to the church pastor. "Would you like to introduce him, reverend?"

Sparks of fury shot from the reverend's eyes to the young lawyer.

"Let me introduce our guest of honor." Joshua turned to the reverend's lawyer. "Say hello to Felix Rawlings. He's flown all the way here from Seattle, Washington, to see your client." Joshua chuckled up to the hulking man on the stage. "This is Orville Rawlings's brother."

Even the reverend was unable to contain his shock at the revelation.

Joshua waited for the gasps that erupted from inside the church to subside before he resumed. "I guess the chaplain didn't get a chance to tell you about his family before you killed him."

Tad got out of his seat to help the elderly man to sit down. On his way to his seat, Orville Rawlings's brother glared up at the man on the stage.

Mannings was too stunned to make any more objections.

Joshua went up onto the stage. "In Hong Kong, the body of a man listed as an American John Doe was found with a bullet in his head in an alley the day this man left. He was stripped of all identification, because Penn took everything, including his Bible. The American embassy in Hong Kong still has the slug from that murder. In the last few days, they compared it to the slug from the Korean fence in Seoul and found a match. The same gun was used in both murders. They will compare the John Doe's dental records to the military's dental records for Orville Rawlings."

Joshua crossed the stage to stand before the man seated on his throne.

"It won't be hard to prove you are Penn. Even your lawyer knows that all military people are fingerprinted when they go into service. Your fingerprints will prove you are Master Sergeant Caleb Penn, which will prove you knew Kevin Rice, which will explain why he was in Chester with this article in his pocket."

There was silence in the chapel when Joshua handed a copy of the magazine article to Clarence Mannings while speaking to the large man, who glowered up at the young prosecutor.

"It has your picture in it with the name of Orville Rawlings. Kevin Rice spent seven years in Leavenworth for following your orders and was accused of killing you. Imagine the fury he felt when he saw that article. Here you were a respected church pastor, making how many tens of thousands a year, while Rice was a convicted thief and suspected killer. It wouldn't have been hard for him to figure out what you did. So, he came here to confront you, maybe even try to blackmail you, and you killed him. By then, killing was easy for you."

"You can't prove Rice even saw this man," Mannings said.

"Oh, but I can." Joshua whipped the bagged murder weapon of Wallace Rawlings from his breast pocket. "This is the proof. It's the gun Hal Poole used to kill Wallace Rawlings. It came out of Wally's gun collection."

Bridgette Poole let out an involuntary shriek and covered her face.

Joshua asked the reverend, sitting in the chair beside where his lawyer stood. "Sergeant Penn, what happened to the gun you were issued when you joined the army?"

Gradually, as the old man came to realize the sequence of events over the years, the pastor's smirk faded.

Joshua crossed the stage and showed the gun to Bridgette Rawlings Poole. "Bridgette, what was the first gun your brother got to start his collection?"

The reverend's daughter peered at the gun in the bag. Her hands trembled when she touched it. She jerked her fingers away as if she had received an electric shock. "It was his thirteenth birthday. Father gave it to him. It was his first gun."

Joshua turned back to the reverend. "The other day, Tad, Jan Martin, and I were shot at. It was not hard for me to see that whoever was shooting at us was a lousy shot. He couldn't hit the broad side of a barn, but he could hit the broad side of a trunk." Joshua took out the envelope containing the slug from the chest. "This slug came from this gun."

Joshua showed the gun to the old man. "Army records show that this gun, with this serial number, was issued to Master Sergeant Caleb Penn. Ballistics would show that the slugs used to kill the Korean fence, Chaplain Orville Rawlings, Kevin Rice, your son-in-law, and your own son, all came from this same gun. Since the first three were killed before your son was even born, and you were in possession of it to give to your son, that puts the smoking gun into your hands."

Silence hung over the church while everyone waited for the man known as Reverend Orville Rawlings to respond to the irrefutable evidence.

The successful church pastor kept his eyes on Joshua Thornton when he raised his bulk out of his seat and crossed to the center of the stage as if to confess his guilt to everyone.

Instead of confessing, the reverend chuckled. Gradually, his chuckle rose to laughter while he casually reached into his inside breast pocket, pulled out a gun, and shot Joshua Thornton in the chest.

CHAPTER 34

▼

The reaction was instantaneous.

Two bullets hit Joshua in the chest. The force of the impact knocked him to the floor.

When the former master sergeant turned to shoot the sheriff, he found himself caught in a hailstorm of bullets coming from the sheriff and a dozen sheriff deputies, state police, and federal agents, all of whom had been hiding in every conceivable place since the memorial service had ended.

Considering the trail of bodies left in Caleb Penn's wake, Joshua Thornton ordered that they had to be prepared for anything.

Anticipating the firefight, everyone dropped to the floor and hid, except for an elderly man from Seattle, Washington, who stood to get a better view.

With a curse, Felix Rawlings shoved Tad away when he tried to help the old man. With a sense of justice, Orville Rawlings's brother smiled broadly as he watched the killer's body riddled with bullets. He had been waiting more than half his life for this moment, and nothing, even deadly danger, was going to rob him of it.

Bridgette Rawlings Poole and Clarence Mannings were the only ones in the chapel not expecting any violence. It took a full moment for the lawyer to realize that they were in the line of fire. Rooted center stage, Bridgette screamed hysterical demands to know what was going on. When Mannings tried to yank her off the stage, Bridgette shoved him away. He was propelled backwards into the same bathtub in which her mother had died.

The gunfight continued while Mannings experienced himself the helplessness that Eleanor Rawlings felt in her last moments of life. Finally, he was able to pull himself up out the sloshing water only to have to duck back down into it while bullets ricocheted off the thick steel walls of the tub.

The firefight only lasted six seconds.

"Hold your fire!" Joshua ordered over the roar of the gunshots.

While lying flat on his back where the force of Rawlings's shots knocked him, the prosecutor had managed to fire off two rounds from his own gun, which he had concealed in a holster strapped onto the back of his belt.

As abruptly as it started, the shooting stopped.

The auditorium was filled with earth shattering quiet.

In disbelief, the man known as Reverend Orville Rawlings looked down at Joshua Thornton, who was sprawled on the floor at his feet.

Ready to shoot again if need be, Joshua aimed his gun up at him. The two bullets Penn had fired into Joshua's chest had exposed the kevlar lining of a bulletproof vest.

Joshua held his breath.

"Holy shit," the old man sneered before he dropped to the floor.

Dead.

Everyone in the auditorium was afraid to make the first move for fear it would be inappropriate.

Felix Rawlings had no such fear. The elderly witness broke the stunned silence with a standing ovation.

*   *   *   *

"I had no idea," Bridgette Rawlings Poole repeated over and over again while dabbing at her eyes.

Meanwhile, the law enforcement officers went about the business of removing the body of the man known as Reverend Orville Rawlings from the church he had built with his father-in-law's money.

Distraught, Bridgette let her drenched lawyer move her to her office located in the business wing of the church, out of Tess Bauer's camera range.

Tess was gloating over personally witnessing the drama, while the rest of the media, called in at the report of the shooting, had to wait along with Joshua Thornton's children outside in the parking lot.

The news journalist discovered that the show was not over when she saw Joshua lead Sawyer, Tad, and Jan out of the worship center and back to Bridgette's office to resume the interview.

Tess ordered her camera operator to continue filming and followed them.

Mannings was appalled when Joshua Thornton knocked on Bridgette's door. "Do you have to get her statement now?"

"We have another puzzle to put together." Joshua forced his way into the office of the heir apparent to Reverend Orville Rawlings's dynasty.

They found Bridgette Poole seated on the sofa with her feet curled up under her. Dry-eyed, she was enjoying a snifter of brandy.

The prosecutor observed with sarcasm, "I'm glad to see that you are not totally incapacitated by the revelation of your family's murderous legacy."

"I knew nothing about what that man did before I was even born." Bridgette snapped.

"But you do know about what happened this summer." Joshua leaned against her delicately designed red cherry desk.

"Talk to my lawyer." Bridgette waved a hand towards Mannings, who resembled a walrus with his glistening wet bald head and bushy mustache dripping water down his chin onto his three thousand-dollar suit.

Joshua spoke to Bridgette, even though he looked at Mannings. "You were the one who called the hairstylist before your husband's and brother's deaths to change the standing appointment. You wrote the suicide note, which you e-mailed to your father twenty minutes after your husband's time of death. It came from your laptop, which you had plugged in at Wally's secretary's desk and used her phone line."

Joshua took a copy of the suicide note from his breast pocket to show Bridgette's lawyer. "The church has a whole network of computers on their account with their server. Most of them belong to members of the Rawlings family. Their server keeps very good records. It wasn't hard to track down from what phone number, not commonly used, this e-mail was sent. It was sent from Wally's secretary's media line twenty minutes after our witnesses heard the two fatal gunshots."

"Your witnesses are wrong about the time they heard the shot," Bridgette said.

Clarence Mannings shook his head. "You can't narrow their time of death down to twenty minutes. Hal could have been alive when he sent that e-mail from his wife's laptop, from Wally's secretary's phone line, before killing himself."

Sheriff Sawyer disagreed with a shake of his head. "We have two witnesses who heard the shots that killed Wallace and Hal. The couple living in the house behind the school heard them. They thought the noise was a car backfiring. That's why they didn't call the police. They were watching a movie and recall the exact point in the movie when they heard the shots. We called the television studio, and they placed the time of the shots as being ten minutes after one."

Joshua held up the e-mail. "This e-mail was sent at one-twenty-eight. The county phone records confirm the time the line was in use."

Before Mannings could object further, Joshua added, "Why would Hal use his wife's laptop to log on under his father-in-law's password to go into the reverend's e-mail to delete his original suicide note more than an hour after sending it from his own terminal at his home? Then, why did he log off and log back on less than one minute later under his own password to recompose another suicide note to send to the reverend—all on his wife's laptop, using Wally's secretary's phone line?"

Joshua laid his hand on top of Bridgette's computer, which rested in the center of her desktop. "And how did that laptop get here? Who removed the computer from the scene and why?"

Joshua told Bridgette, "You were there when Hal killed Wally. You put him up to it. After they were both dead, you used your father's password to check the suicide note and found that it had something in there that you could not let the police read. Our computer forensics people retrieved Hal's original suicide note from your father's system…with a warrant, of course. Even though something is deleted, it is not necessarily gone."

Joshua took the letter out of his pocket and handed it to Mannings. "In his original suicide note, Hal states that Vicki was killed in a crossfire between God's angels and Satan's demons; but that Bridgette killed Beth Davis, one of the devil's demons sent to destroy the reverend; and that the two of them committed suicide together, because, together, they killed Wally. Hal believed they had a suicide pact."

Mannings's mouth dropped open.

Bridgette responded for her lawyer. "As I'm sure you figured out, Hal was not the sharpest knife in the drawer." She gave Joshua a cocky smile. "If you will recall, I have an alibi for Beth's murder."

Joshua smirked back. "That's right. The tanning salon just a few blocks from the hospital from which Beth was taken after her collapse at the courthouse."

Bridgette snickered while Joshua continued; "Your lawyer did supply us with the sign-in sheet. You signed in at four o'clock, and the clerk does remember you, but there is not a check out time, nor does anyone recall seeing you leave."

"I didn't sign out because there was a line at the counter. I'm much too busy to wait in lines."

"What time was that?" Joshua asked.

Mannings regained his senses. "For all you can prove, it was hours after Beth Davis was killed." He laughed, "If you will recall in Criminal Law 101, the burden of proof is on the prosecution to prove the defendant guilty. All I have to prove is reasonable doubt."

"Bridgette killed Beth Davis, and I will prove it."

"When?"

"Now." Joshua gave Bridgette a glare of disgust. "You duped your husband into thinking the two of you had a suicide pact. He never dreamed you had no intention of killing yourself before he pulled that trigger on himself?"

"I lost my nerve." Bridgette sniffed unconvincingly.

"You never intended to kill yourself."

"You can't prove that." Bridgette gave a silent order to Mannings to stop the interview.

"Why would you schedule a hair appointment for the next morning, if you planned to kill yourself that night?" Joshua asked.

"I refuse to say anything."

"You always had Hal Poole wrapped around your little finger," Joshua said. "It wasn't hard for you to convince him that you had to kill Vicki and Beth because they were Satan's demons. Then, you told him that Wally had to be killed. You convinced him that suicide was the honorable thing to do so you could use him as a postmortem scapegoat for your murders."

Curtis Sawyer agreed. "You probably even convinced him that the order to kill your brother came from God himself."

"Now, why would I want to kill Vicki and Beth Davis?"

"To frame Wally." Sheriff Sawyer reminded her, "You made damn sure that I knew that that gun belonged to Wally."

Tad added, "Wally's fingerprint was found on Beth's finger where it was pressed against the trigger to kill her."

"See!" Bridgette flared. "It was Wally's fingerprint!"

Tad told her, "The fingerprint was upside down. It would have been impossible for Wally to hold his hand over Beth's hand in that position to pull the trigger. It was a mistake on your part."

"I imagine that is how you caught your hair in the gun's chamber. While you were bent over Beth's comatose body, pressing the barrel against her temple, planting that fingerprint on her fingernail before pulling the trigger, a strand of your hair got caught on the murder weapon." Joshua added casually, "That red hair proved that Beth's killer had a sibling connection to Vicki. I'll give you another chance. Care to voluntarily give us some of your DNA so we can compare it? Now that we have Wally's DNA, we have proof that he is Vicki's half sibling, but he's not the perp. With that being the case, the old no-probable-cause defense isn't going to fly."

"You already proved my father was not what he seemed," Bridgette answered with a glare. "It's plain to everyone that he had a secret life. That hair came from one of my father's children from his secret life."

"Prove it. Give us your DNA and clear yourself," Jan challenged.

Joshua smiled at Bridgette like a hawk that had landed his prey. "Even if you and Wally are full siblings, your DNA is not exact. As I stated before, if Wally's DNA proves that he is Vicki's half sibling, which it does, that makes you Vicki's half sibling also. Plus, you're a woman. That DNA left on the scene came from a woman."

Manning's walrus mustache twitched.

His client's smug expression faltered.

Mannings grabbed the prosecutor's arm and forcibly turned him away from his client. "What possible motive would Bridgette Poole have to kill Beth Davis?"

"We hardly even knew each other," Bridgette smirked.

"You two did go to the same high school," Joshua reminded her.

"I was four years behind her."

"Two," Joshua corrected her.

"We did not travel in the same circles at all."

Joshua chuckled. "So you weren't friends?"

"Hardly."

"You didn't socialize together?" Joshua went on to clarify his question. "You didn't go out together? Have drinks together? Go shopping together?"

"No!" Bridgette's tone told everyone in the room that she was insult by the very question.

Joshua asked casually, "So what were you doing in her car?"

"I was never in her car!" Bridgette silently commanded her lawyer to take over for her.

Joshua bent over from where he stood above his suspect and whispered into her ear. "What's the first thing you do when you get into someone else's car to drive it?"

Bridgette snapped, "What?"

Joshua smiled knowingly.

Mannings interrupted them by repeating his question about Bridgette's motive for killing the small-town pharmacist.

"She had two reasons." Joshua held up two fingers. "Self-preservation and greed. She set out to kill two birds with two stones, but someone beat her to the punch with Vicki Rawlings."

Joshua circled the suspect as he told her story. "You didn't kill Vicki. You were going to. That was what you had planned when you got Beth out of the hospital and took her to Vicki's place in her car, which was left at the courthouse. You had ridden to the courthouse with your husband, so you didn't have the problem of leaving a car anywhere. You simply followed the ambulance to the hospital in Beth's car. You went to the salon to establish an alibi. After you were alone in the tanning booth, you signaled the front desk to turn on the tanning bed. Then, you slipped out the back door and went to the hospital to wait for Beth to be left alone so that you could take her to Vicki's trailer to kill her."

Joshua chuckled, "Ironically, when you left your DNA behind, you sent us on a wild goose chase looking for Vicki's illegitimate half sister. It didn't occur to us that you were anything but her aunt until we got your brother's DNA to prove otherwise."

"All circumstantial evidence, Commander," Manning's chuckled. "I can convince a jury that her husband picked up her hair while they were together and he left it behind on the scene while killing those two women. You have no real evidence to prove anything other than what he confessed in his suicide note."

"How did Hal get his wife's fingerprints into Beth's car?" Joshua told Bridgette, "We found fingerprints on the rearview mirror in Beth Davis's car. Adjusting the rearview mirror is one of those little actions no one thinks about when they get into a different car. Those prints will prove you were in her car. You just said in front of everyone here that you and Beth weren't friends. You stated that you were never in her car. Those prints will prove you were lying when you said that. Now, why would you lie about that if you hadn't done something very wrong? A jury will want to know what you were doing in her car, if not to take her to Vicki's trailer to kill her."

Mannings glanced at Bridgette for a sign that Joshua was wrong.

Joshua resumed his case. "After you killed Beth, you drove back home in Vicki's car, a black MG with the personalized tags 'RWLNGS4'. It was registered to her father, Wally, so there was never any question, before now, about why it is at the estate. It was Vicki's car, and she was the primary driver, as a host of witnesses will testify. I myself saw it at the scene when she shot up the First Christian Church in Chester."

Curt Sawyer told Mannings, "Vicki's car was impounded after she shot up the church. After her grandfather posted her bail, the same afternoon she was killed,

Vicki went to the impound yard and got her car. We have Vicki's signature on the sign out sheet."

Joshua noted, "Yet, that car was not at her home when we found her body. Someone had taken it from her trailer to the Rawlings estate."

Bridgette looked up at Joshua, who smiled charmingly at her.

The prosecutor continued his case. "Your intention was to frame Wally for the murders so that you could inherit your father's drug empire. You planned to kill Vicki and make it look like Wally was trying to make it look like a murder-suicide, but someone else killed Vicki first. You got lucky. All you had to do was drag Beth back to the bedroom and kill her. You splattered Beth's blood on your brother's coat when you shot her, like you planned to do all along, and you left his coat in Vicki's closet. I have no doubt but that a DNA match will prove that the hair found on the scene and in the gun belonged to you, which will connect you to both the victim, the coat the victim's killer was wearing, and the murder weapon found in the scene. The security cameras at the hospital show you leading Beth out. It was Wally's coat on a person much thinner than he was."

Manning's bushy eyebrows furrowed as he scowled. "Do you seriously believe that my client killed Beth Davis solely to frame her brother to cheat him out of his share of their father's estate?"

"That, and self-preservation," Joshua clarified. "Bridgette managed her father's drug operations. She laundered some of the money through the church. Most of it, they transferred to overseas banks."

"Those trips your client takes to a retreat in Raccoon every month," the sheriff interjected, "aren't to any retreat. They're to the airport, where she catches a chartered flight to the islands, where she makes large cash deposits in an off-shore bank."

Sawyer responded to Bridgette's gasp, "We've been keeping an eye on you."

Joshua clarified, "We are talking hundreds of millions of dollars accumulated over decades. You see, her father was a sort of CEO. Bridgette is the president. Both Beth and Vicki knew that. Beth was being investigated for her small role, which she was blackmailed into doing. Bridgette saw at the courthouse that they were both weak links. It was only a matter of time before one, or both, of them brought the whole drug operation down on their heads."

Mannings looked at Bridgette and sadly shook his head.

Bridgette sat up straight and looked at each of them. The defiance on her face was an indisputable clue to her genes. "I was not responsible for my actions. Just look at my upbringing. I never stood a chance."

*   *   *   *

"Look at her," Jan ordered Tad to notice the injustice Joshua had committed at her expense.

From the living room window seat, Sheriff Sawyer, Tad, and Jan watched Tess Bauer interview Joshua. The rest of the Thornton family watched from seats out of the camera shot.

The journalist and the subject of her exclusive interview sat in his two leather wing-backed chairs in front of the fireplace. Tess sat up straight on the edge of her seat. She held her clipboard with her list of questions in her lap.

"So much for my exclusive," Jan pouted.

Tad soothed Jan's envy. "Keep watching."

"I guess," Tess concluded, "Reverend Rawlings got there before Bridgette and killed Vicki, who threatened to reveal that she was actually his daughter."

Joshua shook his head. "Vicki thought Tad MacMillan was her father. Besides, even if she did know, Reverend Rawlings would never have killed her."

Tess laughed. "Family loyalty? You just said tonight that he killed his own wife because he was raping his daughter-in-law."

"The man we knew as Reverend Rawlings was not stupid. He knew that Vicki's death would eventually lead to the truth about what he did to Cindy Rawlings, which would mean the downfall of his church. That's why he sent the mail bomb to Tad MacMillan after Vicki died. He was afraid the medical examiner would discover the truth and he'd end up with the same problem he had with Doc Wilson, if not worse. Before Vicki's death, the reverend terrorized Tad with threatening e-mails, which we traced to his laptop, in hopes of driving him back to the bottle, which would eventually lead to discrediting him or, better yet, drive him out of town. The reverend also manipulated Vicki to stalk the man she thought was her father who had rejected her. Orville Rawlings had to get rid of Tad because he didn't know if Cindy had told him about the rapes. Once Vicki was dead, then Tad, as medical examiner, would have physical evidence to reveal that Wally could not be her father."

"Since killing was so easy for the reverend, why not just have Tad killed?" Jan interjected a question to spear-like glares from Tess and her news crew.

Joshua responded with a small grin. "I asked that question myself. It's just a guess, but I think he didn't kill him because everyone here in Chester knew how close Tad and I are. The local media has followed my career and my tenacity is no secret. If someone hurt Tad, I'd be back here in a heartbeat, and no one would stop me from finding out who did it. I don't think that was something he wanted to take a chance on happening."

Tess regained control of her interview. "But you came back anyway."

"Yeah, I did, didn't I?" Joshua returned to the previous question with a slight shake of his head. "The reverend couldn't let anything happen to Vicki, if only to protect himself. That's why, with all the trouble she caused him—the DUIs, the car accidents—he never had her killed."

"But Vicki was going to tell all about Rawlings's drug operations. She told Amber!" Tess pointed out. "Amber saw him kill Vicki—"

"And Beth Davis?" Joshua reminded Tess of Amber's interview with Morgan. "She claimed she saw him kill Beth, too, and we proved Bridgette Poole did that."

"W-well," Tess stammered, "Amber did do a lot of drugs. It must have just looked to her like Reverend Rawlings." She sucked in her breath. Joshua saw a slight grimace before she asked, "Who did kill Vicki Rawlings?"

Joshua chuckled. "That was the murder that tripped me up."

Tess joined in Joshua's amusement before asking with a grin, "How did it do that?"

"Well," Joshua began, "the problem I had was in the way I looked at Beth's and Vicki's murders. We had a crime scene. We had two murders, but we kept looking at it as one crime, even though we knew the murders were committed two hours apart. I thought, assumed, that the two murders were connected."

"But that wasn't the case?"

Joshua shook his head, and then held up two fingers. "When I looked at the crime scene as two separate murders, with two murderers with two separate set of motives, whose crimes just so happened to be committed in the same location, like two puzzles in the same box, then it made sense. Then, I saw what happened."

The journalist laughed nervously. "What happened?"

"Tess, you killed Vicki Rawlings."

Her face blank, Tess stared at Joshua.

Silence filled the room.

Joshua broke the silence. "Remember the glove you made sure everyone at my news conference knew about? The glove no one but the police knew about?"

"A source in the sheriff's office told me about the glove," Tess explained quickly.

"There was a fingerprint on that glove. A bloody fingerprint."

"Amber explained that to me," Tess said. "She said she picked up the glove to see what Rawlings dropped on his way out."

"Tess, you are a respected journalist." Joshua sat up in his seat. "You're up for an award for your series on drugs in the valley. Years ago, you interviewed a presidential candidate in Pittsburgh, did you not?"

"Yes, I did."

Jan, Tad, and Curtis Sawyer stood up from the window seat. The children sat at the edge of their seats while the poised news journalist's composure slowly slipped away.

Joshua spoke in a soft tone. "We got a match on the fingerprint on the glove you picked up after Rawlings dropped it in the confusion when Beth collapsed. We ran it through national security. Did you forget? To interview a presidential candidate, you have to pass security to determine if you are a threat. They take your fingerprints, which remain on file in the government database."

Thinking quickly, Tess observed the people in the room. "There must be some mistake."

Stunned by the change in the tone of the interview, the camera operator forgot about taping the journalist and the prosecutor. The news producer and station manager stepped forward from where they had been watching the interview in the background.

Joshua was shaking his head. "No, Tess, there wasn't any mistake. For years, you've been telling everyone that you blamed the Rawlings for your sister's death. You claimed that you turned down the network offer because you were going to stay here to get the drug dealers who killed your sister."

"Yes."

Joshua indicated his front porch outside. "Right out here on my porch, you told me that drugs killed your sister, and that was why you were after the Rawlings."

"I remember."

"You never mentioned that she bled to death from cuts on both her wrists."

Tess cleared her throat and swallowed. "I was too ashamed to tell you." She added quickly, "She killed herself because drugs were destroying her, and she couldn't stand it. She was weak. The Rawlings fed on that weakness. Vicki got her hooked on drugs, and then she raised the price. Diana never would have killed herself if Vicki hadn't have gotten her hooked."

Joshua watched her closely. He sighed and sat back in his chair. "I was in the Navy when the wall came down in Germany. Then, something interesting came out. You see, during the Cold War, the Soviets were accusing the Americans of all these awful things we were doing: bribery, blackmail, and murder for secrets. What came out afterwards was that the Soviets diverted suspicion from themselves by accusing us of the very things they were doing. It's a very interesting little ploy."

Tess stared at Joshua with wide eyes.

"You killed your sister because she stole your boyfriend."

"No!" Tess cried out.

While the journalist sobbed, Joshua continued, "It was supposed to look like a suicide. When the medical examiner in Hookstown was unable to rule with certainty that it was not murder, because there was no hesitation in the slashes you put on her wrists, you had to make sure no one suspected you. Shortly before her death, you got into a huge fight in front of witnesses because she stole your boyfriend, and then the boyfriend took off and left you. If your sister's death was investigated as a murder, you would be the prime suspect. So, to divert suspicion, you cried foul and pointed your finger at the Rawlings."

Joshua sat forward. "Vicki knew the truth and was blackmailing you. So, you had to win her confidence to get close enough to kill her to stop the blackmail. That was another reason you didn't go to New York. You couldn't afford to live there with all the blackmail you were paying Vicki. By all accounts, Vicki was ruthless, just like her birth father. She didn't know who she was dealing with."

Sheriff Sawyer interrupted. "We checked your bank records. A lot of cash had been disappearing, leaving you barely enough to live on. Not only did it stop disappearing after Vicki Rawlings died, but the day after her death, you got a safety deposit box at the same bank. Care to show us what is in it? Could it be a bundle of drug money that you stole from Vicki after killing her? It seems kind of odd that with all the drugs Vicki was dealing that no cash was found at her place."

"I was lending money to a friend and they finally paid me back! I put it in the safety deposit box so the government wouldn't know about it!" Tess turned back to Joshua and sputtered, "I would never kill my sister. I loved her!"

"We talked to the state police in Pennsylvania." Joshua stated firmly. "A girl with short dark red hair and gothic makeup was seen outside Diana's boarding house the very night she died. They suspected she was the one who supplied her with the drugs. Her description matches Amber to a 'T'."

Tess choked, "Amber killed my sister?"

"As suddenly as she showed up on the drug scene with your sister before her death, Amber disappeared. Then, according to the drug underground—we are talking years later—she reappeared on the drug scene, just in time for your series on the drug culture in the valley and Vicki's murder."

Tess's tears stopped. She shot Joshua a crooked grin. "Amber did it," she whispered.

"And you are Amber."

"That's not true," Tess said with new assertiveness. "You saw my interview with her where she told me on camera about what she knew and gave me the tape! Both of us were on camera."

"No one was there to see it recorded."

"It was two o'clock in the morning! Amber was scared!"

"Tess, what's one of the first things you learn in communications?" Joshua answered his own question while she gazed at him with wide, moist eyes. "Film editing and special effects. One special effect, which is surprisingly easy anymore, is to make double images. To shoot one scene with an actor, and then shoot a second scene with the same actor and splice them together to make it look like you have twins." Joshua indicated his own twin sons.

Jackie, the news producer, confirmed Joshua's statement with a nod of her head. "We have the software to do it right in our own studio. You know how to use it, Tess."

Joshua plunged ahead. "You did so well in diverting suspicion from yourself for Diana's murder that you decided to try it again by accusing and framing Reverend Rawlings of killing his granddaughter, your blackmailer."

Tess was so shocked she didn't wipe the tears that soaked her face.

Joshua continued to present his case. "That was why you left the glove at the scene. But then, I threw a monkey wrench into your plan by refusing to accept the glove as real evidence. Unwittingly, I gave you the idea of using Amber as an eyewitness. I said bring me a witness and I'll arrest Rawlings." He laughed. "Suddenly, out of the blue, Amber showed up to say she saw everything."

"She did see everything!"

"You saw everything! Everything except for Beth's murder, that is!"

"You can't prove that!"

"Yes, I can, Tess." Joshua observed how she held on tightly to her ribs. "You gave it away the night of the murders when you showed up before the police—"

"Amber called me!"

"You were shocked out of your gourd that there were two murders."

"Amber had only told me about Vicki."

"You had only killed Vicki. Bridgette showed up afterwards with Beth while you were back at your apartment changing out of your Amber costume. You gave yourself away in your special report."

"How?"

"You proved that you had been on the scene at the time of Vicki's murder."

The news producer announced, "We gave the prosecutor the unedited tape of your report."

"You said that Vicki was stabbed with a steel stake," Joshua reminded her. "I heard you report that at the scene less than an hour after we found the bodies."

The sheriff told her, "The authorities never released to the media that the murder weapon was a steel stake. We only said it was a stake."

Joshua shrugged, "Why not assume it was a wooden stake? That's what they used to kill vampires, and Vicki was a bloodsucker. The stake was a symbolic gesture on your part. She was sucking you dry."

Her eyes wide to hold back the tears as best she could, Tess laughed. "Amber killed her." She added desperately, "Amber told me it was a steel stake when she called me." She rambled on quickly. "Amber killed Vicki! She killed my sister and then she killed Vicki! She's crazy and she's setting me up!"

"Yes, Amber killed your sister and Vicki." Joshua pointed at the reporter. "And you are Amber."

"You're insane!"

Joshua explained, "The station sent the original tape you brought in of your interviews with Amber to the state forensics lab. They found where it was edited."

"Amber is real! People have seen her! Ask around!"

"But no one ever saw the two of you together." Jackie looked for confirmation to the camera operator, who looked sadly at Tess before shaking his head in response to the wordless question. "You were so good that none of us even realized it until Mr. Thornton asked us. Every time Amber came in asking for you, you couldn't be found. You wouldn't even answer your cell phone."

"That doesn't mean anything!" Tess wiped her running nose on her sleeve.

"Let's look at your interviews." Joshua went to the television and DVD player they had concealed in the entertainment center. As he spoke, the image of Amber in her reddish black hair and lipstick came up on the screen. "You were good, Tess. Amber had a different style and manner of speech. I was fooled for a long time—"

"—I heard Vicki screaming at her old man! I could hear her fighting him. Then suddenly, it was quiet, and that was worse than the screaming because I couldn't tell what was happening. Then-Oh,God!" Amber covered her face with her hands.

The image on the screen froze with Amber, her bare shoulder peaking out of the black sleeveless top. Her hand with her claw-like fingernails covered her face.

Joshua pointed to Amber's shoulder. "Look. No tattoo. Now, I looked at all your interviews with Amber. She had a black widow spider tattooed on her left shoulder. But, in this interview with Morgan Lucas, she has no tattoo. The night she came to my house to give me her statement, the tattoo moved to her right shoulder."

Joshua stepped across the room to Tess. He reached down and took her hand. Wordlessly, he observed her fingernails, which were neatly trimmed and painted a soft pink color. "You have pretty hands. I can see that you take good care of them. You keep your nails short. I noticed that the night you were here. My wife kept her nails trimmed, too. They are easier to take care of, and you can do more when you keep your nails short."

The prosecutor pointed to the screen where Amber covered her face with her long claws. "But, that afternoon that I came to your studio after Amber told the valley about seeing the murders, your fingernails were long and dark, just like Amber's. I wasn't the only one who noticed that you had Amber's fingernails. Morgan did, too. She had to notice. She was sitting three feet from you. When you were ranting and raving at her for stealing your source, you pointed your finger at her, and that was when she realized that you were Amber." Joshua sighed, "That's why you had to kill her."

Tess snatched her hand out of Joshua's grasp.

"You had to glue Amber's nails on over your real nails. In order to remove them without damaging your own nails, you have to soak them in a solution. I think you didn't have the time, or maybe the means, to get those nails off before returning to the studio to go into your act about Morgan Lucas stealing your story."

Joshua looked down at the woman hugging her ribs that ached as she trembled in her effort to not sob.

"When I met Amber, I knew she was not the real thing, just like Morgan Lucas. That was why you had to kill her."

Tess dropped her head.

Joshua observed the pain on her face. "My daughter put up more of a fight than you expected when you came here to attack one of my kids to make me back off." He nodded with pride at Tracy, who was watching from the kitchen doorway. "Tracy has a brown belt in martial arts. Her mother taught her well. She felt your ribs break when she kicked them in, and you knew better than to go to the hospital to have them treated."

Even as she felt jealous of the young woman who had achieved her dreams of being a journalist, Jan felt sorry for Tess.

Joshua leaned towards her. "Take off your wig, Tess."

Tess grasped the crown of her honey blond hair. The wig came off to reveal closely cropped, reddish-black hair.

There was a collective gasp in the room.

"You're wrong about one thing, Mr. Thornton." Tess looked up at Joshua with a tear-soaked face. "Vicki wasn't blackmailing me because I killed my sister. She saw me kill that pig that dumped me for her. The little slut was hiding in his closet."

EPILOGUE

▼

"Okay, we have the ice cream, the chocolate sauce—"

"Hot fudge sauce," Murphy interjected.

"Is the hot fudge ready yet?" Joshua asked Tracy.

"Oh, Tracy," Sarah gave an exaggerated moan, "can you get me a glass of iced tea while you're over there?"

"Sure." After stirring the melting fudge sauce on the hot stove, Tracy yanked open the refrigerator door to retrieve the iced tea pitcher.

Donny came into the kitchen with a pillow, which he tucked in behind Sarah's back at her seat at the head of the table.

Joshua watched the scene with a sense of unease. For his family, things weren't quite normal.

"Is that better, sis?" Donny adjusted and readjusted the pillow for his sister.

"Yes, much." Sarah smiled at him.

Sarah was enjoying the attention too much, and her siblings hadn't realized it yet. Joshua anticipated a war when they did.

"And don't forget cherries." Curt diverted Joshua's attention from the scene of family harmony. "You can't not have cherries." The sheriff looked different dressed casually in jeans and tee shirt rather than his uniform.

Joshua double-checked the jar. "We always have cherries."

"I want mine without any sauce," Tad reminded them from where he observed the making of the sundaes on the other side of the counter.

Behind Joshua's legs, Admiral was hiding from Dog, who was pawing and barking at him while wagging his bushy tail.

"And you call yourself an American," Curt cracked at Tad before telling the ice cream chef, "I'll take his sauce." He sat across from Jan, who was typing away on her laptop at the kitchen table.

Tracy placed the pan containing the hot fudge sauce on the bar. "I think you're ready to go. Serve 'em up, Dad."

"Scoop."

Tracy slapped the scoop into her father's outstretched hand, and Joshua proceeded to prepare the sundaes for the group.

Sarah cleared her throat. "Dad, there is one thing I don't understand."

"Only one?" Joshua snickered. "Consider yourself lucky."

"Why did Tess wait so long to kill Vicki, if she was blackmailing her?"

"Because she was crazy," Murphy answered.

"Crazy like a fox," Tad muttered.

"Are you saying it is all an act?" Jan asked the doctor.

"I'm not a psychiatrist," Tad told them, "but those murders were too well planned to be the work of an insane person."

Curtis Sawyer agreed. "The boyfriend's murder wasn't premeditated. That was the first one. Tess told us where she hid the body, right in the guy's own basement. She carefully planned all the other murders."

Jan asked, "What did she have in that safety deposit box? Was it drug money she stole from Vicki?"

"Yep," the sheriff answered, "over one-hundred-and-fifty-thousand dollars that Vicki picked up on the way home from jail."

Joshua observed, "Of course, the Rawlings couldn't report it missing after Vicki was killed since it was drug money."

"Why did Tess Bauer slice up that reporter's face?" Donny wanted to know.

"Jealousy," Jan answered. "Morgan was pretty and Tess wasn't."

"She wanted to make it look like some crazy person did it," Joshua told them. "Tess admitted in her confession that Morgan gave her the opportunity to confess to the fraud herself and put a bullet in her career, or let Morgan do it for her. Tess came up with another option."

Jan stopped with her fingers over the keyboard. "So why attack Tracy?"

Joshua told her with a coy grin. "When Tess came here posing as Amber, I saw through her disguise. She knew that it was only a matter of time before I revealed the truth, just like Morgan Lucas."

The sheriff added, "She also had enough sources in the sheriff's department to know that the hit was a fake."

"She knew that I wasn't dead. She decided to take the opportunity of everyone thinking I was dead to scare me off. The best way to do that would be to attack one of my kids." Joshua looked at his children. "She would have attacked any of you kids who came into that bathroom. Tracy just happened to be the one who won the race that night."

Jan shook her head. "I knew there was something wrong with Tess Bauer. I just knew it."

Tad laughed as he took his bowl of ice cream and sat next to her. "Come on! You thought I killed Beth," he reminded her.

Jan flushed. "Who told you that?" She shot an accusatory glare at Joshua, who turned away to look for something in the fridge. She retaliated. "Josh actually thought Beth Davis was Maggie's mother!"

Tad gave an exaggerated scoff. "Did he really?"

Joshua caught Tad's eye from behind Jan, who smirked with satisfaction.

"I guess I was having an off day then," Joshua stated with a hint of humility.

Tad grinned at him. His gratitude over Joshua skillfully avoiding to reveal Maggie's relationship to the Rawlings overflowed. His secret was safe for the time being.

"Did Vicki know that Amber was Tess?" Jan asked with her fingers poised over her keyboard to type out the answer to her query.

"I doubt it." Joshua sat on a kitchen stool.

Curt eyed his host's large ice cream sundae with admiration.

Joshua continued, "My guess is that Vicki didn't know who Amber was until just before Tess killed her."

Tad took rawhides out of the cupboard to serve the two dogs. "Tess probably would have gotten away with it if it weren't for her ambition. She just had to be the first one on the scene to scoop everyone else, and, in doing that, she gave away that she had been at the scene of the crime."

While swallowing a mouthful of ice cream, Joshua nodded in agreement.

Tracy sighed with amazement. "I can't get over all the people Reverend Rawlings had killed in his life."

"But he wasn't Reverend Rawlings," Jan reminded them. "He was an escaped murderer."

"All those people he hurt," Tad shrugged, "and he was totally incapable of remorse. He rationalized that it was just what he had to do."

"Even killing his wife," Tracy mused.

Curt snickered, "Yep. And all those members of his church. They have hundreds of members, and they all believed Rawlings was a man of God."

"The church is already crumbling," Tad told them. "The members are jumping ship like rats with all the evidence coming out about the Reverend Rawlings. Believe it or not, there are still some things that you just can't spin enough to cover up."

"That's too bad. They were looking for direction in the right place, just from the wrong man," Jan pointed out.

Tad was somber. "Reverend Rawlings and his family were evil. Most of the people in his church were sincere in their faith. But because of that one man, who was as far from God as you can get, some of his followers may turn their backs on God forever, when God had nothing to do with the reverend and his sins, at all." He added with a snicker, "Except maybe exposing him for who he really was."

The sheriff scoffed at Tad's remark, "What do you mean God exposed him? Josh exposed him."

"Yeah, but I think he had some help."

"From who?" Donny asked.

"From God, you dummy." Sarah slapped her brother's knuckles with her spoon.

"Stupid!" Donny flicked a spoonful of ice cream at her.

The frozen propellant hit her right between the eyes.

Sarah screamed and dove for Donny, but Murphy separated them.

"Dad," Sarah screamed, "did you see that?"

"Yes," Joshua chuckled. "If you two are going to kill each other, please do it in the other room so we don't have to witness against you." Everything was back to normal.

"Slimeball!" Sarah grumbled while Tracy escorted her upstairs.

When Donny saw the look directed at him from the kitchen counter, the boy abruptly swallowed his triumphant glee. Dropping his head, the child turned his attention back to his sundae.

"Come on, Tad," Curtis returned to the subject. "If God wanted Rawlings exposed He would have done it like three decades ago, but He didn't. We had to wait for Josh here to come back home and put it all together." Curt looked up at Joshua who was wordlessly watching them argue. "What do you think, Josh?"

Joshua nodded towards Tad in agreement. "I never would have been able to prove that Rawlings was Penn, even if I had it all figured out down to the last detail, if Bridgette had not taken that very gun out of Wally's collection to give to Hal to shoot at us and kill Wally with."

J.J. screwed up his face. "Why did she want to have Hal kill you guys? I mean, Wally had already hired Sheriff Sawyer to do it."

"She didn't actually order Hal to kill anyone," Curt responded. "She only told him to follow your father to make sure he didn't find out anything that would interfere with their family performing their lordly duties. After Hal had killed himself, and she discovered that Josh really was alive, she had no choice but to call in her old friend Scott Collins." He turned back to Joshua with a snort. "Do you really think God helped you to nail Rawlings, I mean Penn?"

"Answer me this." Joshua licked his spoon. "How many guns did Wally have in his collection?"

Curt shrugged. "Thirty-two."

"And out of thirty-two, Bridgette selected the one gun, the only gun, that could have exposed her father for who and what he really was, fifty years after he had committed his first murder." Joshua clarified, "If his daughter, who grew up to be just as evil as he was—"

"Sins of the father," Jan muttered.

"—had not picked that very gun, Penn would have gotten away with everything, and we never could have proved anything."

"Yeah, but what good would it have done to have the gun if you hadn't had the brains to put it together," J.J. said proudly.

Tad concluded by quietly asking the sheriff, "Who gave him those brains?"

"So, Josh," Curt chuckled with satisfaction, "You did a pretty good job. Three murderers in one day, that's got to be a record. I heard the attorney general was impressed. I know I am."

"You should be." Joshua grinned.

"What's next?"

"I'm taking the kids to the beach," Joshua answered. "For the rest of the summer, I'm going to be the father I'm supposed to be."

"What a swell guy!" Jan sighed dreamily, "Will you marry me?"

"I'm still in mourning."

"You can't mourn forever."

"As much as I hate to interrupt a marriage proposal," Curt cleared this throat to ask Joshua once again about his plans, "What are you going to do after the beach? Are you going to run in this next election? Our county can use a good prosecutor working on our side."

"How about it, Josh?" Jan asked. "My book does need an ending."

Joshua finished off his sundae under the eyes of his sons, Jan, Curtis, and the two dogs.

His answer was a mysterious smile.

The End

0-595-30253-X

Printed in the United States
38252LVS00004B/183

9 780595 302536